THEY HAD THE CAGE DOOR OPEN IN LESS THAN THREE SECONDS...

In three more seconds, Domino and Dominique, the two space cats, were sitting on the windowsill, peering down into the courtyard. There was a wall enclosing the farther end, but it appeared leapable; there was a wire screen just outside the windowpane, but it was fastened down by only a simple hook-and-eye device. The problem was the window itself. It was stuck fast, and they could see at once that any system of levers or counterweights capable of multiplying their combined strength enough to raise the sash would take far too long to construct—assuming they could find the necessary materials.

Only brute strength could force open this laboratory window, the brute strength of an Earthling.

Which of the two had the idea first was irrelevant, for they both acted on it at the same instant. Whatever the purpose of the building, they were not its only prisoners. By not they had a clear picture of its floor plan and knew exactly how to find the human captive they'd seen earlier.

Down from the sill and out the door they went. The oafish noisiness of most of the Earthlings made them easy to evade, and the two bandit-eyed cats stole through corridors, intent on rescuing the one person who in turn could rescue them. . . .

JACK LOVEJOY
OUTWORLD CATS

DAW BOOKS, INC.

DONALD A. WOLLHEIM, FOUNDER

375 Hudson Street, New York, NY 10014

**ELIZABETH R. WOLLHEIM
SHEILA E. GILBERT
PUBLISHERS**

First Printing, March 1994

1 2 3 4 5 6 7 8 9

 DAW TRADEMARK REGISTERED
U.S. PAT. OFF. AND FOREIGN COUNTRIES
—MARCA REGISTRADA
HECHO EN U.S.A.

PRINTED IN THE U.S.A.

CHAPTER I

The two young cats turned from the computer screen, sprang into the weightless air, and glided unerringly the length of the utility module and through an open air lock. Their eight paws rebounded simultaneously from the overhead of the space bridge beyond.

They had been programming their graduation exercises, under the stern gaze of a senior instructress who brooked no adolescent nonsense as she telepathically suggested improvements in the syntax of their coding. The summons had also been telepathic, from a senior crew chief, and overrode all other assignments.

The flexible tunnel down which they glided united their splendid habitat with a primitive space station being constructed by Earthlings in a geosynchronous orbit above their planet. There were no Earthlings now aboard the complex of modules and solar arrays—a golden opportunity to scan the apparatus and circuitry for future appraisal.

Ages ago, when the Masters first reconnoitered the planet Earth, they discovered among its primordial fauna the answer to a dilemma that had long bedeviled their interstellar ambitions, and by selectively breeding the creatures for intelligence and physical dexterity they at last opened an entire arm of the galaxy for exploration.

Gracile, bluish-pearl in color, with bandit masking and forepaws nearly as pliant as hands, the cats only superficially resembled their remote ancestors. Their smallness and light weight economized on stores and fuel, they slept five hours out of six, minimizing the frictions of shipboard confinement and the need for recreational facilities, and their superfeline agility eliminated the need for bulky ramps and ladders; in the weightlessness of outer space they virtually flew from station to station about the ship.

With routine interfacing and maintenance thus relegated, three masters now sufficed where once many times that number had had to endure the tedium and perils of a long voyage, thereby vastly extending both the scope and number of galactic missions.

The cats on board were exclusively female, so that through controlled insemination operatives could be bred and fully trained within months, whenever needed. Lifetime implants quieted the hurly-burly of discordant hormones.

The Master directing the scanning operations stood at the very center of the module, keying data into a portable console with magically supple fingers. His bulbous head was completely hairless and seemed too massive for his spindly little body to support. He was warmly bundled inside an insulation suit, though the air about him was temperature controlled to protect the crude apparatus of the Earthling module from damage.

The glide path of the two young cats was aimed directly at him, but at that precise instant two larger cats sprang at them and deflected their trajectories toward a bank of instrumentation racks in a remote corner. Only by positioning a scanner behind these particular terminals could the innermost circuitry be recorded, but the panels could not be wedged open far enough to admit even the smallest member of the regular crew, without leaving telltale damage. The two young cats barely squeezed inside themselves, though willing paws assisted them by holding aside the clumsy, ill-devised tangle of cables. Never had they so appreciated the wondrous design of their own ship.

Team-think had been conditioned into them since they were blind, mewling kittens, and, cramped as they were, not a single motion was wasted in positioning the scanner. Then they awaited the next telepathic command from their crew chief. What flashed through their minds instead was a General Alarm, and the scanner wriggled away from them like a living thing. They immediately tried to follow, but the tangle of cables was no longer held aside for them and they made slow progress.

Inch by inch, squirming and squeezing, they wriggled toward the narrow opening. At last they could see members of the crew feverishly impelling scanners and other equipment into the space bridge. Yet they were instinctively blocked from alerting any of them to their plight; for no law of team-think was so indelibly impressed into their minds as that neither personal safety nor life itself transcended danger to a Master, and a General Alarm was flashed only in an extreme emergency. They could only continue to squirm and squeeze and wriggle their way through the tangle, without hope of assistance.

Escape was mere inches away when they were momentarily stunned by another telepathic command they were unable to obey. Through the chaos of cables they watched helplessly as the entire crew seemed to explode before their eyes, springing in all directions at once, redoubling their combined momentum by bouncing from the overhead, bulkheads, and deck, and converging with team-think interaction upon the Master, as he labored feebly toward the space bridge. Hundreds of claws hooked into his insulation suit, and amidst a cloud of fur he was borne to safety.

Wriggling free at last, the two cats flew in tandem across the now deserted module—a moment too late. Their eight paws rebounded this time from the air lock door just as it slid shut, tumbling them backward. Still instinctively blocked from calling for help, they panicked as they heard the clamps of the space bridge detaching from the hull outside; then only the silence of eternity. They were marooned.

"Space debris," said Mickey Dunstun from the pilot's seat, as he watched the unexpected blip fade from his radar screen. "It's becoming a regular junkyard up here, Angel. There's the UN Commstat though, dead ahead."

"It'll all be dead, before we're finished," said the man in the commander's seat beside him. The perverse humor that tabbed him "Angel" was the sole familiarity he tolerated, for a less angelic countenance could hardly be imagined. Thick black eyebrows bushed from a jutting browridge, his bullet head was shaven, and a broken nose meandered between brutish jowls; his hunkering shoulders hunched forward over his pot belly as he peered intently into the screen. "That's it, all right." His usual belligerent scowl twisted into a sneer of contempt. "The Big Guy's miles ahead of these UN bozos. A cloud cover over the hemisphere grounded them, but not us."

The unmarked shuttle was stealth engineered to elude detection by any radar beam on the planet, and neither the two men at the controls nor the four crew members carried indentification. In fact, unknown to any of them, a DESTRUCT command was programmed into their computer system, set to respond so explosively to threats of detection that there would be no telltale wreckage to incriminate the owner of the ship.

"He's hopping mad, from what I hear," said Dunstun. "So we'd better do this right." He was a big man by normal standards, but dwarfed by the brutish hulk seated beside him.

"You mean about that snoopy broad?" said Angel. "Yeah, I know all about her. It was me who caught the bozo who sneaked her through security. Busted him up good before I turned him in, you know where." He pointed significantly to the crown of his shaved head.

"So I heard." Dunstun checked a row of position indicators, and reset three switches on the orbital maneuvering system. "I also heard the Big Guy pulled it over their eyes with that *Greenworld Challenger* business. Not a peep out of the newsies."

"Miles ahead of 'em every time." A corner of Angel's mouth twisted sneeringly upward, in the closest he ever came to a smile. "Yeah, I was in on that, too. I've never actually met the Big Guy, but he must be getting good reports about me because now he sends me along on all his big jobs. To make sure nobody does nothing dumb," he added, with a meaningful look.

Dunstun concentrated still more intently on the instrument panels. "But what about the broad herself? Who is she?"

"Her brother was one of them environmentalist bozos aboard the *Greenworld Challenger.* He did some barbell work in college, so he thought he was strong." Angel's mouth twisted contemptuously. "I always did like busting up smart asses. And his snoopy sister wasn't so bright neither."

"You mean you caught her, too?"

"Brought her in just before we took off for Sulatonga. Hated to miss out on the fun, but you gotta do what you're told."

"So that's two for two, the security guy and the broad both."

"That's right. Mr. Grotten himself says to me, 'Good work, Angel.' " He sat back complacently in his seat. "I'm kinda proud of that."

"If Mr. Grotten's in on it, it must be big." Dunston began resetting switches and pushing buttons at strategic intervals. There was a barely perceptible shudder throughout the ship, and he scanned his monitors. "Right smack on target."

"Better be." Angel shot another meaningful look at him, then activated his own monitor screens. "Looks good at this end, too. All systems go, and every Brainer where he should be. Speaking of Brainers, by the way, there'll be one more right after we land back in Ingles City."

Dunstun glanced nervously at him. "Another Brainer? Who do you. . . . Oh, you mean the broad?"

"That's right. Why, did you think I meant you? Nah, you ain't done nothing wrong, Mickey. At least, I hope not, for your sake. The Big Guy likes you, Mr. Grotten likes you, I even like you myself. Sure, I meant the broad." He pointed to the crown of his shaved head. "So I missed out on the fun this time. There'll be other times. Plenty of 'em. Once the Big Guy takes over the space program, there'll be no other commstats but his in orbit. He's already planting Brainers in key spots all over the world. Meanwhile we gotta discourage the competition."

"That's why we're here," Dunstun muttered, his attention concentrated on the instrument panel before him.

With a delicate touch he operated his rotational hand control, and on four separate display screens, monitoring the ship's exterior from four different perspectives, the stealth shuttle could be seen maneuvering between two gigantic silicon wings and alongside the largest module of the UN Commstat. Its long and costly construction, still fraught with political controversy, had just this month reached permanent manned capability. Mickey pushed a button, and in the upper corner of the uppermost display screen a space bridge could be seen extending toward an air lock in the hull opposite. There was a distant clack of metal against metal, and he pushed another button.

"Magnetic clamps fixed," he said. Double-checking the instrument panels, he keyed his password into the computer, freezing the controls. "Ready?"

Angel nodded, and unclasped his seat harness. "We don't need suits, do we?"

"No, the completed modules are air- and temperature-controlled." Dunstun slipped out of his own harness, and propelled himself weightlessly toward the hatchway. "Looks like we got the place all to ourselves, thanks to that unforeseen malfunction at the Cape, and the cloud cover."

"Nothing the Big Guy does is unforeseen," said Angel, pushing off after Mickey. "He's got people everywhere, including the Cape. When it comes to space launchings, the rest of 'em are still in the Stone Age compared to us."

Dunston glanced at the brutish physiognomy of his companion as they floated side by side past a convex bank of electronics racks, and he, too, was reminded of the Stone Age.

"Are you sure we're really alone?" said Angel, checking his inertia against the portal of the space bridge. "Not that I mind a little rough work. But nobody's supposed to know we're up here, or even suspect what's going on at Sulatonga."

"If you're still worried about that blip on the radar screen, forget it. There's nothing up here but space debris."

"Yeah, but what about experiments? You know, bees or monkeys, or stuff like that. You know what the Big Guy thinks about animals."

Dunstun glanced at a dial over the portal, then keyed a bulkhead panel, and the door slid open. "It's all been checked and double-checked, Angel. Believe me, the United Nations wants nothing alive up here that might hurt their precious Commstat."

The corner of Angel's mouth twisted upward. "Wanting and getting ain't the same thing. Okay, you three, lug that gear after us."

The trio of scrubbed and close-cropped young men hovering nearby had the regimented look of boot camp marines, as though nothing could be more alien to their natures than disobedience to a superior. One guided a massive power-supply unit weightlessly into the space bridge, another followed with a magnetic amplifier the size of a refrigerator, while the third lit the way with an electric torch.

The Commstat's emergency air lock was boldly out-

lined with a white stripe. Dunstun metered the gray
hull for interior pressure and nodded to Angel, who at
once set to work with a device of his own and in less
than five minutes jimmied open the door. Stolen blue-
prints had given them a clear picture of what they
would find inside, but nothing could have prepared
them for the spectacle of two bandit-eyed cats looking
expectantly up at them from the deck plates.

But if they were surprised, the two cats were utterly
confounded. The clangor of a space bridge affixing itself to the outer hull had encouraged them to believe
that they were not abandoned after all, and in joyous
tandem they had flown straight back to the air lock. No
circumstances extenuated tardiness in response to a
General Alarm, but they had both endured sharp chas-
tisement from instructresses and crew chiefs during the
months of training, due to a kittenish penchant for mischief, and the punishments of the Masters were never
severe. Besides, no disciplinary action could possibly
exceed the pangs of being marooned.

The most appalling thing about the monsters looming before them in the air lock was their misshapen re-
semblance to the Masters. But where the Masters had
massive heads and puny bodies, these creatures had
massive bodies and puny heads. Then a hideous growl
broke the spell, and the two cats turned in unison and
flew side by side toward the most distant corner of the
module.

"Goddamn it, Mickey! You told me there was nothing up here." Angel glowered at him. "What the hell
do you call that?"

He pointed into the far corner, and the docile young
man beside him obediently shone his electric torch in
that direction. The cats had insinuated their claws into
the overhead, and hung upside down like a pair of flying foxes.

"I don't know, but they can't be experimental animals," said Dunstun. "You know what the Big Guy
thinks about animals of any kind. So Mr. Grotten

checked out that angle himself. Ask him, if you don't believe me."

"And break radio silence?" Angel looked him disgustedly up and down. "Sounds to me like maybe you slept through our briefing in Sulatonga. What else did you miss?"

"Not the part about our having only a couple of hours to do the job up here, before the cloud cover breaks over the only telescope liable to spot us."

He tried to sound confident but could not quite suppress the betraying quaver in his voice. Angel was more resourceful than he looked, and although the ticklish launching from Sulatonga might be beyond his capability, he was technician enough to handle the routine landing back at Ingles City. It was not improbable that he had, in fact, been granted that very option should he for any reason find his pilot expendable.

Angel's jutting browridge beetled still further as he pondered. At last, he turned to the Brainers. "Okay, you two, set up that gear over there, with the beam on full power. I don't want so much as a clock in here telling the right time when we leave. And you, get me something I can use as a cage." He literally sailed the third close-cropped young man back through the space bridge.

"Never saw cats like these before," said Dunstun. "We always had cats around the place when I was a kid. Alley cats, Siamese, Persian, even an Angora once. I don't like cats any more, of course," he hastened to add.

"Better not." Angel scowled at him. "What the Big Guy says is right. 'The only good animal is a stuffed animal.' Got that magno set up yet, you two? Then start beaming it at that memory unit over there. That's right. I want everything in here to look like it was hit by a solar storm, which is what our Media guys will tell the world. In the meantime, while the circuits are cooking, fetch me them cats. And don't leave no clues we were here, or I'll sail the pair of you out an air lock."

The hum of the magnetic amplifier, invisibly reducing electronic circuitry to a condition of permanent malfunction, was at first the only sound inside the module. This was soon drowned by the scrambling of the two Brainers, as they futilely pursued the elusive cats round and round, up and down, from deck to bulkhead to overhead. Angel's bawling of contradictory orders drowned this in turn, while he swung the electric torch wildly back and forth, trying in vain to focus its beam on at least one of the cats, who continued to dodge and leap and soar out of reach with an agility that seemed supernatural. They rebounded acrobatically off each other in midair, reversing their trajectories; they rebounded off the very backs and heads of their pursuers, as though taunting their clumsiness. Angel's curses soon overpowered all other sounds.

"All right, you clowns, get your butts down here," he shouted at last. "Reset that magno in front of them instrument racks over there, while I try and figure this one out. What's this?"

The third Brainer had just emerged from the space bridge, carrying an enameled gray box.

"A power-pack casing, sir," he replied. "This clasp mechanism is designed only to hold the door closed, but should effectively preclude the escape of any creature shut within."

"That's right," said Angel. "They don't call 'em dumb animals for nothing. The trouble is getting 'em inside in the first place. I'd bring down the pair with a couple of bullets, except I don't want to risk punching holes in the fuselage or leaving evidence we were here. What we need is a net, or maybe something like a big flyswatter."

But at that moment, to his surprise and everyone else's, the two cats flew side by side down from their perch atop a bank of electronics racks, and alit on the deck plates directly before Angel, as if beseeching entry into the power-pack casing. Wonderingly, the Brainer held it open, and together the cats hopped tamely inside and settled themselves comfortably while he reset its door clasp behind them.

"Figure that one out." Angel stared in bewilderment. "One minute they're bouncing around here like ping-pong balls, and the next they're curling up like pussycats."

"Perhaps the sight of a cage reassured them," said Dunstun. "When we were chasing them, they may naturally have reasoned we meant them harm."

"Reasoned? They're dumb animals, Mickey. They don't reason, and they don't play chess or write symphonies neither. Though, come to think of it, they are kind of odd. Must be some rare jungle breed, or maybe from the Himalayas somewheres. Anyway, the Big Guy's sure to want 'em for his museum—after he figures out what the hell they're doing here. How long will it take you to wrap things up?"

"Give me an hour or so. The UN mission thinks they're gonna settle permanently into the habitability module, when they finally get up here. But they'll be lucky to salvage even man tended capability, once I get through." He grinned knowingly. "It'll be the news story of the day, all over the world. Our Congress and Media guys are only awaiting the go-ahead to attack the Administration for criminally endangering American lives, for throwing away the taxpayers' money, and so forth. That'll give us all the delay we need to wreck the satellite backup system, too. Project Nimrod is just weeks away from countdown, from what I hear."

"Knowing too much ain't good for you, Mickey. These three used to think they were wise guys, too." Angel nodded toward the Brainers, who were now docilely setting up the magnetic amplifier before yet another rack of electronic circuitry to be cooked. "See what it got 'em. Do what you're told, no more, no less. That's the best way to stay healthy in B.I.T.E."

He propelled himself back into the space bridge, carrying under his arm the locked power-pack casing. There was not a sound from inside.

CHAPTER II

Born and nurtured in space, their every instinct conditioned to low or zero gravity, the only sensations of heaviness the two young cats had ever known were during accelobursts and decelobursts aboard ship and during the periodic physical conditioning they and all their teammates had received. Thus constant gravity was a cumbersome experience, and even locked inside their rude cage they knew that their flying days were over.

An X-ray photograph of the power-pack casing, which Angel had shoved under his meaty right arm as he shambled across a hangar floor aswarm with technicians servicing the stealth shuttle, would have revealed only a pair of gracile, bluish-pearl felines dozing placidly inside. Though they were not actually asleep and their telepathic exchanges were anything but placid.

It seemed that these big, ugly creatures with the puny heads considered them the ones with no brains. The idiotic simplicity of the mechanism confining them meant that escape was only a matter of choosing a favorable moment—and, naturally, of evading recapture. They would be encumbered by gravity, but their oafish captors should be easy to dodge under any conditions. Then what? Being marooned on an alien planet was a vast improvement over being marooned inside a foodless, waterless module in outer space, but they were marooned nonetheless. For it was a primal law never to issue distress signals, or try in any way to contact the Masters, should one ever find herself separated from the mother ship. They were on their own and would have to survive by their own wits.

Taken together these were formidable. Team-think conditioning enhanced their combined intelligence geometrically: one plus one always equaled more than two, a whole greater than the mere sum of the parts. Literally putting their heads together, they tried to foresee the challenges that might soon confront them.

The puny heads and brute clumsiness of the Earthlings were grounds for optimism. But what if these oafs were not the dominant species on the planet? What if they were only conditioned operatives, serving the true rulers of Earth in the same manner that they themselves served the Masters? Only time and further information could resolve that question, so they left it open and instead concentrated their mutual thoughts upon the more immediate problem of escape.

They had no means yet of discovering exactly where they were on the planet. Earthlings communicated, after a primitive fashion, by growling at each other, but these guttural noises were still unintelligible. So general reconnaissance would have to be the first order of business, carried out at the earliest opportunity.

This came sooner than expected. The clumsy jostling of their enclosure was abruptly supplanted by the firmest seating they had ever known. They recognized the growling of the biggest and ugliest of their captors, mingled with the somewhat less hideous growling of another Earthling, as it receded from them. Moments later they heard a shutting sound, followed by a metallic click; then silence. Their keen senses assured them that no hostile life-form remained within their immediate vicinity, and as one, they rose and attacked the lock of their rude cage.

A claw insinuated here, a forepaw pressed there, and the crude mechanism sprang open. Warily they eased open the door and peeked out.

They found themselves atop a rectangular block of some grainy organic material, its surface laden with crude electrical devices; the bulky objects distributed unsymmetrically about the surrounding room were mostly of heavy plastics, some of them contoured like the furniture upon which the Masters sat or reclined. The air was pungent with animal smells and the oiliness of machines. Harsh light shone from three long glowing tubes located directly overhead.

Near them sat a glass dish filled to overflowing with the stubs of tiny white tubes and evil-smelling ashes. They could not even guess what had been burned here or why. More and more strange odors now assailed them out of the unfiltered atmosphere, which seemed richer than the air breathed aboard ship, though uncomfortably stuffy and close. Some primitive electrical and electronic devices stood among the bulky objects crowding the room. The one that most interested them had a display screen like their shipboard training console, and they wondered if it, too, could furnish them with information.

But first they had to test their physical capabilities under the handicap of gravity, and they sprang down from the desk in tandem. The floor was covered with an organic material like coarse fur, but landing on it was still an unaccustomed jolt. Every movement here was like bucking the tension beams in an exercise pod; they had both recently graduated into advanced agility training, and now tried their leaping range with vertical and horizontal springs. They could touch the ceiling with their most powerful leaps, though it was frustrating to discover that no matter how high they bounded, gravity would always pull them down again.

Next came a more thorough inspection of their surroundings. Neither was afflicted with feline nearsightedness, and their vision encompassed the full spectrum of colors. Colorfulness was not, however, a feature of this particular room. It was furnished with unmatched odds and ends, drab and functional; the walls were painted gun-metal gray and decorated with framed enlargements of monstrous weapons of war.

There was a flat, shiny gray box atop one corner of the desk, which looked to be some kind of simple communications device, probably used to transmit the growls of whichever Earthling sat here to others in the huge, sprawling structure, and the two were careful not to touch its keys. The last thing they wanted, while still so vulnerable to recapture, was to alert their captors that they were out of their cage.

They examined the screened console from every angle until satisfied that it could only be some kind of video receiver; none of the other rudimentary devices scattered about the room interested them. The brown plastic trash can beside the desk was empty, and they positioned it upside down in front of the console, so they could reach the controls. Without a schematic, they could master these only through trial and error, and they pushed buttons and twisted knobs until at last they heard a faint sizzling noise and the screen brightened with colorful images.

It took only seconds to reduce the volume to a safe whisper and to master all the other controls. Switching from channel to channel, they were unable at first to discover anything instructive. One Earthling would growl at another, who would growl back, and a maniacal cackling would erupt somewhere offscreen. Or grim-looking Earthlings would race back and forth in roaring vehicles, seeking opportunities to kill each other, or to blow up other vehicles in flaming explosions. They had quickly grasped the prevailing system of time measurement, from a team-think analysis of the round white clock on the wall, and now counted seven Earthlings murdered in less than five minutes.

Switching through a whole gamut of channels, they gained only the impression that Earth was a violent planet.

At last they came to a channel that seemed to promise useful information. A small Earthling, who evidently had authority, instructed three others in the use of a numbered wheel. Each would spin it in turn, and then recite a lesson, to the approval or disapproval of the small Earthling, whose occasional growls evoked a maniacal cackling from the unseen audience.

Meanwhile another Earthling with long blonde hair posed, postured, and danced back and forth in front of a giant display board, where blockish characters appeared in increasing numbers. When the whole board was lined with characters, a clatter of Earthlings slapping their forelimbs together sounded offscreen.

The two young cats watched the program for several minutes, but were not enlightened, and again switched channels.

More violence. One Earthling would hurl a hard white sphere with great velocity at a succession of others, who would try to knock it back at him with still greater violence using murderous clubs. When one succeeded, the team of Earthlings stationed here and there behind the hurler would scramble madly about, chasing after the white sphere and flinging it one to the other, while a terrible multitude roared and shouted at them.

This was the least comprehensible spectacle they had yet viewed. They still desperately needed information, but it was evident by now that they would not get it from this display screen. Only from the backgrounds of the chase-and-murder sequences had they gained any picture at all of this alien world. They would just have to get out, ill prepared though they were, and confront its challenges as best they could.

But how to get out? Behind a set of plastic blinds they discovered a pair of framed glass panels, one of which was raised at the bottom just far enough for them to crawl beneath. Examining it more closely, they were discouraged by a screen of woven metal strands just outside the opening, which was bolted down and could well trip some kind of alarm.

Springing down from the sill, they next discovered the source of the shutting noise they had heard while still inside their makeshift cage. The slablike gray panel had hinges at one side, and was evidently the

usual means of egress. Once again using the inverted
trash can to stand on, they examined the shiny metal
knob apparatus halfway up the side opposite the
hinges. A lock checked the knob from turning, but it
was hardly more complex than the one on their cage,
and with perfect teamwork they needed only minutes
to defeat its mechanism, employing a stiff plastic card
they discovered in the top drawer of the desk as their
principal tool.

They had been conditioned since kittenhood never to
leave a work space without first restoring every last ar-
ticle there to its original place. They put the trash can
back exactly were they found it, relocked the power-
pack casing atop the desk, and smoothed all paw marks
from the carpet. Only then did they crack open the
door and peek into the corridor outside.

A red-and-gold carpet ran its length; some of the
doors along it were solid, others had glass panels, and
there were cubicles without any doors at all. A light
shone in one of these, from which rose and fell the angry growlings of two Earthlings.

It would be safest to head in the opposite direction,
and one braced her forepaws against the jamb, while
the other hopped acrobatically onto her shoulders and
relocked the door. The carpet was a handy place to
hide the stiff plastic card under; it also cushioned the
pressures of gravity as they hurried down it, side by
side, keeping perfect step.

Their ears peaked at the jungle of alien noises; their
nose leathers twitched at the piquancy of exciting
smells. Shipboard life was mute, sterilely clean, and
virtually without odor; above all it was protective.
Never in their young lives had they missed a meal or
gone so long without rest, and their alertness was disturbed again and again by fond memories of their
nourishment stalls, and of donning sleep-learning caps
and snuggling down inside their nice warm pods.

Millennia had passed since their ancestors had
hunted for their own food, and neither of them had any

notion of how to feed herself, much less find a safe place to sleep. Not with Earthlings shooting, stabbing, hurling missiles, beating, burning, and blowing each other up everywhere on this violent planet.

They now perceived more growling sounds, growing louder and clearer as they neared an adjacent corridor, and the cats froze like two pointers on a scent, listening. It was the big, ugly Earthling who had brought them here from outer space; the multiple tread of feet indicated he had at least three companions. Diving into the nearest cubicle, they crouched in the shadows, poised to spring over its partitions, which did not reach to the ceiling, should anyone try to enter.

Their estimate was correct. There were four Earthlings, and it was the biggest and ugliest of them who led the way past the doorway; all were too intent on their growling to glance inside. The instant the last heel swung out of sight, the two cats sprang to the opening and peeked after them.

They saw the big, ugly one fit a key into the door they had just relocked, and hold it open respectfully for a companion who looked every bit as mean as he did, though the newcomer was not so hulking and seemed to wield authority. Then the corridor was deserted again, and like twin shadows, the felines scooted around the corner and out of sight.

The smells were stronger now, but more familiar; they sensed the presence of machines and electronic circuitry and hurried together down the carpeted corridor, forepaws in marching step, until it debouched into a tiled storage area. Crates of various shapes and sizes were stacked against the walls; at the center of the floor loomed a machine they recognized from one of the chase-and-murder episodes on the video screen, in which one demented Earthling ran over several others who had been trying to kill him with exploding weapons. Its forklift was also stacked with crates, balanced so that a narrow space separated them from the body of the vehicle.

It was into this space that they wriggled, as their handiest hiding place, when they heard approaching footsteps. Taking up positions on either side of the opening, they peered warily out in two directions at once; but the footsteps, sounding nearer and nearer, approached directly from the rear, so they could not see who was coming. Then they heard someone clambering atop the vehicle, and a moment later there arose a heavy rumbling directly ahead. The whole wall seemed to be moving, startling them, until they realized that it was just a huge door rolling aside. Then an electric motor began to whir behind them, and the next thing they knew they were moving ponderously forward out of the storage area and into a colossal hangar.

Team-think and the telepathic pooling of impressions brought to their minds a simultaneous picture of their surroundings from both sides of the vehicle at once. The cat peeking out on the left could see the great black stealth shuttle, aswarm with scrubbed and close-cropped young men in white coveralls, stenciled in black letters with the insignia B.I.T.E. The cat on the right had a clear view of the hangar wall, including a number of doors and windows opened for ventilation. They mutually analyzed their escape route while at the same time continuing to pool their opposing impressions.

The instant the forklift halted, the cat on the left side wriggled over to the right. Both were in complete agreement about which shadows to dodge through, which crates, machines, and parked vehicles to use as cover, and the most promising opening in the hangar wall to run for. They waited tensely while the growls of approaching Earthlings grew louder and more distinct; then they heard the driver of their vehicle climb down its left side and emit incomprehensible responses. This was the critical moment, and they slipped from cover, dived together into the nearest shadow, dodged behind a skid stacked with baled rags, and were gone.

"Hey, what was that?" The strapping young forklift driver turned an instant too late to see them. "I think we got rats in here, Steve."

"Don't talk goofy. You know this place is kept like a hospital." The balding, potbellied foreman was accompanied by four Brainers in uniform-white coveralls. "The Big Guy hears about rats in here, or anywheres inside the Restricted Zone, and heads roll. Maybe yours, if you couldn't back it up. Now are you positive, absolutely positive you saw rats?"

"Something small and furry dodged behind them bales over there. I caught only a glimpse out of the corner of my eye, as I was climbing down. But what else could it have been?"

"Forget it, Hal. Tell the Big Guy about rats, and he'll think some enemy is plotting to give him a disease. You know how he is."

"I know how he is with people who don't show him the proper respect." He nodded toward the four scrubbed, close-cropped young men, who were now docilely unloading the crates from his forklift. "Lucky we're friends, Steve."

"Your word against mine, Hal. Mr. Grotten is a stickler for correct police procedure, and you got no witnesses."

"What about these four?"

"Be serious. Brainers don't have an opinion till you give it to 'em."

"I am serious. I just spotted Mr. Grotten himself, heading for office country with Angel, Mickey Dunstun, and the night security chief."

"Oho, so it's brownie points you're after."

"Why not? We're all in it for all we can get. Just like the Big Guy himself always says. Soon's your Brainers finish unloading, I make a U-turn back to office country."

True to his word, minutes later, the driver parked his forklift back in the storage area, hit a button on a nearby stanchion, and strode up the corridor, as the huge sliding door ground shut behind him.

He was taking a risk, of course. He, too, wore the insignia B.I.T.E. on the back of his white coveralls, and knew all too well the paranoid fears and delusions attributed to the founder of Benton Ingles Transworld Enterprises. A report of rats at his restricted air base, the most jealously policed of all his secret operations anywhere in the world—unless rumors about mysterious constructions on an equatorial island were true— would goad him to fury. Heads would roll, or more likely undergo cranial surgery and a readjustment of personality. But each head that rolled or was surgically altered meant a new opportunity for power and advancement—assuming the person who reported the rats did not end up with his own personality readjusted.

The dreaded Chief of Operations of B.I.T.E., second only to Benton Ingles himself in authority, suffered no such fears or delusions. Kurt Grotten was ruthless efficiency personified. After newspaper allegations of corruption and brutality had cost him his captaincy on the Los Angeles police force, the best job he had been able to land was that of night desk sergeant at a third-rate seaside resort.

Soon afterward, Benton Ingles fixed upon the region as the future hub of his worldwide industrial empire—a despoilation of the environment so gross that it had stirred a national outcry—only to find himself stymied by opposition in the legislature. But when, within a few days, the secretary of state drowned under mysterious circumstances, two environmentalist senators were killed in unwitnessed automobile accidents, attributed to drunken driving, and a committee chairman shocked all who knew him by committing suicide—the official verdict of the coroner—there were enough changes of heart among the surviving solons to bias the vote in favor of industrialization.

However these events came about, Kurt Grotten shortly thereafter resigned his job as desk sergeant, and assumed the more arbitrary and lucrative post he now commanded.

He was reputed to keep secret files on friends and enemies alike, in the manner of the late J. Edgar Hoover, so that anyone who dared question his mandates could be coerced back into line by threats of blackmail. No man, not even Benton Ingles himself, had played a more decisive role in the evolution of a cluster of seaside resorts into Ingles City, the fastest growing industrial complex in California, if not in all of America.

His pet means of intimidation was to encourage underlings to denounce their superiors; his door was always open to informers, his ear to furtive accusations against company officials and fellow workers. It was not in his interest that anybody in the organization trust anybody else, and nobody did. There was hardly an official in B.I.T.E. who didn't owe his position to some denunciation or other—or who did not tremble at the thought of being denounced in turn.

Bonuses and promotions on the one hand, hellish inflictions on the other: as the forklift driver turned up the adjacent corridor, he reconsidered the risk he was running, and became less and less sure of himself.

"On my mother's grave, Mr. Grotten, there were two cats aboard the UN Commstat. I knew you'd want evidence, so I brought the pair of 'em down in this here power-pack casing."

The driver recognized the deep, raspy voice coming from an open doorway just ahead, and stopped dead in his tracks. If even a tenth of the rumors about Angel were true, it behooved any man concerned with his immediate health and well-being to be wary. The next voice he recognized was that of Chief Grotten:

"Let's review the evidence. The room door was locked, the power-pack casing was locked, the only window open even a crack has a screen outside that's bolted shut. Are you telling me, Angel, that a pair of cats not only unlocked their cage door from the inside, and relocked it, but also unlocked and relocked the room door without a key? Cats?"

It was the tone more than the actual words that intimidated the driver. Chief Grotten was notoriously sensitive about his high-pitched voice and normally affected a masculine baritone. Only in moments of anger did he lapse into shrillness and squall like an old woman. His voice was now ominously high-pitched:

"Maybe you two are suffering from jet lag. I mean, all the way out to Sulatonga, then up to the UN Commstat, and back here again. That might make anybody think he saw cats. Tell me if I'm wrong, Mickey."

"I think that's what must have happened, sir," Dunstun abjectly agreed. "Under pressure and the jet lag, like you say, we just got a little mixed up. But we did a good job upstairs."

"You get paid to do a good job, Mickey. It's for those who don't that we make special arrangements." His words were measured, but still ominously high-pitched. "Now what about you, Angel? If you still insist you saw cats, I'll naturally bring it to the attention of Mr. Ingles. Though perhaps we should first send you over to the Med Center for a checkup, to make sure you're not needlessly upsetting him without evidence. As you know, we have a very private wing there for treating special cases."

Angel quickly recanted. "I guess I made a mistake, sir. Like Mickey says, we were under pressure, and the jet lag, and all that. Don't hold it against me, sir. I'll do better the next time. I caught that snoopy broad for you, didn't I? If it's not too late, sir, I'd like to get in on her interrogation."

"That's already being taken care of, Angel." Grotten's voice deepened into a baritone. "Now I'm the last man to discourage employees of B.I.T.E. from going the extra mile, or from reporting errors or wrongdoing anywhere in the organization. Just be more careful in the future. That goes for you, too,

Mickey. I've wasted enough time over this non-sense. . . ."

The forklift driver waited not a moment longer to tiptoe hurriedly back up the corridor. He was now pretty sure it had not been rats he saw out in the hangar; though this was definitely the wrong moment (if there ever could be a right moment) for showing up the vindictive Chief of Operations. But the breaking up of the conference had taken him unawares, and he had not quite reached the corner, when Angel shambled out into the corridor, his shoulders thrust belligerently forward, a scowl twisting his brutish countenance.

Their eyes met for only an instant, but the driver knew he had been recognized.

Cost effectiveness was the primary consideration of any B.I.T.E. architect, anywhere in the world, and the sprawling conglomeration of hangars, offices, and workshops was constructed as cheaply as possible out of cinder block and corrugated iron, painted white to minimize the expense of air-conditioning during the hot California summers. Had it not stood in the Restricted Zone, isolated from public view, critics would have denounced it as yet another B.I.T.E. eyesore.

Chief Grotten emerged alone into the parking lot, where his sinister black sedan squatted pantherlike in its reserved space. He had had it custom-built in Germany to police specifications, with bulletproof windows tinted so eyes could see out but not in, creating the same effect as the intimidating dark glasses of a traffic cop.

It was constantly monitored by hidden television cameras. Nonetheless he circled it twice with an infared remote-detection sensor, held at two different levels, to assure himself that it had not been tampered with in his absence.

Sliding behind the wheel, he noticed a light on the telephone recorder and keyed in his password. The message was brief, spoken by a woman with a thick

Italian accent, and he smiled sardonically as he heard her choice for tonight's rendezvous. Darling Carla, he thought, as he swung the black sedan out of the parking lot. Her sense of vengeance was exquisite.

Years had passed since she'd been chosen Second Runner Up in a Miss World contest. As the wife of Benton Ingles, who ranked only after the Sultan of Brunei as the richest man on Earth, she could now indulge in any conceivable luxury, and did. Yet it still rankled her vanity that two women had been judged more beautiful, and her vindictiveness, like her indulgences, grew yearly more extravagant with the fading of her looks.

He had been instrumental in the humbling of her rivals, and her gratitude had served him well.

Miss World would be middle-aged by the time she was released from prison, where she was now serving the maximum term for the possession of narcotics, despite continued protests that the incriminating evidence had been planted. Carla, out of the goodness of her heart, sometimes dropped in on visiting days to cheer her up, and regularly sent her gifts of candy and other fattening foods.

The First Runner Up, a blonde Austrian woman of angelic beauty, had also suffered misfortunes. When her husband took his own life, despairing over inexplicable business losses and the rejection of his every application for credit, she had been left destitute with two small children to care for. A godsent offer of work in the movies lured her to Hollywood, where she was humiliated to discover that the films were the lowest type of pornography. Deceived, stranded, more destitute than ever, the only job she could find was that of waitress and dishwasher at an all-night diner on the outskirts of Ingles City, and even that opportunity came through the influence of her former rival.

Carla sometimes dined there, chauffeured in her private limousine, and lavishly decked out in diamonds and furs. Her commiseration and good humor, when the grateful woman waited on her table, did credit to her nature, though she tipped sparingly.

Glancing at his watch as he sped through a crowded intersection, Chief Grotten stomped the accelerator. The nonsense about finding cats in outer space had cost him precious time, and Carla was not a woman to be kept waiting. She was still sensually attractive, her charms enhanced by the most fashionable hairdressers and cosmeticians in America, her increasingly voluptuous figure garbed more expensively than any queen's. But she was touchy about real or imagined slights to those charms, and there was no telling where one of her rages might lead, at a moment with B.I.T.E. was on the threshold of its most daring enterprise.

His tires shrieked as he wheeled around a corner and sped toward the next intersection, outracing a blue sports car, swerving past a bread truck. His radar detector sounded, but he ignored it and shot arrogantly through a yellow light.

The driver of the squad car parked stealthily just inside the mouth of an alley reached for the ignition; but his partner had had a better look at the speeding black sedan, and checked his hand. No police officer with any expectation of present or future employment in law enforcement would ever think of interfering with that particular car. Not in Ingles City.

Neon, asphalt, reinforced concrete, painted cinder block walls, gas stations, shopping malls, fast-food drive-ins, and the all-pervasive reek of exhaust fumes; the only parks were industrial parks, the only surviving patches of greenery appropriated for subdivisions and garbage dumps. Town after town had withered beneath the metastasizing urban sprawl, and Royal Beach alone, some few miles down the coast, still resisted the contagion. How the Royal Beach Preservation Society could best be undermined, and the last obstacle to the ascendency of Ingles City removed forever, was something he particularly wanted to discuss tonight with Carla.

She herself could be an obstacle, capable of subverting his own secret ambitions for ascendancy, if not handled just right. Voluptuous and wildly passionate, loving power for its own sake, ruthless toward anyone or anything that stood in her way, merciless toward enemies, avenging any grievance: she was a woman after his own heart.

Her husband had lately begun to weary of her indulgences and vanity, and to suspect her of plotting against him; thus relegating her to the same status as the overwhelming majority of the human race. Should his plans to aggrandize B.I.T.E. into a New World Order materialize, she could well become expendable. Grotten had no doubts that disposing of her would then become his personal assignment, or that he would carry it out with the same ruthless efficiency with which he had carried out all such assignments in the past. True, she had given him much pleasure, but only weaklings and degenerates let their personal sentiments interfere with business. Meanwhile she could be useful.

Accelerator floored, tires squealing around corners, horn blowing the traffic aside as he wove in and out, he reached his destination barely to the minute. In fact he was turning into the parking lot of the Amber Light as he spotted Carla emerging through the front door.

Gorgeous in her new ermine cape, glittering with diamonds, she would have been a magnet for every mugger in California, except that he or one of his men had her under continual surveillance, by order of her suspicious husband. He let her believe that their trysts were a grave risk, exciting both her vanity and her passions, while out of old habit as a policeman he covered his butt. Any report to her husband had first to cross his own desk, any wiretap recording of telephone calls to or from himself—the telephones of all B.I.T.E. employees were routinely tapped—was accessible to nobody else.

The stakes were too high, and he was too close to success, to let himself be tripped up now by personal sentiments or carelessness.

"Whatsa matter, you no anxious to see me no more." She sat poutingly at the opposite end of the front seat, her ermine cape drawn haughtily about her. "Always before, you come early."

"I've thought of nothing but this moment all day long, darling. But you know the risks I take in meeting you, and what your husband would do to me if some busybody reported my car sitting here in the parking lot, waiting for you." He took a pair of binoculars out of the glove compartment. "I've been watching you from a safe distance. You seemed to be enjoying your dinner, though your waitress looked upset about something."

Mollified, she relaxed and loosened her ermine cape. "She'sa madly jealous of me." She held up her right wrist and admired the flash and glitter of her new diamond bracelet, which brilliantly reflected the gleam of passing streetlights.

He drove within the speed limit now; there was no longer any hurry, they had the whole night before them, and he wanted to interrogate her before they reached their trysting place. Nor did he take a direct route. He was a policeman every waking hour, and the watch sections were about to change inside the Restricted Zone; the sight of his car patrolling along the fence was always a powerful incentive to discipline.

"They say Miss World don't look so hot these days, up at Stateville." He drew her closer to him. "Forget the regular visiting hours, by the way. I fixed it with the warden so you can visit her any time you like."

"Those stupid judges." She snuggled against him. "If they could see her now, none would vote for her. I think tomorrow I bring her some candy, or maybe the next day."

"Good idea. Just let me know if she don't appreciate all you've done for her, and the warden will make other arrangements for her work assignments and living quarters. Speaking of visiting, have you been to Royal Beach lately?" He asked the question offhandedly, though he had logged her departure and arrival times there with the precision of a railroad schedule.

"Ah, I visit Lola, when was it, three days ago. Despite all her paint and powder, her wigs and padding and foolishness, it is sometimes nice to talk to one from the old country."

"What did you talk about?" He watched her out of the corner of his eye.

"It make her unhappy that other big stars of her day—not many are still alive—get television specials and film festivals, and she gets nothing. So we talk about a new book about old Hollywood. She show me the line where the writer say a nice thing about her, so she'sa buy all his unsold copies, like always. She got the stuff piled up all over the place. Her house look like a palace outside, and a junkyard inside."

From surveillance photographs he knew exactly what the exterior of the ornate old mansion looked like—there were many such in Royal Beach, whose Victorian splendors were its major tourist attraction—but his agents had not yet been able to penetrate its interior. Nor had he found any means of intimidating its bizarre owner.

He turned off the main road, a few blocks short of the UCIC campus, and wound through a new subdivision of cinder block duplexes, roofed with all-weather plastic and painted various shades of pastel, housing mostly faculty members and their families. He stopped before a high chain link fence topped with barbed wire and flicked off the headlights.

"Not here, darling," he quickly reassured her, sensing her dissatisfaction. "This would never be good enough for you. No, I'm taking you to a mansion overlooking the sea, with silk sheets and champagne.

The owner is vacationing in Monte Carlo, and won't return for the rest of this year, perhaps never. We'll have it all to ourselves, whenever we want it."

"He fears what you have on him in your secret files?"

He shrugged. "It's useful to know where the bodies are buried."

Extracting the binoculars once more from the glove compartment, he swept the complex of buildings, hangars, and airstrips within the Restricted Zone. The end of one watch and the beginning of the next was the best time for spotting derelictions of duty. The campus of the University of California at Ingles City was also within his jurisdiction; but eggheads were too foolish and trivial to concern him, and he relegated its policing to subordinates.

Carla was not impatient. It excited her to watch the feared Chief of Operations punish underlings, especially when he used his fists, and she lit a cigarette and settled back, exhaling the fumes of Turkish and Egyptian tobaccos, her personal blend.

"Poor Lola." She sighed dramatically, like a heroine of grand opera, though all the while eyeing him furtively as if bent on a subtle interrogation of her own. "I know she is stop my husband's plans for Royal Beach, but I hate to see her hurt."

"That's business, darling." He took out his pocket notebook, and jotted down a list of violations. A hangar door left unsecured, two watchmen out of uniform, a burned-out light, and a gate guard sneaking a cigarette while on duty. Meting out discipline tomorrow would make his day. "I'm glad you don't meddle with such things. Your soul is too sensitive."

"Alas, it is my weakness." She sighed more dramatically still. "But what can you do to poor Lola? She'sa pay her taxes, and it'sa how many years now since the old scandal about the cocaine? Fifty? Sixty? She was then the big star of the movies, before they talk."

"I've tried to protect her, for your sake. I know how sensitive you are. But business can sometimes be cruel, darling. Should your husband decide she has to be destroyed, the most I can do is tell you about it in advance, though you must promise not to warn her."

"Yes, I know the business does not permit such sensitive feelings as mine, so I will not warn her." She snuggled into her ermine cape, as if it were the arms of a lover, and inhaled voluptuously from her cigarette. "My heart aches for her even now, when I think of how I shall console her to the last, and all the time she will never know what is going to happen to her."

The look on her face reminded him of a cat holding a canary tenderly in its claws, not wanting to rush the fun. He knew, though, that B.I.T.E. was being frustrated from expansion into Royal Beach by more than just one dotty old woman.

Lola Londi was another Italian beauty queen, of a long bygone era. Her brief movie stardom had ended with the coming of the talkies; but her peasant's distrust of any commodity but land had meanwhile served her well. She'd converted most of her untaxed salary into local real estate, then dirt cheap, and her many lovers were soon aware that the gift of an orange grove or a parcel of building lots was more likely to win her favors than showering her with diamonds. A goodly chunk of her holdings later developed into the business district of Los Angeles, and she remained to this day the largest owner of land in and around Royal Beach. Though seemingly dotty about everything else, her insights into property values were still uncannily shrewd.

He had learned this the first and only time he tried to pressure her into selling out. With regal calmness she informed him that she was considering an endowment of all her property to the Federal Government, for public use, as the best means of escaping the bother it was giving her. Soon afterward, a bill was proposed in Washington, by an elderly representative known to have once been her admirer, to declare Royal Beach and all its Victorian splendors a national monument.

Only through expensive congressional arm-twisting did Benton Ingles manage to get the bill tabled. The sequel was that B.I.T.E. never again bothered her about property.

Nor had he been able to exploit the old cocaine scandal. Half a century had passed since headlines blazoned her arrest at a Hollywood orgy. The tabloids would nonetheless have dug it all up again, dragging her through the mud with cheap innuendos and lurid photographs, had she been publically arraigned for possession of narcotics. Fear of so final a degradation would surely have made her more willing to negotiate.

But the agent he sent to plant the evidence, an experienced operative in such undertakings, was caught and thrashed by her chauffeur, a retired prizefighter. That the agent, when he at last got out of traction, was further disciplined by having his personality surgically readjusted did nothing to advance the interests of B.I.T.E. At least, in regard to Royal Beach.

It remained a quandary, made doubly vexatious by the growing power and influence of the Royal Beach Preservation Society.

Benton Ingles suspected them of a conspiracy against him, his inevitable reaction these days to anyone or anything that thwarted his ambitions. Exactly how far those ranged, even to world domination, no one could say with confidence, any more than one could know the full repercussions of his plane crash, eleven years ago. His physical injuries were on the medical records, the maiming of his body visible to all eyes, but no physician could diagnose the extent to which his mind had been left scarred and twisted.

Manipulating him through his paranoid delusions

was an art form, but to what extremes he might be carried by his suspicions that his wife was also plotting against him was a growing concern to Chief Grotten. The beautiful Carla was not intelligent, but her cunning and ruthlessness, stirred by untamed passions, could at any instant bring all Grotten's ambitions tumbling down, perhaps even jeopardize his very life. What he needed was some safe means of release in a crisis. It was her own idle curiosity that at last gave it to him.

Whether by chance or, more likely, intention (she was an inveterate eavesdropper), she had picked up the name Sulatonga from a conversation she was not meant to overhear. All she had learned from a gazetteer was that it was an equatorial island in the Pacific, used during the Fifties for hydrogen bomb testing. All she learned from him was that B.I.T.E. harvested guano there, for the manufacture of nitrates.

This disgusted her, and she had said that she would certainly never take a vacation on Sulatonga, and he had been careful never to make her any more curious. But her possession of the name, with Project Nimrod on the verge of countdown, was potentially more explosive than any nitrates ever detonated.

"Watch out!" she cried, as he started to pull away.

"What? I didn't see anything." He peered into the rearview mirror.

"Two cats. They were crossing the street, and you almost ran them over. You should have turned on your headlights."

"There, now every cat in Ingles City can see me." He drove slowly along beside the high chain link fence, headlights blazing, so that every employee inside the RZ could also see him. "It seems like everywhere I go tonight people see cats that I don't."

He weighed a possible connection, but then shook his head. There were no facts, no hard evidence, not even clues upon which a policeman could justify fur-

ther investigation. Besides, the eggheads and degenerates who lived here in this faculty subdivision often
kept pussycats as pets. Though he knew of at least one
mean dog in the neighborhood.

CHAPTER III

The two young cats crouched side by side in the bushes, their minds in telepathic rapport. They had not realized that engines could smell so foul, or that the big dormant machines parked along the street could spring so unexpectedly into life. But their scheduled feeding time was long overdue, a schedule that had never varied in all their young lives, and a whole menu of strange and enticing aromas had momentarily beguiled them into heedlessness. More caution was needed if they hoped to survive on this violent planet.

Another of the foul-smelling machines rushed past, its forward lights glaring like monstrous eyes. But the cats were warier now and did not leave the sheltering bushes until all was clear. Other lights glowed atop poles spaced at regular intervals before the rude dwellings of the Earthlings; feeble illumination that hardly bedimmed the lights of heaven, constellations familiar to them from shipboard monitors. What surprised them was that here the stars twinkled.

More and more stars were becoming visible to them, as the last patches of clouds scudded across the sky. They sensed Earthlings all around them, and creatures still more primitive, as well as a galaxy of rudimentary electronic devices in operation. They also sensed food nearby, but this time the enticing aroma only made them more cautious. Never out of step, all their movements coordinated, they edged purposefully toward its source.

The moon was rising now, and a bowl of table

scraps, set out in the yard of an Earthling dwelling surrounded by a low metal fence, fixed their attention.
The pit bull whose dinner it was prowled furiously
back and forth, ready to defend it against marauders of
any size or rapacity. It was the ugliest and most savage
creature the two cats had yet encountered on the
planet, and they hung back to analyze their prospects.
The brute was clearly not aware of their presence. But
why was it so angry?

Then they spotted another brute of similar features,
though slighter in build, facing it through the chain
link fence with a taunting demeanor. The coyote was
an old adversary, whose quickness and agility, guided
by a sly cunning, had maddened the pit bull again and
again this season, raiding his house's rubbish heap,
overturning garbage cans on property he was supposed
to be guarding, stealing dinners from beneath his very
nose. With the hated face mocking him from only
inches away, the dog could do nothing but bite the
fence wires in frustration.

But then the coyote sensed an easier meal. Many of
the faculty members living in the subdivision had family pets, and a staple of his diet for months past had
been house cats, with now and then a tasty kitten for
dessert. Such was his quickness that the two young
cats, hanging back in the shadows, did not realize they
were in danger until the brute was almost on top of
them, its fangs bared to rend and devour.

A thousand generations separated them from attacks
by predators, but they sensed that here was a terrible
enemy, and their team-think training had conditioned
them to analyze and respond instantly to emergencies.
On the other hand, hardly a day separated the coyote
from the killing and eating of an Angora kitten, leather
collar and all, and he expected to break the neck of at
least one of these tasty-looking youngsters at a pounce.

What he did not expect was for them to spring simultaneously in opposite directions at the last possible
instant; for the house cats he preyed upon had never

before shown such agility, and were usually too pampered and overfed to fight back. His hungry overconfidence carried him well past the mark.

But his own agility was almost supernatural, and he righted himself in an instant and spun back for another pounce. His mouth began to water as he saw that the two cats had foolishly trapped themselves against the fence gate, on the other side of which the pit bull continued to glare out at him. Here was a chance to break the necks of both cats at once, and eat his dinner right under the dog's nose, and he leapt hungrily for the kill.

It was futile now for the cats to try and run away, and this time he was ready for their agile dodging. But he was again confused when one of them propped her forepaws against the gatepost, while the other hopped acrobatically onto her shoulders and pushed the handle. The next instant they were beyond the reach of his snapping jaws, swinging the gate open behind them. He skidded to a dead halt—muzzle-to-muzzle with the pit bull.

"Yip!" He shot straight into the air, his paws churning wildly, and hit the ground running.

Such was his quickness that, despite the proximity of his enemy, he came within inches of escaping. But unfortunately for him those inches were at the end of his tail, and the jaws that clamped shut on it were like a steel trap. For months now he had been taunting and humiliating the pit bull; but now it was the dog's turn, and the fur literally flew.

Mothers, fathers, and children alike ran to doors and windows up and down the block, alarmed by the wild snarling outside. But had they known the source of the uproar, all would have rejoiced. The heartbreaking loss of house cats and kittens would nevermore grieve their neighborhood.

The two young cats, on the other hand, were horrified. Not even the scenes of violence they had witnessed on the video screen had prepared them for such savagery. Hungry as they were, they forgot all about stealing the pit bull's dinner while he was worrying the carcass of his old enemy and used the opportunity to flee. Shunning the glow of the streetlights, they trotted in step up the asphalt road.

They had climbed without difficulty through the coils of barbed wire atop the chainlink fence, escaping an ugly sprawl of hangars, offices, and concrete runways. The concrete-and-plastic ugliness squatting all around them was still less inviting, and they again looked urgently for some means of escape. At last, turning a corner, they spotted an open campus directly ahead, and simultaneously quickened their pace.

Then they were confronted by a new menace. A hideous yowling noise out of the shrubbery overhanging the road before them, and into the moonlight emerged a creature startlingly like themselves, though it was half again as big and more than their combined weight. Not a crew chief aboard ship was of such dimensions; certainly none had such fangs and whiskers. They stopped and tried to communicate with it telepathically, but sensed in return only brutishness and stupidity.

Back arched, its fur standing on end, it seemed more menacing still as it sidled toward them. Then, without warning, its hideous yowling exploded into a scream of rage, and it attacked. But it turned out to be as slow and clumsy as it was stupid, and they easily evaded the swipe of its claws. Administering team-think discipline to the brute would have served no useful purpose, so they merely dodged around it and continued on their way. It did not pursue them.

Glancing back, they saw it sit plump in the middle of the road and complacently lick its paws, evidently concerned only with the defense of its own territory.

What perplexed them most about this alien world was that it was not completely alien. Earthlings, whom they were now convinced must be the ruling species of the planet, were uncouth reflections of the Masters, and here was a creature so like themselves it was uncanny. Of any ancestral relationship they were, of course, unaware; neither could they know by how much their intelligence exceeded that of any other cat on the planet. Their eyesight was more raptorial than feline, and they distinguished colors with the perceptiveness of a human artist. However, what they followed now were their noses.

The pavement ceased abruptly, and before them swelled a greenery of lawns, trees, and flowering shrubs, interrupted here and there by Earthling structures, which seemed to them little more than piles of masonry. Blossoms of many colors exuded sweet perfumes, and they sensed concentrations of electronic equipment, but what truly excited their senses was the most delectable aroma they had ever smelled. Shipboard food was bland and without seasoning or much natural flavor; but never in their lives had they gone so long without a meal, and they trotted in step over the campus lawns, guided by their twitching nostrils.

They had a fix now on a bank of operational computers, in the windowless brick tower looming directly ahead, the tallest structure they had so far encountered on the planet. The beguiling aroma wafted from the same general direction, growing ever stronger and more delectable as they approached. It was still quite faint, virtually undetectable by duller senses, but theirs were made keen by hunger and remultiplied by a team-think sharing of perceptions, and they followed it unerringly toward the multistoried brick building.

Then they saw a muscular young Earthling in a blue uniform converging on a side entrance of the building and hastened to overtake him. Their super-acute perceptions did not sense in him the violence and cruelty of other Earthlings, and they outflanked him as he turned up the concrete walk toward a steel door over which glowed a small light bulb. Just before he reached it, they cautiously emerged together from the shrubbery.

"Well, well, and what have we here?" He looked curiously down at them. The nameplate on his blue shirt read TIM WAVERLY; he was tall and well tanned, with the physique of a bodybuilder, yet his manner was retiring, almost self-effacing. At last he realized that both cats were staring at the brown paper bag in his hand, and he laughed good-naturedly. "Oho, so that's the attraction. I guess this stuff smells pretty strong, even wrapped in plastic. I'm surprised half the pussy-cats on campus aren't after me."

The two young cats, reassured by his gentleness, looked trustingly up at him. They'd realized by now that they were unable to communicate telepathically with Earthlings, the way that they had with the Masters, and so they simultaneously raised their right paws toward the bag.

He blinked in surprise. He had often seen dogs sit up and beg, or raise their paws to "shake hands," but never cats. Though, of course, he knew little about their ways. His mother was allergic to animal hair, so he had never been allowed to keep pets as a child.

"All right, I've always been a soft touch for panhandlers." He laid his schoolbooks on the stoop, and opened the brown paper bag. "Really, you're doing me a favor. Dad's a fisherman and catches more fish than he and Mother could ever eat. It's a sin to waste food, but I've been eating so much salmon lately that I'm ready to start meowing myself. I can't even give the stuff away fast enough, and have to pay extra fees to use the dorm freezer." He spoke with the wistfulness of a lonely person, all too accustomed to talking to himself for lack of other company, as he peeled open the clinging plastic wrap, and laid the sandwich before the two cats. "Just don't leave a mess, young ladies. We have strict rules on this campus against litterbugs."

In fact, they turned out to be such extraordinarily dainty eaters that he wondered what breed they could possibly be. They were unusually gracile, with a bluish-pearl color and bandit masking he could not re-call ever seeing before; and though their faces were distinctly feline, the peculiar shape of their foreheads gave him an uncanny impression of intelligence.

Or was he just fantasizing again? He knew it was a bad habit; his mother had often corrected his tendency to color everyday events with his own imagination. But whatever the cats were, he himself was still a student working nights to pay his tuition, and if he didn't get cracking he'd be out of a job.

It took him only minutes to sign in, relieve the watch in the main computer room, and verify the data recorded in the log. His duties were not onerous: make scheduled checks of dial readings, record them in the log, keep Security Central regularly informed about the status of all on-line equipment, and sweep, swab, and buff the floor. That left him most of the night free for doing homework, calisthenics, sets of dumbbell exercises, and playing chess against the mainframe. But he did not forget the sandwich wrapper. For whereas student litterbugs might only be fined, university employees who littered were subject to official reprimand.

He slipped out the side entrance just as the cats were finishing their sandwich, dutifully wasting not a crumb. He smiled at the nicety of their eating—until he saw them neatly fold and refold the plastic wrapper into a perfectly square pad, ready for disposal. Only after blinking in astonishment for several moments did he become aware that they were looking expectantly up at him, as if to tell him they were still hungry.

He returned in minutes with another sandwich, which, out of curiosity, he placed before them unwrapped. If he was astonished before, he now fairly gaped as he watched them peel open the clinging plastic wrapper with their amazingly dexterous forepaws, every movement team coordinated to minimize effort and eliminate waste or damage. They even bit and swallowed in unison, like mirror images of each other.

Was he cracking up? Since childhood his parents had encouraged him to pay his own expenses, which they said would help him learn the value of money.

Working all night, grinding out straight As all day in Business Administration, a major insisted on by both his mother and father, and working out at all hours in the campus weight room; it left him scant time for making friends or dating—which his parents discouraged in any case. Just as they frowned upon his acquaintance with Tedworth Vay, though the renowned investigator of the occult also lived in Royal Beach. Had the strain and isolation become too much for him? To his old tendency to fantasize, he had, of late, added the lonely habit of talking to himself. Was he now also beginning to hallucinate?

It was a mystery like those he read about in occult literature. He had to investigate, no matter what the consequences, just as Tedworth Vay would have under the circumstances. But how? Take possession of the cats, obviously—assuming they really existed—though this might get him into serious trouble. Were he discovered bringing animals into the main computer room, he would at the very least be reprimanded, perhaps even fired. That was a risk he would have to face.

There were also risks in annoying a feeding cat; a lesson he had learned painfully as a child, and he rewrapped the partially eaten sandwich with diffidence. But his apprehensions proved unfounded; the two young cats only regarded him aloofly, like a pair of duchesses too well bred to notice the indecorum of the vulgar.

"This way, young ladies, if you please." He held open the side door for them.

Again they astonished him. With no trace of feline skittishness, they not only preceded him unhesitatingly into the building, but continued down the corridor, and straight into the main computer room, somehow divining exactly where he wanted them to go. He had to hurry to catch up.

He secured the door behind him, but it had a spy window through which prowling security officers could make sneak checks on employees, so he led the cats out of sight behind a tape-drive unit, before again placing the sandwich in front them. But instead of unwrapping it at once, they walked off in opposite directions, one exploring the left side of the room, the other the right.

He had heard it was normal feline behavior for a cat to scout every nook and corner for possible enemies, prior to settling down in a strange interior; though the behavior of these cats seemed anything but normal. Systematically, they examined bank after bank of electronic equipment—memory units, line printers, input/output units, disk and tape drives, towering central processing units, CRT terminals, display panels, the very telephone units on the desk—like a pair of visiting technicians.

At last they met at the center of the room and sat with their heads together for several minutes as if silently comparing notes. The University of California at Ingles City had the newest and most expensive mainframe of any school in the country, but they were obviously unimpressed.

Or was he imagining things again? That it should no longer astonish him to see cats daintily unwrap a salmon sandwich and resume their dinner was in itself unsettling. Reprimand or no reprimand, though he lost his job for it, he was now resolved to see it through, to know once and for all whether it was the cats who were peculiar—or himself.

But if he was going bonkers, he was not so addle-pated yet as to forget his job, or the shrill nagging of his parents that he continue to bring home straight As. Unit by unit, he moved from one end of the equipment-crowded room to the other, logging data from scores of dials and display panels. There were no obvious problems, and he phoned in his report to Security Central.

Normally he would now have settled himself at the desk and ground out his homework. Tonight, however, it proved more difficult than usual to concentrate on subjects in which he had no real interest. Try as he might, he just could not seem to relate the "micro" activities of a small business to the volatile cycles of the "macro" world marketplace. Strange cats tended to wander through his economics in such improbable ways that he began to worry that he really had slipped a gear.

Three weeks might pass without seeing the night security chief, or he might drop by three times during the same watch, peeking through the spy window when least expected, coming in to inspect without warning, so his security personnel could never feel secure themselves. What if he came spying tonight? Would he discover anything out of the ordinary, except an overworked student suffering from hallucinations?

He was about to reassure himself that the cats were genuine, when one of them emerged from behind the tape-driven unit, carrying the neatly folded sandwich wrapper daintily in her teeth, and dropped it into the trash can. Then she disappeared again.

Her behavior did little to confirm his sanity, but what choice had he now other than to accept the reality of the cats and make provisions for them? A litter box was essential, and a place for them to sleep.

He himself would have no trouble staying awake tonight, and could leave the storeroom coffee urn unplugged. . . . The storeroom! He quickly unlocked the desk, took a square-bowed key from its secret compartment, and hurried around the bank of memory units that screened the door.

His access to the room violated official regulations, a breach winked at by his supervisor, so there would be no reason for the security chief to peek inside, should he happen to come sneaking around later tonight. Beside a spare word processor stood a metal cabinet, and he detached its bottom two drawers from their slide tracks: one drawer, suitably padded, could be adapted as a sleeping basket, the other could serve as a make-shift litter box. All he needed now was some litter.

Bundles of supply chits, voucher forms, and telephone message pads were stacked along a shelf to the right of the door; but using any of these would have left broken seals, and inventories here at the Computer Center were scrutinized down to the last paper clip. Beneath the shelf stood a row of spare file cabinets, whose empty drawers several computer-room employees had unofficially appropriated as lockers—another infraction winked at by the supervisor.

Tim's own drawer was crammed with textbooks, dumbbells, and educational videotapes, but not so much as an old notebook he could shred for litter, and to rummage through the belongings of other employees would be an infringement of their privacy. Those still employed here, at least. A relief watchman had been fired last month after three reprimands for poor attendance, and Tim opened his drawer in hopes of finding an old newspaper.

What he found instead were two girlie magazines, and he tossed one to the floor while he shredded the other into the makeshift litter box. But when he turned to shred the second magazine, he discovered that the two young cats had followed him into the room and were sitting side by side before its open centerfold, gazing curiously down at the picture of a bosomy naked woman.

They looked up at him, then down at the picture again, then once more up at him, as if puzzled by the bimorphism of the human species. He felt himself blushing.

They understood his litter-box provisions after a single demonstration, after he had shredded the second magazine, but looked doubtful about the arrangements he made for their sleeping—padding the second drawer with two of the green smocks, worn by computer-room personnel during the day, which hung on pegs to the left of the door. That was their problem. He had heard that cats could nap anywhere, at any time, and these two were clearly exhausted; so he took his books, dumbbells, and videotapes, locked the storeroom door behind him, and left them to curl up wherever they would.

If access to the storeroom was against regulations, so was doing homework on the job. But the building supervisor knew how hard it was to find stable employees for this shift, which paid niggardly wages even with a night differential added, and precluded any real social life. So he was not troublesome.

Tim wished he could say the same about his homework. Returning to his assignment, it took some painful concentration and a determined reading and rereading of the dreary text—interrupted by equipment checks, the logging of data, and reports to Security Central—before he finally began to see relationships between small-business activities and the global marketplace. A lack of interest in the subject, more than any intrusive wondering about strange cats, muddled his concentration.

Yet he could not forget them completely, and at precisely half past three he was forcibly reminded of the dangers they posed for him. An uneasy sense of being watched caused him to glance up from his textbook, and he spotted the night security chief peering in at him through the spy window. He waved, and the chief nodded curtly in response and went away. Which he certainly would not have done had he come spying when the cats were out in the open examining the equipment.

Tomorrow would be a heavy workout day in the campus weight room, so tonight he confined himself to light dumbbell exercises. Then came his routine sweeping, swabbing, and buffing of the tile floor, before at last settling down to his nightly chess match with the mainframe.

Tim was still only a novice, though under the tutelage of Tedworth Vay—an erudite student of the game, as he seemed to be of virtually every other subject in the universe—he had made encouraging progress. He had never actually beaten the computer, but could now usually get past twenty moves before having to resign.

The first game was a disappointment. Professor Vay had loaned him one of the classic books on chess, which he supplemented with the newest instructional videos in the field, and he set up the Old Indian Defense used so brilliantly by the great Capablanca. But he let the computer crowd him to one side of the board, then brought out his queen too soon for conditions, and made a stupid move with his king rook. He sighed, and hit the END command, and a new chessboard immediately appeared on the CRT screen.

Professor Vay had advised him that a knowledge of the classic games of the masters was imperative to a mastery of chess, and this time he decided to let Capablanca do the playing. The famous third game of the 1924 world championship was indexed in the book, in parallel columns of symbols, and he deactivated the computer program, and manually keyed the game move by move onto the screen. It was fascinating to watch Capablanca, or at least the ghost of his intelligence, recover from the disadvantage of playing black, gain the initiative, and masterfully press on to victory. It was also humbling, though he now saw where he had gone wrong in his handling of the Old Indian Defense.

He hit the END command and reactivated the chess program. The computer had every other advantage, so he always played white; but as he pondered his opening strategy, he was distracted once more by the uneasy feeling of being watched. He glanced quickly up at the door. Nothing. The spy window was vacant. Shaking his head, he again tried to fix his attention on the game. Yet the uneasy feeling persisted, and at last he glanced behind him—and nearly shot straight out of his chair.

The two cats sat side by side, gazing up at the CRT screen with such intentness that he had the eerie impression they were trying to analyze the game. Still more unsettling was the certainty that he had locked the storeroom door. Had they picked the lock? Cats?

No; he was sure there was a wing knob on the reverse side of the lock for opening its dead bolt, as a precaution against anyone being locked into the room. This reassured him of his sanity, until he tried to envision cats actually turning the wing knob, not to mention the doorknob itself. He took several deep breaths to steady himself.

Then he realized that both cats were now looking expectantly up at him, as if wondering why he had not begun the new game.

"You two are giving me the willies," he said, with a quaver in his voice. What if they had not opened the door at all, but simply evanesced through it like ghosts? "Wait here. I've got to check."

To his relief he found the door ajar, its dead bolt indeed turned from the inside; but he glanced into the storeroom, and his uneasiness redoubled. He had left the cats to figure out their own sleeping arrangements, and they had; though not as he had expected. Instead of curling up on the pair of green smocks he had folded up for bedding, they had stretched them between two storage racks and hitched up their ends like hammocks. Or perhaps more like pods.

He returned to the computer room wondering if his student medical insurance covered psychiatric care.

It was definitely a bad sign that he was no longer astonished to find the two cats sitting before the CRT, keying chess moves into its console with a readier manipulation of computer programs than his own. But it was at least some consolation to see that they had also brought out their queen too soon, and in fact seemed unaware that they were already checkmated. It was marvelous how much they had picked up just peering over his shoulder. He recalled with chagrin how much longer it had taken him to grasp the principles of the game.

Still, they had a lot to learn, and he rose and beckoned them to follow. It was surely an even worse sign to assume that cats could play chess at all, yet what other choice had he now but to believe his own eyes? If the men in white coats dropped a net on him, so be it.

The videocassette was entitled "Fundamentals of Chess." He inserted it into the VCR beneath the training console and hit PLAY. No gestures or dumb show were needed; it was uncanny how familiar the cats were with electronic equipment; they seemed to intuit at once exactly what was intended. Side by side, they gazed raptly up at the display screen.

Taking a deep breath to steady his nerves, he went about his scheduled rounds of the equipment. Never had he inspected it so diligently, or logged the readings of its many dials and gauges with such meticulous care, as though trying to prove to himself that his wits were still intact.

There were still no problems, and he made an effort to sound composed when he telephoned in his report to Security Central. The clerk on the line seemed perfectly matter of fact, without any evident suspicion that he was talking to a madman. Or was he just humoring him while he sounded the alarm at the psycho ward? Fortunately, the university had not yet installed videophones, so the clerk could not see the two cats sitting directly behind him, operating the VCR. That would definitely have sounded an alarm.

He was surprised that "Fundamentals of Chess" had run barely a quarter of its reel. Could he really have completed his rounds so soon? Then one of the cats hit STOP with her paw, then REVERSE, then PLAY again. It seemed they would not move on to the next fundamental of chess until they had mastered the last. He wished his own study habits were as concentrated. Had he learned the game more slowly, he would surely have progressed faster.

"Less haste, more speed." He recalled from his

readings for a survey course in history that that had
been the motto of one of the old Roman emperors;
though without five multiple choices to select from he
was no longer sure exactly which. He regretted having so little time to read history, especially ancient
history, for he truly enjoyed the subject; certainly
more than plodding through wearisome courses in
Business Administration. But his parents always dis-
paraged such interests—be it ancient history, classics,
poetry, or occult literature—or any pursuit other than
the major they had chosen for him: "There's no
money in it."

And nothing in himself. His faculties were still
sound enough to feel hunger, and he sat at the desk and
unwrapped his last sandwich. The cats had had their
fill of salmon for one night, and were unlikely to have
much taste for apples, so he ate his frugal meal with a
bottle of chilled mineral water from the department
frostfree—another indulgence by the supervisor—and
watched them patiently work their way through "Fundamentals of Chess."

They had turned off the volume, and analyzed the
tape solely through its pictorial sequences, like a silent
movie. This led him to the consoling belief that they
were ignorant of human speech. Had they talked, he
would immediately have gotten out his student insurance policy and checked the benefits.

In fact, he had not heard them meow or purr or make
any sound whatsoever, as if they were mute or had
been raised in an environment of utter silence. Yet they
had to communicate with each other somehow. How
else could the uncanny coordination of all their actions
be explained?

They were also extraordinarily well mannered.
When they had at last mastered the contents of "Fundamentals of Chess," one of them hit REWIND and,
after a few minutes, EJECT; the other replaced the cas-
sette neatly in its box, while the first hit the POWER

buttons on both the VCR and the console, turning them off. Then they sat for several minutes with their heads together.

He was no longer surprised to see them operate a VCR so confidently after only one demonstration. It was just rather unflattering to recall his own first blunders with videocassettes. But they were cats nonetheless, and they needed their sleep. Side by side they walked back to the storeroom.

Now what? How was he to deal with them, if they existed? Or with himself, if they did not? Keeping pets in the dormitories was strictly prohibited. For whatever its official status, the policies of UCIC were still dictated by Benton Ingles, whose neurotic dread of animals as disease carriers was as widely known on campus as his public campaign to relegate all unprofitable species to museums. But what species was he dealing with here? Whether somebody's exotic pets, or escaped laboratory animals, these two cats were like none he had ever seen before. There were rumors about sinister experiments at the Med Center, one whole wing of which was restricted to scientists with special security clearance. Were people out searching for the cats at this very moment?

He telephoned the Administration Center. "Hello, Chuck? Tim Waverly. Would you please check the bulletin board for me, and see if anybody's lost a pair of cats. That's right, two females not quite full grown. Yeah, I'll wait."

"Nothing, Tim," the report came back a few minutes later. "There's a picture of a ginger tom on the board, but it's been there for a week, and there's no recent entry in the log about lost cats. What's up?"

"Tell you about it later, Chuck. Got to wrap it up now for the night. But thanks, I appreciate it. See you around."

That all but eliminated the chance that the cats were only lost pets. His readings in occult literature suggested other possibilities, beyond mere figments of an overworked brain; but he was shy about consulting Tedworth Vay until he had firmer evidence. The most likely explanation was that they were escaped laboratory animals. A fellow bodybuilder had a girlfriend who was doing graduate work in biology. She might know something about animal experiments in her department or could at least make inquiries of the right scientists. But he'd have to wait until morning to contact her. What was he to do with these weird cats in the meantime?

He recalled the old comic song, "The Cat Came Back," in which the singer laments all he's done to get rid of an unwanted cat, only to have it come back again and again. In his own case, he wanted the two cats to come back. If they were smart enough to play chess, surely they were smart enough to come back to where they had been fed and cared for. He had little choice but to trust to their feline natures.

It was thirty minutes before the end of his shift when he entered the storeroom. Both cats had rolled their makeshift hammocks around themselves like pods, but for some peculiar reason they slept with their paws wrapped over their heads like caps. He had the silly notion that they missed the nightcaps they normally wore to bed—which turned out not to be so silly after all.

"Reveille! Reveille! Let's go, you two. Rise and shine."

While they wriggled out of their pods and yawned and stretched, he replaced his dumbbells and videotapes in the file-cabinet drawer, and carried the makeshift litter box out to the dumpster. Tomorrow he would buy a plastic box and fill it with ground clay, not shredded girlie magazines. That is, if the cats came back.

He himself was back within minutes. The shocks had come so hard and fast tonight that he now wondered if he were becoming inured; he was barely flabbergasted to find that the cats had already taken down their hammocks, rehung the smocks on their proper pegs, and neatly rewound the electrical wire they had used to sling them. They looked up at him as if asking, "What next?"

"Well, first of all, you should have names," he decided. "You both look like you're wearing masks, so I'll call you with the black tip on your tail Domino, and you with the black right forepaw I'll call Dominique. Now at least I can tell you apart. This way, Domino and Dominique, if you please."

The last few days had been overcast, but the sky was now cloudless and graying with dawn, as he led them out the side door of the building. Once more they looked quizzically up at him.

"I'm afraid you're on your own for the rest of the day, young ladies. Meet me here tonight—same time, same station—and I promise you salmon galore. Meanwhile I'm going to try and find out who or what you are. Discreetly, of course." He caught himself, and glanced in all directions. His habit of talking to himself was bad enough, but to be overheard talking to cats might start rumors. Besides, he already knew they could not understand human speech.

What about time? If they learned so readily to operate a VCR, why couldn't they learn to tell time also? He knelt and showed them his wristwatch; then cycled its hands around to twelve, and then around to twelve again. They continued to gaze raptly at the dial, and he repeated the demonstration thrice more, pointing in each instance to the illuminated clock tower over the Administration Building, and pantomiming their returning here when the hands of its giant dial had rounded to twelve a second time.

He was beginning to feel foolish, kneeling down on the sidewalk, when all at once they both seemed to understand, at exactly the same instant, and abruptly disappeared into the shrubbery.

He returned thoughtfully to the main computer room, and gathered up his homework materials, wondering whether the cats really would come back. Stranger things had happened tonight.

CHAPTER IV

Angel was sullen and belligerent at the best of times, and today he was in a bad mood. He had been humbled, he had been humiliated, and though he had abjectly recanted, he was certain the two cats really existed. They were not the delusions of overwork or jet lag; he had seen them with his own eyes, and if he had to search from one end of California to the other, he was determined to find them.

He alerted pet shop owners throughout Ingles City and its suburbs—none of them were able to identify the breed of cat from his description—and waited ill-humoredly the rest of the day for the evening shift to come back on duty, his browridge beetling in a malevolent scowl, his meaty fists clenching and unclenching with impatience to tear somebody to pieces. But he would have to investigate with caution. Chief Grotten considered the matter closed, and had left no doubt about what would become of anybody who insisted on keeping it open. The operation at the Med Center was called "personality readjustment," and his own head was already shaved, ready for boring.

He found Steve Heinsohn in a corner of the hangar, directing a crew of uniformed Brainers in the repair of a wheel assembly, and drew him aside.

"Cats?" The balding, potbellied crew chief raised his eyebrows. "But I guess it's not really surprising we should get a cat in here, though the Big Guy hates animals of any kind. Traps or poison take too long. Want to get rid of rats, give me a tomcat every time."

"Rats?"

"That's what we're talking about, ain't it? I mean, you were with Mr. Grotten last night when Hal Larmer reported seeing the rats, weren't you?"

"Oh, yeah, that's right. Where's Hal now?"

The crew chief glanced around the colossal hangar. "There he is over there, working his forklift."

The driver had just positioned his lifting fork beneath a skid stacked with wooden crates, when he spotted the hulking figure, shaven bullet head carried menacingly forward, descending upon him. His first panicky impulse was to throw the vehicle into reverse and make a dash for office country, but he knew it was too late.

"Get down from there, you," Angel growled at him, and he obediently scrambled down from his seat, smiling ingratiatingly. "I got some questions, and I want some answers. Now Steve over there tells me you spotted rats in here last night. Why the hell didn't you report it?"

"I was going to, Angel. Honest. I was on my way. But I really wasn't sure, and Mr. Grotten sounded, well, kind of pissed off about something. So I never got around to it."

"What the hell do you mean, not sure? Did you see rats, or didn't you see rats?"

"Yeah, I saw a couple of small animals running past, but only out of the corner of my eye, and they were gone before I got a good look." He grinned weakly, nervously licking his lips, his heart pounding with fear. "What else could they have been but rats?"

Angel had a pretty good idea, and suspected the driver did, too, but he did not press the point. "I'll let it go this once. But the next time something like this happens, you come straight to me." He seized Hal by the shirtfront, and lifted him helplessly to his tiptoes. "Got that?"

"Right, Angel. I mean, yes, sir. Thanks for the

break. It won't happen again, I promise. I'll come straight to you."

"You'd better." Angel set him down again, and with a last ugly scowl stalked from the hangar.

Slowly, his heart still pounding, the driver climbed back into the seat of his forklift. It had been a close call. He could see the gang of Brainers, toiling docilely around a wheel assembly at the far side of the hangar, and nervously tried to rub away the tingling he felt at the crown of his head.

Meanwhile Angel rounded up Mickey Dunstun, and informed him of his discovery. "We got to ask around till we come up with the right answers. We can't go back to Mr. Grotten with only a story about some bozo who saw something out of the corner of his eye. We need hard evidence."

"Very hard, before I get involved again," said Dunstun. "But why the Administration Building?"

"Best place to start," said Angel, parking his car behind the functional brick-and-glass building, above which an illuminated clock tower rose into the evening sky, now fading from red to grayish-purple. Students ambling down the campus walk glanced curiously at him as he passed, as if they had never seen anything quite so gruesome outside of an old horror movie. "You know how sappy these eggheads are about pets."

"The bulletin board? Yeah, maybe somebody found 'em and posted a notice. Unless they got greedy. An odd breed like that might fetch a nice buck."

"Way ahead of you, pal," said Angel. The functional interior of the building would have better served a bank or insurance company than a modern university; its sole decoration was a blockish mural: "The Triumphs of Industry." "Every pet shop owner for miles around knows who to call, should anybody come in selling cats. Here we are."

They scanned the bulletin board in silence.

"Nothing," Dunstun said at last. "Parakeets and hamsters for sale. A lost ginger tom. Books and furni-

was it all right. Though how those two damned cats ended up at the Computer Center was a puzzle. Were they still there? No, the supervisor of the main computer room was a pussy, but not so stupid as to defy Benton Ingles and allow animals on campus. But what about the young watchman himself, this Tim Waverly? He was a student and maybe hadn't learned yet what became of people who defied the interests of B.I.T.E.

"Thanks, boys." He removed the earphones. "I won't forget this."

"Any time, Angel," said the quartet, and four whitey-bald heads nodded him to the door.

He did not say another word until he and Dunstun were out of earshot, well up the corridor. "You wanted hard evidence, Mickey. I think we got it. Mr. Grotten is making a special inspection of the RZ later on, on account of some violations he spotted there. The night security chief always goes with him, so maybe certain wise guys here on campus will get to thinking it's safe to break regulations."

"Maybe so," said Dunstun, who all this while had been racking his memory for any careless remark he might have dropped lately over the telephone. "But don't tell me these dirty old men record the phone calls of Mr. Grotten, too?"

"Never." Angel hit the elevator button. "That's the one exception in all Ingles City. Unless, of course, he happens to be talking to . . ." He trailed off, a peculiar look crossing his face. "Anyways, we got a few hours to kill before this wise guy comes on watch again. A couple of beers at Lena's would hit the spot."

Tim Waverly hummed the tune of "The Cat Came Back" as he returned to the side entrance of the Computer Center shortly after midnight. His cats had indeed come back, punctual to their time; but he could not let them into the building until he had the main computer room to himself. Meanwhile he left them a packet of smoked salmon.

They were just folding its plastic wrapper into a neat little pad, ready for disposal, as he opened the door. They seemed well nourished, though from the relish with which they ate the salmon he suspected they were unused to such tasty fare. He also found it curious that they never meowed or purred, as if they had never learned how.

"All right, young ladies, the coast is clear."

Trotting along together, they preceded him into the main computer room. The storeroom door was already open for them, and he filled the new litter box he had bought for them with ground clay, and demonstrated its use by setting them one after the other inside it, as one normally does with cats. They submitted to the demonstration, but looked reprovingly up at him. Did he think they were idiots?

He set out a water bowl, a salmon sandwich (unwrapped) from his lunch bag, and two smocks and some lengths of electrical wire. He was curious to see them string their hammocks, but his hourly report was already late, and he hurried off with the equipment log.

Stringing hammocks was indeed the first order of business for Domino and Dominique. It had been a long and troubled day for them, evading without rest or comfort the perils of this alien world, and the Earthlings of all shapes and sizes who swarmed beneath its sun. The very heat and brightness of day were unwonted afflictions. Then at sundown more and more creatures primitively like themselves emerged. These were easily dodged or outwitted, for they had only negligible powers of telepathy. And their own powers were, if anything, rendered keener by the omnipresence of danger.

They were stringing their second hammock together when they detected an ominous presence, and they shot out the door into the main computer room, ready to meet or evade yet another peril. Somewhere in the vicinity was the big, ugly Earthling from whom they had so recently escaped, but the surges of electromagnetism all around them at first muddled their locator sensibilities. Too late they looked up at the spy window in the door.

Heavy-lidded eyes stared malevolently down at them. Instantaneously they analyzed their new predicament: it was useless now to try and hide, and they braced themselves for evasion and flight. The moment the door opened, they would scoot between the legs of the great shambling oaf and be out of range, if not out of sight, before his clumsy reactions could set him bending and grabbing for them. Minutes passed, then more minutes, but still the door did not open. At last the malevolent eyes withdrew, and soon all sense of enmity faded from perception.

It was no more useful to worry about matters beyond their control than to speculate with insufficient data, so the cats rolled themselves podwise into their hammocks for a snooze. The absence of the sleep-learning caps they had worn through every nap since kittenhood made them more uncomfortable than any imminence of danger, and they slept with their paws wrapped atop their heads.

Tim was even more perplexed about their behavior than he had been last night. The biology student he had contacted was not aware of any escaped laboratory animals or experiments with cats anywhere on campus; though neither she nor the professors she queried for him knew what secret research might be going on in the restricted wing of the Med Center. He could carry his own investigations no further. Tomorrow or the day after he would have to consult Tedworth Vay.

Right now he had an especially dreary homework assignment to complete, while keeping up with his regular equipment checks and reports. Domino and Dominique reappeared before he was finished, so he gave them "Master Strategy in Chess," a new videocassette he had just acquired, to study in the meantime.

It was well after three before he at last finished grinding out his paper for Problems in Personnel Management 343; deadly dull, of no possible interest to anyone, least of all himself, but meeting every department requisite for a high grade. With a sigh of relief he hit PRINT on the word processor, free at last from the drudgery of Business Administration, and accessed the chess program on his CRT terminal.

"All right, young ladies, ready for your first lesson? Since you're beginners, you can play white, and I promise to take it easy on you."

The cats leapt onto the systems desk with an alacrity that was disconcerting. Still more disconcerting was the adroitness with which they maneuvered their chessmen into a Sicilian defense, and then move by move inexorably closed in on his king. He had read somewhere that *checkmate* was a corruption of the Persian *shah mat,* "the king is dead." But whatever the source of the word, it was soon evident that his own king was as dead as the old Shah himself.

He sighed. "You win, but you needn't gloat about it."

Domino and Dominique gazed at him with looks he knew to be perfectly expressionless yet which somehow conveyed the impression that they were grinning like a pair of Cheshire cats. He had worked all spring to hone his playing skills and until tonight believed he was making progress. It was no confidence builder to be checkmated by two cats playing their first game. But he wanted to show he was a good sport, and so he scratched their ears and petted them.

They were obviously perplexed by the gesture. Bred and trained exclusively as working animals, they had never known affection and for several moments looked quizzically at each other as if conferring on how they should react. On the whole they rather liked being petted, so he petted them again.

"Give me another chance?" He hit CLEAR, and a fresh setup appeared on the CRT screen. "But this time I'll play white, and you have to promise to take it easy on me."

He opened with his king's pawn, expecting the cats to respond by setting up their Sicilian defense again. Instead they vanished, diving in tandem from the systems desk and scooting out of sight behind a central processing unit. The next instant the door burst open, and several men rushed into the room.

"You saw 'em, Mr. Grotten." Angel pointed at the CPU. "Just like me and Mickey here first saw 'em aboard—"

"Before they escaped from the Med Center, you mean," Chief Grotten cut him off sharply, nodding toward the astonished Tim.

"Right as always, Mr. Grotten. The less these college punks know, the better." Angel sneeringly looked Tim up and down. "Gimme that cage, Mickey. This time I'll lock it myself, so's they won't run away again. Now come here, you goddamn cats."

Domino and Dominique had reappeared, peeking out from behind the enameled gray processor unit. But as Angel bore angrily down upon them, brandishing the animal cage, Tim stepped into his path. He had recovered by now from his first surprise and did not budge even when he stood chin to chin with the gruesome hulk, so close that Tim was disgusted by his smell of stale sweat and the beery foulness of his breath.

"Out of my way, punk," growled Angel, threatening to crown him with the wire cage.

Tim knew that his gesture was futile, that nothing he could now say or do would save the poor cats from being caged, but there was something so loathsome, so hatefully brutal about the hulk menacing him that he was ready to oppose Angel to the very death.

Nor was the gesture, no matter how futile, missed by Domino and Dominique. They understood, better than Tim himself, how futile any resistance was at this time, but also appreciated his gallantry in stepping forth to defend them, a gesture they would not forget. Besides, the Earthlings evidently still considered them idiots;

for the lock on this new cage looked even simpler to pick than the one on the last.

"Put that cage down, Angel," Chief Grotten snapped at him. "We don't want any incidents here."

Glowering, his meaty fists aching to pound the face before him to jelly, Angel nonetheless obeyed the command of his superior. He and Tim continued to measure each other, neither showing any inclination to back down. It was Domino and Dominque who separated them by calmly walking over to the cage and letting themselves be locked inside. Angel had seen them do exactly the same thing aboard the UN Commstat, and so was less surprised than Tim.

"Come over here, Waverly." Chief Grotten read the nameplate on his shirt and drew him aside. "You've probably noticed some peculiarities about these two cats," he said, lowering his voice.

Tim considered this the understatement of the season, but he merely nodded. At least there was no longer any doubt that the cats were real, and that he wasn't headed for the loony bin after all. The lenient manner of the dreaded Chief of Operations probably meant that he wasn't headed for the unemployment line either.

"Not half a dozen scientists in the world know about what I'm now going to reveal to you," continued Chief Grotten, dropping his voice still more. "I realize you haven't the proper security clearance to hear this, but under the circumstances I have no other choice. These two cats are part of a top-secret experiment at the Med Center. Their cage door was carelessly left open, and they escaped. The scientists will be happy to get them back. They were afraid they'd be savaged by the first stray dog or cat that came upon them.

Tim doubted that Domino and Dominque were quite so helpless, but it now appeared that his original surmise about them was correct. "Then they're just part of some experiment in genetic engineering? Yes, I suspected as much. But you can rely on me, Mr. Grotten. I promise not to reveal their existence to anyone."

"I'll hold you to that promise, Waverly. And as for your disobeying regulations and bringing animals on campus, I'll give you a pass this time." He stared him down with the cold menace of a traffic cop. "But only this time. Do you understand?"

"Yes, sir. And thanks. It won't happen again."

Domino and Dominique gazed forlornly back at him through the wires of their cage, as Angel, after challenging him with a last contemptuous sneer, carried them out the door.

In a way he felt as miserable as they did; though he knew there was nothing more he could have done to protect them. The idea of genetically engineering species of animals—foreshadowing as it did the genetic engineering of human beings—was itself depressing. But again, what else could he have done?

There was no place for ethical questions in Business Administration, or even for speculative ideas—except insofar as they might be exploited to raise corporate profits—and he completed his hourly equipment checks with a heavy heart.

Floor wax and disinfectant mingled their sterile aromas in the filtered air of the Med Center; the wall tiles were a pastel green; fluorescent light panels shone down from a ceiling of yellow acoustical tile. Bottles and metal instruments clattered somewhere in the distance. Both Angel and Chief Grotten wore black gumshoes, which barely whispered as they strode the length of the corridor. Domino and Dominique could not have been more silent if they had been fast asleep in their cage.

"I kept you from stomping the punk, Angel, because we can't have any newsies sniffing around just now," said Chief Grotten, checking his watch. "The story about massive malfunctions aboard the UN Commstat is ready to break all over the country, and Project Nimrod is only weeks from countdown. But don't worry. When the time comes to bring the punk here for personality readjustment, I'll give you the job."

"Thanks," said Angel, balling his meaty right fist. "That's one job I'm looking forward to. What's that sound?"

"Be right back." Chief Grotten silenced his wrist beeper, and headed for the nearest telephone.

Staff doctors, nurses, and clerical workers, uniformed in pastel-green smocks with the insignia B.I.T.E. in black letters over the breast pocket, glanced curiously at Angel and at the cage he held under his left arm, but they were careful not to seem inquisitive. The restricted wing of the great hospital complex was too close at hand, and Angel looked too mean and belligerent even for friendly comments about the two cats.

Chief Grotten rejoined him within minutes, and they continued down the corridor.

"Mr. Ingles is still in teleconference with Washington, so I wasn't able to get through to him." He kept his voice down, and spoke only when out of earshot of the staff. "His congressmen are all primed to attack the funding of the satellite communications network, but the timing of their attacks is critical. One thing I did learn, though. Details about your wreckage of the UN Commstat, blaming it on a solar storm and faulty equipment, have just been leaked to the Media. The story should hit the airwaves first thing tomorrow."

Angel nodded with grim satisfaction. "He's miles ahead of 'em. With all the newspapers, magazines, and radio and TV stations he owns, he can make the news come out any which way he wants."

"Not yet, Angel. Not by a long shot. That's why control of the satellite network is so important to him, and why we don't want any newsies sniffing around just now. The Media hate his guts, and want nothing better than to make him look like a public enemy. They've never forgiven him for building Ingles City, and mock his university here every chance they get."

His eyes narrowed vindictively. "They'll behave better—after they've had their personalities readjusted."

They turned down an adjacent corridor, and were confronted by a sign in bold letters: NO ADMITTANCE. Stepping around it, they proceeded toward a green steel door.

"I don't blame you for being sore at 'em," said Angel. "You were doing a great job in East L.A., till the newsies started blubbering about police brutality and corruption. They're the ones who gave you a bad name."

"I have their names in my safe," said Chief Grotten. "Their time will come, too, just as with this Waverly punk. His file says he's from Royal Beach, and belongs to that bodybuilder club we chased off the beaches here when they were privatized. Looks to me like a troublemaker."

"Him and that whole Royal Beach crowd needs to be taught a lesson," said Angel.

"We have to be careful there, at least for a while. The Royal Beach Preservation Society not only has money behind it but clout and access to the Media. Don't worry, though, they won't stop the spread of Ingles City much longer. Meanwhile, what happens to the Waverly punk should indeed teach them a lesson. He's a big strong kid, the kind we can always use in warehouse country."

"How about in the hangar instead, sir? Steve Heinsohn, the crew chief, needs all the Brainers he can get, and I owe him a favor. He gave me the tip I needed to run down these goddamn cats."

"We'll see."

They slipped their ID cards into a slot beside the green steel door, and faced a TV camera. There was a metallic buzz, and the door sprang open; but no sooner had they entered than Chief Grotten's beeper sounded.

"It's the Big Guy this time. You go on ahead, Angel. Dr. Carlson is waiting for the cats." He hurried to the nearest telephone but did not pushbutton its digits until his companion was out of earshot.

Tiles of pastel green also covered these walls, but some of the rooms here had steel doors, and the harsh and cloying smells of strange chemicals wafted through the pervading aroma of floor wax and disinfectant. All exterior windows either had bars and panes of wired glass or were bricked over.

Angel felt uncomfortable, if not foolish, standing alone in the middle of the corridor with a cage full of cats. Not that any member of B.I.T.E. could ever feel really comfortable in the restricted wing of the Med Center. The green steel door three rooms ahead was marked SURGERY; the red DO NOT ENTER sign above it was lit. Somebody was being operated on; maybe that snooping broad he had caught spying. His capture of her had brought him to the attention of Benton Ingles himself; his recapture of the two cats would bring him more recognition still.

"I'll take them now."

The bearded man who came bustling toward him down the corridor wore thick spectacles, and a nameplate over the breast pocket of his green smock: R.N. CARLSON, M.D., Ph.D. He carried a folded white cloth over his arm.

"We'll just drop this over their cage." He unfolded the cloth. "We have some tests prepared, and we don't want them to be too nervous or excited. It might skew the results." He frowned as he peered through the wires. "Hmmmm, Mr. Grotten said they were a rare breed. I'm not sure what they are myself, but then zoology isn't my field. We'll know more after the staff zoologist gets here. He's written several papers on species Felidae."

He took the cage from Angel and covered it with the white cloth, though neither Domino nor Dominique evidenced the least twitch of nervousness or excitement. Two pussycats dozing before a fireplace could not have seemed more tranquil, or so remote from the keen analyses of their surroundings that were, in fact, passing between them.

Chief Grotten came striding up.

"Test the cats thoroughly, Doc, and be sure they're X-rayed." He wrote on a card and handed it to him. "I can be reached through that number, no matter what the time. By the way, any problems with that Malmrose bitch?"

Dr. Carlson pointed to the crown of his head. "Tonight."

"Good. Did you get anything more out of her?"

"No, we're certain now that she was acting alone, and that her story about coming here to look for information about her brother is essentially true. The drugs we gave her are irresistible, especially when used in conjunction with, shall we say, certain physical discomforts." His face assumed an expression more cruelly feline than any ever worn by Domino or Dominique.

"Too bad she didn't ask me about what happened to her precious brother and his pals." Angel's mouth twisted into a sneer. "Squealed like pigs, the whole lot of 'em."

"You don't want to repeat that story too often, Angel," said Chief Grotten. "Call me when you got something, Doc."

"Hey, where are we going?" asked Angel, as he was hurried down unfamiliar corridors. "This ain't the way we came."

"Mr. Ingles wants to see us both, right away. But first we have to take antiseptic baths and change into fresh clothes."

"Baths? Fresh clothes?" Angel's heavy browridge lowered in bewilderment.

"We've been handling animals. Mr. Ingles thinks his enemies may have put disease germs into the fur of the cats, so that when he petted them he'd sicken and die. Also, he wanted them X-rayed, in case bombs have been sewn inside them."

That cut off all further discussion, and they entered

the locker room, its air heavy with steam and disinfect-ants, and began stripping off their clothes. Each had been too intimately involved in the aggrandizement of B.I.T.E. ever to trust the other with the least disparag-ing remark or attitude about the neuroses of their leader.

CHAPTER V

Factories, oil refineries, industrial parks, canneries, shopping malls, asphalt parking lots, office buildings of raw concrete, houses of painted cinder block and aluminum siding, smoke, stink, and pollution: Ingles City spread along the once sylvan coastline like a tumorous growth. At its center rose the palatial residence of Benton Ingles, from which extended like the radials of a spiderweb the visible telephone wires and invisible radio beams by which he detected the least tremor anywhere in his transworld enterprises. Electrified fences discouraged intruders, and so responsive was the security system that the metal tips on a pair of shoelaces would trip a general alarm.

Chief Grotten, along with his hulking companion, both now antiseptically scrubbed and wearing the borrowed coveralls of maintenance men, had to park outside the main gate and submit to close scrutiny before being admitted. All seemed dark, but he knew, as he led the way around to the side of the looming structure, that every inch of the grounds was flooded with black light, and that their every movement was now being observed on television monitors fitted with special filters. The steel door buzzed open a step before they reached it.

"Ah, Kurt my boy, how nice of you to drop in." Benton Ingles greeted them genially in the grand salon. "And this, I believe, must be Angel. You don't object to my calling you that, I trust? Good. Your work has been reported favorably to me, and I've looked for-

ward to meeting you personally. Nothing so gratifies
me as recognizing the meritorious services of my employees."

Armaments, aerospace technology, electronics,
chemicals, military and commercial aircraft, heavy machinery, oil refining, and shipping were among the
most lucrative ventures of B.I.T.E. Exactly how immense its worldwide holdings had grown in recent
years was known to one man alone, and it was not
Chief Grotten. Nor could he do more than speculate on
just how vast was its media contingent, for newspapers, magazines, and radio and television stations were
secretly being bought up through dummy corporations
all over the planet. Ingles had once remarked to him
that the most valuable lesson he had drawn from his
readings on Hitler was that absolute power could be
achieved only through absolute control of public opinion.

Tall, spare to the point of emaciation, his iron-gray
hair brushed straight back from his high forehead,
Benton Ingles was an imposing figure. Eleven years
had passed since the crash of an experimental air-
plane had left him so torn and mangled that no doctor
at the time had given him any chance of life. Yet such
was the strength of his will that he had not only survived but gone on to new heights of wealth and
power. His left arm was virtually useless, and a steel
plate crowned his skull; but he still held himself rig-
idly erect, and the penetrating keenness of his intel-
lect was feared throughout the business world.
However, not even his doctors could say to what degree the heavy dosages of amphetamines and painkillers he needed to keep himself going affected his
mind.

The white gloves he changed regularly throughout
the day were not worn to conceal deformities; plastic
surgery had erased the most visible scars from everywhere on his body. He was morbidly cautious about
contracting diseases, and even with gloves on did not

shake hands with his two underlings, or let them approach within ten feet of him.

"Sorry about our appearance, sir," Grotten apologized. "After taking antiseptic baths at the Med Center, as you ordered, we discovered that these coveralls were the only fresh-laundered uniforms available. I considered the matter too urgent to lose any more time over clothes."

"Sound judgment," said Ingles, still keeping his distance. His voice was firm and cultured, but with a peculiar metallic timbre, the consequence of the surgical repair of his larynx. "That's why I made you my Chief of Operations. Please be seated." He nodded toward a gray plastic sofa with black armrests, and sat halfway across the room in a matching armchair; furniture reminiscent of a dentist's waiting room. Bursts of Napoleon, Julius Caesar, and John D. Rockefeller sat atop black metal pillars; the walls were gun-metal gray, and were hung with paintings and enlargements in ebony frames, depicting in a vividly representational manner some of the great military and industrial triumphs of history. "All right, Angel." He fixed him with his steely blue eyes. "Let's hear your report."

Stammering, repeating himself, tripping inarticulately over his own tongue, forgetting what he had said each time he met the penetrating gaze of his superior, Angel slowly and clumsily detailed everything that had happened, from his first encounter with the two mysterious cats aboard the UN Commstat until their recapture tonight at the Computer Center. Benton Ingles glanced sharply at his Chief of Operations, when he heard how the original report about the cats had been disregarded, but otherwise followed the stumbling narration intently to its conclusion.

"Anything to add, Kurt?" he asked.

"No, sir. What Angel says is substantially correct." Chief Grotten was not disconcerted at having his own earlier report about the cats tested in his presence against the report of a subordinate. He often used the same technique himself. The important thing now was somehow to get himself off the spot. "I freely admit, sir, that dismissing Angel's first report was a mistake, which I'm determined to rectify very soon. But when I examined the evidence, it was clear to me as a professional investigator that the cats, assuming they actually existed, could not possibly have escaped their confinement without assistance."

"Assistance?" Ingles began to tug at his white gloves. "Are you implying treason? Within my own organization? My own employees conspiring to kill me or steal my property?"

"I'm convinced of it, sir. I've been investigating the possibility of a conspiracy extending beyond Ingles City—"

Ingles held up a gloved hand to silence him. "Angel, wait for me in the library, please. It's the third door down the corridor, on the right." He waited until the hulking man had shambled from the room, and when he resumed speaking the metallic timbre in his voice made him sound like a recording. "Now let me get this straight, Kurt. Are you saying that one or more of my own employees let the cats escape? Why?"

"To cover their tracks, sir. I've never forgotten our first interview, when you appointed me your Chief of Operations. You said, 'Suspect everybody.' That's been my guiding principle to this very day. Though in this particular instance my suspicions were misplaced. You see, Angel and his pilot, Mickey Dunstun, had in a very short period of time made a nonstop flight to Sulatonga, been launched into space, reentered the atmosphere, and landed back here in the Restricted Zone. I suspected they were suffering from some kind of jet-lag disorientation. After all, cats aboard a UN Commstat?"

Ingles tugged thoughtfully at his gloves for several moments, as if trying to draw them more protectively over his hands.

"All right," he said at last. "I understand how you

could have made your mistake, and why conspirators would want to recover any telltale evidence before their failed plot was exposed, whether intended to infect me with some incurable disease or kill me outright with a bomb. What I don't understand is why they would let the cats loose, after going to so much trouble and danger to get them back again."

"I'm guessing that the cats just plain ran away. In any case, my preliminary investigation has already turned up some highly questionable associations." Grotten proceeded cautiously, never underestimating the risk involved in playing upon the paranoid fears of his superior. The mind of Benton Ingles, though twisted by strange manias and delusions, was almost morbidly keen and penetrating, as ruined business competitors down through the years had discovered when it was too late. "It may only be a coincidence, but the young security guard who had possession of the cats lives in Royal Beach."

Ingles listened so keenly that he seemed almost to vibrate, but he did not interrupt.

"Naturally I'm investigating him," Grotten continued. "But if he's involved at all in any conspiracy against you, it's probably as the stooge of more determined and resourceful people. I fobbed him off with a tale about the cats being escaped laboratory animals, and got his promise of silence. Not that I rely on that, of course," he hastened to add. "I was just mindful of your orders to avoid any incident the newsies could drum up against you, and decided we should wait to silence him more reliably until after you've monopolized world communications. Then the newsies won't matter."

"Your decision was correct," said Ingles. "Cries for the privatization of the space program are growing louder and louder, from coast to coast. But all the coordinated efforts of my people in the media, the Congress, and the business community to manipulate public opinion could be derailed by just such an incident. We must at all costs preserve media silence until Project Nimrod is operational. The launching from Sulatonga is now only a few weeks from countdown."

"That's good news, sir. But it wasn't from Sulatonga that the two cats were launched. Now whether they were planted aboard the UN Commstat with the intention of infecting you with an incurable disease, or, as you suggested, with bombs sewn inside them, the fact remains that somebody knew we were coming."

Ingles tugged fretfully at his white gloves. "It wouldn't be an ordinary disease, like plague or leprosy," he said, as though thinking out loud. "They can genetically engineer diseases these days for which there is no known cure. Bombs can be detected with X-rays, but not diseases. That takes testing in a laboratory."

"I'm awaiting a call from the Med Center at this very moment, sir." Grotten watched him shrewdly. "The staff zoologist had not yet arrived, when I left to come here and report."

"Zoologist? What kind of cats are they?"

"That's just the problem, sir. They're some odd breed nobody seems to recognize, and may themselves have been genetically engineered especially for this mission. We'll know soon. Whether we'll ever know who tipped off your enemies at the Cape about our mission to the UN Commstat remains to be seen. But it must be somebody close to you, sir. Somebody who might be also in a position to tip off your enemies about Sulatonga."

Ingles gave the wrist of his left glove an angry tug. "I know what you're driving at, Kurt. You don't like my wife, do you?"

"That's not my place, sir. I'm just a policeman doing his job. You informed me yourself that she had dropped the name Sulatonga in conversation, which could only mean that she had eavesdropped on some private conference of yours. At your direction, I've kept her under close surveillance ever since. Though her visits to Royal Beach still frustrate my efforts."

"Royal Beach again," muttered Ingles.

"She visits Lola Londi there at least once a month. They're both Sicilian, and I guess it's only natural she should want to talk occasionally to somebody from the old country."

"Yes, but what do they talk about? How much does my wife betray to her about my affairs? This Londi woman, this fossil, is the chief financial support of the Royal Beach Preservation Society, which has checked my every industrial move in that direction. I've often had the feeling they're somehow forewarned."

"Your feelings in that respect, sir, have always been extraordinarily acute. The evidence for a Royal Beach conspiracy against you is now so strong that I believe some decisive action is warranted, before it's too late."

Ingles did not reply for several moments, tugging at the fringes of his white gloves one after the other as if silently counting off points of consideration. "All right, Kurt," he said at last. "Before we commit ourselves to any decision, let's be sure we know exactly where matters stand." He lowered his voice, though the entire house, from cellar to chimney, was electronically monitored for bugging devices at least once each month. "We've now achieved our preliminary goals. First, the UN Commstat has been rendered inoperative, without any suspicion of sabotage so far. Second, a media blitz has discredited NASA, denouncing engineering flaws, cover-ups of radiation hazards, fraud, profiteering, the loss of American sovreignty to UN bureaucrats, political corruption, and so forth. Meanwhile the seeds of a public demand to privatize the whole global communications network are being planted throughout the country."

"All the evidence, real or manufactured, of vice and corruption, needed to alienate the American people from spokesmen for the UN program is also being planted, sir," Grotten added.

"Good work," said Ingles. "For as soon as the Administration has spent itself into bankruptcy, throwing good money after bad, banking its reputation upon the viability of the UN program, every satellite still in orbit will mysteriously go dead, thereby discrediting forever every present and future plan for free access by all to world communications."

He gazed into the distance, his eyes clouded over with the grandeur of his master vision, like a dictator gazing down from the podium upon a million servile faces reflecting his own omnipotence.

"The stakes are mountain high," he continued, "as high as the risks, but the game is worth the winning. With control of the worldwide exchange of information, I'll not only be in a position to bend international politics in whichever direction is the most profitable for B.I.T.E., but able to manipulate a network of servitors infiltrated into high places everywhere across the planet. Ultimately, DNA testing at birth will determine which particular brain implant is the most suitable for which particular infant, or whether its continued existence is warranted. All profitless individualism and disobedience to superiors will soon thereafter pass from the Earth."

"A beautiful concept, sir," Grotten said with genuine admiration.

"Yes, but no concept, no matter how beautiful, is foolproof so long as fools are allowed to meddle with it."

"Verna Malmrose is scheduled for personality readjustment tomorrow, sir," said Grotten. "If that's the incident you're referring to."

"It is," said Ingles. "It took all my power to quash a congressional investigation into the sinking of the *Greenworld Challenger,* even when all evidence placing it within a thousand miles of Sulatonga had been obliterated. Had Angel not brought in that snooping bitch when he did, who knows what kind of public outcry her environmental friends might have raised against me." He pondered this a moment, then rose stiffly to his feet. "Wait here, please. I'll be right back."

Every wall of the library was lined with rare first editions, medieval folios, incunabula, and matched sets bound in calf, not only impressive to visitors but a sound investment, acquired under standing commissions by brokers all over the world. It was the innermost sanctum of the great industrial empire, its showplace and most secluded conference room, where no bugging device could be introduced without tripping alarms all over the city. The furniture was upholstered with quilted leather; the logs crackling in the fireplace were of aromatic cedar.

Angel sat on the edge of his chair, feeling (and looking) like the proverbial bull in a china shop, afraid to touch anything around him for fear it might break. Some might have counted it an honor to be here at all, but no employee of B.I.T.E. was ever permitted to feel secure about himself or his position, and he had left the restricted wing of the Med Center barely an hour ago.

His ears pricked up at the whisper of approaching footsteps, and he leapt to his feet as he saw the doorknob twist.

Benton Ingles refused the support of a cane, and by an effort of will, despite a left hip prosthesis and a steel rod bracing his right femur, walked erectly and without a noticeable limp; though all his movements were slow and robotlike. He motioned Angel back into his chair, as he crossed the room to the leather sofa a healthy ten feet away.

"I'll come right to the point," he said. "I've long searched for just the right man to resolve the impasse at Royal Beach, but so far without success."

"Give me a chance, sir," Angel blurted out. "I handled that *Greenworld Challenger* business for you, didn't I? And that snoopy broad who was trying to give you trouble. I caught her when nobody else could."

"So you did. In fact, several good reports about your work have lately come to my attention." Ingles gazed judiciously at him for several moments. "Yes, you may be the very man I've been searching for." His voice now sounded ominously metallic. "The time for compromise has passed. The Royal Beach Preservation Society has not only spurned my most generous offers, but in their arrogance they have publicly impugned my efforts to improve their local economy."

Angel shook his head in disgust. "People just don't appreciate all you done for 'em, sir."

"Nor do they appreciate yet what I can do to them," said Ingles, his eyes narrowing with rancor. "The security guard who had possession of those two infernal cats turns out to be a member of the Royal Beach Preservation Society, which can hardly be a coincidence. But he's a bodybuilder, a young and powerful man. He could be dangerous."

"Only to himself." Angel sneered. "Don't worry, sir, he'll get his when the time comes." He pointed to the crown of his shaven head. "I'm your man, sir. Any job, no matter how tough."

"Very well, I'll give you the chance. You'll report directly to me, and to me alone. Frankly, Chief Grotten has not performed toward Royal Beach with the effectiveness I require of employees, and we are too near our final triumph to accept any standard less than perfection. What we need is zeal, not complacency. Those grown lax in their duties must be replaced by more vigorous men."

Wild new ambitions flitted through Angel's dull wits as he sat nervously on the edge of his chair, answering question after question about tonight's events. He was too slow of comprehension to suspect how shrewdly Ingles was probing him for discrepancies between his account and that rendered by his superior, Chief Grotten.

Grotten himself knew, just as he knew why he'd been left here alone in the grand salon. Separate interrogation had been the standard procedure when he was a Los Angeles police captain, and he pondered where he might be vulnerable, where some enemy might penetrate a chink in his armor to injure him. It was dog eat dog up and down every hierarchy of B.I.T.E., and only the strong and resourceful long survived the merciless grappling for enrichment and power, much less prevailed as top dog. There was only one direction a man in his position could go—and only one way out.

Yet even while he groped through the abstract dangers and prospects hovering spectrally all around him, his policeman's mind never lost its clear grasp of routine details. Surely the tests on the two cats had been completed by now. Why hadn't someone from the Med Center contacted him?

"Suspect everybody" had been his guiding principle long before his first interview with Benton Ingles. Nonetheless, he checked his initial impulse to investigate. It would be dangerous at this time to be found by Ingles, who suspected his every subordinate of working collusively against him, on the telephone without himself being present.

Then he became aware of a potentially still more dangerous situation. About no one was Ingles more suspicious these days than his wife, whom he also regarded as a subordinate, and there she stood, the voluptuous Carla. Nodding in the direction of the library, he put his finger to his lips. She caught his meaning at once, and without a word turned and, swaying her hips enticingly, slipped back out of the room.

Ingles reappeared through another door moments later, and slowly crossed to a chair some distance from Grotten.

"Those infernal cats are the key to everything," he said. "That they are a rare and exotic breed could give us a clue to the homeland of the enemy who planted them aboard the UN Commstat. Meanwhile we can proceed to ferret out any traitor or traitors in B.I.T.E. who may have conspired with that guard."

"Lie detector tests for all employees are already standard procedure, sir. Scopolamine injections can be administered to those whose tests give questionable results, with forceful interrogation reserved for special cases. Angel is our best man for that because he enjoys the work."

If this was meant to draw Ingles into revealing what he had just discussed with Angel, or why he was still keeping him in a separate room, it failed.

"Why hasn't the staff zoologist you said was coming to the Med Center reported yet?" he asked, adding suspiciously, "or has he?"

"Not yet, sir. I waited to call until you could listen in on an extension, in case you had any questions."

"Good thinking. Go ahead, make your call. I'll listen in over here." Slowly and mechanically he crossed the room to the extension.

"Carlson? Chief Grotten here." He kept his eyes firmly on his superior, all the while he spoke into the telephone. "Why haven't either you or the staff zoologist reported to me by now? Didn't I tell you the examination of the two cats was to be given top priority?"

"Yes, sir. But there have been unexpected problems." The voice on the line sounded flustered. "Dr. Rottwald, our staff zoologist, has only this minute given me his preliminary report."

"Problems?" said Grotten. "I thought this Rottwald was a world authority on cats."

"He is, but not on cats like this. DNA testing—we made a second test, by the way, because the results of the first were so startling—indicate an enormous genetic drift from species Felidae."

"They're cats, aren't they?"

"It's not quite that simple, Mr. Grotten. You see, the two specimens you brought us are so unrelated to any known cat on Earth that we can't as yet confidently fit them into a taxonomic classification. Dr. Rottwald sees certain affinities to the Brazilian margay, but any relationship even there must be considered extremely distant. Our working hypothesis is that they evolved on some remote island, in compete isolation for millions of years from any other feline species. For instance, they don't mew or make any other sound like ordinary cats. Their plates suggest internal differences more profound still."

"Have your X-rays revealed anything potentially dangerous to someone who might handle them?" Grotten noticed how intently Ingles now listened at the extension. "A bomb, for instance?"

"A bomb?" There was a long silence on the line. "No, I was referring to the plates of their brain scans. The cranial capacity of the two specimens is somewhat more extensive than normal for cats of their size and weight. But what is really astonishing is their cerebral complexity. The convolutions of their brains look almost human."

"Are you telling me they're smart?"

"That could well be the case, Mr. Grotten. The exact relationship of cerebral convolution to intelligence is still controversial, but the preponderance of evidence suggests a high degree of correlation. We are now preparing to administer to the specimens the familiar maze test, and if their performance warrants it we will then proceed to challenge their intelligence with tests of graduated complexity."

"Have the cats given you any trouble?" asked Grotten, struggling to keep his patience. The academic tendency to dither over trifles infuriated him.

"Not the slightest. They don't mew or make any other feline sound, as if they had been raised in a mute environment. Dr. Rottwald has commented that he's never known any species of cat to be so cooperative under examination. No house cat could be more docile."

"Doesn't that strike you as odd?" said Grotten.

"First you tell me they're from some wild island, and now you're saying they behave like pussycats." He watched Ingles for his reaction. "But more important, if these cats are from some unknown place on Earth, isn't it possible they're carriers of yet undiscovered diseases?"

There was another long silence on the line. "We never thought of that, Mr. Grotten."

"Well, start thinking, and start testing. Call me the moment you have something, any time, day or night." He looked across the room to see if there were any further questions, but Ingles shook his head. "This is top priority, Carlson. Nothing, and I mean nothing, is more important to you than getting me your report. Understand?" He hung up without waiting for a reply.

A frown darkened Ingles' face as he recrossed the room to his chair. "I want this Carlson replaced the moment he submits his report," he said. "He should have thought about genetically engineered diseases. And be sure the pelts of the two cats are sterilized, when the taxidermist prepares them for display at the museum." He brooded for several minutes before continuing. "Something here doesn't ring true, and I have a keen ear for false notes."

"None keener, sir," murmured Grotten, afraid for an instant he had overreached himself. It was all too easy, and therefore all the more dangerous, to forget that this physical and psychic wreckage of a man still possessed a mind brilliant with contrivance and insight. Some resource was needed to divert his sharp scrutiny elsewhere, and out of the corner of his eye he found it. Leaning forward, he lowered his voice almost to a whisper: "Have you considered the possibility, sir, that the false note you detect may be near at hand? That someone close to you, at the very heart of B.I.T.E., may be betraying you to your enemies at Royal Beach?"

Before Ingles could reply, his wife entered the room,

and a new look of suspicion hardened his features. Chief Grotten was less surprised by her appearance, for he had seen the doorknob twist, and guessed correctly who was about to enter the room. He rose courteously to his feet, as Ingles advanced slowly and mechanically to meet her."

"I hear voices as I pass the door." She accepted her husband's peck on the cheek without enthusiasm. "But if you got business, I will leave."

"How long did you hear voices on the other side of the door, Mrs. Ingles?" Grotten assumed a look of cold dislike.

This was her cue, and she defied him like a heroine of grand opera.

"Whatta you think, I'ma spy on my own husband? Big cop! Go ahead, arrest me."

"My sole concern is protecting your husband's safety and well-being, Mrs. Ingles." Grotten played his own role less melodramatically. "That's my job."

"Your job?" She looked his denim coveralls up and down. "You look like your job should be carrying out the garbage."

"Now, now, my dear." Ingles intervened. "This is no time for squabbling." Though the mutual enmity of subordinates always pleased him—as both his wife and the Chief of Operations were well aware. "But it's true we have important business to discuss."

"It would only bore you, Mrs. Ingles," added Grotten. "Not only wouldn't you understand the subject matter of our discussion, but I doubt you would even know its geographical location."

This was another cue for her to pick up, though of a more insidious kind.

"If you talk about Sulatonga, I know where it is, because I look it up in a book. Right in the middle of the Pacific Ocean, right on the equator. They got schools in Italy, too, Mr. Big Cop."

"And very good schools, I'm sure," he said, with a

significant glance at Ingles.

"Let's all have a drink," he said. "My dear, would you invite the man in the library to join us, while I do the mixing. He's called Angel. I'm told he helped you with your luggage at the airport, a few weeks ago. Do you remember?"

"Big, ugly man like a bald Frankenstein? Who could forget?"

"If you're afraid of him, Mrs. Ingles," said Grotten, "I'll go and get him."

"Afraid? I am afraid of nothing." Lifting her nose with disdain, she strode haughtily from the room.

"I believe she's right about a lack of fear, sir," said Grotten. "Or should I say a lack of prudence? In any case, dare we risk Project Nimrod and the world supremacy of B.I.T.E. on the whims of a woman? A single inadvertent remark to her friends—and your enemies—at Royal Beach might well launch a congressional investigation. When I say inadvertent, I'm of course giving her the benefit of the doubt."

Ingles eyed him narrowly. "Go on."

"You just heard what she said about Sulatonga. What else does she know, and who else has she divulged it to? Only someone very close to you could have known about our raid on the UN Commstat. The cats found on board, and the docile way they allowed themselves to be brought here, suggests they were put there for the purpose of getting to you, by someone who knew we were coming."

The seeds of suspicion were already planted; it remained only to cultivate them. Dear Carla. Weeks had passed since she first asked him about Sulatonga, between bouts of lovemaking one night, and he had nursed the information for just such a moment as this. She had picked up her cues exactly as he knew she would.

"She's cunning, and has pried into my affairs before," said Ingles. "Divorce proceedings, or even a formal separation, could well goad her into making inconvenient disclosures to the Media, at a moment when I can ill afford notoriety. So we must proceed with caution. Once Project Nimrod is operational, and we gain exclusive control of global communications, then you may deal with her as you see fit. Meanwhile keep her under close surveillance."

"Very good, sir," said Grotten.

Everything was turning out exactly as he had anticipated. The knowledge that he would soon have the job of silencing the voluptuous Carla forever would spice their lovemaking. He would indeed keep her under close surveillance.

Meanwhile Carla herself was being surveyed by other eyes. Angel had been encouraged tonight to believe he might soon supplant Kurt Grotten as Chief of Operations, and now he longed to supplant him as well in the arms of the ravishing Mrs. Ingles. He knew of her trysts, for he had secretly followed her to them, and now ogled her brazenly as he followed her back down the corridor to the grand salon.

His lecherous gaze did not disconcert her; men had regarded her that way since she was twelve years old. It was her husband's recent lack of regard that caused her apprehension. She was of the race of Machiavelli and Lucrezia Borgia, with a sixth sense for murderous conspiracies, and all her instincts warned her to be careful. She had recently come to distrust even her lover, who had proved so useful to her.

Her favorite American drink was sherry cobbler, which her husband mixed to perfection; though he himself drank only bottled mineral water, and only from bottles he had opened with his own hands, after a close inspection of the seal.

Chief Grotten always made a point of drinking canned beer, as befitted his station. Angel joined him, making a social effort tonight by drinking from a glass.

"Here's mud in your eye," said Ingles.

"Here's mud in your eye," repeated his guests.

But it was guarded, not muddied, eyes that watched furtively over the rim of each glass as it was raised in the corny old toast.

CHAPTER VI

It was a near thing. The two young cats had proceeded systematically in their search. One took her turn standing guard at the laboratory door, while the other reconnoitered the corridors. There were Earthlings with bandaged heads in some rooms—in one room an Earthling with a shaven head lay strapped down—but they could discover no means by which to escape from the building. And now it was night again.

It was Dominique who flashed the telepathic alarm which brought Domino racing back in time to reclose the room door, relock the door of their cage, and pull its covering cloth back into place moments before three scientists entered. Then the cats pretended to doze, while the cloth was lifted and bespectacled eyes peered in at them.

"I still believe that your maze will be too complex for them, Rottwald," said Dr. Carlson, re-covering the cage. "It took me several minutes to puzzle it out myself."

"A solution is irrelevant," said Dr. Rottwald, the staff zoologist, a tall, spare man who took himself very seriously. "Observation of their behavior while confronting the maze will tell me all I need to know. Physiognomical evaluation can take us no further."

"Then you still can't identify their species?" asked Dr. Carlson.

The zoologist lifted an eyebrow at him, as if his professional competence were being challenged. "Clearly they are hybrids. The improbably large genetic drift indicated by our DNA tests is an illusion, the result of artificial crossbreeding. Lester, bring the cage."

"Yes, sir." His assistant was a prematurely bald young man with the thickest spectacles of them all. He gingerly picked up the cage and followed the two senior scientists up the corridor outside.

"After maze testing," said Dr. Rottwald, "all I should need for my final report is routine vivisection. You can then hand the carcasses over to the taxidermist. They should make a handsome exhibit at the Ingles Museum of Natural History."

"Remember, they must still be examined as possible carriers of disease," Dr. Carlson reminded him.

"Haven't I already told you that they had no fleas, lice, ticks, or other parasites, and that their blood was amazingly free of pathogens? Disease carriers?" The zoologist looked him up and down. "You're beginning to sound paranoid, Carlson."

"The examination was requested by our Chief of Operations, at the behest of Mr. Ingles himself, who is concerned about the spread of infection," Dr. Carlson said quietly, with a meaningful glance over the top of his spectacles.

"Yes, yes, nothing could be more important. I see that now. In my anxiety for thoroughness and accuracy, I may have been hasty." The zoologist glanced back at his assistant, toting the animal cage behind them, as if fearful of betrayal. A terrible retribution for any inappropriate words or behavior in the service of B.I.T.E. was never far away in this wing of the Med Center. "In fact, a comprehensive report on the status of pathogens should have been our first consideration."

"My research assistants are preparing the report at this very moment," Dr. Carlson reassured him. "But I'm reluctant to hand the cats over to be stuffed for exhibition until we know Mr. Ingles is satisfied that no further testing is required."

"I agree completely," said the zoologist. "Perhaps I could help with the report myself."

"I'd appreciate that. I'm operating tonight, so I can't give it my personal attention."

"Operating at this hour?"

Dr. Carlson pointed to the crown of his head. No other explanation was necessary, and they turned right and proceeded down another corridor, and then turned left.

Neither Domino nor Dominique had reconnoitered this sector of the restricted wing, and, peering down between the floor of their wire cage and the bottom of its cloth cover, they added its configurations to their mutual picture of the floor plan. Then they were confronted by another kind of floor plan, whose purpose was not immediately evident.

Compliant behavior was the best strategy for lulling their captors, and they had offered no resistance when hair was snipped from their tails, or when blood samples were drawn from them. Domino was tameness itself as she allowed herself to be lifted from the cage.

"Keep the other one covered, Lester," said the zoologist. "Now pussycat, let's see how smart you are."

The maze was supported by sawhorses and took up over half the room. First Domino was shown a bowl of cat food at its exit, and then carried back around to its entrance. She realized now that it was only a simplistic test in problem solving, and that the Earthlings regarded her as an idiot. Still, the food did smell rather tasty, though not so delectable as salmon.

Methodically eliminating false paths, she quickly sensed the pattern of the maze, and picked her way without difficulty to its exit. The cat food was even tastier than it smelled, and she discovered among its ingredients something not unlike salmon.

"Remarkable." The zoologist checked his stopwatch, and made an entry in his notebook. "Ever see anything like this before, Lester?"

"Never, sir. Not even the otters are anything like so fast. Amazing time. Truly amazing."

"Faster than mine," muttered Dr. Carlson, disgruntled.

Domino was allowed only a few nibbles, but did not resist being carried back to the cage. Nor did Dominique object to being carried away in her place. The rigmarole of showing her the bowl of cat food and setting her down at the entrance of the maze was repeated. Without hesitation, she shot through the true path so fast that the scientists were left gaping.

"Incredible!" Lester blurted out. "Not a single false move. It's as if she already knew the way."

"She did," said the zoologist. "Somehow the two cats are communicating with each other. There can be no other explanation."

Domino and Dominique were, in fact, in continuous communication, as if their remultiplied intelligence combined two halves of the same brain, or two units of the same mainframe. Even while solving the idiocies of the maze, they continued to exchange information and hypotheses for the solution of a far more urgent problem.

The windows they had come across during their explorations of the restricted wing all had bars and panes of wired glass. The one in this room had neither, and though it seemed to look only into some kind of inner courtyard, it was the most promising means of escape they had yet discovered. While the three Earthlings stood together exchanging growls, their own telepathic exchanges concentrated on the most efficient use of levers and counterweights for prying open the heavy window.

"Nowhere in the literature have I found such convincing evidence of animal telepathy." The zoologist closed his notebook and handed it to his assistant. "Write up my notes on the maze test as soon as possible, Lester."

"Yes, sir," the younger man said, resigning himself to a sleepless night.

"A Hedspeth-Moltke perception test will show

whether our first observations are conclusive," continued the zoologist. "There's a laboratory just down the corridor with the necessary apparatus."

"The report on possible diseases carried by the animals," Dr. Carlson reminded him.

"Yes, of course. That investigation must be given our highest priority." He glanced furtively at his colleague, as if still apprehensive about betrayal. "Lester here will be glad to help with the report."

"Very glad." The flunky repressed a sigh.

"Meanwhile, return this specimen to its cage. We'll keep the pair together until the last moment. Separating them for the Hedspeth-Moltke will raise their threshold of distress, thereby enhancing their telepathic sensitivity."

"My understanding of the Hedspeth-Moltke is that the subjects must be increasingly distressed throughout the observation," said Dr. Carlson, checking his watch. "Fear, pain, and ultimately death are administered through a graduated scale. Do you intend to kill the subjects at this time?"

"It's true that without ultimate distress the results of a Hedspeth-Moltke must remain somewhat unsatisfactory. But we obviously can't kill the specimens until assured that Mr. Ingles no longer wishes them alive."

"I'm not scheduled to operate for an hour yet," said Dr. Carlson. "I'll telephone the Chief of Operations as soon as we get the apparatus set up. Perhaps I can get you the permission to apply ultimate distress."

"That would maximize the accuracy of the results. Afterward, Lester can deliver the carcasses to the taxidermist." His inability to classify Domino and Dominique had left the zoologist feeling vindictive toward them, as if they were at fault for bringing his professional competence into question. "Leave their cage here for now, Lester. We don't want them disturbed until we're ready to begin observations."

Barely three seconds elapsed between the closing of the room door and the opening of the cage door. Three more seconds, and Domino and Dominique sat on the windowsill, peering down into the courtyard. There was a wall enclosing its farther end, but it appeared leapable; there was a wire screen just outside the windowpane, but it was fastened down by only a simple hook-and-eye device. The problem was the window itself. It was stuck fast, and they could see at once that any system of levers or counterweights capable of multiplying their combined strength enough to raise the sash would take far too long to construct—assuming the necessary materials were available.

Only brute strength could force open this window, the brute strength of an Earthling.

Which of the two first had the idea was irrelevant, for they both acted on it at the same instant. Whatever the purpose of the building, they were not its only prisoners. By now they had a clear picture of its floor plan and knew exactly how to reach their objective.

Down from the sill and out the door; the oafish noisiness of the Earthlings made them easy to evade, and the two bandit-eyed cats stole unerringly through the corridors.

For the first time in her young life Verna Malmrose knew despair. Strapped immobile to a hospital bed, her head shaven and constrained from even turning by metal clamps; the cruel surgery to which she had been condemned would leave her with a functioning organic brain but no mind of her own, a kind of human vegetable. Her one remaining hope was to die on the operating table.

Drugged, pierced with needles, jolted by electric cattle prods, beaten by thuggish fists, kicked and starved; her long ordeal had left her too exhausted for sleep. Or was her insomnia a nervous reaction to the scopolamine injections? Mercilessly, her interrogators had tried to force from her a confession that she was part of a conspiracy against Benton Ingles. She was unsure exactly what they did force from her, but it could hardly have implicated anyone because she had acted alone.

She had personally recovered the effects of her twin brother Vernon, after he perished at sea along with the entire crew of the *Greenworld Challenger.* They had purportedly been investigating endangered fauna in the Marquesas Islands, but certain hints before his departure suggested a more perilous objective, one he dared not reveal even to her. What that was, she still did not know, except that it must somehow have threatened the industrial empire of Benton Ingles.

If Verna was too exhausted to sleep, neither was she fully conscious, and she lapsed continually into waking dreams. Scenes from college life replayed before her eyes like old film clips. She had been elected Facilitator—a goofy title, she still thought—of her school's film society and had procured for it vintage films from collectors and museums all over the country. Her major in Art and Design was wonderfully exciting, and she had enjoyed working in her family's health-food shop in downtown Albuquerque. Yet she had not hesitated to leave that all behind to investigate the true manner of her brother's death, to persevere no matter how often she was put off, abused, misled, deceived, discouraged, and menaced.

Her brother and his friends died heroically in a gallant cause. She was more certain than ever that she had done the right thing, though it would now cost her her rational mind.

Scenes from old films began to mingle vividly with her other reveries: Lon Chaney at the organ in *The Phantom of the Opera;* Marion Davies strapping scrubbrushes to her feet and skating back and forth across a soapy floor, scrubbing it the easy way; Vilma Banky carried off by villains, riding across the sands of the desert with Rudolph Valentino in pursuit. Again and again in her utter exhaustion she drifted to the borderlands of unconsciousness, only to be jolted back by auditory hallucinations of bangs, whistles, thumps and shouts. Then she was suddenly wide awake with terror.

As in a nightmare she watched the door slide noiselessly open, but no doctor or hospital orderly entered the room this time, only a pair of bluish-pearl cats with bandit masking. Strapped and clamped helplessly immobile, she watched them glide toward her without making a sound, closer and closer, and then leap in tandem onto the foot of the bed, as if one were a mirror image of the other. All she could think of were grisly tales about elderly people, paralyzed or too ill to reach a telephone, trapped in their homes with hunger-maddened pets. She, too, was paralyzed, too stricken with horror even to cry out.

Or had her auditory hallucinations now given way to visual hallucinations? After all, cats had stubby little paws not handlike organs more supple than any raccoon's. Nor had cats the dexterity to unbuckle the leather straps holding her down, or to unscrew the metal clamps fixing her head in place. At least, not pussycats. What hellcats or feline apparitions were capable of, she hadn't the vaguest notion. . . .

Whether she swooned from shock or drifted again toward the borderlands of unconsciousness, the next thing she knew all her bonds had been cast off, and she lay covered by only her skimpy hospital gown, her freedom of movement restored. But the cats were still there, sitting side by side at the foot of the bed, and she stared at them now less in terror than in bewilderment. They, in turn, stared at the clock on her bedside table, as if they had an appointment to keep. . . .

She awoke with a start. One of the cats had jabbed the bottom of her bare foot with a single claw, and now both were pushing her in tandem, as if she were a log they were trying to roll. At last through her wooziness she realized they wanted her to get up, and she slid her legs over the side of the bed and levered herself into a sitting position. But she was still groggy, and once more began to slide toward unconsciousness, until startled awake again by another claw jab.

The next thing she knew she was toddling dreamily toward the door, with the two cats scurrying around her like border collies herding some big dumb sheep. Up one corridor and down the next they kept her moving, literally shoving her out of the way of approaching danger into the nearest vacant cubicle. In one of these she again noticed them staring at a clock. It was now twenty minutes to twelve. Why was midnight so important to them? Was that when their spell was broken, when they turned back into pumpkins?

Single claws simultaneously jabbed both her bare feet, and she shook herself. Even through the clouds of wooziness she understood by now that the cats were trying to rescue her; though how this could be, or why they were doing it, still eluded her wandering mind. She could only try to remain alert and let them lead her wherever they would.

They shoved her at last into a vacant laboratory, but this time not because of approaching danger. A huge animal maze took up half the room. She was given no time to wonder about this; they herded her straight to the window, leapt up onto the sill, and together pushed at the sash by way of demonstrating what they wanted her to do.

So that was it. They were not apparitions after all; nor were they rescuing her so much as getting her to rescue them, and for the first time in days she smiled—until she saw her own image reflected back at her from the dark window. She was completely bald; all her beautiful auburn hair had been shorn away, as if she really were a sheep. She hazily recalled an orderly shaving her head in preparation for surgery, but only now did she see what had actually happened to her, and hot tears welled in her eyes. She felt hideous.

She also felt angry, and tried to rip open the sash at a yank. It scarcely budged. This did not discourage her—obstacles just made her that much more determined—and she braced herself for another effort. Her brother had been the bodybuilder of the family; she had pumped iron more to develop symmetry than bulging muscles, but she was nonetheless exceptionally strong for a woman of her age, with a full-breasted, beautifully proportioned figure.

Her reflection warned her that some of those proportions were now much too evident. All she had on was a thigh-length hospital gown, tied loosely at the back, but this was hardly the time to worry about modesty.

Positioning herself as she would for a squat press, she added the thrust of her strong, shapely legs to her second effort, and this time the frozen window snapped loose. Before she had jammed it as high as it would go, the two cats had already unlatched the screen, and she followed them into the courtyard outside. The effort left her momentarily giddy, but the cool night air revived her. It also made her conscious of the loose flimsiness of her hospital gown, and she fumbled behind herself at its strings, trying to draw them tighter.

A gibbous moon stood halfway up a sky awash with glittering stars. Three sides of the courtyard were bounded by the restricted wing of the Med Center, the fourth by a cinder block wall coped with plastic tiles. One cat was sitting atop a plastic contour chair, the other atop the round serving table beside it. The instant they caught her eye, they raised their left forepaws in unison and pointed at the wall.

Put the chair on top of the table and climb over. Obviously. She should have figured that one out herself, with no need to have it pointed out to her. Literally pointed out, by cats. She again felt giddy.

For more than one reason she hoped no one spotted her climbing over the wall in the moonlight. The tie at the back of her hospital gown had come undone, and anyone looking her way would indeed have seen a moon.

She dropped to the grass on the other side. The two cats waited while she retied her hospital gown, then once more raised their left forepaws in unison, beckoning her to follow. She was glad they avoided walkways, where students coming home late might see her from behind, and whenever possible used trees and shrubbery as screens. But there was something peculiar about their movements, and at last she realized they were trotting along in step, like soldiers in double time. Twice she noticed them glancing anxiously up at the illuminated clock atop the Administration Building, and quickening their pace.

She was anxious herself, not just to see whatever magical event these strange cats expected to befall them at midnight, but to put as many miles as possible between herself and Ingles City. If her escape had not already been discovered, it soon would be. Steal a car from the parking lot? She could hardly use public transportation dressed, or rather undressed, as she was, and in any case she had no money. But the first excitement had worn off, and she found it harder and harder to concentrate.

Where were the cats taking her? She followed them passively across the dark and deserted campus; they seemed to know where they were going, while she herself tended to relapse into dreaminess with every step. The cool grass felt pleasant beneath her bare feet; the air was soft and fragrant; moonlight caressed her with silvery beams. All at once a windowless brick building loomed before her, seeming to rise forever into the night sky. The cats led her past its side entrance, where a single bulb glowed over a steel door, and into a stand of flowering shrubs nearby. Then they turned back.

Dreamily she started to follow them, but this time they rose up together and placed their forepaws against her knees. Evidently they wanted her to remain in concealment, and she was too disoriented to resist. Then she was alone. The brick wall beside her radiated back the warmth it had absorbed during the day; the flowering shrubs rose about her like a giant bouquet, breathing their sweet perfume into the night. A pleasant languor stole over her, and she yawned and sat upon a fluffy patch of grass, wondering what she was doing here. Midnight was now only minutes away, and she fumbled at the strings of her hospital gown, trying to retie them. . . .

Tim Waverly was always punctual. His blue uniform was freshly laundered and pressed, he wore his blue Los Angeles Dodgers baseball cap turned backward, and carried as usual a stack of books, notebooks, and manila folders in one hand, and a brown paper bag in the other. He was surprised to find Domino and Dominique waiting for him at the door.

"Sorry, young ladies," he said. "All I have tonight is peanut butter and jelly. I didn't expect to ever see you again, or I would have emptied the freezer of salmon." He looked down at them in perplexity. "Now what am I going to do with you? I'm not even supposed to know you exist."

The Chief of Operations himself had confided to Tim that the cats were part of a top-secret experiment in genetic engineering, and he knew it was his duty to return them to the Med Center. But he had a strong aversion to condemning any living creature to a cage.

The cats themselves solved his immediate dilemma—and created for him one far more dangerous and perplexing. First they simultaneously pointed with their forepaws toward the shrubbery; then each hooked a claw into one of his pants legs, and tugged him in that direction.

"Don't tell me you've brought friends?" He had a wild fantasy about Domino and Dominique staging a prison break, and leading every laboratory animal on campus here. "All right, I'm coming. Don't tear my pants off."

He set his books and lunch bag on the stoop and followed them into the shrubbery, half expecting to encounter there a menagerie of escaped cats, dogs, monkeys, rats, guinea pigs, and rabbits. Though never in his wildest fantasizing could he have expected to encounter a bald girl asleep in the moonlight. She was scantily clad in a hospital gown which had come untied at the back, revealing a truly splendid figure. Nor did it help his composure when she sighed comfortably in her sleep and rolled over.

"Now what am I going to do?" He made a gallant effort to look only at the two cats, but was not entirely successful. "You've gotten me into a fine mess this time, young ladies."

He wondered if they really had staged some kind of prison break. The girl was bald and wore only a skimpy hospital gown. Was she also part of some top-secret experiment in genetic engineering? If Domino and Dominique had been given human qualities, perhaps she had been created in the laboratory with the nature of a cat? But whoever or whatever she was, he could not just leave her sleeping in the moonlight.

He doffed his blue uniform shirt and covered her with it; then he shook her arm, softly at first and then more vigorously. But all she did was moan and try to push the shirt off herself. Now what? It looked like he might have to carry her. But where?

"Wait here, young ladies," he said. "I'll be right back."

He was allowed two personal business days off a year, and so far had not used them. Requests were supposed to be tendered at least twenty-four hours in advance, not three minutes, and only because he had perfect attendance and had often subbed for others on short notice was an exception made this time. But he would have to act fast.

He was now certain that Domino and Dominique had first been traced here through his telephone call to the Administration Building. The call he had just made to Security Central would also be monitored, and it would seem just too much of a coincidence that he requested emergency time off, on the very night the two cats escaped again and a beautiful young girl disappeared from some hospital, not to rouse suspicion. The Chief of Operations and his goons might be on their way here at this very moment.

He found the girl curled in a fetal position when he returned and tried shaking her again, but she only curled tighter still. There was no help for it; he would just have to carry her. But Domino and Dominique once more solved his dilemma, jabbing the soles of her bare feet with needlelike claws.

She blinked sleepily up at him for several moments; then all at once her eyes widened in alarm, and she gasped and sat bolt upright, instinctively holding his shirt in front of herself.

"It's all right, I'm not going to hurt you," he said. "But we must hurry. This is where they found Domino and Dominique the first time they escaped, so they're sure to come looking for them here again."

"Domino and Dominique?"

"The two young ladies sitting beside you. The one with the black tip on her tail is Domino. Dominique has the black right forepaw. That's how I tell them apart."

She started to reply, then noticed she was holding a man's shirt in front of herself. "Where did this come from?"

"It's mine. You weren't wearing . . . that is to say, I thought you might, well, be more comfortable, you know, at this time of night. . . ." He trailed off in embarrassment.

Reaching quickly behind her, she discovered to her own embarrassment that her hospital gown hung completely open. She looked steadily into his eyes.

"How was I sleeping when you first saw me?"

"Very soundly. Now let's get going." He didn't mean to be brusque, but the posse would soon be gathering, if it was not already heading this way, and he set her firmly on her feet.

She continued to hold the shirt in front of her, but now realized that it was part of a uniform, and drew away in alarm. "Please don't take me back to the hospital. It was awful. They were going to turn me into a vegetable."

He looked curiously at her. She had obviously suffered an ordeal but did not speak or behave like a laboratory experiment.

"We'll talk about it later," he said. "Right now we have to get moving, and fast. I know where I can borrow a car, so I can take you out of town to people who will protect you. But we must hurry."

She sensed in his manner, like Domino and Dominique before her, something fundamentally decent and trustworthy. In any case, she had no choice now but to trust him.

"All right, but you go on ahead. I'll catch up with you in a minute."

Resignedly shaking his head over the vagaries of women, he pushed his way out of the shrubbery and gathered up his books and lunch bag. But true to her word, she emerged into the light scarcely a minute later, now wearing his shirt with its overlong sleeves rolled up at the wrists.

"Lead on, Tim Waverly." She tapped the nameplate over the shirt pocket. "I'm Verna Malmrose. Now, exactly where are you taking me?"

"I live in Royal Beach and have friends there who can help and advise you." He used the trees and shrubbery to screen them, avoiding the walkways. "Verna Malmrose?" he said thoughtfully. "I know a Vernon Malmrose. Any relation?"

"My twin brother." She decided that this was the

wrong time to go into details. "We attended the California Strength and Health Club convention in Royal Beach together, just last year."

"Of course, now I know you. We weren't introduced, but I remember Vernon pointing out his sister to me one day on the beach. I didn't recognize you."

Tears welled in her eyes, and she covered her head with both hands. "Those dirty swine cut off all my beautiful hair."

"Sorry I mentioned it." He put his Dodgers baseball cap on her bald head. "It'll all grow back before you know it. Now let's hit the road."

"I hope that road has a fast food place on it."

"You mean they starved you, too?"

"I'd kill for a cheeseburger."

"How about peanut butter and jelly?"

"Gimme." She fairly ripped open his lunch bag, and bit ravenously into a sandwich. "Yum, yum. Strawberry jam and chunky peanut butter. Absolutely, utterly delicious. It's been days since I've eaten. I just hope I don't fall asleep between bites."

She had begun to stumble, and he was afraid he might end up carrying her after all, but she bravely carried on. Then his attention was attracted by flashing lights, and in the distance he saw police cars, one after the other, skid to a halt in the parking lot behind his dormitory. The posse was already on their trail.

Dead ahead, the faculty subdivision slumbered in the moonlight. Despite the hour, he should have no trouble borrowing the car of an assistant professor, who was also a fellow weight lifter, and he began working out their best means of reaching Royal Beach in safety.

All the while Domino and Dominique trotted along in step behind them, silently working out their own best means of survival on this strange and violent planet. Service to the Masters had been imprinted upon them every waking and sleeping hour since birth. That these conditioned instincts should now be transferred to their Earthling benefactors, who not only bore a likeness to the Masters but like them sometimes needed looking after, was inevitable.

CHAPTER VII

"You can never trust a broad, not even when you got her doped up and tied down." Angel seized a course workbook in his meaty hands and savagely ripped it in half. "I nailed that first security guard for you. Looks like she's got another one wrapped around her little finger."

"Take it easy, Angel." Chief Grotten glanced over the shambles of books, papers, notebooks, hangers, and clothing, scattered about the dormitory like the debris of a windstorm. "Tearing up the place doesn't do me any good. Waverly never came back here after calling Security Central. His roommate says so, and says he doesn't know where he's gone. That right?"

The roommate, a fledgling CEO, sat abjectly on the edge of his bed. He nodded vigorously, anxious to please, as though apologizing that he had no information to betray.

"Try Royal Beach, sir," said Angel. "That's where this bluebird punk lives. He's got the broad, he's got the cats, and that's where he took 'em. Bet on it."

"Perhaps, perhaps not," said Chief Grotten. The cold aloofness with which Benton Ingles had accepted his report about the escape of both the girl and the cats had shaken him. He was sure now that one of his subordinates was being groomed to supplant him, and it was not hard to guess who. Not since a coalition of journalists and civil libertarians had hounded him off the Los Angeles police force had he felt so close to ruin. "But you'll soon be able to investigate there yourself. I understand you've been given a special assignment at Royal Beach."

Until this moment he had had only suspicions, but Angel's guilty reaction confirmed them. Benton Ingles, too, was a past master at playing subordinates off against each other.

"You'll be reporting directly to Mr. Ingles," he continued, and again his suspicions were confirmed by Angel's confusion. "But you're welcome to any men or equipment you may need from Special Operations. This is a big assignment for you, and I want to give you all the help I can."

"Thanks. I, uh, appreciate that, sir." The lowering of Angel's heavy browridge betrayed both his perplexity and the eternal insecurity of B.I.T.E. employees. "You got anything more for me to do here, sir? Then I'll get started for Royal Beach. You know, the sooner the better."

With a last glower at the thoroughly cowed student on the bed, he strode belligerently from the room. The hasty slamming of doors up and down the corridor outside evidenced how startlingly his grim appearance had discouraged the curiosity of other students in the dormitory.

Chief Grotten made a last inspection for clues to the whereabouts of Tim Waverly. Only when his policeman's thoroughness had been satisfied did he again notice the roommate, who all the while had never taken his eyes off him.

"Here's my telephone number. You're to call me the instant you have any information at all about Waverly. Is that understood?"

"Yes, sir."

"This is a confidential matter, so you won't mention it to anybody. Is that understood?"

"Yes, sir."

"Then start cleaning up. This mess is nothing to the one you'll see if I have to send Angel back here to check up on you. Now is that understood?"

"Yes, sir."

The obsequiousness of the young Business Administration major in accepting a rotten job, the groveling self-effacement of his truckling to authority, and the fawning servility with which he held open the door for a man he feared and disliked, were attributes that would one day serve him well in his climb up the corporate ladder.

The idea came to Chief Grotten as he descended the rear stairway. It would be easy to ensure that any report Angel sent from Royal Beach, no matter how privately, would also come to him. More difficult would be to ensure that nothing the Malmrose girl reported publicly jeopardized Project Nimrod. There was already a dragnet out for her, but recapture was too much a matter of chance. Somehow anything she might divulge to the police or the Media had to be discredited beforehand—and now he knew how. That the device would also punish the fools who let her escape would be appreciated by Benton Ingles.

The rotating beacons atop three police cars flashed their red lights round and round through the night as he crossed the parking lot to his car, smiling grimly to himself.

"God, that was embarrassing." Tim Waverly set the green plastic shopping bag beside him on the front seat of the old Plymouth. "He winked at me."

"Winked at you?" Verna repressed a grin.

There was only one other car in the parking lot. Through the window of the all-night convenience store a respectable-looking old man could be seen leaning on his elbows beside the cash register.

"Please do your own shopping in the future." He frowned, gripping the steering wheel with both hands. It was an hour before dawn; traffic was increasing along the coastal highway, beyond which the Pacific Ocean glistened metallically in the waning moonlight. "I put the bra and panties on the counter, hoping he'd just ring them up with the other purchases. But he leaned over and whispered that he had sexier stuff in the back room. For special customers. Extra large, even in my size. My size! I told him the things were for someone else, and that's when he winked at me."

"Oh, Tim Waverly." She laughed merrily. "Anything in the morning papers?"

He drew a newspaper from the shopping bag. "The headline story is about the failure of the UN Commstat. Looks like the whole space program has been grounded, pending a congressional investigation. Here, read it for yourself."

"Oh, this is terrible. 'Billions of tax dollars wasted,' 'Corruption at the United Nations,' 'Faulty design,' " she read the subheadings. "Somebody's really playing this up big."

"Benton Ingles owns half the newspapers in the state, including that one, and nearly all the local radio and television stations."

"Yes, I saw him in a television interview, on one of his own stations, explaining why the entire satellite communications network should be privatized." She yawned. "Uh-oh, I think all that coffee I had at the Burger King is wearing off."

"We're almost there. I called Tedworth Vay, the man I told you about, and left a message on his answering machine. He'll be interested in hearing your story, and in meeting our two curious friends." He nodded toward the rear seat, where Domino and Dominique lay with their paws wrapped over their heads, curled asleep like a pair of furry question marks.

"I've never read any of his books," she said, "though I've seen them on the racks in supermarkets and drugstores. All about the occult. He's not a weirdo, is he?"

"Anything but. He's converted his mansion in Royal Beach into a popular tourist attraction, the Museum of the Unexplained. His lectures help support his clinic."

"Oh, then he's a doctor?"

"Not in the medical sense. His Ph.D. is in classical literature, but he felt cramped by the modern university, and the demand for narrower and narrower specialization. He wanted to write books people would read, not just pothole monographs for publication credit. He's interested in everything, from archaeology to zoology, but especially in manifestations of psychic powers and disorders. People from all over the world consult him."

She looked curiously at him. "You sound like an enthusiast yourself. Funny you should major in, of all things, Business Administration."

He frowned. "I'm mostly doing it for my parents. You see, I'm an only child, and they've done so much for me, and made so many sacrifices on my behalf, that I didn't want to disappoint them."

"But aren't you working your way through school? If your parents live in Royal Beach, they must have money."

His frown deepened. "Well, I suppose they're comfortably well off, though certainly not rich. We've never actually sat down and discussed family finances together. They believe that if I pay my own way through college, I'll grow in character and gain a better appreciation of the value of money. It's for my own good, really."

She saw that it was a painful subject for him, and changed it. "When do we meet your famous friend? I'm getting sleepy."

"We still have a couple of hours to kill. Why don't we stop somewhere for coffee? After all those cheeseburgers, french fries, and peanut butter-and-jelly sandwiches, you probably couldn't eat a full breakfast."

"Watch me. Those dirty swine starved me for days. But first you'd better take a walk, so I can get dressed." She rummaged through the shopping bag. "Hmmmm, I hope this bra fits."

"It was the closest they had to what you asked for," he said innocently. "There wasn't a larger size on the shelf. You know, wearing that loose shirt, I never realized you were so ... I mean, when I first saw you sleeping on your stomach ... uh, yes. ..." He broke down and stared fixedly out the windshield. Even in the dim light of the parking lot she could see he was blushing.

"Take a walk, Tim Waverly." Her shoulders trembled with suppressed laughter.

The Santa Lucia Mountains loomed purple against the eastern sky as Tim turned the old Plymouth down Lengendary Lane. At its head rose the most resplendent Victorian mansion in all Royal Beach. Originally built in the decade following the Gold Rush, by a speculator in mining shares, it had been renovated in the decade following the Volstead Act, by a speculator in rum; then renovated again into the Museum of the Unexplained.

"I think I feel some stubble." Verna ran her fingers gingerly over the crown of her hair. "Five o'clock shadow at seven in the morning." She donned the Dodgers baseball cap again, and gazed out the window at the parade of gaudy and bedizened relics of the Age of Opulence, lining either side of the brick-paved street. "These places really are spectacular. Is this where you live?"

"No, this is the Gold Coast. My parents' house is up there in the hills, in the new section of town. We call these beauties the Painted Ladies."

"They're beauties all right, and some other ladies seem very interested."

He glanced back as he turned the Plymouth up a brick driveway, originally designed to accommodate horse carriages. Both cats stood on their hind legs, Domino peering out the left rear window, Dominique peering out the right.

"What one sees, the other knows," said Verna. "Like two sets of eyes in the same head. They're uncanny."

"Here's the place for explanations of the uncanny,"

said Tim. "And there's the man who can do the explaining."

Tedworth Vay awaited them beneath the carport, at the side of the mansion. He was tall and aristocratically slender, with thick, graying hair combed straight back from a high forehead, and a neatly trimmed Vandyke. He reminded many visitors here of the Sorcerer in a tarot deck.

"Hello, Tim. And you must be Miss Verna Malmrose." He introduced himself, and bowed with old-world courtliness as he assisted her out of the car; his poise immediately put them both at ease. "And there, I presume, are the extraordinary Domino and Dominique." Both cats, still standing on their hind legs, examined him curiously through the same rear window. "This way, if you please, one and all."

Before Tim could let the cats out the back of the car, they slipped out the front, and entered the house with the air of visiting duchesses, walking side by side in perfect step.

"If your professor figures those two out, he's a genius," said Verna, both touched and amused by the courtesy with which Tim held open the door for her, like the leading man in an old movie.

Her first impression was an eerie sense of having wandered back through time. The Museum of the Unexplained, it turned out, occupied only the basement of the mansion; the clinic, presently unoccupied, and the old carriage house were at the rear of the grounds. But all around her was another museum of Victorian elegance, ornate with fine furniture upholstered in velvet and brocade, rare paintings and statuary, silk wall coverings, mahogany wainscoting, antique bibelots, golden tassels, and hand-loomed carpets and draperies.

She stepped through a doorway curtained with strings of coral beads into the most congenial room she could imagine. Never had she seen armchairs and sofas so comfortably overstuffed, or such thick-piled carpets, or such beautifully embroidered draperies, or so cheerful a fireplace, or lamps that cast so warm a glow. She sank into the cushions of the sofa with a grateful sigh.

The velvet smoking jacket, silk neck scarf, loose flannel trousers, and doeskin slippers worn by Tedworth Vay blended smoothly into his comfortable surroundings. He seated himself in the armchair on the opposite side of the fireplace, on whose mantlepiece was a photograph of a formidably beautiful woman standing before the ruins of some ancient city. Books and a decanter of old port sat on the table beside him; but it was too early for drinks, and Tim and Verna, having breakfasted, declined either coffee or tea.

Meanwhile Domino and Dominique separated and systematically reconnoitered their new environment, meeting again at the center of the room to exchange impressions. Tedworth Vay observed them with shrewd curiosity, but had to defer any investigation of their peculiarities until after he had settled more urgent matters.

"First things first," he said. "Tim here informs me that your captors abused you, Miss Malmrose. Are you in need of medical attention?"

"What?" She blinked sleepily at him.

"I say, are you in need of medical attention?"

All her accumulated weariness had hit her like a blow the moment she sank into the overstuffed sofa, and tears of exhaustion now welled in her eyes.

"Those dirty swine cut off all my beautiful hair." She yawned and caught herself nodding. "I'm sorry, what were you saying?"

"She's utterly exhausted, Professor." The voice was that of a child, and came from just outside the beaded curtain. "I sense only disconnected images, like scenes from old movies, flashing through her mind. But she's not in pain."

The most striking reactions to the voice, or perhaps to some more profound communication, were that of Domino and Dominique. Side by side, heads forward, eyes watchful, they faced the curtain with a vibrant intentness.

"Come in, Rhoda," said Tedworth Vay, more curious than ever about the two cats. "I thought you were going upstairs to the game room, to watch television."

"There's nothing on now but news specials and talk shows about the mess in the space program."

A child of ten, dressed in fringed buckskin and Indian beads, entered the room. She was as struck by Domino and Dominique as they were by her, and gazed intently down at them. After a few moments, she smiled.

"They're talking to each other, Professor. Or maybe not exactly talking, but tuning in together on the same image. It's hard to explain, because I've never sensed anything like it before. Ghost Eagle could summon animals from all over the reservation, and said they can summon each other from far greater distances."

"There's a scientific controversy about that," he said. "In any case, let me introduce you. Tim Waverly, Verna Malmrose, my ward Rhoda Dawn. Now as for Domino and Dominique, perhaps it was they who drew you downstairs from the game room. Ghost Eagle told you before he died that your powers were stronger than his, the strongest, in fact, that he had ever known. Your powers may be developing as you grow older."

"I don't know about that, Professor," she said. "But I do know that these are not ordinary cats."

"You can say that again," exclaimed Tim. "Our Chief of Operations told me they were part of some secret experiment in genetic engineering. But whatever they are, they play a mean game of chess."

"Chess?" Tedworth Vay looked quizzically at him. "You mean they can push chessmen across a board as directed?"

"No, Professor, I mean that they play chess. They picked up the fundamentals by watching videotapes, and mastery by watching me replay a Capablanca masterpiece. I did no better against them than I do against the mainframe."

Tedworth Vay thoughtfully poured himself a glass of port. He was too experienced an investigator of the occult ever to dismiss phenomena, no matter how strange or unaccountable, merely because they did not jibe with official science. That was Academe's way, not his. He reached out and tugged the bell pull beside the fireplace.

"Before we investigate anything," he said, "we should first get Miss Malmrose to bed."

It was only now that Tim realized that Verna was sound asleep on the couch beside him.

"Poor kid, she's had a rough time of it. Her brother was aboard the *Greenworld Challenger* when it went down under suspicious circumstances, and she came to Ingles City to find out what really happened to him. Her investigation must have been getting close to something big, or they wouldn't have gone to so much trouble to stop her."

"No doubt, but exactly what she was getting close to and who *they* might be still remains to be investigated. Alas for my telephone bill. Most of my queries must be directed to sources in Washington."

"Do you think she's right, that the shipwreck really was suspicious?"

"I thought so at the time, because of certain discrepancies in the official account, and because Media controlled by Benton Ingles protested too much that it was true. Ah, Chesterville. Prepare one of the guest bedrooms for Miss Malmrose here, please."

"Very good, sir," replied the butler.

He was a large, florid-faced man in his late forties, with snow-white hair combed straight back in emulation of his master, who carried a butler's inherent superciliousness above and beyond the call of duty. A jocular tourist had once referred to him as a "walking sneer."

"Allow me, sir."

He lifted the sleeping girl off the couch and carried her out through the beaded curtain as ceremoniously as if she were a silver salver to be presented at a state dinner, with the disconcerted Tim tagging unavailingly along behind.

"Have you been able to remember anything yet before the night Ghost Eagle chanted over you in the spirit circle?" Tedworth Vay asked his ward. "You must have been about four years old at the time."

She shook her head. "I've tried and I've tired, but it's still like I'm staring at a brick wall. Everything after that night is as if it happened only yesterday. I have the feeling that people were cruel to me, and that I was beaten again and again, but who they were and why they hurt me, I just can't seem to remember."

"You may not want to remember, dear," he said. "And perhaps it's best that way."

He had legally adopted the child only recently, though her antecedents remained a mystery. Her blue eyes, strawberry blonde hair, and fair complexion ruled out an Indian origin. Exactly how she came into the hands of the old Jacarilla medicine man was also still unknown. "Rhoda Dawn" was an anglicized form of the Indian name, which a linguist at the University of New Mexico informed him meant "Spirit Eyes," implying second sight.

When Ghost Eagle died, the tribe, in superstitious dread, turned her over to the local Indian agent who, in turn, brought her here. She was the most powerful natural medium he had ever tested, and her reaction to the two strange cats, and theirs to her, further confirmed the extraordinary range of her clairvoyance.

"They're sleepy," she said, still gazing intently down at Domino and Dominique. "But what are we going to feed them? There's no cat food in the house."

"Try salmon," said Tim, reentering via the beaded curtain. "They're passionately fond of it. We put Verna in the bedroom at the top of the stairs, Professor, the one with all the jade carvings. She'll sleep for hours."

"What about you, Tim?" he asked. "There are twenty bedrooms upstairs. Take your pick."

"Thanks, but I'm not sleepy. Normally I'd be in Econ 231 at this time." He frowned. "If you don't need me for anything right now, I think I'd better go home for a while. My parents will be upset about my missing classes, but they'd really be hurt if I was in town and didn't see them."

"Go ahead, I'll call you if I need you. Right now I have some other calling to do, long distance. By the way, if you call anybody back at the university, or anywhere else in Ingles City, be careful what you say. The Royal Beach Preservation Society protects residents against local wiretapping, but it's powerless at the other end of the line."

"Don't worry, Professor, I've already got my story worked out. I'm going to tell my roommate that I'm on my way to Las Vegas, to try my new card-counting system at blackjack. He'll buy that, because he's always trying to work out his own system for beating the house. In fact, it seems to be the ambition of every instructor in the Business Administration department to beat the house with some card-counting system or other."

"That was my experience in the Classics department, too. Drop by late this afternoon, if you can. Miss Malmrose should be rested by then, and we can all hear the story of her adventures, as well as yours about these mysterious cats. Chess?" He raised his eyebrows. "Well, we shall just have to see about that. Give my regards to your parents."

"I will, Professor," he said tactfully, with no intention of actually doing it. Mentioning the name Tedworth Vay in front of his parents was like waving a red flag in front of a bull. "I'll see you again this afternoon. Rhoda, Domino, and Dominique, have a good day."

"You'd better be off now, too, Rhoda," said Tedworth Vay. "Take our friends here upstairs, and find them somewhere they can nap. Maybe the television programs will be more interesting for you now."

"I doubt it," she said. "Probably just more stuff about the big space station that flopped, and scientists making excuses about it, and congressmen pretending to be angry and saying the people are being swindled out of their tax dollars. I'd rather read the book about hobbits you gave me. It's wonderful."

"Yes, and there are thousands more books in the library down the hall, each with its own delights. You'll make many wonderful discoveries there in the years to come. But run along now. I'll have Chesterville pick up all the necessary paraphernalia for the boarding of cats."

He sat alone in the grand salon for nearly an hour, in the overstuffed armchair by the fireplace, until he had carried his reflections to the limit of his information. Then he took out his pocket notebook and ran his fingers down a list of telephone numbers.

Chief Grotten congratulated himself as he led the Ingles City Chief of Police up the corridor of the Med Center into its restricted wing. His brutal stratagem had allayed the suspicions of Benton Ingles, perhaps even regained him some of his lost favor, discredited beforehand anything the Malmrose girl might divulge to the Media or the authorities, and punished those who let her escape in so gruesome a manner that discipline would tighten naturally throughout all B.I.T.E. Against so many advantages, what did the lives of three scientists matter? The country was lousy with eggheads.

"It's not pretty," he said. "No matter how long you're a cop, you never quite get used to scenes like this. By the way, I've put our staff pathologist on the case. I didn't see any need to drag your department guy all the way out here, when the murders took place right in a hospital."

"Exactly what I would have done myself," the Chief

of Police agreed, just as he would have agreed to any other disposition the formidable Chief of Operations of B.I.T.E. chose to make. He had no illusion about who wielded the real police authority over Ingles City and all the townships for miles around: a single telephone call and his job, his pension, and perhaps his very life would be forfeit. "And thanks for sealing off the area so promptly. Saves me the trouble."

"Well, Hutton?" Chief Grotten confronted the guard posted at the laboratory door. "Any new developments?"

"No, sir. The state police have the girl's description, but so far there are no leads."

"The newsies are on their way in full force, including TV crews. Give me the high sign, the moment you spot them."

"Yes, sir."

The Chief of Police wondered about the usefulness of so much publicity, but his colleague was right about one thing: no amount of police experience ever hardened a man to so grisly a scene. This was not murder, it was butchery. He winced as he fought down a wave of nausea.

The three scientists, including the staff zoologist and his young assistant, had evidently been taken unawares by the escaped madwoman; the young assistant had been literally dismembered. He picked up a sealed plastic bag; the surgeon's knife inside was clotted with blood.

"It's like a butcher's knife with the edge of a razor," he said. "But it's still hard to conceive of a lone girl committing such carnage."

"Glance at this." Chief Grotten handed him a hospital data sheet. "You'll see why we're alerting the public about her escape."

Halfway down the page the Chief of Police raised his eyebrows; at the bottom he whistled and shook his head.

"I see what you mean. A weight lifter, no less." He

made a wry face. "Nothing so turns me off as a broad with muscles. And it was her own brother who committed her here?"

"An environmentalist loony," said Chief Grotten. "He was aboard the *Greenworld Challenger* when it went down. Commits his sister to an institution just so he can go off and save the whales. You know the type."

"Don't I, though. California's crawling with tree huggers these days." He turned away as the pathologist and his assistant eased one of the corpses into a body bag; its throat was sliced nearly through. "Looks like these three were just in the wrong place at the wrong time."

"That's my guess, too," said Chief Grotten, now handing him a police fact sheet in addition to the hospital data sheet. He had personally created both documents not two hours ago, and double-checked every "fact" in the case with professional thoroughness, to ensure there were no discrepancies in the official account.

"Here they come, Mr. Grotten." The door guard poked his head into the room. "TV cameras and all."

"All right, Hutton. Give them any assistance you can." He turned back to the Chief of Police. "You have all the facts there. I'll leave you to handling the briefing. If anything else turns up, I'll let you know."

He slipped from the room and out a guarded exit just as the crowd of newspaper and television reporters, photographers, sound technicians, and TV cameramen, all laden with their various paraphernalia, came surging down the corridor like a tidal bore. He had taken precautions against their curiosity straying beyond this one sealed-off and guarded corridor anywhere else in the restricted wing. Meanwhile he was curious about a few things himself.

"Whipple?" His call over his car telephone was answered after a single ring. "What's happening at Royal Beach?"

"It's just like you figured, boss." The voice on the line was high-pitched and nasal. "Angel staked out the houses of the Waverly punk, all his known pals, including some weird professor with a museum, and that dotty old movie star you told me about. I got the job watching her, just like you wanted. I'm in the telephone booth across the street from her mansion. Boss, it's like something out of an old movie. This whole section of town's like that."

"Don't worry, Whipple. Their days are numbered. Just keep your eyes open. You know how to reach me, the minute anything happens. Especially if Mrs. Ingles should visit there."

"Oh, now I get it. I was wondering why you wanted me staked out at this particular house."

"It's not healthy to wonder too much, Whipple. Just do what you're told. No more, no less."

"Right, boss. You know me, I never second-guess nobody. Ever. Whoever shows up here, whatever happens anywheres in Royal Beach, you'll know first thing." There was now a whininess in his nasal, high-pitched voice.

Chief Grotten hung up without another word, leaving his spy in a state of servile apprehension—the attitude he considered most useful in a subordinate. No event in Royal Beach would now be hidden from him. Whether or not the Malmrose girl was taken there by young Waverly, she would sooner or later be recaptured, sedated, and returned to the Med Center for personality readjustment. Sooner, if she tried to contact the authorities, with the public conditioned to believe her a homocidal maniac. Any accusation she made would be dismissed as the ravings of an escaped madwoman.

The two mysterious cats had escaped at the same time; but the less publicity about them, the better. Keep your story simple, and stick with it. If criminals ever understood that, half the jails in the country would be empty.

His custom-built black sedan appeared more than usually sinister as he sped unheedingly to his tryst through the workaday streets of Ingles City. The voluptuous Carla awaited him in the mansion by the sea. His story of the means he had used to discredit the Malmrose girl would excite her to a wild sensuality. It was a pity that he would soon have to kill her.

CHAPTER VIII

"Watch yourself, Professor," warned a voice over the telephone, in a thick Middle Eastern accent. "Remember your investigation of the Vampire Tong. Don't get so close this time."

Tedworth Vay had been on the telephone all morning, and with each call he made the picture had grown more ominous, until the entire country, the very planet itself, seemed on the brink of destruction. The insidious Vampire Tong disguised its murders, to obtain transplant organs for aged millionaires, behind the superstitious dread of vampires. His exposure of its operations had more than once imperiled his life. Only the Missionary's Curse affair, eight years ago in New York, had ever brought him so near death. But never had the stakes been higher than they were now, or the forces arrayed against him so ruthless and overwhelming.

"Don't worry, Kelly, I won't take any unnecessary risks," he said. "Did you get the details?"

"I always get the details, Professor," said the voice. "That's why you pay me so much for my services. You'll see what Benton Ingles wants the public to believe on the evening news. That your Verna Malmrose escaped a hospital for the criminally insane, carved up three doctors like she was the butcher and they were the pigs, and is now on the loose, armed and dangerous."

"I hadn't heard anything about murder."

"You will soon, and so will the whole country. She

never did it, of course. My guess is she got something to tell that Benton Ingles don't want nobody to hear. Her house in Albuquerque is being watched, which means they don't know where she is yet. My belief is that it's got something to do with the sinking of the *Greenworld Challenger,* because her twin brother was aboard. Can you doubt that Benton Ingles was behind that, too?"

"Not anymore. Stay with it, Kelly. But you watch yourself. This is shaping up as the biggest thing either of us has ever tackled."

"I think so, too, Professor. But Khalid Aslanov, sometimes known as Kelly, has survived the fall of dynasties, the wrath of drug lords, war, revolution, and four wives. I will indeed stay with it, as you say, at my usual exorbitant fee. But I will telephone you only when I am here at Royal Beach, where the telephone lines, happily, are still untapped. In the meantime, when you are thinking about this case, Professor, think also about the space program. My details, such as they are, all point in that direction. Adios, ciao, and farewell."

Tedworth Vay hung up the telephone with a sense of despair unusual for him. The slaughter of three scientists, merely to cover up the flight of a poor, tortured girl, did indeed point to stakes as high as the space program. Clues dropped by his sources in Washington now acquired new significance, and he sat for several minutes with his fingertips pressed lightly together, pondering. Then he became aware that he was no longer alone in the library.

"Well, Rhoda?"

The girl stood in the doorway, a finger to her lips. "Domino and Dominique are excited about something, and I think I know what it is." She lowered her voice to a whisper. "The house is being watched."

He glanced toward the curtained window and started to rise, but she checked him.

"You can't see them from here, only from the bedroom windows upstairs. Domino and Dominique sleep with their paws covering their heads, as if they're missing something. Anyway, they were curled up on my bed, and I was reading in the chair, when suddenly they both awoke at the same instant and ran to the window. I peeked out, too, and saw three men across the street looking up at the house."

"They may just be tourists," he said. "Tomorrow is a T-day, and the agency is sending three full busloads for each lecture."

"No, Professor, these men look more like gangsters, and I think Domino and Dominique know them from somewhere."

"Let's have a look," he said, following her from the room.

The second floor of the mansion mingled elegance with nestlike comfort in a manner sniffed at by art snobs. Plush carpeting, colorful tapestries, satin wall coverings, furniture of an antique richness—gifts from admirers all over the world—enameled vases blossoming with fresh-cut primroses and peonies; opulent nudes and flowery still lifes hung in gilded frames from every wall; the statuary was extravagantly rococo. Tourists were often more impressed by the luxuries of the upper stories than by the mysteries in the basement.

Rhoda's bedroom might have graced the indulgences of a Cora Pearl, or some other voluptuous grand horizontale of the Second Empire. Mirrors were everywhere, and the bed so piled with feather mattresses that a sleeper could sink from view into its fluffs of downiness; its canopy of rose-red silk was supported by four posters of shimmering brass.

"It's their tails." Rhoda pointed to twitches at the bottom of the drawn curtains. "They're standing on their hind legs, looking out the window. It's hard to tell whether they're angry or just very excited."

Tedworth Vay crossed the room, opened the curtains an inch at one side, and peered down. A long black automobile was parked across the street; two men in dark business suits stood beside it, listening to instructions from a third man, a grisly hulk with a shaven head. All the while their eyes wandered furtively over the house, as if they were casing it for a robbery.

"I'm afraid we must waken Miss Malmrose," he said. "I can guess who those three are, but we must be certain, and we must know right away."

"I'll get her," cried Rhoda, and the fringes of her buckskin dress swirled about her as she ran out the door.

It was a dull and puffy-eyed Verna Malmrose who stumbled into the room minutes later, dressed incongruously in a man's silk bathrobe and a Dodgers baseball cap.

"What's the trouble, Professor?" She stifled a yawn, and felt unconsciously beneath her cap for stubble.

"Take a look." He held the curtain aside a crack. "See anybody you know?"

Her startled reaction gave him his answer. Some of the things she angrily muttered were also revelations about modern womanhood. Nor could he recall any women of his own day with so robust a physique. They had lifted teacups then, not barbells.

"Thank you, Miss Malmrose." he dropped the curtain. "I had to be certain of the identification before I could act."

"What are you going to do?"

"First I'm going to warn young Waverly not to return here this afternoon. Then I'll make arrangements for your safety."

"Make them good, Professor," she said. "The goon with the shaved head out there is cunning and sadistic, and doesn't smell very good either. He actually laughed, while he was kicking and punching and slapping me around, before he handed me over to be turned into a vegetable."

"He's not your gravest peril, Miss Malmrose. He can't know you're here, or even in Royal Beach, or he would have done more than merely stake out the house. The police are after you, too." And he related the brutal murders at the hospital from which she had escaped. "Above all," he added, "don't try to contact your parents. I've learned that their house is being watched, so we may be sure their telephone is also being tapped, and their mail intercepted."

She was stunned. "But I never hurt anybody. I couldn't have. I was so weak and dopey I could barely crawl out a window, much less attack three grown men. Who'd believe such a thing?"

"The millions who watch the evening news, and every police department in the country. Of course you're not a murderess. I know that, Miss Malmrose. The three scientists were killed so the blame could be fixed on you, and anything you might reveal about the operations of Benton Ingles thus discredited beforehand. Your enemies are ruthless and unprincipled men, so the sooner we got you to a place of safety the better."

"Why can't I just stay here?"

"Tourists. Monday, Wednesday, and Friday are T-days here, when I lecture in the Museum of the Unexplained and conduct tours of the house. Your enemies will not miss so golden an opportunity to reconnoiter, and it would be too risky to try and hide you. Though I believe we can rely upon the sagacity of Domino and Dominique to keep themselves out of sight. Besides, I still wish to test the precise range of that sagacity.

Domino and Dominique emerged from behind the curtain at that moment, and looked up at Verna like a pair of examining physicians.

Tedworth Vay replaced them at the window. The long black automobile was gone, and the two men in dark business suits now leaned against a lamppost, smoking cigarettes as though they expected a long vigil. That meant it had been the goon with the shaven head who had also been recognized by the two cats.

But it did not take a physician's eyes to see that

Verna needed more rest, and he led her, blinking sleepily, back to her bedroom. Leaving Rhoda to tuck her in, he descended once more to the library, where he found Chesterville leafing through a calf-bound volume of etchings.

Thousands of other volumes, the classics of many diverse fields, some rare, others plucked from used-book stalls, lined the shelves. But regardless of cost or binding, all had the one invariable characteristic of readability, and all had over the years been fondly read and reread.

Chesterville, who rose upon his master's entrance, was himself a great reader, though mostly of literary curiosities and the biographies of eccentric people. Of old prints and etchings he had expert knowledge, and had once made a handsome living from the sale of signature prints by such modern masters as Dali, Miro, Picasso, and Buffet. The prints were of the finest quality, and in demand among collectors all over the art world. Even the curator of a famous New York museum admired their craftsmanship, with the sole reservation that they were certainly forgeries.

During his consequent sojourn at a public-supported institution in upstate New York, Chesterville had no less than three years and no more than five to reconsider the error of his ways. His conclusion was that he had missed his true calling. For whereas a supercilious manner and an innate cynicism toward the pretensions of mankind—concealing his sneers for the gullibility of the very marks he was duping had never come easy to him—limited his success in the field of sharp practice, these very qualities made him a natural butler.

He had selected the name "Chesterville," from among the many aliases he had juggled during his career in international sales and service, as the most distinguished possible for his new calling.

That he was a thorough scoundrel actually enhanced his value to Tedworth Vay, whose own calling often brought him into situations where he needed more from his butler than mere good service and reliability. Chesterville was both street smart and resourceful, with good judgment as to how far he could carry his devices without earning himself another stretch at Statesville. His master was the one man on Earth he regarded with unqualified respect, even awe, and never questioned the expediency of his least commission.

"Cat food, cat litter, a litter box, and a selection of doll's hats, two of each kind." He jotted down the strange shopping list without batting an eye. "Very good, sir."

"Have the articles delivered, so you won't be encumbered walking back from the shopping center."

"I presume this has something to do with the two men watching the house? Yes, I thought as much. Shall I lose whichever of them tails me?"

"Pretend you don't know you're being tailed. This is by way of a test run. I want to know exactly how good they are, so we can determine the degree of evasiveness needed to shake them off whenever necessary. Also, I want to know who they are."

"Very good, sir. I'll fax telephotos of them to the FBI. You should have positive identifications within the hour. Anything else?"

"One thing. It's possible they may strike up a conversation, and try to inveigle you into betraying the whereabouts of Miss Malmrose."

"As to that, sir, I should say their chances of winning the state lottery would be infinitely greater. That this concerns Miss Malmrose is not surprising. The massacre in Ingles City has for the nonce preempted the space-program fiasco from the news broadcasts. As you know, Loo keeps four television sets, tuned to four different channels, operating continually from four sides of the kitchen. The ceaseless noise and commotion may remind him of the village marketplace in his homeland. Be that as it may, he is fascinated by the luridness of the crime and speaks of Miss Malmrose in glowing terms."

"He won't speak about her outside the house. We can be sure of that. But you don't seem to think she was involved in the crime?"

"No, sir. My judgment of her is that she is a redoubtable young woman, with intelligence and an independent spirit not easily intimidated. A type which is alas becoming all too common in America these days." He narrowed his eyebrows in disapproval. "But as to any complicity in the Ingles City massacre, I find that hard to believe. Courageous self-defense, yes. Wanton brutality, never."

"I concur, except in your opinion of modern women. Take your telephotos and fax them to the FBI, before you leave for market. Meanwhile I must entice Loo away from his television sets long enough to prepare his most sumptuous repast. Lola Londi is coming to tea."

Chesterville looked quizzically at him for a moment; then his face brightened and he nodded his appreciation, a shrewd twinkle in his eye.

"Very good, sir. Very good indeed."

Verna Malmrose examined her full-breasted nakedness in the bathroom mirror. She was refreshed by the soundest sleep she had enjoyed for weeks, and invigorated by a hot bath in a Victorian bathtub shimmering with Oriental porcelain and gold. Yet her reflection did not please her. Sedentary confinement had left undeniable hints of softness around her middle, which threatened to droop completely into flab. Perhaps Tim Waverly could get her an aerobics video.

Though one physical development was encouraging. The sandpaper roughness of her scalp, the first stubbly regrowth of her beautiful hair, proved how irrational had been her fears of permanent baldness.

She smiled as she slipped into her bra and panties, recalling poor Tim's embarrassment over buying them for her. But it evidently had not dawned on anybody in this bachelor establishment that she might need new clothes, so she had no choice other than to slip back into the flowered shirt, sandals, and beach shorts he had bought her at the same convenience store. Donning her blue baseball cap, she descended the ornate marble staircase.

She could not remember climbing these stairs; much about her arrival here was now dreamy and vague, and as she descended she looked around with growing wonder and curiosity.

She could almost hear the modern art critics gnashing their teeth over the representational beauty of the paintings and statuary; no doubt these same pundits would also have reviled the lush coloring and exquisite craftsmanship of the decor, perhaps decried the very humanity of its conception. Yet it seemed to her the loveliest and most congenial house she had ever been in. Its lusciousness was like a bouquet of camellias, and, indeed, the air was sweet with the fragrance of garden flowers.

She heard voices as she crossed the foyer, which she remembered as in a dream having crossed once before; one of the voices spoke with an Italian accent. Through a curtain of coral beads she could discern the outlines of an old-fashioned tea party, in the antique setting of the grand salon, and looked on with a growing sense of unreality. It was like a scene from an old B movie: quaint people gathered about the fireplace of a country mansion, waiting for the great detective to reveal the identity of the murderer.

The quaintest of them all was a woman of indeterminable age, dressed flamboyantly in no identifiable style, who sat regally in the middle of the overstuffed sofa, with her back to the window. The repast laid out before her might have tempted the palate of a queen, but for some reason she seemed put out.

"Why do these creatures stare at me so? It's as if they were trying to hex me with the Evil Eye. How can one be expected to digest properly in the face of such impudence? Look at them!" The trilled R's of her Italian accent rendered her tones grandiloquent. "Whatever can they mean by it?"

Moving nearer the beaded curtain, Verna could now see Domino and Dominique seated side by side on the plush carpet, gazing up at the woman with unblinking curiosity, like two scientists examining a new species.

"There's an old adage, Lola," said Tedworth Vay, seated in the overstuffed chair across from her. " 'A cat may look at a king.' The adage, I presume, refers to royalty in general, so we can also say that a cat may look at a queen."

There was a raspy chuckle from a corner of the grand salon still blocked from Verna's line of sight, which the woman on the sofa pointedly ignored.

"You always understand these things, Professor," she said. "That is why I never hesitate to bring you my insights and opinions. Yes, I suppose these lowly creatures are more sensitive to true refinement than are certain incorrigible ruffians I could name." She glanced pointedly toward the blind corner of the room.

Verna did not know of any mannerly way of making her presence known through a beaded curtain—she could hardly knock—so she just parted the strings and entered.

She was not noticed at first, and now saw that the man seated in the blind corner was dressed as a chauffeur. He was only of middle height, but barrel chested, with powerful arms and shoulders; his hair was fringed like the tonsure of a medieval friar, and his eyebrows disfigured by scar tissue. A retired prizefighter? He certainly looked able to take care of himself, and his florid complexion and potbelly suggested that he took very good care of himself indeed.

But it was only when she looked more closely at the woman seated regally on the sofa that her growing sense of unreality struck her with full force. She knew her from somewhere, yet was sure they had never met before. Wearing an elaborate black wig and a mask of cosmetics, and seated strategically with her back to the light, it was impossible to guess her true age. If Professor Vay reminded her of the Sorcerer in a tarot deck, there was something about this outlandish old woman that reminded her of a sorceress. Then all at once she knew what it was.

"My goodness, it's Lola Londi," she blurted out, attracting all eyes. "I saw you in *Sidonia the Sorceress* for the third time, just last month. You were wonderful." Then she blushed, and for an instant was tempted to dive back through the beaded curtain.

"Ah, here she is now." Tedworth Vay rose courteously from his chair, and beckoned her forward. "Lola, this is the unfortunate young woman I told you about, Miss Verna Malmrose. It seems she already knows you, at least as a fan."

"I'm the Facilitator of my school's film society, Miss Londi. I can't tell you how thrilled I am to meet you." Verna knew she was gushing, but it really was a strange sensation to meet someone out of history, as if she had just curtsied to Cleopatra or shaken hands with Joan of Arc. "There wasn't an empty seat in the house for our latest screening of *Sidonia the Sorceress,* and we plan to screen it again next quarter."

She did not add that the film was regarded by most college students today as a comedy, all the funnier because the humor was unintentional, or that a recent showing of *A Woman Scorned,* a stagy old melodrama, had had the more irreverent students rolling in the aisles.

"I wish I had a pen, so I could get your autograph."

"Time enough for that, child," said the old woman, obviously gratified. "Come sit here by me. Professor Vay informs me that you are in grave peril, so I've consented to take you under my protection. You're to live with me until all danger has passed."

Though she trilled her Rs and flicked her eyes melodramatically into the distance, it was quickly evident to Verna that she could neither see nor hear very well—spectacles or a hearing aid would have marred her glamour—and that she was probably closer to ninety than eighty. Her brief vogue in Hollywood, in the last golden years of the Silent Era, had ended with the coming of the talkies; and though her dark, voluptuous beauty had faded and gone, she still held herself erect, a queen among women, with the regal bearing for which she had once been so renowned.

"These events have not taken me entirely by surprise," she continued. "Professor Vay will bear witness how often I've declared my forebodings over the Lost Continent of Mu."

"Very often, Lola," he said dryly.

"Again and again I have repeated the warnings of the Sleeping Prophet. If this matter proves to be another evidence of the evil ambitions of the War Priests of Atlantis, then the Battle of Doom may have already begun. Though you, Professor, remain cautious."

"I'm still investigating, Lola." He remained tactful. "So before you take Miss Malmrose under your wing, I must ask her a few more questions. First of all—"

"No. First of all, the poor child must eat. See how she's looking at the food. Graziella, why are you just standing there?"

Her maid was a buxom peasant girl, who for some reason wore a conspicuous red wig. She poured Verna a steaming cup of coffee, and heaped her plate with the flakiest buttered croissants she had ever seen. Tasty little sausages lay smoking hot in a chafing dish, among a delicious array of cakes, tarts, pastries, scones, and other savories, and she forgot all about the softness around her middle, and tucked in with a will. One sip of the coffee told her she had entered another world.

"An Arabian mocha," said Tedworth Vay, in answer to her nod of appreciation. "By all means enjoy your breakfast, Miss Malmrose. But we mustn't forget that our time is short, and your danger imminent."

"Yes, and the impudent wretches have threatened even me." Lola Londi assumed an air of theatrical outrage. "Shortly after you telephoned, Professor, and informed me that your house was being watched, Graziella reported a spy outside my own house. I sent Maximo out to thrash him."

Verna caught the eye of the chauffeur, who balled his fist and winked. He was a large and powerful man, but she knew it wouldn't take her many more breakfasts like this one to match his girth. The sausages especially, crisped in a sweet-and-sour sauce that was literally mouth watering, were irresistible. She wanted to offer one to Domino and Dominique, who continued to gaze curiously at Lola Londi.

"I also sent Chesterville out, but only to gain information," said Tedworth Vay. "With his usual subtlety, he learned that Benton Ingles dispatched his myrmidons here to Royal Beach only because Tim Waverly— the young man about whom I spoke, Lola—departed the UCIC campus the same night Miss Malmrose escaped."

"Thanks to Domino and Dominique," added Verna. She held out a sausage to them, but they were not interested.

She did notice, however, a coquettish glance toward Maximo by Graziella when the name Chesterville was mentioned, but this time he balled his fist without winking.

"They've been well fed, Miss Malmrose," said Tedworth Vay. "I would have put them under Lola's protection also, except that I want to observe their behavior. Besides, there's Lakme."

"Lakme?"

"My Siamese cat," explained Lola. "Perhaps not the best natured of the breed I've ever owned, but my darling nonetheless. Though I can't understand yet, Professor, why my house was being watched. I don't know this young Waverly at all, and have never until this moment met Miss Malmrose here."

"Remember, Lola, who's behind the spying," he said.

She reflected a moment, then nodded shrewdly. "I

see what you mean. Yes, I suppose it's natural for Benton Ingles to suspect his wife of using my house for trysts with lovers. She doesn't, but I'm not at liberty to divulge what other arrangements she's made."

"Exactly what arrangements have you made for me, Professor?" Verna at last pushed her plate away. "Those two men are still outside. How can I possibly leave the house with Miss Londi without them spotting me?"

"Oh, they'll spot you all right," he said. "The trick is they'll think you're someone else. They saw a maid with red hair enter the house with Lola Londi—whom they will surely know visits me regularly, my most welcome and honored guest—and they'll see a maid with red hair leave the house with her."

"I like it," said Verna, glancing speculatively at Graziella. "Especially the part about wearing a wig."

"Poor child," said Lola. "I know how you must suffer from the loss of your hair."

Verna suspected that she knew all too well—and also about the loss of teeth, eyesight, hearing, and digestion. But the Lost Continent of Mu? War Priests of Atlantis? She hoped the old woman hadn't lost her grip, too.

"It's growing back, Miss Londi." She felt under her baseball cap for the reassuring stubble. "Some women these days wear crew cuts, so in a couple of weeks I shouldn't look too weird."

"Crew cuts yet." The old woman melodramatically lifted her eyes, with a sigh of despair. "But you mustn't call me Miss Londi, my dear. It has ever been Lola to my fans. Wherever I went, night or day, everywhere in the world, they would gather in their thousands and shout, 'Lola! Lola! Lola!' A woman was still admired then for beauty and elegance."

"You're still admired, Lola, and always will be," said Tedworth Vay. "But speaking of night or day, we had better not delay your departure with Miss

Malmrose much longer. The men outside may become suspicious if you leave after dark."

"Graziella, why are you just standing there?" Lola turned upon her buxom maid. "Get that spare uniform you brought, and help Miss Malmrose dress. The morning room should be unoccupied."

When Verna returned, not many minutes later, she was costumed like a parlor maid with flaming red hair. She carried her own clothes, including her Dodgers baseball cap, in the package that had contained the spare uniform, which the two men across the street had seen Graziella carry into the house."

"Excellent," said Tedworth Vay, and tugged at the velvet bell pull. "You'll be safe and comfortable with Lola, Miss Malmrose. Meanwhile I have some loose ends to draw together, before we make our next move. Ah, Chesterville."

But the butler had not entered the room alone. Nor was he the first to speak.

"Hello, Lola. Hi, Max. Hi, Graziella." Fringes of buckskin flounced about Rhoda as she skipped into the room. "So here you are." She looked down at Domino and Dominique. "They watched that videotape about chess you gave me, Professor, but then disappeared. Are we going to play a game tonight?"

"We're all going to play chess tonight." He, too, looked down at Domino and Dominique. "And if these two are as good as young Waverly claims, it will be a game to remember. But run along for now, dear, and take your mysterious little friends with you." He turned to his butler. "Chesterville, Graziella is staying the night. Please see that she's made comfortable."

"I shall do my utmost, sir. This way, if you please."

Verna did not miss the byplay that accompanied their departure. While Chesterville, an expression of indefinable slyness on his face, very pointedly did not look in the direction of the chauffeur, Graziella made a point of doing just that, tauntingly, almost provokingly. Whatever the rivalry here, it was a sullen and glowering Maximo who held open the rear door of the antique Packard for her and her "mistress," minutes later.

She had seen parlor maids played so often in movies that she had no trouble assuming the role. Neither of the two men in business suits, smoking cigarettes beneath the lamppost on the opposite side of Lengendary Lane, heeded her as the glistening black limousine swung past them.

Tedworth Vay, reentering his mansion from the carport, was also satisfied with the performance. Graziella, dressed in street clothes, could mingle with the T-day crowds here tomorrow—among which, no doubt, would be one or both of the men now watching the house—and thus return inconspicuously to her mistress. In fact, she was inconspicuous for the rest of the night. Nor was Chesterville to be found at any of his usual occupations.

His own occupations included a game of chess with his young ward. Tonight, though, he was less interested in observing her progress at the game than he was in the reactions of its spectators.

The library was an eminently cozy room; its easy chairs were the easiest in all of Royal Beach; a portrait of William Butler Yeats, the great poet and student of the occult, hung over the marble fireplace, where an evening fire crackled pleasantly. An ormolu lamp cast its mellow glow upon the chessboard which was set up on the teakwood coffee table between two easy chairs.

A cup of sweetened cocoa, a glass of rare port, and a classic chess manual sat ready to hand at one side of the board; at the other sat Domino and Dominique, watching the progress of the game with fixed attention. Simultaneous twitches of their tails, sometimes even of their paws, suggested a temptation to kibitz—especially whenever Rhoda moved a piece. She was a child prodigy, of gifted intelligence, but a child nonetheless, and only just learning the game. The result was inevitable.

"I should have castled sooner, Professor," she said,

finishing her cocoa. "Then I let myself get crowded to one side of the board. But I think I'm improving, don't you?"

"Your progress is remarkable, dear," he said. "Now I want to see how far our mysterious little friends here have progressed."

He opened the chess manual to a bookmarked page, and set up one of the most baffling of all classic problems on the board. It could be solved only by a single unusual move: King bishop to N-6. He noticed the intentness with which Domino and Dominique gazed down at the pieces.

"Now off to bed with you, dear," he said, picking up a volume of Restoration comedies from the library table, and following her and the two cats out the door, which he deliberately left open.

"Aren't you going to read in the library tonight, Professor?" asked Rhoda.

"No, tonight I'm going to read in the grand salon. Sleep well, dear. We shall see what we shall see, in the morning."

CHAPTER IX

Tim Waverly felt as if the walls were closing in. He had phoned his dormitory at UCIC, with a prepared excuse for his absence from classes, only to be pumped for information about his real intentions and whereabouts in a manner that suggested his roommate had been either bribed or coerced into playing the spy. He never doubted that all telephone calls there were being tapped.

Still more depressing was the suspicion that his calls were also being monitored at this end of the line. His mother reentered the television room at the same instant he did, from the direction of the dining room extension phone. He had long suspected her of eavesdropping on his personal calls; until he started college she had openly read his mail, out of "concern for his moral rectitude." He avoided her gaze, and the I-know-what-you're-up-to look that had always made him feel guilty as a child, even when he had done nothing wrong.

The couch and chairs were slipcovered with durable plastic, the tables surfaced with stain-proof glass; laundered throw rugs strategically protected the carpet from wear, and shoes were replaced at the front door, even by visitors, with house slippers. There was nowhere in the world Tim felt less comfortable than in his own home.

His father sat exactly in the middle of the plastic-covered sofa, directly in front of the television screen, shaking his head in disgust over the evening news.

"Just look at this mess the Administration had made out of our space program." There was a plastic bowl filled with salted peanuts on the coffee table before him, and he palmed a handful and funneled them into his mouth. "No wonder our taxes are going through the roof. The whole goldarned thing should have been turned over to private industry from the start. Haven't I always said that, Marge?"

"You're right, Fred." She lounged back in her plastic-covered chair and lit a menthol cigarette.

Both were stolidly middle-aged, with the cheesy fatness that comes from too much junk food and a lack of exercise. Their only real interests were watching television and fishing.

"Every time the Administration bungles, they raise our taxes," he continued to gripe. "Our scientists told 'em it wouldn't work, but they went and did it anyway. Now this thing. . . . What's it called, Marge?"

"A solar storm, Fred."

"That's right. Billions and billions of our tax dollars for all this here fancy hardware, and one solar storm and none of it works." He snatched up another handful of peanuts. "They should have listened to Benton Ingles in the first place. He said he'd set up the system, take all the risks himself, and run it at a profit, so it wouldn't cost us taxpayers a goldarned penny. Remember when he said that, Marge?"

She started to nod but then looked more closely at the television screen. "Speak of the devil, there he is now."

The network was owned by Benton Ingles, and he was interviewed with a deference usually reserved for heads of state. In fact, the questions and answers struck Tim less like an interview than a catechism. But it was an effective performance.

"World communications is a business, the same as any other," said Ingles, seated imposingly behind a giant mahogany desk. "It should be built by American know-how, and run according to American business principles. The failure of the United Nations Commstat shows what happens when our leaders let a gang of Third World bureaucrats lead us by the nose."

"How would you tackle the problem, Mr. Ingles?" asked the interviewer, as though reading from a cue card.

"I would not only replace the faulty system we've got now with a better model, without further squandering the taxpayers' money, but I'd assume all maintenance costs myself. The Administration is telling us they can repair the defective commstat for five billion dollars. Check the records. That's more than it cost new, so we can be sure the American people are not being told everything."

"Have you heard the accusations of corruption against the United Nations, Mr. Ingles?"

"Yes, and I've also heard the accusations our own Administration is trying to cover up, to dupe the American taxpayers with a lot of phony assurances that the network of auxiliary satellites up there is capable of assuming the full load, while the main commstat is being repaired. I'm not a scientist myself, never pretended to be. All I can go by is what my engineers tell me, and I have the best in the world."

"What do your engineers say about this matter, Mr. Ingles?"

"That the UN Commstat is beyond repair, and that if we overload the network of auxiliary satellites, it will fail, too. In short, that the Administration is throwing good money after bad."

"Thank you, Mr. Ingles. As always, you've been most informative." The interviewer looked like he wanted to genuflect. "We'll be back after these messages."

"Haven't I said the same thing, Marge?" said Mr. Waverly.

The commercial now on the television screen displayed a laser-print copier manufactured by a subsidiary of B.I.T.E.

"You're right, Fred." His wife lit a fresh menthol cigarette from the stub of the old one. "And let's not forget that the good money the Administration intends to throw after the bad will be our tax dollars."

The next segment of the news was so lurid that it seemed like the crime of the century. Every gory detail of the murders at the UCIC Med Center was lingered over with morbid sensationalism. Photographs of Verna Malmrose, including one with her head shaved, were flashed across the screen while an overvoice referred to her as "Jacqueline the Ripper." A national manhunt was already under way.

"Now isn't that terrible," exclaimed Mrs. Waverly. "A girl brought up in a good home, with every advantage, and she does something like this. What's become of our country?"

"It's these feminists who are behind it." Her husband finished off the last of the salted peanuts. "Haven't I always said they're wrecking the country, Marge?"

"You're right, Fred."

Tim had been forewarned about these grisly events. He and Tedworth Vay had a system of precautions, in case of maternal eavesdropping. The signal was a lone ring on the telephone, and he would go to the nearest public phone booth, and call back. He'd learned today that not only had poor Verna been framed for murder, but that his own house was being watched, and that he must not return to Legendary Lane until further notice.

The cynical ruthlessness of Verna's persecutors, butchering three of their own merely to silence her, made him shudder to think what would happen if they ever recaptured her. Nor could he forget how lovely she'd looked, sleeping in the moonlight.

Pack-rat accumulations of books, magazines, and yellowed newspapers constricted some rooms of the old mansion into mere aisles. But here in the drawing room, appointed like the grand reception chamber of an empress, reigned only the splendors of a bygone era. The television set seemed an anachronism.

Verna was horrified by the evening news. Lola Londi, now wearing spectacles and hearing aids in both ears, sat beside her on the Empire divan, while Maximo lounged on a satin-upholstered armchair nearby. All watched the screen with rapt attention.

The commercial that interrupted the lurid coverage of the murders on the UCIC campus portrayed an oil company owned by Benton Ingles devoting its technology to improving the quality of the environment. Verna sneered. She had seen firsthand the devastation wrought by that particular oil company in northern Mexico. Then she realized that she was being observed.

"That's right, my dear," said Lola Londi. "Sneer at them. Frankly, my regard for American women has never been high. Always trying to be nice is a sign of thin blood. But you have shown me that one should not be prejudiced."

"But I'm innocent," Verna protested, wondering if the old woman had already forgotten everything Tedworth Vay had told her.

"Of course you are, my dear. And you're wise never to change your story, even among friends. It is too easy to become confused when policemen grill you and shine lights in your face. Say too much or change your story, and they trap you."

Maximo nodded his agreement. "Omerta rules."

"Not that such vulgar matters have ever concerned me," she continued, her bearing now wonderfully regal. "My father was Prince Giuseppe di Cattanetta, and for seven generations not one member of his family did a day's work. Would you like to see my family album?"

Verna naturally wanted to see it very much. Half the police in the country were now out looking for her, and she had nowhere else to go. Still, she was innocent. She waited while the old woman rose, paused to let her blood pressure adjust, and strode from the room. Then she leaned over, and spoke in a low voice:

"Max, I never killed those men. Professor Vay told her that, and I thought she understood."

He shrugged. "Who can say what she understands anymore? Everything to her is like an old movie or a scene from grand opera. If harboring a murderess brings drama into her life, then she's harboring a murderess. The only thing she's completely sane about is money, and about that she's very sane indeed."

"Then her father really wasn't a prince?"

"In Sicily, every man is a prince." He chuckled slyly. "If he isn't a count or a duke. You see, hundreds of years ago the King of Spain auctioned off titles of nobility, in order to raise money for his wars. The trouble was that once somebody became a prince, or a count or a duke, it no longer befitted his dignity to work. So he didn't. Neither did any of his sons, for centuries."

"Was her mother a noblewoman, too?"

He now laughed delightedly. "Her mother wore her first pair of shoes to her own wedding. She was a shepherdess the prince paid calls on whenever he was out hunting. But her brother was a mafioso, and when she became pregnant he put a shotgun under the prince's nose. Don't mention sheep in this house, if you can help it."

"Here we are, my dear." Lola reappeared, carrying an antique leather album with gold hinges. "No, Maximo, remain seated. You know I never allow anyone to touch this book. The memories are too precious." She reseated herself on the Empire divan.

Verna was startled when a Siamese cat leapt up beside her. Whether by accident or out of meanness, it clawed her leg in passing. She noticed Maximo twist his hands in opposite directions, throttling the animal in dumb show.

"Behave yourself, Lakme," said Lola, opening the

album across her legs. "Here is the founder of our dynasty, the first Prince of Cattanetta."

"A striking figure of a man," Verna said tactfully.

The photograph was an old painting, and though the pose was flattering, the background lavish, and the portraiture romantic, here was a bandit if ever she had seen one. His first three descendants reminded her of cardsharps, while the last two, including Lola's father, looked as stiffly aristocratic as Gilbert and Sullivan caricatures. Many of the women in the photographs were strikingly beautiful.

"And here is Aunt Santuzza, our family saint," Lola said with evident pride. The photograph was of a dumpy little woman, with her pudgy hands folded in prayer, and her eyes turned so piously heavenward that only the whites were visible. "She was tempted by the Devil, but spurned all the riches and delights he promised her in his letters."

"She received letters from the Devil?" Verna glanced at Maximo, whose face looked respectfully solemn, though she thought she detected a twinkle in his eye. "What kind of letters?"

"Their contents are mysterious to this day. I was only a child when a papal nuncio came and sealed them forever. Three times they were soaked in holy water, yet pious noses can still detect their smell of brimstone. Pilgrims visit the convent from all over Sicily to sniff them."

"But couldn't your aunt simply have refused delivery of the letters?" asked Verna.

"It was a test of faith, child. She regarded it as her sacred duty, not just to accept delivery of the letters, but to read each to its wicked end. You see, as the Devil multiplied his temptations, she multiplied her own sanctity in resisting them. Such was her piety, that on no Sunday was she known to show anything but the whites of her eyes."

"Was that because letters are never delivered on

Sunday?" asked Maximo, the twinkle in his eye now unmistakable.

"Santuzza was a saint." Lola lifted her own eyes heavenward. "Though the good fathers at the Vatican still quibble over her beatification. She would have accepted a letter from the Devil on any day of the week."

"But what if he didn't put enough stamps on it?" Maximo glanced slyly at Verna. "Would she have paid the postage due?"

The old woman frowned thoughtfully. "That's a difficult question, because if the blessed Santuzza had once paid the postage due, the Devil would have tried to cheat her on the stamps every time he mailed her a letter. Besides, she was a holy sister, vowed to poverty. It's a question only the holy fathers could answer."

"Yes, the holy fathers love questions like that. But right now, I think it's time we locked up for the night."

"What? Oh, yes, of course. Also, please see that Lakme has food and water. Graziella won't return until tomorrow afternoon, and someone must take care of my darling."

"It would be my pleasure to take care of your darling, bella signorina." He looked daggers at the cat. "Shall I light the urn now?"

"By all means. Miss Malmrose has had a trying day. A nice cup of tea would relax her."

"Your tea would relax a volcano," he muttered as he rose and lighted an antique samovar, setting out a tea service for two. "I remain at your call, bella signorina." He picked up the cat as if he wanted to throw it out the window but only bowed with surprising courtliness and carried it gingerly from the room.

"An incorrigible ruffian." Lola raised her eyebrows in long-suffering resignation. "But what about you, my dear? Malmrose? It can't be Sicilian, unless you've Americanized it. My own name was too long for theater marquees, so I shortened it when I came to Hollywood. I am the youngest daughter of Giuseppe

Leoncastellammare, Prince of Cattanetta." She looked expectantly at Verna.

"Oh, that's really great. I mean, I'm not surprised," she stammered. "That is, you always look, well, so regal in all your movies."

"It was my forte. But you seem nervous, my dear, and no wonder. I know all about your days of torment and cruelty, and understand your feelings. For I, too, have suffered at the hands of sadistic villains. I still shudder with horror whenever I recall how the evil Duke of Toledo sujected me to the tortures of the Spanish Inquisition. Lying helpless at the brink of a pit, a blade of razor sharpness pendulating closer and closer. I escaped his clutches only by swimming a moat filled with crocodiles."

Verna blinked at her in wonder. Did the old woman have senile lapses in which she confused her old movies with real events? *The Castle of Toledo* was a favorite with university film societies, and the scene with the rubber crocodiles, the operations of whose spring jaws tended to be eccentric, invariably brought down the house.

"But what about yourself, my dear?" The old woman seemed to emerge once more into reality. "Have you a lover?"

"Well, I dated, of course." Verna was disconcerted by so direct a question. "But what with my schoolwork, my film society responsibilities, my fitness program, and tending the counter at my family's health food store, I really don't have much time to get seriously involved with anybody."

"A pity, for youth should be the time of love." She sighed melodramatically. "In the old country we understand these matters better than you do here in America. Ah, the passion of my first lover. Three times he put his knife to my throat, but I only laughed at him in disdain. Such was his desire for me that in his fury he would tear the bark from trees with his teeth. Have you ever seen the Springbreath Deodorant Soap commercial? Or the Harzweiser Beer commercial?"

"Uh, yes, almost every night," said Verna, startled by so abrupt a change of subject. Though she was beginning to distinguish the old woman's lucid intervals from her cobwebs of fantasy. "They were both shot aboard some luxurious old yacht."

"It's mine." The old woman beamed triumphantly. "The *Sidonia*. It was built especially for me by a New York stockbroker, in 1928. The next year he jumped out of a window, poor man. Movie leases and private charters have always made it profitable, but never more so than today. Though I feel sorry for those beautiful young people I see cavorting aboard it on television. How empty their lives must be when they can find nothing better to sing and dance about than deodorant soap and beer." Her eyes seemed to gaze fondly across the years. "In those wonderful, mad, glorious days when I was a star, our parties lasted for weeks, as we sailed the world. We drank champagne, and nobody cared how they smelled. Is the water boiling yet, my dear?"

"The water? Oh, in the samovar. Yes, I believe it is. Shall I pour the tea?"

Steeped under the explicit instructions of the old woman, it was like no tea Verna had ever tasted. She felt herself relaxing after a single cup.

"It's very good. What kind is it?"

"My own special blend. The leaves are from a South American bush, fermented in the sun."

"Coca?" Verna understood now why she was beginning to feel strangely euphoric. "It will definitely make me less nervous, if nothing else."

"Are you sleepy, my dear?"

"No, I slept all day, so I'll probably be up half the night."

"Do you play gin rummy?" the old woman eyed her avidly.

"As a matter of fact, I'm considered a good gin

rummy player. Most Greenworld conventions end after supper in a gin rummy game, and an old geology professor taught me how to win. I usually do, by the way."

The old woman smiled complacently, and the next thing Verna knew she was seated across from her at a card table of inlaid tortoiseshell and ivory, with a fresh cup of tea, watching her riffle the cards with Las Vegas dexterity.

"What shall we play for, my dear?" she asked.

"I'm afraid all I can play for now is an IOU," said Verna. "Those swine who cut off my beautiful hair stole everything I had." She ran her fingertips gingerly over the stubble of her shaven head.

"Then I shall put up the stake myself."

Placing a shiny coin in an ashtray of carved jade, she fanned the deck across the table for the opening draw.

Verna assumed that the coin was only a penny, a token wager, but on closer inspection it turned out to be a twenty dollar gold piece. As she sorted her cards, she had the odd feeling of stepping out of the mainstream of time into some lost eddy. Or was it just the dreamy effects of the tea? Whatever the case, it was apparent that she had better keep her wits about her. Lola Londi was a gin rummy shark.

As the game progressed, Verna noticed that whenever the old woman felt herself beginning to dither, she would gaze at the gold in the jade ashtray, and each time her wits would be avariciously whetted. But if her card play thus remained focused, her conversation tended more and more to ramble.

"Professor Vay tells me your brother died for science," she said, snapping up a nine of hearts from the pile.

"My twin brother Vernon, yes. His body was washed ashore on the island of Nukuhiva, in the Marquesas. I flew there to supervise the funeral and take possession of his belongings."

She studied her cards, finding it harder and harder to

concentrate. Should I knock on eight or play for a better hand? she wondered. Her last knock had been undercut.

"Ah, the South Seas." The old woman sighed, a faraway look glazing her eyes. "How romantic it was, dancing by the firelight, swimming the midnight lagoon with my beloved, beneath the tropical moon. He was an American sailor, who bravely fought a giant squid to save my life. I shall never forget the creature's writhing tentacles."

Neither will the school film society, thought Verna. The giant squid in *A Princess in Paradise* had raised more howls than even the rubber crocodiles in *The Castle of Toledo,* though the young Lola Londi was superb as the tragic Princess Luanda.

"Knock on three." The old woman discarded and laid out her hand.

To her chagrin, Verna could not lay off a single card. She toted up the count, and drew yet another line under her opponent's score. It was her deal, and she gathered up the cards and shuffled.

"So much that is romantic and beautiful has passed from life," continued the old woman. "A friend from the old country, the wife of the famous Benton Ingles, loathes the South Seas. All because her husband mines bird droppings there. Though it does seem a beastly thing to do in the tropics."

Verna dealt the new hand. She had known that the wife of Benton Ingles was an Italian beauty queen, though it came as a revelation that the woman was intimate with Lola Londi.

"I've had ugly experiences with Benton Ingles," she said dreamily, as she carelessly discarded the first card her hand touched. "He must be an awful man to live with."

"He is violently jealous and tyrannical, like all real husbands." The old woman pounced on the discard. "So Carla deceives him and squanders his money, like all real wives. Being a woman of spirit, she accepts his

attempts to conceal things from her as a challenge."
She pounced on another careless discard. "You don't
seem to be concentrating on the game, my dear. Pour
yourself another cup of tea. It will soothe your nerves."

Verna filled both their cups. "Doesn't your friend re-
sent being treated so badly by her husband? I would."

"Ah, but you Americans are a young people, and
still callow in the ways of marriage. Deceiving a jealous and tyrannical husband and discovering his secrets
are a wife's happiness. Gin." She laid down the best
hand of the night.

"Ouch!" Verna winced at the mittful of face cards
she had been caught with, and despairingly began to
add up the points.

She forced herself to concentrate, and the next game
went better. The old woman played her cards with un-
diminished skill, though she now tended to stare at the
twenty dollar gold piece for longer stretches of time,
and her conversation was becoming stranger and stranger.

"The Lost Continent of Mu was located in the South
Seas," Lola said, snapping up a ten of diamonds and
discarding a useless four of clubs. "Some say it was
torn from our planet by a passing comet and formed
the moon. Others believe it sank beneath the waves
and will one day rise again. The Sleeping Prophet says
that day will be soon, and that the jealousy of the War
Priests of Atlantis will not avail them. . . ."

Verna herself was now experiencing intervals when
she was less than lucid, although the old woman had
drunk two cups of tea to her one. Exactly when the
game finally broke up, or faded into dissolution, she
was uncertain, but she suspected it was not far from
dawn. The old woman bade her good night like Princess Luanda sending forth the doomed warriors of the
island to battle the forces of evil.

She seemed to float across the room. Glancing back
from the doorway, she was swept up into a vortex of
unreality such as she had never known. Lola Londi,

like a revenant from a world long passed into eternity, stood majestically amidst the velvet draperies, silk upholstery, polished mahogany furniture, painted screens, and ormolu lamps of a Victorian drawing room that could have been used as the set for one of her own movies. Her pose, expression, and gestures were reminiscent of the triumphal scene in *Sidonia the Sorceress,* a mood perhaps suggested to her by her triumph in the card game. Or did she wander the house fantasizing like this every night?

The winding staircase was like a scene from some period melodrama or horror movie, where a beautiful heroine in a long satin gown is preceded through the ghostly old mansion by servants bearing candelabra, or perhaps by a mad doctor or Count Dracula himself. She reached the second floor in a dream. Her bedroom was the second on the left—Maximo had seen that she memorized the way, as if dire consequences awaited her if she opened the wrong door—and she seemed to float toward it through an eerie twilight. Velvet tapestries alternated along the walls with paintings of Italian landscapes.

"Ow!" she cried, as a sharp pain bit the calf of her right leg.

Startled from her dreaminess, she whirled around in time to spot a Siamese cat slinking into the shadows. Normally she adored cats—her very life had been saved by two cats—but she could now understand why Maximo might want to throttle this particular brute.

Nursing her bitten leg, she hobbled down the corridor to her bedroom.

Cats were also on the mind of Tedworth Vay, the following morning. It was a T-day, and he was exquisitely barbered and appareled in an embroidered black smoking jacket and silk neck scarf fastened with a ruby pin. He smiled as he examined the chessboard. Sometime during the night the white king bishop had been moved to N-6, solving the classic problem.

Where Domino and Dominique had gone he did not know, but a whole new field of investigation now lay open before him. That is, after more pressing investigations had been completed. He picked up the telephone and touch-toned a long-distance number.

"Hello, Tedworth Vay speaking. Is the senator available? Yes, very important. Thank you, I'll wait."

He sat back in his overstuffed chair and pondered. The two mysterious cats had solved a chess problem with an unusual move, but he could make no move against Benton Ingles until the problem itself was defined. The fate of the *Greenworld Challenger* and the murderous persecution of Verna Malmrose could only mean that Ingles was up to something big, and probably illegal, somewhere in the South Pacific. But exactly what? And where?

The desire of Ingles to privatize the satellite communications network, under the suspices of B.I.T.E, was now being pushed by his entire Media empire and every political lobbyist he had in Washington. But what possible connection could there be between the space program and the South Pacific?

His eyes drifted back to the chessboard. If Domino and Dominique were really experiments in genetic engineering, what conceivable reason could Ingles have for breeding super-intelligent cats? Were there three problems to be solved here—or only one?

"Yes, I'm still waiting." A few moments later he was greeted by a voice familiar across the nation, and replied: "Good afternoon, Senator. I know you're busy, so I'll come straight to the point." And item by item he detailed the latest machinations of Benton Ingles, excepting only the persecution of Verna Malmrose.

There was a reflective pause before Senator Worthing answered. "I'm glad you brought this to my attention, Ted. I knew some of it, but not all. Ingles is trying by hook or by crook to discredit the Administration because of the failure of the UN Commstat. Our scientists have assured us that any flaws in its design will soon be rectified, and that its network of auxiliary satellites can meanwhile handle the full load. Assuming their assessment is correct, the program—and it's truly a noble endeavor, from which all mankind will benefit—shouldn't fall too far behind schedule."

"Assuming they are correct," added Tedworth Vay. "But my understanding of the deployed communications system, Senator, is that the UN Commstat was to have functioned something like a main generating plant, and the auxiliary satellites only like its substations? Won't throwing a full load on them bring the whole network dangerously near its maximum capacity?"

"That's essentially correct." The pause was longer this time, and when Senator Worthing resumed speaking his voice sounded tired. "I'll level with you, Ted. Ingles has the Administration out on a limb, and his wolves are gathering below. All I can do is pray our scientists are right. If the satellite network fails, after all the bad press he's given the failure of the UN Commstat, the whole thing could collapse around our ears."

"That explains his recent media blitz, but not what connection this could have with his interests in the South Pacific."

"I don't know that one myself, Ted. I'll check my sources, and get back to you if I find anything."

"I'd appreciate that, Senator. By the way, where does the *Greenworld Challenger* investigation stand now?"

"It doesn't stand anywhere at present. Ingles has had his stooges here close the books on it, after sweeping all its loose ends under the carpet. But thanks again for the information, Ted. I'll get back to you soon."

After hanging up, Tedworth Vay sat pondering for nearly an hour. The more he knew about the problem the less sure he was about his next move. Chesterville appeared precisely at noon.

"The first busload of tourists has just arrived, sir," he announced.

"Then we'd better take our battle stations. Where's Graziella?"

"In the kitchen, teaching Loo her family recipe for spaghetti sauce. He's making it in a wok. Shall I send her to you?"

"No, just be sure she understands when and how she's to leave the house. We're still being watched, and the spy Max thrashed at Lola's house may have been replaced. We don't want anyone to start wondering why she was here."

"Rely on the girl, sir."

"Yes, Lola considers her extraordinarily capable."

"She is certainly that, sir," Chesterville said dryly. "Anything more?"

"Just one thing. The agency has oversold both lectures today, so we may have tourists prying into every corner of the house. Please remind Rhoda to keep Domino and Dominique out of sight. Where are they now, by the way?"

"Playing Nintendo upstairs."

"Nintendo?"

"Yes, sir. Something called 'Space Invaders.' Young Rhoda is an adept at the game, though not a patch to the two cats. I observed them run up a score which I doubt even the manufacturers considered possible."

"Nothing surprises you, does it?"

"Working for you, sir, has long since inured me to surprise. I'll alert Loo about the large crowds descending upon us today, so he may prepare his refreshments accordingly."

Chesterville assumed the look of supercilious arrogance that American tourists expect of a butler in a Victorian mansion, and strode haughtily from the room.

Pondering for a few moments, Tedworth Vay at last rose and parted the brocaded velvet drapery an inch at one side. Two men in dark business suits leaned against a lamppost on the opposite side of the street, smoking cigarettes. He felt increasingly trapped in his own house, as if all the world were now closing in on Royal Beach.

CHAPTER X

Verna wondered, as she descended the circular staircase that afternoon, whether she would ever get her clock reset. For days she had been so stretched out from lack of sleep that she was like a zombie; now she felt dull and logy from too much sleep, and her eyes still burned from staring at the pips of gin-rummy cards.

No doubt Lola Londi had always been a late sleeper, perhaps, like Count Dracula, never seeing the sun. The cleaning women, who flitted like shadows among the dust-catching stacks of books, magazines, and Hollywood memorabilia that crowded the great mansion all seemed to be old hands at working in silence, so as not to disturb the mistress. Though the mop and bucket dropped carelessly in the foyer looked brand new.

"Good morning," Maximo greeted her as she entered the morning room. "I hope you slept well."

"Too well." She yawned. "Or maybe I just have a tea hangover."

He chuckled. "What you need is a good breakfast. Waffles and maple syrup? A buttered croissant? Ham and eggs? Pancakes? Rashers of bacon? An omelet? Whatever your heart desires."

"It desires only a bowl of cereal, thank you." She was hungry, but had not forgotten the hints of softness around her middle. Then she yawned again. "Also, a strong cup of coffee, please. By the way, one of your cleaning ladies dropped her gear in the foyer. Somebody might trip over it."

"That was Graziella." He shook his head in exasperation. "She slipped out of Professor Vay's house with the tourists, then bought a mop and bucket, so anybody who saw her come here would think she was just another cleaning lady, arriving late. Clever, but unnecessary. The jerk who was spying on the house isn't there anymore. I've checked."

"I heard you beat him up."

"Knockout in the first round." He winked, and threw out his barrel chest as he strode off to get her breakfast.

She felt gingerly under the polka-dot red bandanna she wore this morning, and was reassured that the stubble on her head was softer, a sure sign that her hair was growing back.

The room had an old-world charm that was also reassuring. The walls were a gallery of old photographs and publicity stills of Lola Londi in her days of stardom; the view was of a splendid garden, whose statues of naked Greek gods and goddesses might have graced the palace of a Renaissance prince. Her humble Cheerios were served in a vessel of engraved porcelain; the sugar bowl, creamer, and coffeepot were of antique silver.

As she finished her cereal and poured herself a second cup of coffee, she was startled to find Lakme gazing balefully up at her. She decided to try and make friends with the cat, who may only have resented her as an intruder in the house, and poured cream into the cereal bowl and set it on the floor.

But the cat only sniffed disdainfully at her peace offering, apparently spoiled by richer fare. Then, with a sneaky quickness, it bit her on the shin and darted from the room.

She replaced the bowl on the table, and hobbled up and down the carpet, nursing her leg. This was the second time she had been bitten; but fortunately her skin was not broken, only bruised, so there was no danger of rabies. She generally liked cats, just as she generally liked people, though in both cases there were exceptions. Lakme was one of them.

Resuming her seat, she stirred cream and sugar into her coffee, but as she lifted her cup she realized that there were now people outside. Nine very old men moved very slowly about the garden, arranging it for a party. From time to time they would stop and gaze into the distance, as if trying to remember why they were here.

"The Sons of Paradise," said Maximo, entering the room. "La Bella Signorina's last and most loyal fan club," he explained as he cleared the table. "They worshiped her when they were young, especially after seeing *A Princess in Paradise*. They're all widowers now, grandfathers and great-grandfathers, who out of loneliness started corresponding with each other after many years. Then they refounded their old fan club, the Sons of Paradise, and moved here to Royal Beach so they could serve the goddess of their youth."

"Oh, how sweet!" Verna felt sentimental tears well in her eyes. "The poor dears. I suppose all they have now is their memories."

Maximo shrugged. "As to that, who knows how much they remember about anything nowadays. What's wrong?" He noticed her nursing her leg.

"Lakme bit me again. I tried to make friends with her, but now I don't know what to do."

"I know what I'd like to do." He made a neck-wringing gesture with his hands. "La Bella Signorina has a pet cemetery out in the garden, and Lakme's plot is already marked out. We must be patient. But the guests will be arriving soon. Is there anything more I can do for you?"

"No, thank you. If there's going to be a garden party, I'd better stay out of sight in my room."

Maximo carried the breakfast tray out to the kitchen. When he returned, he found her peering curiously out the window.

"If you're looking for the pet cemetery, you can't

see if from here," he said, adding with a twinkle in his eye: "It's already very crowded. La Bella Signorina names all her cats after the heroines of grand opera, but there have been so many cats, over so many years, that she ran out of Italian names. Lakme is her first cat named after a French opera, which explains many things."

The new mop and bucket still lay carelessly in the foyer, and with a look of resignation he put them safely out of the way in the hall closet.

"Not that I'm prejudiced against the French," he continued, as they ascended the grand staircase. "I just know that the greatest soldier of France, Napoleon, was Italian. So was the greatest writer of France, Zola. I say no more."

"Where's Miss Londi now?" asked Verna, at the top of the stairs.

He jerked his thumb toward a nearby dressing room. "The assembly line."

As if in answer to his irreverence, the door burst open at that instant, and Lola Londi herself emerged half assembled. Her maid Graziella appeared in the doorway behind her.

"Maximo, I'm surprised at you. Graziella tells me there are spies outside. I won't have anyone peeking in my window, do you hear me?"

"No, no, bella signorina, calm yourself. Yesterday I caught the spy and thrashed him. I've checked, and checked again. Nobody is now watching the house."

"Oh, yes, I see him." Graziella stepped forward, with a taunting look. She was a buxom girl, with thick raven hair and dark eyes, and spoke with a charming Italian accent. "I get off the tourist bus and buy mop and bucket, just in case some smart guy is watching the house. At first I see nobody when I walk past. But there he is, hiding in the bushes right across the street, and he thinks I don't know he's there. But I do," she added with an impudent smirk.

"Excuse me, bella signorina," said Maximo through

his teeth. "I got some unfinished business to take care of."

Thrusting out his barrel chest, his powerful shoulders hunched belligerently forward, he descended the stairs like a heavyweight about to enter the ring. His scowl boded no good for spies.

"Please excuse me, too, Lola," said Verna, using the familiar address the old woman insisted upon. "Your guests will be here shortly, so I'll go to my room now. I have a good book to read."

"No, no, child, you are my guest, too. Wear your red wig and sunglasses, and nobody will recognize you. I have so many rich and powerful men among my admirers that it is only natural you should be nervous. We'll have a nice cup of tea before we go out into the garden. That will relax you. But hurry now. The sun is setting." Though barely half assembled, she strode back into her dressing room with the carriage of an empress.

Verna prudently looked up and down the corridor, especially where there were shadows or hiding places, before starting for her own room.

"Have you lose something, signorina?" asked Graziella.

"No, I just wanted to make sure that cat didn't sneak up on me again." She nursed her bitten leg.

Graziella's eyes narrowed and she made the same neck-wringing gesture Maximo had. Lakme was evidently no favorite in this household.

Maximo slipped out the rear door into the garden, where the Sons of Paradise, by fits and starts, through lapses of strength and memory, were steadfastly arraying the grounds for an evening gala. There was a double-winged gate of solid oak in the rear wall, in an archway broad enough to admit a truck; but he cut instead through the carriage house, and into the brick lane that separated unbroken rows of other garden walls. By circling the block, he was able to sneak up on the clump of bushes across the street from an unexpected direction.

He knew that Graziella, like her mistress, tended to dramatize; but there really was a man peeking out through the bushes, and he tiptoed up behind him intending only to scare him off with a few cuffs and backhanders. Then he noticed that his left ear was bandaged, exactly where he had clobbered the man spying here yesterday. That the wretch should now dare return was an affront to his honor, and he began to sputter in his anger like a toy steam engine.

Whipple had, in fact, been keeping the sharpest lookout of his life. His right eye was black and partially closed, his left ear and cheekbone swollen, and both lips puffy; for not only had he been soundly thrashed by the Londi chauffeur, but Angel had knocked him around afterward for letting it happen. Nor had Chief Grotten offered the least sympathy when he reported to him behind Angel's back. Then an odd sputtering sound caught his attention, and slowly he turned.

One look and he ran for daylight. But Maximo was an old club fighter, a brawler who knew how to cut off the ring from quicker and more agile opponents, and it was not daylight that Whipple ran smack into.

There was a jolting flash of blue, and a sparkling of stars, followed by a vague awareness of staring up at the evening sky, with grass tickling the back of his neck. Then he was on his feet again, though positive he had never gotten there under his own power; then there was an explosion directly between his eyes, and once more he found himself staring at twilight. Then he was up again, then down; then up yet again, and the world flashed and popped and sparkled around him like the Fourth of July. The last thing he saw was grass directly in front of his eyes, before the lights went out altogether. . . .

"Get up, you clown!" The voice was harsh and raspy, and seemed to come from far away. "Twice I give you a simple job to do, and twice you let some bozo kick your butt. I think maybe your personality needs readjustment."

This jolted Whipple like a bucket of ice water, and he gazed up through a fog at the hulking forms of Angel and Mickey Dunstun, hovering over him. The sky was redder now, and the shadows of the trees and bushes around him had lengthened. He groaned at the pain in his ribs; his head felt swollen out of shape, and he could see better out of one eye than the other.

"I'm gonna give you one more chance, though you don't deserve it," Angel growled down at him, lowering with menace. "Blow it this time, and you're a Brainer. Now get up!"

Whipple staggered to his feet; his right eye was now so swollen that he had to cock his head to one side in order to see. And what he saw made him suspect that his mind was still wandering. Both Angel and Mickey Dunstun sported long hair and beards, and were dressed in sweatshirts bearing environmentalist slogans.

"Put this on."

The sweatshirt Angel thrust at him was stenciled with the logo SAVE THE WHALES. Stripping off his suitcoat, shirt, and tie, he donned it as ordered. Only now did he notice the placards stacked on the lawn nearby.

"The others will meet us behind the house." Angel checked his watch. "They can buy this environment junk anywheres. So we'll be ready to move the minute the tractor gets here."

He wore a green sweatshirt stenciled ANIMALS ARE PEOPLE, but his phony hair and beard only made him look like an undercover cop. He peered through the bushes toward the long line of chauffeured limousines parked across the street.

He sneered. "Just look at these rich bozos lined up, and all to see some goofy old broad who must be close to ninety. Nickel-and-dime punks compared to the Big

Guy, even this Delfred Bassett we're going after. Refused a fair offer for his company! But the Big Guy's miles ahead of 'em. We won't be killing two birds with one stone here. More like a flock."

That one of his own men should get beaten up had angered him; that the same man should get beaten up a second time had so infuriated him that he was on the scrambler before Whipple had even regained consciousness. The decisive response from Benton Ingles still awed him; for it was both ingenious and boasted a detailed knowledge of the situation he would not have thought possible in someone not actually on the spot.

Not only did he already know about the twilight garden party, but knew the actual names of Lola Londi's old admirers who were invited to attend. Among these was the notorious fish tycoon, Delfred Bassett. Environmentalists all over the world regularly organized protest demonstrations against him and the "clean sweep" trawling of his fishing fleets, which so depleted the coastal fishing grounds of Third World countries that some now suffered destitution. It was not unusual for protests to erupt into violence, and if certain persons who had lately made themselves a nuisance to B.I.T.E. happened to be maimed or killed in a demonstration here tonight, B.I.T.E. newsies would see to it that the environmentalists got the blame.

The concise manner in which Benton Ingles had outlined it all for him over the scrambler left Angel deeply impressed, and he counted off on his fingers: Delfred Bassett, Lola Londi, her chauffeur, the whole Royal Beach Preservation Society, and environmentalist dingbats in general. Five birds with one stone. He chuckled sardonically to himself. Miles ahead of 'em every time.

"You two carry these printed signs around back of the old broad's house," he said. "I'm gonna round up the troops. If the tractor gets there before I do, tell the driver to keep it out of sight."

The Sons of Paradise formed an aisle for the grand entrance. Dressed in their club uniforms of sky blue, with shiny brass buttons and maroon-and-gold piping, they were like the ushers at some old movie palace of the Silent Era. Verna Malmrose, peering down into the garden from behind her bedroom curtain, found it all charming in its tinsel splendor.

And Lola Londi really was magnificent. She wore a gown of shimmering red silk, a ruby necklace, and a tiara of diamonds, and strode into the roseate glow of sunset like the empress of some exotic land.

Small wonder that her old admirers, though now stout and white-haired (if they had any hair at all), greeted her with such adulation. All were rich and powerful men, tanned, expensively tailored, and immaculately groomed, with chauffeured limousines awaiting them outside. Yet none had ever forgotten, in the treadmill accumulation of ever more money and power, the fantasy created for him in his youth by the exotic Lola Londi. All extinguished their Cuban cigars before stepping up to greet her.

Verna had not wanted to spoil the effect by intruding herself, and so had delayed her own less conspicuous entrance into the garden, Resettling the red wig more firmly on her head, she donned sunglasses, and started to turn from the window; but then something incongruous caught her eye.

The stone wall surrounding the garden enclosed a full acre of ground; it was coped with brick tiles, and there was a gate of solid oak. Beyond it ran a tree-shaded lane paved with brick, dividing rows of garden walls, and evidently serving the mansion owners as a kind of refined alley. She had noticed people gathering there, and assumed they had merely come to listen to the music; but now she saw that they were protest demonstrators.

Yet something here was all wrong. She had marched in too many demonstrations with her brother not to know what they were really like, and what kinds of people really participated in them. These demonstrators were too uniform in age and sex (there were no women), and behaved too much like the popular conception of radicals to be the real thing. Who were they, she wondered, and what were they really up to? They had begun to chant slogans, but she was too far away to make out any words.

The flush of twilight lent a healthy glow to the wrinkled, jowly faces of the millionaire guests. Lola was still the cynosure of their adulation, and stood with her back turned strategically to the setting sun, graciously accepting their homage. This was her hour, and Verna skirted the crowd at a discreet distance.

She selected a demitasse of Turkish coffee and a glazed marzipan from the buffet table, and strolled inconspicuously down the walk toward the oaken gateway. Twilight in the manicured gardens of Versailles or medieval Florence must have been something like this, though she could not picture either the Sun King or any Renaissance prince ever suffering protesters to use his name in vain.

"Delfred! Delfred! Delfred! Woof! Woof! Woof!" the demonstrators chanted over and over again, a chant she had heard before at more authentic demonstrations. They raised their placards so high now that they were visible over the top of the garden wall.

This put a damper on the reception, though she doubted that Lola Londi herself was at all perturbed by what was happening, or even aware of it, since she was not wearing either her spectacles or her hearing aid; unless she may have noticed an unusual inattentiveness among her court of admirers. They knew exactly what was happening, and didn't like it one bit.

One of them, a poochy little man who looked more like a neighborhood grocer than an international tycoon, seemed especially upset. He stood somewhat apart from the others, where he could help himself from the buffet table with unwatched greed. His houndish face was anything but memorable, yet Verna felt certain she had seen it somewhere before.

"Delfred! Delfred! Delfred! Woof! Woof! Woof!" continued the chant outside the garden wall.

Then all at once she knew. It was Delfred Bassett, who had arrogantly dubbed his fishing fleets "sea factories," and sent them forth with unprecedented greed to despoil the coastal regions of the Third World. Their trawl nets were miles long, and swept the ocean so clean of living things that they were likened to giant vacuum cleaners. Her brother had once organized a demonstration against the relentless extermination of porpoises, sea otters, and pilot whales by "clean sweep" trawling, on a weekend she had had to spend studying for exams.

She knew that Bassett's name stood high on the enemies list of every environmentalist group in the world, but not until this moment had she ever seen him in person.

The "Woof! Woof! Woof!" being chanted by the protesters was authentic. Her brother had informed her that the chant was standard at all protests against Delfred Bassett, referring to his houndish appearance, or perhaps his houndish greed. But the placards bobbing up and down over the wall—SAVE THE WHALES, CLEAN AIR NOW, BOYCOTT GRAPES, ANIMALS ARE PEOPLE, and so forth—could have been purchased at any specialty shop in town, and looked as if they had. Like the ridiculous beards and long hair worn by the demonstrators themselves.

She didn't need a closer look to write them off as fakes, any more than she would have needed to microscope a three dollar bill to know it was phony. Who they were and what they were really up to would have to wait upon events. Right now she was curious to get a closer look at Mr. Delfred Bassett. She had never understood why a man with so much money could think of nothing better to do with his life than just to pile up more money, which he didn't need and would never spend. Especially when his greed condemned so many helpless men, women and children to so much misery and want.

Returning her empty plate and demitasse to the table, she sidled over to the poochy little man. Besides Lola and her maid Graziella, there were no other women present. She hoped he would not think she was a gold digger putting the make on him.

"Delfred! Delfred! Delfred! Woof! Woof! Woof! continued the chant on the other side of the garden wall.

CHAPTER XI

Black velvet hung with paintings and photographs of renowned masters of the occult, covered the walls of the lecture theater. Twin mummy cases flanked the dais, and there were displays of memorabilia from noted investigations into the strange and mysterious. Draperies of black velvet led to the Museum of the Un-explained, the uncanny extent of whose weird and mystifying collections baffled many visitors. Nor was this spaciousness an illusion. For vast underground vaults had been secretly delved here by a bootlegger, the better to conceal his wares, and extended well beyond the apparent dimensions of the house.

The second lecture today was so crowded that several tourists had to stand behind the last row of wooden chairs. It had been well received, and Tedworth Vay had already sold over a hundred autographed copies of his books. Though sometimes people made uneasy by his presentations tried to reassure themselves, like whistling past a cemetery at night, that they were really superior to it all.

A potbellied retiree in a flowered shirt, who looked like he would much rather have been out on the golf course today, had asked a silly question. Some women in the audience, miffed at what they thought was intentional disrespect, gave him their opinions of his character and intelligence. Tedworth Vay took charge of the situation before it became acrimonious.

"No phenomenon, ladies and gentleman, whether it exists in reality—whatever that may be—or solely in the mind, is unworthy of investigation. Take flying saucers, for instance. Now even if the skeptics were correct in dismissing them as mass delusions, that would still leave the nature of mass delusion itself to be studied. Alas, the academic mind is so closed to any phenomenon not officially approved, that the investigation of flying saucers, from any perspective whatsoever, is academically forbidden."

He had had tough audiences at both lectures today, but each time had succeeded in winning them over. It was his principle never to disparage any question, no matter how frivolous it seemed.

"Now I've been asked what has become synonymous with the unanswerable," he continued. " 'Which came first, the chicken or the egg?' Let's see if it has an answer. Tell me, sir." He turned back to the retiree in the flowered shirt. "What is a chicken?"

"A bird," he answered, and there was some mocking applause from the audience, most of whom were disgusted with him.

"See, he's not as dumb as he looks," a fat woman commented ironically.

"Yes, a chicken is indeed a bird," said Tedworth Vay. "But a bird with specific characteristics, different from those of, say, a canary or an ostrich. Now we know that all birds have evolved over millions of years from reptilian ancestors. Some fanciful scientists have categorized birds as the last dinosaurs. Be that as it may, we can assume that at some point in evolution a creature not quite a chicken laid an egg that hatched into the first true chicken. Now, sir, perhaps you can answer your own question. Which came first, the chicken or the egg?"

The retiree blinked a moment, then brightened. "oh, I get it. The egg came first. Say, that's terrific. I never thought of it like that before."

This time the applause was genuine. But some questions inevitably breed others, and Tedworth Vay was pretty sure what the next one would be.

"I hope this don't sound like, well, you know, too simple," the fat woman began hesitantly.

"It is the simple questions, madam, that often turn out to be the most profound," he encouraged her.

"That might be, Professor, because none of us, me and my family, I mean, could ever figure this one out, though we've argued about it for twenty years. Not every day, of course, but, you know, like once in a while. Anyways, if a tree falls down in the forest, but there's nobody there to hear it, does it make any sound? My husband here says yes." She jerked a thumb at the fat man beside her. "But I don't think so."

"Then you are correct, madam. No matter how tremendous the crash, if there is no one present to hear it there is no sound."

The woman gloated at her husband, but he would not yet acknowledge defeat.

"Yeah, but how do we know that, Professor? I mean, if nobody's there, how do we know what's going on?"

"Listen." He cupped his hand behind his ear. "Can anyone hear a radio playing?"

"I don't hear anything," and "Quiet as a tomb," were among the replies from the audience. Some imitated him by cupping their hands behind their own ears; others shrugged, or exchanged quizzical looks, or just shook their heads. "There's no radio here."

He now turned to a teenager in the second row. "I see that you have a portable radio hooked to your belt, young man. Please unplug your earphones and turn it on."

The small theater was instantly beset with the discordant howling and thumping of rock music.

"Thank you, that's quite enough of that," he said dryly, and there was a ripple of laughter and applause as the radio was turned off again. "The point of this demonstration is that this room, in fact this entire planet, is saturated with radio waves, across a broad band of frequencies. But where there is no receiver to detect and amplify them, there is no radio. Now let's go back to the question of whether a falling tree makes a sound, if nobody is there to hear it."

"Okay, I get it," said the fat woman's husband. "So I was wrong. A falling tree makes sound waves, but no sound if there's no ears to detect 'em. You're a smart man, Professor. We've been trying to figure that one out for years." He smiled as his wife gave him a conciliatory peck on the cheek.

Tedworth Vay acknowledged the applause with a showman's flourish. He knew that a lecturer's ability to field questions after a lecture always left a more indelible impression upon his audience than the lecture itself. The questions following the day's first lecture had fixed upon the pyramids of Egypt and their relationship to the occult. His knowledge of the subject had so fascinated that audience that they might have been in their seats yet, but for the timely intervention of Chesterville.

"I'm sorry to disturb you, Professor." He had emerged dramatically out of the black velvet curtains at the rear of the theater. "An important telephone call."

His urgent manner, the hint of awe in his voice, and the pressing earnestness of his demeanor had all implied that the caller was no less than a world statesman. This was his usual device for clearing the theater whenever an audience showed signs of hanging on. But in this case there really had been a telephone call, and the caller was indeed a world statesman.

"Sorry, I'm so late getting back to you, Ted." The voice of Senator Worthing sounded hoarse and tired over the receiver. "It's been a long day here, fending off attacks on the space program by the stooges of Benton Ingles. With all his newspapers and television stations working overtime to whip up a national scandal, he's got the Administration over a barrel."

"Any problems yet with the satellite network?"

"So far, so good. We've all got our fingers crossed. But I'm still running into stone walls trying to discover what Ingles is up to in the South Pacific. He won't keep me in the dark much longer, though. There are no stone walls high enough to keep a committee chairman from peeking over. We should know as soon as I get back from Charlotte."

"A policy speech?"

"Yes, I'm driving down there tonight for a university commencement. It gives me an opportunity to defend the Administration and its space program. I'll be back here the day after tomorrow, and should have something concrete for you by then. I'm getting a bad feeling about this, Ted. Ingles wouldn't be going to so much trouble to cover his tracks, unless he was up to something really dirty. You'll be hearing from me soon."

Tedworth Vay hung up the telephone with a bad feeling of his own. But there was nothing he could do about it until Senator Worthing called back except be patient. . . .

Keeping his patience with this second lecture audience, and the inane tendency of their questions, was a trial of his good nature and professionalism. He now fully expected to be asked what would happen if an irresistible force met an immovable object. It was a relief to be asked instead about the Indian rope trick. A common question, but at least within the realm of the occult.

"First of all," he said, "we may be sure that the traditional Indian rope trick, in which a rope is thrown into the air and a boy climbs up it and disappears, has never actually been performed. It's a visual hallucination imposed by a skilled magus or fakir upon a suggestible audience, and perhaps belongs more to the psychology of hypnotism than to magic or the occult. A viceroy of India, in the days of Queen Victoria, once offered ten thousand pounds, a tremendous sum at that time, to anyone who could demonstrate the trick. There was no claimant."

"Then it's all just a hoax?" asked a young woman.

"No, I'm sure the trick was once part of the repertoire of Indian fakirs. But its success depended solely upon their ability to induce a visual hallucination in a credulous and highly suggestible audience, after first creating an atmosphere of intense expectation and high emotional strain. One suspects that many of the miracles of religion were created in exactly that way."

He was afraid for a moment that he had created too expectant an atmosphere in his own audience, but the reliable Chesterville emerged dramatically through the black velvet curtains right on schedule.

"I'm sorry to disturb you, Professor," he announced in pompous tones. "An important telephone call."

"Thank you, Chesterville," Tedworth Vay shrugged apologetically to his audience. "Please excuse me, ladies and gentlemen. You've been a wonderful audience, and I hope that in my small way I've helped enlighten you about the true nature of the occult. There are many mysteries of heaven and earth yet to be explained, and closing our minds to them won't make them disappear. So farewell, till we meet again. It's getting late, and I doubt that many of you would care to remain here after dark."

There was laughter and applause, which he acknowledged with a last bow and flourish, and disappeared through a curtain behind the dais. Wearily ascending a secret staircase hidden in the walls (another legacy from bootlegger days), he entered the library from behind a revolving bookcase. Once again there really was a telephone call. Chesterville handed him the receiver.

"Young Waverly, sir."

"I'm at the corner drugstore, Professor." Tim sounded anxious and confused. "I circled my house, then I circled the whole block, just to be sure. Nobody's watching anymore. Do you think they went away?"

"More likely they're up to something," said Tedworth Vay. "Exactly what, remains to be seen. I'll get back to you, Tim. Thanks for calling."

He sat back in his overstuffed armchair, contemplating the ceiling as if it were a chessboard. Outside in the driveway he could hear the bus drivers cautioning the tourists to "Watch your step, please," as they loaded their buses for departure.

"Oh, here you are, Professor." Rhoda Dawn entered the room dressed in her fringed buckskin shirt, strung with Indian beads. "Domino and Dominique are asleep in their little hammocks. They chose the toy football helmets, from all the doll hats and things Chesterville bought, and now won't sleep without them on."

"Are they tired of playing Nintendo?"

She shook her head. "I had to turn it off. Once they learned how to play, I couldn't get them away from it. They're the world champs. But I don't think they'd be allowed to compete in any contest."

"Why not?"

"Because they play as a team. One watches the screen, while the other works the controls. They talk so fast to each other that all I can pick up is a blur of images. Hello, Chesterville. Are the tourists gone yet?"

"Salutations, dear child," he said, reentering the room. "They are indeed gone, as are the men who have been spying on the house. Though exactly when they left, I can't say."

"I can. It was about an hour ago. I know because Domino and Dominique got excited and ran to the window, just like yesterday. I saw the two spies get into a long black car with some others, and drive off."

"Tim Waverly just reported the same thing," said Tedworth Vay. "He wondered if they were going away for good. Do you think they are, Chesterville?"

"No, sir. I should say rather that they're regrouping for something nefarious, perhaps involving Miss Malmrose."

"Yes, I'd considered that myself. Get the Londi residence on the phone, please."

As Chesterville reached for the telephone, it rang. He picked up the handset with unruffled aplomb.

"The residence of Professor Tedworth Vay. May I help you?" A sneer curled his lip, and he covered the receiver with his hand. "The Londi chauffeur. He wishes to speak to you, sir. He says it's urgent."

"I'll take it. Yes, Max?" He listened a moment. "A protest demonstration? No wonder Miss Malmrose is suspicious. Yes, I believe she has considerable experience in such matters. I'm on my way."

He depressed the plunger, and touch-toned a new number. "Tim? That's right. We may have an emergency. Round up as many friends as you can, as fast as you can, and get over to the Londi residence. There's a protest demonstration going on, in the lane behind the house. No, we're not sure who they are yet. Yes, hurry."

"I'll get Domino and Dominique," cried Rhoda. "They'll know if these demonstrators are who you think they are."

Within minutes they were all seated at the front of Tedworth Vay's black Duesenberg, with Chesterville at the wheel, racing up Legendary Lane through the dusk. Domino and Dominique lay calmly across Rhoda's lap, unfazed at being roused from a sound sleep, for both they and their ancestors for thousands of years had been bred specifically to handle emergencies with dispatch and efficiency.

Maximo opened the front door. He raised his eyebrows at the sight of the two cats, but was too awed by the knowledge and accomplishments of Tedworth Vay to question his motives. He led the way to the morning room. The sun had just set, and through the window they could see the Sons of Paradise lighting colored lanterns, whose fairy radiance, mingled with the fading reds of dusk, cast over the garden a pagan unreality.

"Look, Professor," said Rhoda, "That settles it. That goon is here somewhere."

The moment Domino and Dominique entered the room, they darted for the settee beneath the window, and sprang onto it in tandem. They now stood on their hind legs, forepaws braced against the sill, peering toward the gateway at the farther end of the garden, their tails twitching angrily back and forth.

"Yes, that settles it all right. I'm only surprised Miss Malmrose herself didn't recognize her persecutor."

"They're wearing funny costumes, Professor," said Maximo. "Wigs and beards and weird clothes. I've already called the cops, but so far not a single one has shown up."

"Call them again. This time ask for Chief Farquarson himself, in my name. Meanwhile, other help is on the way."

Maximo was back in two minutes, shaking his head. "The line's dead, Professor. They must have cut it."

"Send Graziella to the police station."

"Too late. I ran upstairs for a quick peek at what these phonies are up to. They've thrown down all their protest signs and are now hooking a chain to a tractor."

"A tractor? That can only mean they're going to pull down the gate and storm the garden. Rhoda, dear, there's going to be trouble. Stay here with Domino and Dominique till I get back. Let's go, Max."

Rhoda knelt on the settee beside the two cats, and gazed with them out into the garden. Colored lanterns glowing magically, colonnades overgrown with blossoming vines, lush beds of flowers and flowering shrubs, bronze fountains, marble gods and goddesses; and there was Lola Londi herself, regal in her gown of shimmering silk, her diamonds and rubies twinkling upon her in the lantern light like tiny stars, surrounded by an elegant court of admirers. Yet beyond the charm and splendor she sensed a lurking malevolence, and she knew that Domino and Dominique sensed it, too.

She spotted Verna Malmrose in a red wig and sunglasses, in conversation with a poochy little man, who looked uncomfortable. Then Professor Vay and Maximo appeared off to her left, hurrying together past a fountain and up the garden path toward Lola Londi.

But scarcely had they reached her, when the entire magical scene dissolved into chaos.

There was a grinding crash as the heavy oaken gates were torn off their hinges, and into the lantern light poured a score of big men with long hair and beards. Most rushed directly at Lola Londi, but she was already being escorted back to the house by Maximo and Professor Vay. Nor did all the danger and commotion cause her to lose her regal bearing.

The first assailant who made a grab for her was felled by a bludgeoning right from Maximo; the next was sent reeling by a left hook to the side of the head. Then ranks of old men in what looked like fancy ushers' uniforms formed a protective cordon between her and the rest of the onrushing pack, sacrificing themselves to aid her escape. And though they were shoved and cuffed and hurled to the ground, they gallantly refused to yield until she was out of harm's way.

Then suddenly the assailants became the assailed, as a score or more of powerfully-muscled young men, led by Tim Waverly, charged through the mutilated gateway and hurled themselves into the fray, just as the big hairy men had started to move upon the house. Despite their size, they found themselves at a disadvantage in every struggle against the muscular young men. Their leader, an ugly Frankenstein wearing a phony beard, shouted and cursed at them, but to no avail. Path by path, flower bed by flower bed, they were driven inexorably back toward the gate.

Rhoda could see Professor Vay now taking charge of the defense, while Lola Londi's elegant court of admirers huddled fearfully behind the statue of a naked goddess, where a bronze fountain put a kind of defensive moat between themselves and the brawlers. But what had become of Verna? Had she escaped into the house? Then she realized that Domino and Dominique were straining forward, their noses pressed to the windowpane, peering off to their right.

And there was Verna. She had evidently been trying

to draw the poochy little man with her to safety beneath a marble colonnade, which ran the length of the garden. But they had been spotted, and two big hairy thugs were now upon them. The poochy little man, instead of trying to defend her, actually shoved her into the arms of the thugs, so he could save himself by running away.

Nobody else saw what was happening. One of the thugs had clapped his hand over Verna's mouth so she couldn't cry for help, while they dragged her toward the other end of the garden, using the vine-shrouded colonnade to screen them from detection. Two more minutes, and poor Verna would be dragged out the gate and lost forever.

"Wait here!" she cried.

Leaving the two cats at the window, she raced out of the room, down the back stairs, and out into the garden. Professor Vay was too distant to hear her shouts, but there was Tim Waverly. He had momentarily separated himself from the fray, and was now looking anxiously around for someone.

"She's over there, Tim!" Rhoda pointed emphatically toward the colonnade. "Two men are dragging her out the gate. Hurry!"

He did not hesitate. Night had fallen, and while the colored lanterns still cast a fairy radiance over the central garden, its outer walks and shrubbery faded into darkness. He dodged through a pool of blue light, rounded a patch of red-violet, and plunged into the shadows. A writhing dark mass was just emerging between the last two pillars of the colonnade, and he hurled himself upon it.

Verna's sunglasses had been knocked awry, her red wig was twisted over one ear, but she continued valiantly to kick and struggle, as she was dragged relentlessly toward the gate. The nearest assailant was the one with his hand clapped over her mouth, and Tim seized him from behind by the hair—only to be left standing with a grubby wig in his hand. Tossing it aside, he spun him around and drove a fist crashing into the side of his jaw.

Verna was now free to whimper and wring her hands in fright. Instead, she went after her other assailant with a vengeance, kicking him in the groin for starters, and whaling away with an abandon that drove him reeling backward.

Tim watched her with mixed emotions, admiring her prowess but with a vague sense of disillusionment. Shrinking damsels in distress, it seemed, were more likely to be found nowadays in musty old romances or the films of Lola Londi than anywhere in modern California.

"Are you all right?" he asked with concern, as the two assailants lurched and stumbled out the gate.

"I'll do, no thanks to Mr. Delfred Bassett." She stamped her foot in anger, twisting her wig farther down over her ear. "The hound! Oh, I'm so mad I'd like to demonstrate against him myself. Woof! Woof! Woof! He actually pushed me into those goons. Hound is too good for him."

"But are sure you're not hurt in any way?" He was also concerned now to calm her down.

His solicitude reminded her how near she had again come to ending up a zombie of Benton Ingles, and she settled her wig more securely on her shaven head, and smoothed her clothes.

"Thanks, Tim. You were great." And she let him slip a protective arm around her, and lead her out of the shadows into a pool of golden light.

Now that the last of the thugs had been driven from the garden, rich old men were everywhere coming boldly forth from cover, to snort and threaten, complain about the degeneracy of the times, and relight their Cuban cigars. Delfred Bassett alone still hung back, peeking stealthily from the concealment of a rose arbor. There was something in Verna's demeanor, as she was accompanied by a powerful young man into the lantern light, that suggested to him that it was not yet a propitious moment to reappear.

The Sons of Paradise, none of whom had been badly injured in the melee, bore their scrapes and bruises like badges of honor; they were already cleaning up the mess, picking up chairs and rearranging the buffet table, in hopes their goddess might return tonight in all her splendor. She did, and they at once dropped whatever they were doing, arranging themselves into parallel ranks and forming an aisle so she could reenter the garden with due ceremony.

She appeared regally on the arm of Tedworth Vay, who considerately avoided all green, blue, and yellow patches of light, and deposited her among her reassembled court of admirers, in the glow of a rose-colored lantern. Then he drew Maximo, who all the while had hovered protectively near, out of earshot.

"Lola will be safe now, Max," he said. "But events are moving faster than I had anticipated. We have to get to the police station as soon as possible, before more damage is done.

Maximo shrugged. "I called them, but no cops showed up. The neighbors must have complained about the uproar here, but still no cops. Something's wrong, Professor."

"That's why we have to act fast. Where's Rhoda? Ah, there she is." He beckoned. "If what I think has happened has, she may be able to help us. Are you all right?" he asked, as the child hurried up to them.

She nodded. "It was a great fight, Professor. Better than any on television."

"She deserves a medal," said Tim, joining them with his arm still around Verna. He recounted the attempted abduction, praising the timely warning given him by Rhoda. "It was Verna they were after, Professor. This whole phony demonstration was rigged up by Benton Ingles to recapture her."

But Verna herself disagreed. "No, it was Lola they were really after. The demonstration against Delfred

Bassett was only a pretext. Though they would probably have kicked his butt, to make things look right, if
they'd gotten hold of him. Too bad they didn't. The
hound! It was only when he shoved me at them, and
my wig slipped off, that their leader spotted me. And
don't worry, I spotted him, too."

"The one like a big hairy Frankenstein?" said
Rhoda.

"Yes, I got a good look at him also," said Tim. "He
works for Benton Ingles. His name is Angel."

"That's the one," said Verna. "He's the goon who
captured me the first time, and he wasn't very nice
about it either." She glanced off into the darkness.
"There he is now."

"Angel?" Tim followed her gaze.

"No, Delfred Bassett. He's ducked back now, but he
was peeking at me out of that rose arbor over there.
Oh, I'd like to slap the teeth right out of his face."

"We'll settle all that later," said Tedworth Vay.
"Right now we have to settle with the police. Remember, Miss Malmrose, you're still wanted for murder."

"How could I forget?" She tidied her wig and put
her sunglasses back on. "Maximo has shown me the
perfect hiding place, should the cops ever show up.
Meanwhile, I'd better stay close to Lola, in case those
goons come back."

"Can you and your friends stand guard, Tim?" asked
Tedworth Vay. "At least long enough to get the gate repaired."

"As long as you want, Professor. Once word gets out
that Benton Ingles is behind this, bodybuilders and environmentalists from all over the state will be calling
to offer help."

"They can't call here," said Maximo. "The phone
don't work."

"Let's find out why," said Tedworth Vay. "Ready?"

It was not until they were actually parking the limousine behind the police station that Rhoda clapped her
hand to her forehead.

"Oh, my goodness. Domino and Dominique! I forgot all about them, Professor."

"They should be all right," he said. "Cats generally know how to take care of themselves, and I suspect none better than those two."

Maximo did not comment as he switched off the ignition. There was no point in reminding them now that Domino and Dominique were not the only cats in the house.

CHAPTER XII

Domino and Dominique watched the whole melee through the window in the morning room. They were glad to see the biggest and ugliest of the Earthlings driven from the garden, though why all creatures on this strange planet were so prone to violence still bewildered them. The Masters had always been calm and rational.

Simultaneously, they turned from the window and sat side by side on the settee cushion, facing the doorway. Earlier they had sensed a creature primitively like themselves somewhere in the house, and now here she was. They tried to communicate telepathically with her, just as they had with similar creatures before but again failed to achieve empathy. Perhaps it was this very inability to understand each other that made Earthlings so violent.

Lakme was a mean cat at the best of times, and the noise and excitement tonight had put her in a bad mood. Vague images now teased her brain; she did not understand them, and this tended to irritate her still further. The kitchen door was shut, and she sat plump on the threshold of the hall doorway, blocking the sole means of escape from the morning room. Her tail began to twitch ominously back and forth.

She had long been the terror of Royal Beach. All neighborhood creatures, great or small, fled from her path wherever she prowled the night; dogs gave her a wide berth, other cats cringed and yowled in fright. That these two youngsters had not only trespassed into her territory, but should not respond to her dread appearance only by gazing impudently down at her, roused in her a murderous fury. Low growls vibrated deep in her throat as she padded toward them across the carpet.

But she did not strike at once. It was always more gratifying to toy with victims first, especially those trapped and helpless, even letting them believe they might escape destruction, before at last falling upon them fang and claw. Nothing in the end escaped the savagery of her pounce; not the squirrels she delighted in tormenting, not the pet bunnies whose necks she broke, not the songbirds whose nestlings she devoured. She sat down a few feet from the settee, to enjoy the terror of her helpless victims. There was no hurry; they could not escape her.

Domino and Dominique had no intention of escaping though they could easily have done so. Both had been unusually mischievous as kittens, continually in trouble with their crew chief, until in exasperation she had awarded them corporal punishment. This was meted out only once, where continued breaches of regulations had to be checked before they jeopardized ship discipline, and the experience lasted a lifetime. They had learned their lesson; now it was time to teach one.

Their continued impudence seemed to Lakme a defiance; faster and faster twitched her tail, louder and more savage vibrated the growls deep in her throat. Then in an explosion of fur and fury she sprang at them, fangs bared, claws extended, ready to slash and rend.

To human eyes her pounce would have seemed lightning quick, but to Domino and Dominique it was as if she were moving in slow motion, a brutishly clumsy oaf. Her claws might have left deadly wounds, had they slashed anything but thin air; her fangs might have pierced to the bone, had they bitten anything but feather cushions. Nothing had ever before escaped her pounce with such contemptuous ease, and before her dull wits could react, she found herself rendered powerless.

Domino hooked four sets of claws into her left flank; Dominique like a mirror image did likewise on the right; each took one of Lakme's ears punitively in her teeth, and preliminary discipline began. Lakme was not really intelligent; but she had a keen sense of discomfort, and quickly learned that her degree of squalling and struggling was visited proportionally upon her ears. When she at last lay still, Dominique insinuated a single claw into a nerve at the back of her neck, while Domino smacked her back and forth across the chops, and pulled her whiskers. The punishment humiliated her, but she had to take it. With the claw stuck like an acupuncture needle into her neck, she was powerless to resist.

Then discipline began in earnest. With boot camp rigor, she was marched up and down the room until she learned to march in step. She tried once to bolt, but with a quickness that seemed almost invisible Domino swiped her hind legs out from under her, while Dominique batted one of her forepaws into the other, and she burned her nose leather along the carpet as she skidded into a heap. Rising dizzily to her paws, she found her two drill instructors bouncing back and forth like the balls of a juggler, blocking her path to the door. Her hair stood on end, and her ears flattened in shock; but she never tried to bolt again.

Her treacherous attempts to claw and bite were immediately punished, and she soon learned that arching her back and spitting was unacceptable behavior. Her mean disposition was an obstacle, but through relentless drill and swift discipline that, too, if not overcome, was finally subdued.

Only when Domino and Dominique sensed that their recruit was properly abashed did they reward her, and march her between them, in a roundabout way, out to the kitchen.

Though Lakme herself knew this was where food was kept, all her previous efforts to pilfer some had been frustrated. But the refrigerator was no challenge for Domino and Dominique. Their uncanny teamwork and dexterity in opening its door, passing down a bowl of chicken croquettes, and removing its plastic cover so daunted Lakme that she never recovered.

In a snug corner of the pantry they divided the goodies into three equal portions, on a fresh dinner plate. The minced chicken smelled delicious, though Lakme was soon made painfully aware that her training was not yet over for the day. She had always been a sloppy eater, and tended to bolt her food in gobbets. But now, through having her whiskers pulled or her nose tweaked at each expression of grunginess, she learned to be a nicer dinner companion.

"That's all we've got, Ted." The Chief of Police turned off his tape recorder and sat back. "How big is this?"

Reginald Farquarson was a dapper little man who, out of uniform, looked more like a high-school principal than a policeman. He had, in fact, been a professor of jurisprudence, until he sickened of academic backbiting and specialization.

"It's getting bigger by the minute, Reggie," said Tedworth Vay, seated across the desk from him. They were alone in the office; Maximo was meanwhile escorting Rhoda from department to department throughout the police station. "Benton Ingles is behind it all, for reasons yet unclear, and he never does things in a small way."

"No, and he never lets justice stand in the way of a profit. But why Lola Londi, of all people? What harm could that old zany possibly do him?"

"For one thing, she's the chief financial support of the Royal Beach Preservation Society. For another, she's visited regularly by Ingles' wife. Also, her chauffeur thrashed one of Ingles' thugs—twice, in fact—whom he caught spying on her house."

"We have no record of that either. But knowing Max, it's unlikely we would have." He answered the telephone. "Yes? All right, thanks." He hung up and reported, as he touch-toned a new number. "Remling's staked out in Grove Corners, so let's get the ball rolling there. Hello, Sergeant," he spoke into the receiver. "Chief Farquarson, in Royal Beach. Listen, a friend of mine will be at your station in a little while. His name is Tedworth Vay. That's right, I've read all his books, too. Anyway, he's meeting some state officials and decided it would be safest to meet them outside the city limits. Yes, very secret. He's on his way out to Grove Corners at this very moment. You will? Thanks, Sergeant, I appreciate that."

He hung up, but before he could speak there was a knock at the door. "Come in."

Maximo and Rhoda entered, with a big, clumsy man in plainclothes.

"Nothing, Professor," said Rhoda. "Everybody here is just like everybody else."

"Then our next stop is the telephone company," he said, rising. "I'll check in every half hour or so, Reggie, to see how things are going out at Grove Corners."

"I'm interested myself. But if I'm not at my desk, Detective Prine here will keep you informed."

"My office is across the hall," said the big, clumsy plainclothesman. "Just come to me, if the chief's not around. Or even if he is. Glad to help."

"Thank you, Detective." Tedworth Vay waited till the man had left the room. "Then there's nothing you can do for Verna Malmrose, Reggie? It's all a frame-up."

The Chief of Police shrugged helplessly. "Even if it is a frame-up, Ted, the case is too big for me. It's in all the newspapers, it's on national television, and I'm still getting bulletins about her every day. If I arrested her here in Royal Beach, she'd be snatched out of my jurisdiction within an hour. Though, of course, I don't think she's here in Royal Beach, so I'm not actively pursuing the case." He looked meaningfully across the desk. "As for the thugs who broke into the Londi property, they're believed to have left town. But if you're right about them, Ted, they probably haven't gone far. Watch yourself."

"Thanks, Reggie. I'll keep in touch."

The telephone company, of all corporations in America, alone rivaled B.I.T.E. in the cost-effective dreariness of its structures. The multistoried pile was windowless and faced with slabs of laminated gravel; its interior was floored with cheap asphalt tile, its cinderblock walls painted white to economize on illumination. It was the eyesore of Royal Beach, though no stockholder complained about his dividends.

Few things depressed Tedworth Vay so much as functional architecture, and he tried to keep his mind exclusively on the business at hand as he, Maximo, and Rhoda were guided from floor to floor by the night supervisor. A call from Chief Farquarson had gotten them complete cooperation, but not until they entered the Directory Assistance Unit, on the eighth floor, did they discover anything out of the ordinary.

"There's one, Professor. Just like you said," whispered Rhoda, pointing to a scrubbed, close-cropped young man in a dark business suit, wearing headphones, and seated before an exchange console. "Ghost Eagle told me that the souls of people reach out from their bodies, and can be detected by spirit people. I can sense an aura in everybody else, but that guy over there is a blank. It's like he has no soul."

The supervisor looked quizzically at her. "Smith? Why, he's the most perfect employee I've ever had. Really knows his stuff, too, which is more than I can say for most management trainees these days. He transferred here from Ingles City, let's see, about three weeks ago."

"Have you any more employees like him?" asked
Tedworth Vay.

"No, but I wish I had," said the supervisor, whose
polka-dot bow tie accentuated the fleshiness of his
double-chinned neck. "He works early and late, and
never thinks about anything but his job."

Tedworth Vay sadly shook his head. "What a pitiful
thing to do to a fellow human being. Max, please ask
the young man over there, the one with the headphones, to step down to the supervisor's office."

"The guy who looks like a sterility symbol? You got
him, Professor. See you down there."

The scrubbed, closely-cropped young man followed
Maximo into the office a few minutes later with
robotlike docility.

"You wanted to see me, sir?" he asked the night supervisor.

"Have a seat, Smith. This is Professor Tedworth
Vay. The Chief of Police has given him the authority to
ask you a few questions."

A slight tremor passed spasmodically through the
young man's body, and his face assumed the disoriented look of a patient coming out of ether. But he sat
where he was directed, and offered no resistance to an
examination of his scalp.

Tedworth Vay saw clearly through the cropped hair
a perfectly round scar, like a tiny manhole cover lifted
for repairs and then replaced precisely at the crown of
the head. Again he sadly shook his head.

"Now I know what became of your call to the police, Max," he said. "And why no complaints from
your neighbors reached them, as well as the reason
your own telephone went dead at the critical moment."

He started to address the night supervisor, but was
alerted by the look of horror on his face. Only now did
he realize that the young man had fallen into an epilep-
tic seizure; his limbs jerked oddly back and forth, his
face rippled with spasms, while the rest of his body
was contorted by wracking paroxysms, as if he were

being jolted again and again by charges of electricity. He emitted not a sound, and with a last violent tremor slumped down in his chair.

Tedworth Vay checked his pulse. "Poor fellow. But he was already dead in any meaningful sense. An autopsy will reveal exactly how it was done to him. Where can I make a private telephone call?" he asked the supervisor.

"What? Telephone call?" The supervisor's jaw disappeared into his double chin as he gaped at the dead man. "Try the office across the hall. Better get an ambulance, or call the police."

"That's who I am going to call right now."

Flicking on the lights in the deserted office, he sat at a secretarial desk and touch-toned a number.

"Hello, Reggie? Tedworth Vay. Anything to report yet?"

"Looks like you were right, Ted." Chief Farquarson's voice sounded tired and remote. "Remling just got back from Grove Corners. Not twenty minutes after I called the station there, telling them you were on the way, the building was surrounded by armed thugs. Turn up anything at your end?"

He explained in detail what had just happened. "The autopsy should be revealing," he added. "By the way, I'd suggest having the ambulance escorted to the hospital. We don't want this body to disappear."

"I'll make the arrangements." There was a pause on the line before Farquarson spoke again. "I'll also take down all notices about the Malmrose girl from the bulletin board. This is getting so big it frightens me. Be careful, Ted."

The next number he touch-toned was long distance. The ruse at Grove Corners proved that Benton Ingles was wire-tapping all calls from Royal Beach. He knew that Senator Worthing was out of town, but wanted to alert him by phone mail the moment he returned to Washington. But instead of a recording telling him to leave a message when the tone sounded, he was answered by the tearful voice of the senator's personal secretary.

"He's dead, Professor," she sobbed into the telephone. "That great, good, dedicated man is dead. It's all lies. He never drank. The political cartoonists used to caricature him like Carrie Nation, breaking up saloons with a hatchet. The liquor lobby hated him. Now they'll ruin his good name, too."

He finally calmed her down enough to learn that Senator Worthing was reported to have crashed his automobile into a bridge viaduct while driving in an intoxicated condition. That the staunchest proponent in Congress of stiffer penalties for drunk drivers should so die would be a national scandal, over which the liquor lobby would rejoice.

"Oh, yes, I nearly forgot," she continued, choking down her sobs. "I'm so upset I hardly know what I'm doing. The senator left a message for you." She read: " 'Tell Professor Vay, if he calls, that I couldn't get anything out of the Pentagon, except a tip to query an official I know over at the Atomic Energy Commission. I'll get back to him as soon as I do.' He didn't say what it was all about, Professor, but he seemed very upset. And now he's dead. . ." She could no longer restrain her sobs.

He started to console her, but a commotion out in the hall forced him to sign off abruptly and rush to the door. Greasy smoke hung heavy in the air, and men with fire extinguishers were plunging one after the other into the supervisor's office. The supervisor himself, his jaw swallowed in the folds of his neck, leaned against the wall for support.

"Smith was a perfect employee," he muttered, his eyes wide with horror. "Came early and worked late. It's weird. Crazy. Like something out of the 'Twilight Zone.' He just burst into flames."

Rhoda stood nearby with Maximo. "It was just awful, Professor. His face started to swell like a balloon, then his entire head suddenly was on fire, and we got out of the room as quick as we could."

"Forget about autopsies, Professor. I think we need big help on this one." Maximo looked nearly as stunned as the night supervisor. "Like maybe the President and Congress, and the Army, Navy, and Marines. Throw in the Air Force, too. I never saw anything so ugly."

"We need help all right, Max," Tedworth Vay said thoughtfully as they descended to the parking lot. "But it's beginning to look more and more as if we're on our own. We're being isolated from the whole rest of the world."

"It all started with those damned cats," said Benton Ingles, seated in the library a sanitary distance from his Chief of Operations. "Everything was proceeding like clockwork, until they popped out of space and then vanished again. Are they hoodoos?"

"Nobody has explained yet what they are, sir." Chief Grotten tried to appear calm, though he felt his power slipping inexorably from his grasp.

Death in a drunk driving accident was a technique he had perfected years ago; it not only eliminated political opponents of B.I.T.E., but so discredited them with the public that any close investigation was effectively quashed. The powerful Senator Worthing had just been dealt with in exactly this manner, though he himself had not been entrusted with the job. Control of events at Royal Beach had also been taken out of his hands.

He had to admire the ruthless efficiency with which Benton Ingles had mobilized his forces. All his most powerful agents in business, politics, and the media were now assembled upstairs in the conference room. None had been trusted with the details of Project Nimrod, prior to countdown, for fear of betrayal. They were here tonight only to receive their marching orders, which each would obey implicitly and without question, to prepare their respective spheres for an imminent world catastrophe, so it could be exploited to the utmost in the interests of B.I.T.E. Yet he himself was excluded from the conference.

Ingles counted off the points on his gloved fingers: "I'm sure the cats, whatever they may be, are somewhere in Royal Beach. I know for a fact the Malmrose bitch is in Royal Beach because she's been seen there. My wife has betrayed me in Royal Beach, conspiring against me with that dotty old movie star, to pass secret information to my enemies. Young Waverly, the security guard who betrayed his post to spite me, lives in Royal Beach. Never fear, neither he nor that Malmrose bitch will ever betray me again, once they've had their insolent personalities readjusted. And I've already had a special display case built at my museum for those damned cats."

Chief Grotten listened intently to the strangely metallic voice. He suspected that Ingles, to compose himself for tonight's conference, had taken an extra dose of amphetamines and painkillers, a side effect of which was to intensify his megalomania and sense of persecution.

"Fools, degenerates, bodybuilders, environmentalists, dabblers in the occult." Ingles continued to count off on his gloved fingers. "They would be a contemptible lot of butterflies, and their Royal Beach Preservation Society as easily blown away as a dandelion tuft, but for one man."

"Tedworth Vay? He nearly fell into my trap, sir. I discovered that he was leaving Royal Beach for a secret meeting with state officials, at the nearby town of Grove Corners, and had men posted there in force. But luckily for him, he never showed up."

A begrudging look of admiration twisted the gaunt features of Benton Ingles. "He's a worthy adversary."

"Why is that, sir? Because he lucked out of my trap?"

"No, because you fell into his. He now knows that

every telephone line out of Royal Beach has been tapped, and will henceforth act accordingly. It behooves us, therefore, to keep him from acting at all."

"Let me handle him, sir. Angel flubbed what should have been a routine job in Royal Beach. The Brainer we infiltrated into the telephone exchange there has kamikazeed. But I've never let you down, sir. Never."

"I realize that, Kurt, my boy. I'm just reserving your talents for a more sensitive job. As for Tedworth Vay, for the Malmrose bitch, for those two damned cats, for that whole pack of Royal Beach meddlers, I regard them as I would any infectious disease that threatens my well-being. The town is now being quarantined. Nobody gets in, nobody gets out. You'll personally take charge of the operation, after you complete the other job I have for you."

"And what's that, sir?"

"Kill my wife." Ingles tugged fretfully at his white gloves. "It was you who first alerted me to her treason. I know you've never liked her."

"Liking or disliking your wife is not my place, sir. What I don't like is the danger her indiscretions pose for B.I.T.E. I've tried never to let my personal feelings influence any job at hand."

"I appreciate that, Kurt, my boy," said Ingles. "No operative of mine is more cunning and merciless in serving the interests of B.I.T.E."

"Thank you, sir."

Once more Ingles counted off on his gloved fingers. "Do the job right, so no suspicion of foul play reaches the hostile Media, and there should be no official inquiry into the death of my wife. I'm the governor's largest single campaign contributor. The state police won't interfere with the quarantine of Royal Beach. My own media people are standing by with a cover story. Terrorists have stolen a vial of plague bacteria from a biological warfare depot. They are believed to be hiding out in Royal Beach."

The timbre of his voice was now so metallic it sounded almost like a robot speaking:

"A concerted attack by my people in Congress, the Media, and the business community upon the failure of the UN Commstat. Fraud, unfair taxes, loss of American sovereignty, mismanagement, cover-ups, corruption, and so forth. Public opinion will be outraged. So any failure of the auxiliary satellite network, in this election year, will topple the administration."

"Then we launch Nimrod?"

"Then we launch Nimrod." Ingles went on counting mechanically on his gloved fingers. "I'll take the Administration off the hook, in exchange for privatization of the space program. Then nothing incompatible with the interests of B.I.T.E. will ever gain access to global communications. All voices now raised against me will be silenced forever. Royal Beach will be incorporated into Ingles City. Its recalcitrant citizens will be corrected as I deem appropriate. Including Professor Tedworth Vay." A begrudging look of admiration again twisted his gaunt features.

"He can't hurt us if he's isolated in Royal Beach, sir. Not with every phone line to Washington tapped, and with any contacts he might still have there shaking in their booties at the ghost of Senator Worthing. He'd better go back to investigating his own ghosts, or he may end up one himself."

"All in good season, Kurt, my boy." Ingles checked his watch. "I'm flying to Sulatonga immediately after the conference tonight, to take personal charge of Project Nimrod. Countdown must now begin sooner than originally scheduled. Just be sure the job I've given you is handled discreetly. Any further adjustment in our timetable, because of adverse publicity, could jeopardize the very establishment of my new world order."

"Rely on me, sir. We're on a seacoast, and Ingles Construction is right on the waterfront. An empty barrel, a bag of cement, and a motorboat ride. That's how we handled street people and guys the courts let go too easy, when I was on the L.A. Police Force. Short, sweet, and no traces."

"Any way you like, so long as there *are* no traces."

Ingles rose stiffly from the quilted-leather sofa on which he had been seated, and proceeded with slow, robotic movements to the door. Chief Grotten hurried forward to open it for him, and together they left the room. Though unknown to either of them they did not leave it deserted.

There was a second quilted-leather sofa in the room, and from behind it rose the voluptuous Carla, her raven hair disheveled, her clothing in disarray, looking less like a beauty queen than some wild bacchante of the midnight hills. She had listened to her husband order her killed, and overheard her lover agree without a qualm, as though she were a mere fly to be swatted, and her dark eyes glittered with a rage for vengeance.

She'd seen her husband grow colder and more distant, but not until tonight had her suspicions been truly aroused. A conference at this time could only mean some crisis for B.I.T.E. was in the offing. Curious, she had lingered deviously near the front door, and seen one powerful official after another arrive with briefcases and anxious looks. Strangely, the mighty Chief of Operations was not among them, and she began to worry that her husband had discovered their affair— which would explain his recent coldness—and had him murdered. If so, it would be her turn next.

In her first anxiety she had made wild plans for flight—back to Sicily, to some mountain hideaway, to Timbuktu (wherever that was), to Sulatonga, though the notion of mining bird droppings still disgusted her—until Grotten arrived after all. But he shook his head when she tried to approach him. That he did not proceed at once to the conference room upstairs could only mean that he had been summoned to a more secret conference with her husband, and that meant the library. She had slipped behind the sofa only minutes before they entered the room.

They were gone now, but what was she to do next? It was hard to concentrate while raging for blood, though she knew any thoughts of going down to the kitchen for a butcher knife were idle. Escape first, vengeance later. But would she be allowed to leave the premises, let alone fly to Sicily or Timbuktu?

Smoothing her dress and hair, she started for the door, only to be driven back into hiding again by the sound of approaching footsteps.

"I have only a few minutes to spare," said Ingles, as he reentered the room. "Disturbing reports have reached me about events at Royal Beach. What really happened there, Angel?"

Carla breathed as softly as she could, lying behind the sofa. She listened intently as Angel recounted his failed assault on the mansion of Lola Londi, and its sequel. All Royal Beach was now being quarantined, as if it had been hit by the black plague. All telephone lines out of the city were now tapped, which meant any call for help she made to Lola would have to be in the secret language of Sicilian schoolgirls. But if she could somehow get past the blockades and into Royal Beach, it might prove exactly the sanctuary she needed. . . .

"I'm disappointed, Angel," said Ingles.

"I hope not with me, sir. I followed your orders exactly as you told me, but somebody must have tipped them off because they were waiting for us. Still, nobody got left behind to squeal, and the newsies are now blaming it all on environmentalists."

There was a pause before Ingles spoke again. "It's interesting that you should believe they were forewarned."

"Not a doubt about it, sir. At least fifty bodybuilders jumped us, and there's no way they could have been there, excepting somebody told 'em we were coming. But the real proof is that they nabbed the Brainer we planted at the telephone company. Tell me how they could have known he was there, or even existed, unless they were tipped."

"They knew, and I know how they knew," said Ingles. "But that matter is already being handled. I'm more concerned now about our Chief of Operations. Do you feel he's become a less reliable man that he was?"

Angel hesitated. "Well, I dunno, that's not really for me to say, Mr. Ingles."

"Ah, but it is for you to say, and to say with facts and evidence. Do I make myself clear?"

"Yes, sir. I'll get on it right away, and I know just how to do it. Some gaffers over in the wiretap unit owe me a favor, but they might be afraid to help me out on anything this big."

Even from behind the leather sofa Carla could detect a note of brutal triumph in his harsh, raspy voice.

"You may give them my authorization for any assistance you need," said Ingles. "I'm flying to Sulatonga tonight, but you can inform me of any discoveries you make over the scrambler."

"Yes, sir. Have a nice flight. It's terrific what you're doing there, miles ahead of them bozos at NASA and the United Nations. And, if I could, I'd really like to be on hand for the launch, sir."

"I intend that you should be, Angel, after you complete your assignment here. But now I must return to the conference. I'm pressed for time, all of B.I.T.E. is pressed for time, thanks to Professor Tedworth Vay."

"Them eggheads make me sick. They can't park their bicycles straight, and they want to tell the world what to do. You should make Brainers out of the whole lot of 'em, sir."

"That's under consideration," said Ingles in a metallic voice. "Meanwhile I don't expect to hear of any more meddling from Royal Beach."

"Sealed tight as a drum, sir. Here, let me get that door for you."

Carla lay still behind the leather sofa until their footsteps had retreated into silence down the corridor outside. Then she sprang into action, hurrying to her bedroom, changing clothes, and stuffing her pockets with all the loose cash she could find. Her husband might already have ordered his security guards not to let her pass; but that was something that had to be risked, and she drove her red Ferrari straight up to the wrought-iron gates, and boldly sounded her horn.

"My husband he is in conference," she explained to the guard, who appeared at the barred window of the security booth. "If he ask for me, tell him I get bored and go to movies."

The guard disappeared again, and she waited tensely behind the steering wheel, afraid he was calling the house for instructions. But then the gates swung silently open, and with a sigh of relief she stomped the accelerator, and shot through them into the night.

She had no illusions about anonymity. No doubt every cop in Ingles City who spotted her car would report its whereabouts to Chief Grotten. They probably had orders to do so. But right now she wanted him to know—or rather, think he knew—exactly where she was going. She parked her conspicuous red sports car conspicuously in the driveway of the deserted mansion by the sea, which had lately become their favorite trysting place, and went straight to the telephone inside.

"Kurt, darling, I am afraid I hear only a recording. Guess where I am now." She was aware that even his car telephone had the capability to trace instantly any call he received. "Oh, I can't even fool you. You always know these things. Yes, yes, I see you are busy with the conference, but that is so boring, and it is such a lovely night. About three? Of course, darling, but don't keep me waiting. I'ma wear the French panties you like. Ciao."

That the traitor was himself now in jeopardy of treason, from a brutal underling, was some satisfaction to her; though she ultimately wanted vengeance of her own. Meanwhile her ruse had bought her a few hours' leeway. Grotten was a thorough man. He would first complete all his preparations for disposing of her body, and for averting any suspicion over her disappearance, before coming here to kill her. Nor would his crafty mind ever credit a mere woman with the craftiness to overreach him.

The owners of the mansion were somewhere in Europe, but their station wagon was still parked in the garage. A head scarf pulled forward, and driving so inconspicuous a vehicle, when Grotten had no reason to have the police of Ingles City track her whereabouts, she was unlikely to be spotted. She could not call Lola and leave a quick message in schoolgirl code on her recorder until after three. Meanwhile she really would take in a movie.

She passed the hours until show time in a confusion of anxiety and rage, pacing up and back like a caged panther, glancing every few minutes out the window, expecting at any moment that the suspicious Kurt Grotten would telephone to check up on her.

He never did, but before she finally left she wrote him a note: "Went to drugstore. Be right back. Love. C."

That would buy her still more leeway, and she drove to the Midway Theater, which had a midnight show. As she crossed the parking lot, she noticed private aircraft rising one after the other from her husband's private airstrip in the Restricted Zone and dispersing to all quarters of the globe. The last plane of all headed westward over the Pacific.

Drawing her head scarf still more concealingly forward, she paid for her ticket and entered the darkened theater. On the screen, a hulking goon was attacking a semi-naked woman with a chain saw.

Chief Grotten was at that very moment watching the same planes rise into the night sky. The waterfront construction company was a subsidiary of B.I.T.E.; its work yard, tiered with lumber and building materials, lay still and deserted all around him; beside a forklift nearby stood an empty oil drum and bag of cement. This was one disposal he intended to handle personally, without help or a single eyewitness.

The motor launch would stand crewed and ready at the docks, an hour before dawn, just as always. A sealed barrel would be winched on board, to be dumped far out at sea, just as usual. There must be no change of procedure that might start rumors flying to the ears of hostile newsies.

Nor was there any hurry. It was a sultry night, the fragrance of orange groves mingling exotically with the briny tang of the ocean, and he thought fondly of how charming Carla looked in French panties. The debate in his mind, as to whether he should just kill her outright or enjoy her voluptuous body one last time beforehand, was quickly settled.

CHAPTER XIII

Rhoda and Tedworth Vay paused before the Londi mansion, to watch the airplanes lift one after the other into the cloudless black heavens over Ingles City some miles up the coast. Maximo parked the vintage limousine in the old carriage house, behind the garden.

"They don't hold air shows at night, do they, professor?" she asked. "The planes seem to be heading in all directions."

"Yes, but I suspect with a single purpose."

Their situation appeared hopeless. Royal Beach now stood like a beleaguered citadel, alone against the hordes of darkness, with no hope of relief, with no resources but their own courage and ingenuity. Nor could they alert the world to its danger, without also alerting the henchmen of Benton Ingles.

But if the city itself was no true citadel, at least the home of Lola Londi now had adequate defenses. Tents of various shapes and hues had been set up throughout the garden, front lawn, and surrounding parkways, though not with the orderliness of a boy scout jamboree.

"The tents at the Snake Dance festival are much prettier," said Rhoda. "I hope you don't let them trample the flowers, Max," she added, as the burly chauffeur rejoined them just before they reached the front door, where two powerfully-built young men stood sentry.

He glanced meaningfully from one to the other. "Don't worry, little Indian, they've been warned."

"It's been a long day for Lola, Max," said Tedworth Vay. "Let's hope the excitement wasn't too much for her."

"No excitement could be too much for her, Professor. Believe me, this has been her happiest day in years. It's like she was back in one of her old movies, a beautiful princess standing courageously against the forces of evil. If there were a giant squid or a few crocodiles, she'd be even happier. I say that with respect," he added.

"I know you do, Max." They watched the last plane rise from Ingles City and head out over the Pacific. "We're running out of time," he muttered as they entered the house.

They found Lola Londi seated at the very center of her Empire divan. The velvet draperies were drawn, a lamp cast its soft illumination upon the Victorian splendors around her, and she did indeed seem to be enjoying herself. No queen could have accepted their salutations more graciously.

Verna sat in a silk-upholstered armchair nearby, with Tim Waverly hovering protectively behind her.

"I've got fifty men posted around the house, professor," he reported. "And all have martial arts experience. It would take an army to break in here now."

"Well done, Tim. But our toughest problem now seems to be, not keeping our enemies from getting in, but finding some means of getting ourselves out. Royal Beach has been effectively quarantined, and its telephone lines tapped. Though I doubt that any moves will be made against us unless we try to move first."

"But it's illegal, Professor," said Verna. "I mean, they can't just tap people's telephones like that. Haven't they ever heard of Watergate?"

"Men like Benton Ingles consider themselves above the law, Miss Malmrose. Nor can the people defend themselves against such lawless arrogance if not enough of them are informed about it. Perhaps no one but Benton Ingles himself knows exactly how many newspapers, magazines, or radio and television stations he controls, or how many state and national officials he has in his back pocket. Look at the way the attack on the house tonight was played up in the media."

"They scarcely mentioned my name," said Lola, with a toss of her head. "Nothing but nonsense about environmentalists picketing Delfred Bassett. As if he or his fish really mattered to anyone. Reporters once crowded hotel lobbies, waiting hours for me to emerge from the elevator. Yet not one has even telephoned me tonight. Delfred Bassett indeed! How humiliating to be ignored in favor of a man who looks like he should be chasing rabbits."

A faraway look crossed the face of Verna Malmrose, like the first glimmer of an idea still just beyond her grasp; but then she shook herself and concentrated on what Tedworth Vay was saying.

"All we can surmise at this moment is that Benton Ingles is determined to privatize the space program, and that the key to his machinations lies somewhere in the South Pacific."

"Where he murdered my brother," added Verna. "And where a couple of Delfred Bassett's ships have mysteriously vanished."

"The Limbo of the Lost," said Lola Londi. The vacant look in her eye suggested that this was not one of her lucid intervals. "Some call it the Devil's Sea, some the Lost Continent of Mu, the realm of forgotten lore. Hundreds of ships have vanished there down the centuries. Thousands for all we know. . . ."

Tedworth Vay allowed her to ramble harmlessly on about races of giants, space children, planetary tunnels, the pyramids of Egypt, and other mysteries now relegated by academics to the loony bin of science. Only when she began to curse her old enemies, the War Priests of Atlantis, did he ease her back to reality.

"We face the same problem with this mystery, Lola." He held her eyes, and spoke in a firm, authoritative voice. "Our evidence is too questionable for people of judgment to accept what we all know to be true. Are you listening to me, Lola? Yes, you are listening to every word I say. That's very good."

He paused to assure himself that she had indeed returned to lucidity before continuing:

"The death, or I should say murder, of Senator Worthing has so shocked Washington that nobody there is now inclined to defy Benton Ingles about anything. Only with concrete evidence can we expect any sort of investigation. And if we don't get that evidence ourselves, nobody will."

"That's exactly how my brother felt," said Verna. "He and his friends were supposed to be going out to investigate endangered fauna in the Marquesas. But he hinted they had other objectives, so secret he couldn't reveal them even to me."

"If we could somehow discover what those were, we'd have something concrete to investigate," he said. "Think, Miss Malmrose. Did your brother leave any clues about the real destination of his voyage?"

"One thing did make me curious at the time, now that you mention it. A few days before Vernon sailed, he checked out a book on the physical effects of radioactivity. He never mentioned the subject in conversation, but several times I saw him reading the book, and taking notes."

"Radioactivity? That is curious, because Senator Worthing, just before he died, was about to make inquiries at the Atomic Energy Commission. Your brother probably knew what Benton Ingles was up to, somewhere in the South Pacific. Alas, the knowledge died with him."

"Maybe not, Professor." Rhoda Dawn now spoke for the first time. "His visions may still speak to us."

"No, I've already gone through all his belongings, searching for clues," said Verna. "Every book and notebook, every drawer and box, every piece of clothing he owned. There was nothing. The natives who recovered his body in the Marquesas turned all his possessions over to the authorities, even his pocket change and wristwatch. Nothing there either."

"Did the wristwatch have a crystal?" asked Rhoda.

"Yes, it was a sea quartz watch, and had a liquid crystal display," said Verna, who now saw what the girl was driving at. "I also recovered the love crystal my brother wore. He believed they have special powers."

"They have," said Rhoda. "Can you get it for me?"

She shrugged. "I don't see how. It's in Albuquerque, but the house there is being watched, and the telephone tapped, and we're surrounded here in Royal Beach. Isn't that so, Professor?"

"Yes, but I have other resources. Write a note to your parents, reassuring them of your safety and innocence, and asking them to turn over to the bearer your brother's love crystal. Lola, have you some stationery Miss Malmrose can use?"

But she had again lapsed from complete lucidity, and replied to the question only by daydreaming out loud:

"The Lost Continent of Mu was the original home of the White Gods, and in a secret cave beneath the Sea of the Emerald Moon are hidden the Books of Lore, where the War Priests of Atlantis shall never find them. . . ."

They let her ramble on, while Maximo went for a writing pad, ballpoint pen, and portable desk for Verna, and Tedworth Vay went to the hall telephone. He returned just as the letter was being sealed.

"There," said Verna, handing it to him. "Now what?"

"Now we wait. My messenger has certain preparations to make before running the blockade. Are you finished with the portable desk? I have some writing of my own to do."

"Oh, I just thought of something," said Rhoda, rising hurriedly to her feet. "Domino and Dominique. With so much excitement, I forgot about them. I'd better go see if they're all right."

Verna gasped. "You mean they're here in the house? With Lakme on the loose. Oh, my goodness, she's so mean she might kill the poor things."

"I should have thought of that myself." Tedworth Vay put aside the portable desk. "We'd better find them right away. There's no time to lose."

They were all on their feet now, and the urgency in his voice jolted Lola Londi back to lucidity.

"Graziella, Maximo, help them search for their cats. Lakme has an unfortunate temperament, and may do them a mischief. Oh, had I only known the poor helpless creatures were at her mercy. With Minnie or Cio Cio or even Tosca we need not have worried. They were such darlings, and I miss them so. Why are you all just standing there? Save the poor kittens, if it is still humanly possible." She assumed a tragic pose, as though resigning herself to their doom.

But while everyone was indeed still standing around, who should come prancing into the room but Domino and Dominique themselves, parading Lakme between them like a center-ring act at the circus. They at once put her through her paces.

First they marched her around the room in perfect step; then they had her sit up and beg, then roll over, and at last dance on her hind legs. It was so incredible a performance that the audience was too flabbergasted to applaud.

"What a nice pussycat." Maximo chuckled.

"Come to mama, my darling." Lola patted the cushion beside her. "I never knew you were so clever."

Lakme hesitated to respond, and glanced from Domino to Dominique and then back again, as if asking permission. Evidently she got it, for she leapt joyously onto the divan, and purred and rubbed herself against her mistress with kittenish affection, in a feline transport of rapture, so happy was she to escape the restraints of her drillmasters.

"See how she loves me, Maximo," said Lola. "Just like dear Tosca. You remember how cuddly Tosca used to be?"

"Who could forget Tosca, bella signorina?" he said dryly.

"Ah, so many of my darlings now laid to rest, so many of my old friends now passed to eternal bliss." Lola seemed to gaze across the reaches of time, her expression one of melodramatic pathos.

Maximo knew what was coming, and settled himself in his armchair to listen. Lola was a fascinating raconteuse, and genuinely entertaining with her reminiscences of old Hollywood, especially to newcomers who had not heard her stories a hundred times before. This passed the time amiably, while they waited for Tedworth Vay's messenger to arrive.

At last Tim spotted one of his sentries standing hesitantly in the doorway, and excused himself. He was back in a few moments and whispered to Tedworth Vay:

"There's a man at the front door, Professor, who identifies himself only as Kelly. The sentries didn't want to let him in, and frankly I don't blame them. He looks like an assassin."

"That's Kelly, all right. Tell him I'll be right there, please."

He finished writing the third of three notes, sealed the envelopes, and slipped unobtrusively from the room, so as not to disrupt Lola's Hollywood anecdotes.

"Roscoe played as many pranks off screen as he did in front of the cameras." She now spoke about a famous comedian of silent movies she had known. "There was no such thing as air-conditioning in those days, and at the dining table, when somebody wasn't looking, he would catapult pats of butter with his knife so they stuck to the ceiling, right over the person's head. Then slowly the butter would melt, and the pats drop one by one into the person's hair. It was hilarious to watch their reaction. . . ."

It was after midnight before Tedworth Vay returned, and his first concern was for his young ward.

"Don't worry about me, Professor," said Rhoda. "Ghost Eagle taught me that we can reach the spirit world easiest at night, so I was always up after midnight on the reservation. When will Kelly get back with the crystal?"

"Tomorrow evening, if nothing goes wrong."

"That's the perfect time," she said. "Are we staying here tonight?"

"I'm not. I still have some work to do. But Lola has offered the rest of you her hospitality and protection. We should have no further worries about Domino and Dominique, now that they get along so well with Lakme." He glanced at Maximo, who chuckled again. "By the way, Tim, there's a telephone call for you in the vestibule."

He returned a few minutes later, looking sheepish.

"I think I'd better go home for a while, Professor," he excused himself. "That was my . . . that is, both my parents are worried about me and, well, they'd rather I slept in my own bed. So if you don't really need me for anything right now?" He reddened, careful not to look at Verna.

"I'll go with you, Tim," said Tedworth Vay, helping him out of his embarrassment. "If you don't mind dropping me off at the other side of town?"

The gathering was now breaking up for the night. Maximo lighted the samovar, and Graziella led young Rhoda, with Domino and Dominique trotting along in step behind her, up to her bedroom. Soon Verna was alone with Lola Londi.

"You look nervous, child," said the old woman. "A nice cup of tea will relax you."

"Oh, I'm sure it will," said Verna, who was in fact not sleepy at all, having again slept through most of the day. "Shall I make it? I remember your recipe."

"Would you, my dear?" Lola extricated herself with some difficulty from the affections of Lakme, who seemed never to want to let go of her again, and purred like a tiny motorboat. "Shall we play for the same stakes?"

"Stakes? Oh, gin rummy. Yes, that will be fine."

* * *

The following evening, in the soft blush of twilight, Verna felt herself transported across thousands of years into the pagan world of antiquity. The garden seemed now like some ancient Greek palestra, where among the statues of naked gods and goddesses living demi-gods worked out with barbells, dumbells, high and low pulleys, abdominal boards, exercise bikes, dipping sta-tions, thigh and knee machines, and various other bodybuilding equipment. There seemed to be a sepa-rate machine for every muscle in the human body, and these were splendid human bodies indeed.

Lola Londi strolled among them with the air of a connoisseur.

"Poor Carla." She sighed dramatically. "Naturally I want to help her in any way I can, but under existing circumstances I don't see how. Perhaps Professor Vay will find a means."

Verna felt self-conscious, among so many young men, about the feathered headdress Lola had insisted she wear to cover her shorn head. She much preferred her Dodgers baseball cap.

"When did Mrs. Ingles call?"

"Last night, while we were playing gin rummy. Maximo always turns on the telephone recorder before retiring to bed. The message was brief because Carla is on the run from her husband, and he's tapping all our telephones. Beastly man! She'll call back tonight, if he hasn't already murdered her by then."

. "Let's hope not," said Verna, wondering what Mrs. Ingles could tell them about her husband's machina-tions, should they somehow be able to bring her in from the cold.

Graziella had devoted long hours with her mistress on the "assembly line," and the results were eye-catching. She was painted to the gills. Though her frilly red parasol and gown of crimson lace might have been more appropriate on the set of *Jezabel* or *Gone With the Wind*. Some of the young bodybuilders were so startled by her twilight apparition that they literally dropped their barbells and gaped. Mistaking the true cause of their reaction, Lola was visibly pleased, and tended more and more to simper.

"It is some satisfaction to find that I am still admired, if only in a limited circle." A blond Hercules stared in astonishment at her as she passed, and she flashed him a smile with teeth as white and flawless as any factory in America could make them. "Though my work is still denied its due appreciation by the tasteless and uncivil audiences of today. Television commercials have numbed their senses. Yet even here I really shouldn't complain. The shooting of commercials aboard my yacht has been quite profitable for me."

Again Verna was struck by the glimmer of an idea just beyond her grasp. But then she noticed Maximo emerge from the house, with Lakme trotting along at his heels.

"School's out." He nodded toward the cat and grinned. "Her drill sergeants are now playing Nintendo games upstairs with young Rhoda."

Verna was chary about her legs, but Lakme was all affection now, especially toward her mistress.

"Mama's darling." Lola smiled as the cat purred and rubbed against her leg but did not risk disassembly by bending down to pet it. "How much she now reminds me of my dear Tosca." She took Verna's arm. "Come, my dear, I'll show you where all my darlings go in the end."

Tall clipped hedges, rose arbors, and a wrought-iron fence secluded a remote corner from the rest of the garden, like a family plot. An extraordinary number of graven memorials, mostly of cats but with an admixture of pugs and poodles, radiated from a central fountain: two bronze cats holding a conch shell, from which an endless stream of water plashed over a litter of playful bronze kittens.

"All my darlings are here," said Lola, "and all still dear to me."

Verna tactfully did not comment on how many pets

Lola had outlived; the oldest memorials were already corroded with verdigris. But it was the oldest of all that held her attention. A stylized leopard? she wondered.

"Ah, I see you're curious about Natasha." The old woman twirled her parasol coquettishly as she noticed one of the bodybuilders gawking at her over the hedge. "She accompanied me everywhere, and the newspapers ran stories and pictures of her, and how I kept a fierce jungle leopard on a golden chain. It was good publicity for a while, and amusing to see whole crowds shrink from her in hotel lobbies or train stations. For, you see, Natasha was really just an ocelot, and as playful as a kitten."

"There was a leopard in *Sidonia the Sorceress*," said Verna. "That's who I thought it might be."

"Not among my darlings," said Lola. "Mike was the name of that nasty brute. He wasn't housebroken, and his breath would have wilted your hair. After he bit the cameraman, did his business on the producer's shoes, and ate the wax fruit at a banquet scene, we donated him to the Los Angeles Zoo."

"Pardon, bella signorina," Maximo finally got a word in. "Professor Vay called to tell you that his messenger has returned from Albuquerque, and that he himself will be here shortly before midnight."

"The perfect hour for a seance," said Lola. "Professor Vay always knows these things. Oh, and look how my darling knows that I have a place here for her, too."

Lakme lay warming herself in the last rays of sunlight, among effigies of Siamese cats engraved with such names as "Minnie," "Cio Cio," and "Tosca," along with their respective dates. Maximo caught Verna's eye, and silently mouthed the word "Soon," twisting his hands as if he were wringing a neck.

"Oh, one thing more," he added aloud. "Mr. Waverly called and asked me to tell you that he couldn't return here until late. He promised his mother he'd stay home for dinner."

Verna sighed, and for an instant her own hands felt the urge to wring somebody's neck.

Tedworth Vay reappeared in the grand salon just before midnight, with a letter for Verna and her brother's love crystal.

"We're on our own," he reported. "I've pulled out all stops, contacted everyone of political importance I know, and not one dares make any move against Benton Ingles without concrete evidence in hand. The administration is reeling under the concerted attacks of his media empire upon failures in the space program. Congress is paralyzed by the death of Senator Worthing. The United Nations have just convened an emergency session."

"The part about the space program was on the evening news, professor," said Tim. "The president is trying to restore confidence in American technology, by demonstrating how efficiently the satellite network is carrying the communications overload, while we repair the UN Commstat."

"Did you watch the news while you were having dinner?" asked Verna, a bit too sweetly.

Tim reddened and looked sheepish. He knew he shouldn't have deserted his post to go home for dinner, but it had been easier at the time to yield to his mother's shrill insistence. Rather than argue with her about returning here tonight, he had shinnied down the drainpipe outside his bedroom window. He did not look forward to seeing her in the morning.

Everyone was present, including the three cats and Graziella, who had pleaded with her mistress to be allowed to attend a real seance, in hopes of learning from her uncle Luigi what he had done with a lost property deed. Nor could she be dissuaded by explanations of the real purpose of tonight's assembly.

Verna was more skeptical about their chances of learning anything about her late brother. She knew that Tedworth Vay regarded young Rhoda, dressed as usual in fringed buckskin, as the most powerful natural medium he had ever investigated. She had heard that Domino and Dominique played a mean game of chess, and with her own eyes had seem them rack up Nintendo scores she was certain were not humanly impossible. Yet even to have suggested, in any classroom back on campus, that occultists might not all be rank imposters, or that all spiritual phenomena were not hoaxes and delusions, would have gotten her nothing but sniggers and mockery.

Perhaps nothing so narrowed one's perspective these days as a college education. But she was determined to keep an open mind.

Her notion of a seance was a circle of people sitting in a darkened room, holding hands around a table, while a medium in gypsy clothes spoke in strange voices and exuded ectoplasm. Nothing like that happened tonight. The room was dark enough, with only a single lamp burning; but there was no table, no holding of hands in a circle, no strange voices or ectoplasm. Only Rhoda sitting Indian fashion in the middle of the floor, with a sketch pad open beside her.

"Ready, dear?" Tedworth Vay placed the love crystal on the carpet directly beneath her eyes, and faded back into the shadows.

No signal was given, but through some mystic rapport Domino and Dominique seemed to know exactly what was expected of them. They placed themselves on either side of the crystal, and gazed down at it with an intensity matching that of Rhoda herself. Minutes passed into minutes; then more minutes; then a quarter of an hour. There was not a sound.

The first disturbance of the eerie silence came in fact from the other side of the room. Lakme had been drowsing beside her mistress on the divan, her forepaws tucked nicely beneath herself, when she suddenly became agitated. Her fur stood on end, her ears flattened back, and she began to emit low plaintive sounds from deep in her throat. Lola calmed her with difficulty.

At last Rhoda began to sketch, slowly at first, then faster and faster. When the first sheet of her pad was cluttered with lines and shapes, Tedworth Vay emerged silently from the shadows, removed it, and faded back again. He repeated this operation again and again, until he had a whole sheaf of sketches. Then he noticed that Rhoda's hand had begun to tremble, and at once halted the proceedings.

Slipping the love crystal into his pocket, he carried her gently from the room, murmuring soft words of comfort and encouragement. Domino and Dominique also looked exhausted from the ordeal, but followed them in perfect step nonetheless.

Graziella was disappointed at not learning something about her uncle Luigi's estate, being milked by lawyers in a Sicilian probate court for decades, and received permission to retire. Verna, on the other hand, was not sure what to think—until she had actually seen what the girl had sketched. Lakme alone now seemed content, and purred and rubbed herself affectionately against her mistress on the divan.

"Lola, have you an atlas in your library?" asked Tedworth Vay, as he strode back into the room.

"Why are you just sitting here, Maximo?" she said. "You know where the atlas is, for I often consult it in my studies."

While Maximo was gone, Tedworth Vay laid out the sketches in a mosaic on the carpet, and thoughtfully walked round and round them, pondering over the disjuncted outlines, rough and careful drawings, jottings, and doodles from various angles.

"Here it is, Professor." Maximo handed him the oversized tome. "A work of art."

"Plate forty-seven is the most significant," said Lola. "It shows the ocean depths of the South Pacific in varying shades of blue. Looked at with an unprejudiced eye, one can detect the outlines of a great sunken land mass. Some believe this to be the Lost Continent of Mu."

Tedworth Vay nodded tactfully, and he was indeed comparing the shapes of Pacific land masses to one particular sketch on the floor, the most carefully drafted of all, which was clearly that of some mountainous island. Other sketches showed part of a boat, various birds and sea animals, and human faces.

Verna recognized three of the faces, and at least two more looked vaguely familiar, and hot tears welled in her eyes. The last time she had seen any of them they were still alive, and she covered her own face with her hands.

Meanwhile Tedworth Vay sat down with the sketch of the mountainous island, and pored over the atlas, map by map, plate by plate, with the meticulousness of a scholar. He seemed increasingly perplexed, until it all came to him in a flash.

"Radioactivity! That's it! Now I understand." He snapped the atlas shut and leapt to his feet. "This book is indeed a work of art, Max. But it was published in 1903. Please excuse me. I'll be back in an hour." And he rushed out the door with the sketch of the mountainous island.

"Where's he going now?" Tim wondered.

"Maybe home to dinner," Verna said dryly, but immediately apologized. "Sorry, Tim. That was mean. I'm just tired, and some of those sketches are of my brother's friends."

"I understand," he said, "and I'm sorry, too. I should never have deserted my post, for any reason. It's just that, well, my parents have done so much for me, and they're concerned about my missing so much schoolwork."

"The Business Administration department will still be there when you get back. Though if you're not really interested in the subject, I don't see why you'd be in any hurry to get there."

"It's a matter of being responsible, and I'm a responsible person. At least, I try to be. A career in the manufacturing or service industries can be as rewarding as any other. We can't go through life doing just the things we like."

She looked curiously at him. "Speak for yourself, Tim Waverly. I have the feeling you're letting others speak for you. You'll never be happy that way."

"People can be just as happy working to achieve market leadership for a major corporation, say, as starving in a furnished room, painting pictures nobody wants to buy."

"That's true, I suppose. But only if your heart is truly in the work. What could be sadder than consigning the best years of the only life you'll ever have to drudgery at some job you take no pride in? And for what? To make more money than you really need to live comfortably? Before you squander your youth and health, working yourself into migraines and ulcers, just to make a lot of money, mostly for other people, I think you should have some meaningful use for that money. If you don't, no matter how rich you become you'll never be happy."

"We all have to work," he said, frowning. "Except, of course, a privileged few. Why not make it the most profitable experience we can?"

" 'What shall it profit a man if he gain the whole world and lose his soul?' " she quoted. "Work, by all means. The happiest people I know have dedicated their lives to work. Happy, because they've found work that is more interesting than play." She glanced at him, and smiled disarmingly. "Don't mind me, Tim Waverly. Live and let live is always the wisest policy. I've been alone too much lately, trying to find out what really happened to my brother, and lonely people are prone to soul searching."

"I understand what you mean by loneliness." Now it was his turn to look curiously at her. "And it's true that the word happiness is not in the vocabulary of Business Administration courses."

"The happiest man I ever met," she said, "was an accountant from New York. That is, he had been an accountant there before he moved to Albuquerque. He was past the usual retirement age, but said he loved his work too much ever to retire. We sold his toys at our shop."

"Toys?"

"They were beautiful, and every one handmade. But it's a long story, and it's getting late."

"Tell it," he said. "We have nothing else to do until Professor Vay returns."

"All right, and it really is interesting. Mr. Shamsky, the man I'm talking about, owned a successful accounting firm in New York. He was a widower, with three children he had sent through expensive colleges, but he never saw them except when they needed money. He had worked six and seven days a week for years, under high pressure, and so spoiled his digestion that he was living on skim milk and baby food. But it was only when his children started urging him to set up living trusts for them, to avoid probate court, that he began to reflect seriously upon his life. He couldn't think of a better epitaph for himself than 'He Paid His Bills.' Which is not much to show for a lifetime of hard work and denial."

A snuffling sound attracted their attention, and they both glanced toward the divan. Lola had awakened from her doze, and looked about herself in bewilderment, as if not quite sure where she was. But then her eyelids began to flutter, and soon drooped shut again. Maximo stood at the window, peering stealthily out into the street from behind the draperies.

"Anyway," Verna continued, "Mr. Shamsky remembered the motto for a happy life taught him as a child by his grandfather: 'Find something you like, and stick with it.' His grandfather had been a toymaker in the old country, and a jolly soul till the day he died. By comparison, there had been little happiness in his own life. He had only become an accountant because his parents convinced him that it was his best chance to make money."

Tim winced but did not interrupt.

"So he started spending his Sundays away from the office, then his Saturdays, too, in a little workshop he secretly made for himself in his basement. He was clumsy at first with his tools, and for two years made nothing that really pleased him. But as his skills improved so did his enjoyment of the work, and he persevered. Then one day he made a mechanical elf that bowed and rolled its eyes, and actually sold it to a local toy store. He says it was the happiest moment of his life."

"But I thought you said you sold his toys at your shop in Albuquerque."

"I'm coming to that. After selling his first toy, he sold his accounting business, set up college trust funds for all his grandchildren, and that's when he moved to Albuquerque. He now gets up in the morning before the alarm rings, anxious to start his day's work, looks twenty years younger, and eats his tacos with red peppers. His one regret is that he lost so many precious years living according to somebody else's formula."

Tim had several economic and social objections he might have raised against so self-indulgent a manner of existence; but he saw now that they would really have been somebody else's objections, and that he, too, was living according to somebody else's formula. He stared thoughtfully at the carpet for several minutes without speaking.

Verna was afraid she may have hurt his feelings, or sounded too much like a nag, and they spoke of other subjects until at last Tedworth Vay returned.

"Here we are." He entered the room carrying two oversized volumes. "Praise be to librarians. What would life be without them?"

"Pretty dull and stupid, if you ask me," said Verna. "But what did you mean before about radioactivity?"

"That was the key. Lola's atlas is indeed a work of art, but it's nearly a century old."

"Land masses, even South Sea islands, don't change much in so short a time, professor," said Tim.

"They do if you drop enough hydrogen bombs on them."

He opened the two atlases, old and new, on the coffee table, placing beside them the sketch of the mountainous island. Lola had awakened at his entrance, and now slipped on her thick spectacles, curiosity momentarily overcoming vanity. The others gathered around.

"See how the island has changed," he said, "and how exactly its new configuration matches Rhoda's sketch. Miss Brandt, bless her heart, got out of bed to open the public library for me. I took some notes, and she'll get more information for me tomorrow. Sailing charts, and so forth. Though we still have to discover a means of getting there undetected by Benton Ingles."

"Where?" Tim peered from atlas to atlas.

"Sulatonga." Verna laid her finger in a green-and-brown patch, surrounded by solid blue. "But can we be sure, professor? After all, we have nothing here but the dream sketch of a little girl."

"We can't be sure," he admitted. "But we have nothing better to go on, and no way of verifying our discovery in the short time we have left, without also alerting Benton Ingles."

"Carla would know," said Lola, slipping her spectacles out of sight again. "A Sicilian wife looks upon any attempt by her husband to conceal his business from her as a challenge. What time is it, Maximo?"

"Time to bring you the telephone, bella signorina. It's almost the hour Mrs. Ingles said she'd call you again, if they haven't murdered her." He hurried from the room.

"Lola, this is very, very important." Tedworth Vay sat down beside her and gently took her hand. "You must not even hint at the name Sulatonga over the telephone. Everything you say will be recorded, and the least suspicion we've discovered their base of operations—assuming we have—would be the end of us all. I'll try to get Mrs. Ingles to a place of safety, and discover whatever she knows without her knowing it. But I can only hope to succeed if Benton Ingles and his thugs never suspect that we're on to them."

"Omerta rules," she said.

Maximo returned with the cordless telephone, and they all sat around the coffee table watching it.

CHAPTER XIV

The call was sure to be traced, so the conversation was no more than a brief exchange of code words, in a Sicilian dialect strange even to Maximo. Yet Lola adroitly picked up all the information they needed.

"Carla will be in the twenty-four-hour supermarket in Cedar Lake, at midnight tomorrow," she reported. "She can be there no more than ten minutes, because not only her husband's thugs are now after her but also the state police."

"I'll have a reliable man there, to take her to a safe refuge," said Tedworth Vay, taking notes. "Did Mrs. Ingles understand the password? And you're sure no eavesdropper will understand what she told you? An Italian translator, for instance."

"Benton Ingles has a low regard for the capabilities of women. Any translator he hires is sure to be a man, and we spoke in the code language known only to Sicilian schoolgirls. It was charming to hear again, after so many years. Carla and I did not, shall we say, attend classes at the same time. But these things never change."

"Sulatonga has certainly changed," said Verna, comparing the two atlases. "How many H-bombs were exploded there anyway, Professor?"

"That's still classified information. Miss Brandt is researching the matter for me at the library, and perhaps we'll have more data tomorrow. All we know at the moment is that Sulatonga was a major test site for hydrogen bombs, in the early Fifties."

"Does anyone live there now?" asked Tim.

"That's another mystery," he said. "For some reason, the original native population has never been repatriated. Exactly why, or what's going on there now, or where Benton Ingles comes in, I'm relying on Miss Brandt to discover for me."

"I doubt that she'll find much," said Verna. "If my brother, with all the resources of the Greenworld Society at his disposal, had to risk his life to discover what was going on there, it's a sure bet that Benton Ingles has covered his tracks."

"Yes, and it's beginning to look more and more as if we're in the same boat. And speaking of boats, your brother and his friends had at least a means of investigating their suspicions. Right now, we can't even get ourselves out of Royal Beach."

"Consider the *Sidonia* yours, professor," said Lola. "It's been completely refurbished for television commercials, with all costs written off my taxes. I have a lucrative new contract from a beer company, and my agent is now negotiating with a manufacturer of aftershave lotion. So I can write off the expenses of any voyage you make, be it to the Lost Continent of Mu itself."

"That's generous of you, Lola," he said. "But has your yacht anchored anywhere near Royal Beach lately?"

"Now that you mention it, I haven't seen the *Sidonia* myself, these thirty years. Except, of course, on television. But there, at least, it seems as beautiful as the day it was first given to me, by that poor man who jumped out a window."

"It is a beautiful yacht, Lola. What I mean is that we're in the bag, surrounded by thugs who are waiting only for the right moment to move in and liquidate us all. The arrival of the *Sidonia* here would at once tell Benton Ingles that we were on to him, and force his hand."

"Then there's no chance of bringing Carla here, professor? I've often suggested to her that she have her lawyers negotiate a settlement with her husband— beastly man!—and live here in Royal Beach. She plays a fair game of gin rummy. In any case, she's earned her service stripes by now."

"Too dangerous, Lola. Kelly will see to it that Mrs. Ingles comes to no harm, but he himself had trouble running the blockade. Royal Beach is off the beaten track, with tourism as its sole industry, and a very minor one at that. It's because so few people come here that Benton Ingles has been able to quarantine us so effectively."

"We need more people coming here," said Verna, in a flash of inspiration. "Thousands, tens of thousands, flooding every road and byway into Royal Beach. Any blockade of the town would be overwhelmed by sheer numbers."

"Yes, but why would so many people come here at the same time?" He looked curiously at her.

"A film festival. The Lola Londi Retrospective Film Festival, to be exact. That's what I've been trying to think of for so long. Sure, and it's really long overdue. Your films have never gotten the recognition they deserve, Lola."

"I've never been one to complain." She assumed her haughtiest demeanor. "But since you've raised the subject, I must say that it is a national disgrace."

"A brilliant concept, Miss Malmrose," said Tedworth Vay. "But I'm afraid that the organization and publicity needed to make such an event a success would require far more time than we have at our disposal."

"Maybe not," she said. "Look how fast Tim rounded up his friends to guard the house. There are thousands of bodybuilders in California, women as well as men, and they have friends, lovers, spouses, and relatives. There are more thousands of environmentalists, still more thousands of movie buffs, and student film societies all over the state. They'd be on the road within hours after getting the word—Benton Ingles. His name would act like a talisman, an Open Sesame! to everyone who loves freedom, nature, and humanity. We can start mimeographing invitations first thing in the morning."

"We don't have to wait that long," said Tim, and strode decisively from the room.

"Excellent, Miss Malmrose," said Tedworth Vay, caught up in her enthusiasm. "Your idea also solves the problems of bringing the *Sidonia* to Royal Beach, without also bringing an avalanche of thugs down on our necks. So famous a yacht would naturally be featured at any Lola Londi film festival. How soon could you get it here, Lola?"

Her right eye half closed as she calculated. "Three days, perhaps four, under its own power. But the advertising agencies that use it for commercials always have it towed on location."

"So could we," he said. "And that would solve another problem, assuming we can make suitable arrangements. It's a long way to Sulatonga for so frail a vessel as the *Sidonia,* but your admirer Delfred Bassett owns some of the largest commercial ships afloat, and they sail everywhere."

"Especially the coasts of defenseless Third World countries, whose economies they ruin for years to come," added Verna. "Though I'd swallow even that—for now, at least—if it would help us get the goods on Benton Ingles. But after the cowardly way he behaved at the garden party, he'd never see me."

"He shall see you, my dear," said Lola Londi. "He's staying at the Royal Beach Astoria, under the pretense of a vacation, but really in hopes of winning my favors. The presumptuous hound! Once you let a cad like that buy you diamonds, he thinks he can go right on doing it." She tossed her head, and assumed a regal bearing impossible to surpass. "He'll see you, or he's bought me his last diamond."

Tim returned, looking pleased. "The response to

your idea, Verna, was terrific. Eddie Sutton teaches high school English, and Nick Featherman works in a print shop. They'll have the invitations ready for mass mailing by the time the post office opens in the morning."

"And I shall telephone Mr. Delfred Bassett before then," said Lola, with another toss of her head. "Assuming he's not already out somewhere, chasing rabbits."

The Royal Beach Astoria was a relic of the Gilded Age, a painted lady of gabled roofs, leisurely verandas, and sumptuous decor. It had indulged the robber barons of one era, pampered the bootleggers of another, and now, renovated to all its pristine swank, coddled an international clientele of jet setters, coupon clippers, corporate raiders, and CEOs. Increasing numbers of Japanese businessmen enjoyed themselves here in Occidental luxury, relaxing from the exertions of buying up the country. Among the American businessmen resident was Delfred Bassett, the fish tycoon.

"Mr. Bassett is taking tea, Miss Jones," said the desk clerk, a sniffy young prig costumed in a frock coat and salt-and-pepper trousers. "He's expecting you."

Verna's own costume included a flamboyant turban, which, though it concealed her shaven head, made her feel like Carmen Miranda. It was late afternoon, and she had needed several cups of strong coffee to get herself going, after a night of gin rummy with a samovar bubbling nearby. Was she becoming a tea junkie? She had been dealt good hands, and had played them skillfully enough, but had still been unable to wrest the twenty dollar gold piece away from her opponent, whose lucid intervals, except for occasional babble about the War Priests of Atlantis, had been nearly continuous.

Sometime during the night Lola had left a message here for Delfred Bassett, virtually a command for him to see a "Miss Jones" the following afternoon. There were too many policemen now on the lookout for a Miss Malmrose.

Verna removed her sunglasses as she entered the charmingly old-fashioned tea room, and glanced around. Three Japanese business people, two single gentlemen, and an elegantly groomed young woman, dominated the center of the room. A scattering of America guests, including a pair of matrons who looked as shrewd about money as Lola herself, sat at remoter tables. But there was no sign of Delfred Bassett.

Puzzled, she was about to retreat, when she caught the eye of the busboy. He may have been costumed in Victorian formality, but his self-assured impudence was California modern. He winked and flicked his eyes toward a corner table. More puzzled still, she advanced hesitantly across the room toward it.

The first thing she noticed was a shoe peeking out from beneath the linen tablecloth, then a foot inside the shoe, then a trousered leg. Still advancing, she at last realized that there was a man hiding under the table, and that the man was Delfred Bassett. She stopped and waited.

Finally, a baldish head with long, floppy ears rose tentatively over the edge of the table, and a pair of baggy eyes peered stealthily around the teapot, to see if the coast was clear. What they met, instead of the re-assurance of a few civilized people sedately enjoying their tea, were the eyes of a determined young woman loaded for bear. With a surprised grunt, the head vanished again.

But it was clearly no use, and after a couple more minutes the baldish head and baggy eyes reappeared, followed by the rest of Delfred Bassett. There was a tinge of red about his long, floppy ears as he dusted his trousers.

"I dropped something under the table," he explained lamely. "Lola, that is Miss Londi, left a message that

she would be sending a Miss Jones here to see me this
afternoon. I had no idea it was you."

Verna had already guessed as much. He had evidently seen her before she saw him, and reacted as cra-
venly as he had at the garden party.

"I'd like to discuss an important matter with you,
Mr. Bassett," she said.

He suppressed a groan. "Won't you join me in a
sugar bun and a cup of tea?" he asked discouragingly.

"I prefer coffee, thank you," she said, sitting down
without his assistance, which he made no gesture of
offering in any case.

As the coffee was being served, she again caught the
eye of the busboy, who continued shamelessly to enjoy
the scene. The Japanese trio on the other hand were too
polite to stare, but it was clear they considered the behavior of Americans inscrutable.

Assuring herself the others were out of earshot, she
came straight to the point, resolutely exploiting the influence of Lola Londi to support her request.

Delfred Bassett suppressed another groan, squirmed
in his seat, and sighed disconsolately. Never had she
seen so hangdog a look on any human face.

Miles away and hours later, Carla Ingles also tried to
conceal herself beneath a restaurant table. There were
few other customers in the Amber Light. The midnight
rush, when the second shift ended at the nearby industrial park, when longhaul truckers broke their over-
night runs, and the local movie houses let out, had not
yet begun. She had hoped to outwit her pursuers, but
succeeded only in outsmarting herself.

She had long known of Kurt Grotten's sadistic brutality toward underlings; on three separate occasions
she had watched him mete out discipline with his own
fists; but only now did she appreciate the deviousness
of his mind. The last place he should have searched for
her was anywhere so public and familiar as the Amber
Light. Yet here he was; she could hear him out in the

vestibule, near the cashier's counter, interrogating the waitress in his affected baritone.

She held her breath. The waitress was none other than the First Runner Up, in the ill-fated Miss World contest of years ago, who might naturally be expected to give her away. That she did not was a wonder.

Then through the clatter and murmur of the main dining room she heard approaching footsteps, and tried to scrunch herself tighter beneath the table, thankful for its overhanging cloth. Kurt Grotten trusted nobody, and would inevitably test with his own eyes any disavowal of her being here. She now regretted that she had spent so much time in other restaurants, not to mention all the banquets, receptions, and dinner parties, and that she could not scrunch herself together tighter still.

The table was in a remote corner of the dining room, almost an alcove, where she could not be seen through any window. She had hoped to lie low here until it was time to keep her midnight rendezvous in Cedar Lake. In fact, she had been just preparing to leave the restaurant, when she was startled by Grotten's voice in the vestibule, and dived for cover.

The suspense was unnerving, but at last the footsteps retreated, and moments later she heard the tinkle of the front door opening and closing. She sighed with relief, unwound herself, and stiffly climbed out from beneath the table. Grotten would certainly keep the roadhouse under surveillance, while he searched for her elsewhere, so she dared not use the front door herself. She had plenty of money, thousands in cash, and laid a hundred dollar bill beside her coffee cup.

"The man ordered me to call him if you came here tonight," said the waitress, whose first angelic beauty had gained character from her years of disappointment and travail. She spoke with an Austrian accent that made her quiet voice sound both sad and charming. "I said that yes I would, but I would never help such a man. He is like the evil men who ruined my country when my mother and father were young."

"They ruined my country, too," said Carla. "Can I get out the back door? The front door is sure to be watched."

"Follow me," said the waitress, and led the way through the kitchen and out into the night. "See that fence around the dumpster there, and the trees and bushes behind it? They will screen you from sight."

"Thanks for everything," said Carla, with a humility new to her. "You've saved my life."

"It is my pleasure to help you, who have done so much to help me. I would never have gotten this job except for you, and my dear children would have suffered. God bless you and keep you from harm."

Carla did not feel very proud of herself as she slipped into the night. Glancing over her shoulder, she circled the dumpster fence, screened herself behind a stand of bushes, and skirted the employee parking lot undetected.

The suburban bus stop was not crowded at this hour—a fat woman with a package, two factory hands with lunch pails, and a sailor—and she concealed herself behind a shuttered newsstand close by. She wore a headscarf pulled forward, blue jeans, and a Los Angeles Dodgers warmup jacket; a shrewd disguise, but Kurt Grotten's police resources were overwhelming. It was a miracle she had evaded recapture this long. Should the agent being sent to her aid fail to make contact, or had the hasty exchange of schoolgirl code words over the telephone been misunderstood, on either end of the line, she might never get another chance.

With the grind of ill-fitted brakes and the whoosh of compressed air, the grimy blue-and-yellow bus pulled up at the curb and opened its front door. She waited till the sailor, the last passenger in line, had his foot on the step, before rushing out of concealment and boarding right behind him.

Luxury sport cars and chauffeured limousines, with an occasional taxicab, were her customary means of transportation. This was her first bus ride in America, and she watched to see how much money the sailor put into the fare box, and did exactly the same. The driver handed her a transfer. She was not sure what she was supposed to do with it, but did not want to make herself conspicuous and stuffed it into her pocket, and took a seat at the back.

Her ruse of switching cars would not long fool so cunning a policeman as Kurt Grotten, and she checked her bus schedule. Cedar Lake was the next suburb after Lionel, and she listened alertly to each stop called out by the driver. People got on the bus, people got off the bus: shabby, ill-dressed people, grubby and cheesy fat: the under class of America. She pulled her headscarf forward, and kept her face turned from the window. The sailor had made a pass at her; but that was one situation she had always known how to handle, and he did not persist.

"Lionel!" the driver called out at last.

The time between stops was longer now, and she did not want to attract attention to herself by standing too long at the rear door, where she might also be spotted by a passing squad car. She sat tensely on the edge of her seat, until the driver finally called out "Cedar Lake!"

Two other people got off with her, a fat man with a newspaper under his arm, who immediately lit a fat cigar, and a dumpy little woman carrying two shopping bags. The bus stop was in front of an old movie theater, already closed for the night; but she could not see the supermarket where she was supposed to contact the agent, and had to ask directions.

"It's right in the middle of the Eagle Shopping Center," replied the woman with the shopping bags. "Go down Main St. here to the Valley Lanes bowling alley, and turn left. You can't miss it."

Carla thanked her, but as she started off in the direction indicated she noticed that the fat man with the cigar was staring at her. Was he suspicious? Or was it only the usual reason men stared at her?

She was certainly stared at in the bowling alley. Nothing else was open this late, and midnight was still thirty minutes away. The supermarket was sure to have a security guard, and she could hardly push a shopping cart up and down the aisles for that long without looking suspicious. Nor could she wander the deserted streets of Cedar Lake unnoticed. The lanes were surprisingly crowded for this time of night, and the thunder of rolling balls and the explosive clatter of pins were deafening. There was nothing she could do about the stares, but by moving continually around she avoided inconvenient passes.

It was exactly three minutes to twelve when she strode through the automatic doors of the supermarket. And there stood the security guard, in the blue uniform of a B.I.T.E. affiliate, something she had not expected this far outside of Ingles City. Kurt Grotten sneeringly referred to these guards as "bluebirds," but that would not stop his mobilizing them to help track her down. In any case, it was too late now to retreat.

The fluorescent lighting was hard and garish, and there were mirrors or miniature surveillance cameras everywhere to discourage shoplifters. She detached a shopping cart from the long file just inside the entrance, and wheeled it down an aisle stacked with colorful boxes of breakfast cereal, trying to look inconspicuous. But just before she reached the head of the aisle, she could not resist a glance back. The bluebird was watching her intently.

She turned down an aisle stacked with canned goods on one side and cookies and crackers on the other, out of the guard's direct line of vision. But there was no evading the omnipresent mirrors and surveillance cameras, and she forced herself to move slowly along, dropping random cans, jars, and boxes into the cart, trying to look inconspicuous. She had picked this supermarket from a newspaper advertisement, mostly because it was out of Ingles City and the words "cedar" and "lake" had code equivalents in her schoolgirl language. Now she wondered if she had made the right choice for a rendezvous.

It was completely self service. The twenty or so other people wheeling shopping carts through the vast glitter of merchandise were all of the same grubby, cheesy-fat type she had seen on the bus. The only employee she saw was a butcher, in a white cap and bloodstained apron, sorting packets of meat at a freezer rack. But there was no sign of the agent who was supposed to contact her.

At last she glanced at her watch: thirteen minutes past twelve: she dared wait no longer. Wheeling her cart around a produce table, cobbled with fresh grapefruits, she cut through the pet-food section, and passed racks of gaudy paperbacks and magazines, on her way to the cash register.

She would toss her purchases in the nearest bushes, and let herself get picked up at the bowling alley. Whatever else that entailed, she would at least gain a safe place to stay the night. Knowing Kurt Grotten, there was by now probably no hotel, motel, or bed-and-breakfast in all California without her photograph at the reception desk.

There was only one cash register in operation; the other seven check-out lanes were plugged with shopping carts, leaving a single exit from the store. But as she approached it, she noticed through the front windows that the bluebird was now outside at the curb, where three unmarked cars had just pulled up. Doors flew open, and a squad of thuggish plainclothes men vomited onto the sidewalk. She quickly wheeled her cart down an aisle stacked with towels, napkins, toilet tissue, lunchbags, plastic wrap, and paper plates, struggling with every step to conceal her panic.

She was relieved to find that not a single customer now browsed the tiers of freezer racks, opulent with fantastic selections of dairy products, cold cuts, delicatessen items, cartoned juices, eggs, fish, meat, and poultry. A stanchion screened a corner here from any mirror or surveillance camera; it was the one blind spot she had noticed in the entire store, but she froze as she emerged from the aisle of gourmet foods. The butcher she had seen here earlier still stood at the same rack, sorting the same packages of meat.

Hurrying footsteps were now audible several aisles away. Panic nearly overwhelmed her, and her knees felt both weak and stiff as she began to retreat.

But then she hesitated. A butcher, working at this time of night? In California? So far as she knew, every butcher in the state was a union man, and never worked past five in the afternoon. And was it just a coincidence that he had not budged all this time from the store's one surveillance blind spot? Cautiously, she wheeled her cart back toward him.

A closer inspection was not reassuring. He had the look of an assassin, and she checked to see that he had no meat cleaver within reach, before edging any closer. She was now safely within the blind spot, right behind him. But still he did not seem aware of her presence.

"Omerta rules," he whispered without looking up at her, and disappeared around the end of the tiered freezer racks.

That was the password, and she peered around the rack after him, and discovered a curtained doorway. The hurrying footsteps were closer now. With an anxious glance over her shoulder, she wheeled her cart into a dim enclosure smelling of dead animals. Then a hand took her firmly by the elbow, and led her through a steel door and out onto a loading dock.

The next thing she knew, she was crouching on the floor of a delivery van as it sped into the night. Not until they were several blocks from the supermarket did the driver at last nod to her, and she unwound from her crouch into the passenger's seat beside him. Without his butcher's cap and apron he looked more than ever like an assassin.

"I am Khalid Aslanov, sometimes known as Kelly," he introduced himself. "My instructions are to keep you safe until further notice. And so, beautiful lady, you may consider yourself safe—until further notice."

A glimpse of feline humor flitted across his assassin's countenance. He drove the van within the speed limit, but with one eye fixed on the rearview mirror.

CHAPTER XV

It was a hectic week in and around the mansion of Lola Londi. Her name was blazoned on billboards, placards, banners, and illustrated posters all over Royal Beach; thousands poured into the city for the opening of her film festival; every hotel, motel, and bed-and-breakfast for miles around was booked to capacity, and motley tent cities made the parks and beaches look like an invasion of Arabs.

Opportunistic vendors were already peddling Lola Londi coffee mugs, Lola Londi T-shirts, Lola Londi pennants and bumper stickers, Lola Londi statuettes of "durable cast stone" (i.e., plaster), and a colorful Lola Londi pasta cookbook, along with reprint posters of all her major films.

The Fremont, Royal Beach's oldest and most palatial movie house, was gauded up as for a Hollywood premier, replete with a tinseled bandstand and searchlights, for the first presentation of *Sidonia the Sorceress*. The very organ that had accompanied the original showing of the film here, well before the installation of sound equipment or air-conditioning, would accompany its reshowing tonight, courtesy of the Hallelujah Baptist Church, which had gratefully accepted its donation some sixty years past.

The Sons of Paradise, resplendent in new gold-braided uniforms, with shiny new flashlights, were to be installed at tonight's presentation as Honorary Ushers of the Fremont Theater, in recognition of their long service and fidelity. Three members of the club had, in

fact, been ushers at the Fremont at the original showing of the film. All were untiring in their efforts to
make the festival a memorable success, in homage to
their goddess.

Verna Malmrose was exhausted. There were dark
circles under her eyes, the result of the too hectic festival preparations by day and staring at too many gin-
rummy cards at night. But at least she was no longer
softening into flab. She now had two aerobics tapes,
bought for her by Tim Waverly, which she alternated
for her daily workouts.

Domino and Dominique also seemed to miss regular
conditioning, and both worked out with her each afternoon in front of the television set. Their vigor and
agility made her feel positively oafish, and she sometimes lost concentration by stopping to watch them.
They exaggerated each exercise to an extraordinary degree, with a team coordination that was almost supernatural. Their pushups carried them a good six feet off
the floor.

Fresh from the shower, she donned an old-fashioned
summer frock, as bright and flouncy as anything in
Maytime or *Meet Me in St. Louis*. This was Lola
Londi's day of days, and the old woman dismissed
contemporary fashions as "clothes for golliwogs."
Verna did not waste any time primping before a mirror,
because she still had so little to primp. Her burr head
and period frock made her look uncomfortably like a
Prussian officer in drag. But the house was quiet for
the first time in a week as she descended to the morning room.

She found Rhoda watching Domino and Dominique
rack up yet another astounding score at Nintendo. As
in everything else they did, the two cats worked as a
team. While Domino concentrated on the screen with
vibrant intentness, Dominique manipulated the
controls—never once glancing up—faultlessly and at
nil reaction time. They never missed.

A whole crate of Nintendo games and instructional

videos had been acquired for their entertainment, so there should be no trouble leaving them behind. Certainly not from Lakme, who seemed almost a nice pussycat these days. Rhoda, on the other hand, would accompany the voyage to Sulatonga. Her clairvoyant powers could prove invaluable in identifying the will-less servitors—whose ranks had very nearly included herself—now being insinuated into key positions everywhere by Benton Ingles.

As expected, his name had worked like a talisman, conjuring up tens of thousands to attend the film festival, whose swelling numbers swept every road leading into Royal Beach clear of barricades. His media empire had waged a pitiless campaign of sleaze and innuendo, to discredit both the cinematic achievements of Lola Londi and the festival itself. But as is ever the case with giving anything a bad press, he succeeded only in doubling the box office.

Tedworth Vay had meanwhile used his own contacts in the Media to promote the festival, and to lay the groundwork for the news bombshell that would follow any discoveries on Sulatonga. Something big was in the offing, something big in some manner connected with the space program. Yet there still lingered the nagging doubt that they were all going on a wild goose chase.

Miss Brandt, the librarian, though hampered in her researches by the need for absolute security, had nonetheless uncovered every scrap of information about Sulatonga available from local sources. She was told only that any query about the subject to repositories outside Royal Beach would have dire consequences, but that had been enough to insure her perfect discretion.

Getting to Sulatonga would be the easy part. Delfred Bassett had promised a tow by one of his sea factories—his first doggish reluctance overcome by a second telephone call from Lola Londi—and the *Sidonia* already rode at anchor off Royal Beach. In fact, it was to read abut the docking of the palatial yacht that Verna had come down to the morning room. She sat quietly by the window, so as not to disturb the Nintendo players.

Lakme lay drowsing on the next cushion, her paws tucked beneath her chest, her eyes seemingly closed, but aware as always of the exact whereabouts of Domino and Dominique. Verna reached across her without apprehension, and unrolled the *Royal Beach Mirror*.

And there was the *Sidonia*, with all her pennons flying, in a full color spread on the front page. A caption referred the reader to page 14 for more pictures, and there were twinned stories about the respective careers of Lola Londi and the yacht. Prominent in the latter was the news of how popular the *Sidonia* had become for television commercials, and of how it would soon be leaving again, for a mini-series about a Hollywood scandal of the Twenties.

Verna rerolled the newspaper. Yes, the *Sidonia* would soon be leaving all right, but not for Hollywood. They would rendezvous with their tow ship in the Revillagigedo Islands, hundreds of miles off the coast of Mexico. Then on to Sulatonga—and what? The exposure to some greedy and illegal scheme against humanity? Or a thankless and miserable death, like that of her brother and all his shipmates? Perhaps the worst scenario of all would be for them merely to end up on a desert island, while Benton Ingles assaulted the freedoms of the world from some other base of operations.

That problem was being wrangled at this very moment by Tedworth Vay, the most resourceful man she had ever met. All had played their individual parts in orchestrating the Lola Londi Retrospective Film Festival, but throughout the enterprise he had been the conductor, the maestro who alone understood the complete score, what it meant and how best to achieve a harmony of purpose. Where he was now, or exactly what he was doing, nobody knew.

She glanced toward the video screen, and smiled at

how strangely the human mind could accustom itself through familiarity to the weirdest and most improbable things. Here were two cats playing Nintendo with supernatural skill, and poor Tim Waverly, try as he might, had yet to defeat them at chess. Though he claimed that in one game he did so exceptionally well that he might have offered a draw—had he known how to communicate the offer.

The cats gave an uncanny impression of always knowing what was happening around them, sometimes of even comprehending human speech. But any attempt, by whatever means, to discover their origins met only a stone wall of resistance, as if their very instincts had been conditioned against exactly such probing.

Yet they themselves were into everything, although never destructively like other cats. Artifact by artifact, they analyzed with superfeline curiosity each new manifestation of humanity they came across, and seemed to comprehend within minutes its inner workings. Their usual reaction was like adult condescension toward the playpen contrivances of children. Unless that was only her imagination.

Tim said that he also tended to impute human reactions to Domino and Dominique, insisting he could sense their glee whenever they beat him at chess. But as to how they had acquired their astounding intelligence, he could offer no better explanation than to repeat what he himself had been told—that they were escapees from a top-secret experiment in genetic engineering. It seemed plausible, because she had nearly ended up a top-secret experiment herself.

Verna could never forget Tim's courage in rescuing her, or the sacrifices he had made on her behalf ever since, though she could have wished that his mother did not telephone him here quite so often, and that he did not look quite so guilty afterward. She wondered if he had mustered the fortitude yet to inform her about his forthcoming absence from both school and home.

The story about his attending a Greenworld rally was credible, and all reasonable objections had been prepared for in advance. But had he told her yet? It could be a disaster if she made inquiries of the police while Tim was voyaging to Sulatonga.

Lakme had snuggled into her lap, and was reluctant to lose a potential ally against her relentless drillmasters. But since they were both within ten feet of her, she allowed herself to be set back on the cushion without so much as a meow of protest. Both cats shot her a simultaneous look of admonition, and she at once closed her eyes and began to purr.

Verna thought whimsically about teaching them how to play gin rummy; perhaps during her absence they could give Lola more of a challenge than she herself ever had. The Nintendo score they had just achieved was phenomenal.

"I hate to leave them behind," said Rhoda, as Verna rose to depart. "But Professor Vay thinks they're the greatest mystery he's ever come across, and he's afraid of their being lost or hurt before he can investigate them properly. I guess it's pretty dangerous where we're going, isn't it?"

"Yes, I believe so." Verna appreciated how Rhoda refrained from mentioning the name Sulatonga, even between themselves, just as Tedworth Vay had cautioned them. This strange little girl was nearly as mysterious to her as Domino and Dominique themselves. "Are you afraid?"

"No, I don't think so," she replied, after pondering a moment. "Not so long as Professor Vay is with us. I always feel safe when he's around, like no matter how bad things get he'll always figure a way out."

Verna felt that way herself. She left Rhoda playing Nintendo—the girl also ran up record scores, though only human records—and started toward the rear door. But an unexpected bustle in the front hallway of the mansion attracted her curiosity, and she turned that way instead.

Several of Tim's bodybuilder friends, who were billeted to crew the *Sidonia*, were unpacking an unmarked crate. Its contents surprised her. She knew that Tedworth Vay had secretly been assembling various odd equipment, but why radiation suits? Forty years and more had passed since Sulatonga had been an H-bomb site. With all the other perils they would have to face, were they also in danger of radiation poisoning?

She ran her fingers lightly over the crown of her head. It would be a shame to lose her hair all over again, now that she had grown at least a respectable crew cut. Tim said she looked cute that way, but she knew he was only being kind. He did seem to be a genuinely kind person. He might sometimes be puppyish in his attentions, with old-fashioned manners and opinions—about some things, at least—but a welcome relief from the macho jerks who were always hitting on her on campus. They asked for a date as if they were conferring a blessing.

She looked everywhere for him out in the garden. A dozen young Apollos, also set to crew the *Sidonia*, were working out on bodybuilding machines; but Tim was not among them. She found him at last beneath the colonnade where he had rescued her from abduction, the night of the raid. Unfortunately, he was not alone.

A blue haze of cigarette smoke fouled the air. The middle-aged woman with Tim had probably once been attractive, but decades of heavy smoking, overeating, junk foods, and lack of exercise had taken their toll. Her thick spectacles suggested that she spent most of her waking hours with her eyes glued to a television screen; though the eyes were still cunning and suspicious. She was obviously accustomed to getting her own way.

"Mother, this is, uh, Cynthia," said Tim, painfully embarrassed. "She's going to the Greenworld rally, too. Cynthia, this is my mother."

"Hello, Mrs. Waverly," said Verna. "I'm happy to meet you."

She saw at once that the feeling was not mutual. The woman responded with a curt nod, and her eyes narrowed with suspicion and dislike. But why Cynthia? Was Tim so embarrassed that he could not remember her real name?

Then it struck her like a thunderclap. She had been so sheltered and protected here that she had nearly forgotten that she was wanted for murder, and that her picture, both with hair and without, had been shown on television screens throughout the country. Her hand started to move toward her shorn head, and though she checked the reflex, it was evident that it had not been missed. Mrs. Waverly's eyes narrowed still more with hostility and suspicion.

"I just came out to tell you we're nearly packed, Tim." Verna was now painfully embarrassed herself. But Tim had already told his mother the story about the Greenworld rally, and that was the main thing. "The rally is in Tucson, Mrs. Waverly, so we're driving down there at night, to miss the desert heat. Please excuse me now. I'm so happy to have met you."

Mrs. Waverly again responded with only a curt nod, and watched her with a vaguely puzzled look, as though trying to remember something, while she strode back to the house through the shadows of late afternoon. Then she turned once more to her son.

"I'm surprised at you, Timothy. You used to be a more responsible person. First you leave your studies, without so much as a word to your parents, after all the sacrifices your father and I have made to see that you got a good education. Now you're traipsing off like a hippie to God knows what kind of orgy. You never used to be interested in that sort of claptrap."

"I've already made arrangements to make up for lost schoolwork, Mother," he said, unable to hold her eye.

"It's not that girl who's leading you astray, is it?" She nodded with suppressed anger in the direction Verna had just taken. "How many times have I warned you, like a good mother, that you have to be careful about which people you associate with? Don't you realize, Timothy, that all your past acquaintanceships will be investigated by any reputable corporation you work for, when you go out into the business world? Especially your female acquaintanceships. . . ."

She brusquely lit another menthol cigarette, tossing aside the match as if she were slapping his face, as she continued to berate her son. It was the sharpest tonguelashing he had endured in years, and though it left him feeling thoroughly miserable, for once he did not yield.

More than anything, it was this resistance to her will that goaded her to anger, and her mood was not sweetened by the drive home. The family station wagon was economical on fishing trips, but cumbersome in heavy traffic, and the afternoon streets were thronged with festival crowds. Their very youth and good health, above all their high spirits, seemed to taunt her; she felt as if they were enjoying themselves at her expense. By the time she arrived home, she was so thoroughly vexed that she could hardly think straight.

Lighting a menthol cigarette, she sat down on the plastic couch beside her husband, to watch the evening news.

"I just wonder what this ridiculous film festival is going to do to our property taxes," she said peevishly.

"What about our income taxes?" He nodded toward the television screen, where a sequence of space-program failures alternated with interviews of prominent opponents of the administration. One and all denounced the cost and faulty design of the UN communications network. "This space boondoggle is bleeding the country to death with taxes. I say privatize it, and let us taxpayers keep our hard-earned money. Benton Ingles told us that from the beginning, and he's a man who knows. The polls prove it. Three to one in favor of letting private money pay for it all." He snatched up a handful of tortilla chips from the bowl in front of him. "By the way, did you get to see Tim?"

She nodded in exasperation, and exhaled a cloud of menthol smoke. "Dr. Weirdo and those bodybuilder types were bad enough. But now he's taken up with a gang of hippies, and won't listen to me anymore. His own mother. Fred, if you could have seen the girl he introduced me to. Bold as brass, and her chair clipped so short that she looked almost bald."

"You mean like that one who murdered those three doctors up at UCIC? Must be the new hair style with the weird set. Looks ugly, if you ask me." He started to reach for more tortilla chips, but noticed his wife staring wide-eyed at the wall. "What's wrong, Mother? Aren't you feeling well?"

She startled him by shooting from the couch, and marching resolutely to the door.

"Where are you going?" he called after her.

"The police station. Now I know where I've seen that girl before."

Tedworth Vay arrived at the Londi mansion just after dark, and at once gathered his argonauts—eighteen crewmen, along with Verna and young Rhoda—in the salon for a last briefing.

"We weigh anchor at nine," he said. "Our supplies have already been boated out to the yacht, which leaves only our baggage, our special equipment, and ourselves to get aboard. We'll pick up our tow southeast of San Benedicta Island, in the Revillagigedos, and then on to Sulatonga. Any questions?"

"You've been forthright with us from the start, professor," said a young bodybuilder with extraordinary biceps. "Except where do we stand now? I mean, how sure are we that what we're looking for is really on Sulatonga?"

There were nods and murmurs throughout the room, indicating that this was still the question of questions. Tedworth Vay raised his hand for silence.

"My most enterprising agent is on his way into Royal Beach at this very moment, with someone who should know the answer to that question, one way or the other. For obvious reasons they can't give us the information over the telephone. As I'm sure you're all aware by now, to lose absolute surprise in a mission of this nature is to lose everything. Perhaps our very lives. I've never underestimated to you the risks involved, and I won't now."

"Will your agent bring this person here to the house?" asked another bodybuilder, whose head looked almost too small for his massive shoulders.

"No, because spies from B.I.T.E. have surely been infiltrated among the festival crowds, and may be watching this house specifically to intercept the person in question. For the same reason I've made special arrangements for you too, Miss Malmrose."

"Do they involve a maid's uniform and a red wig?"

He smiled. "It worked before, and I see no reason why it shouldn't work again. You'll make the switch with Graziella after everybody else is gone, to divert suspicion. Now are there any further questions?"

"Are you sure Domino and Dominique will be all right while we're gone?" said Rhoda. "I wish we didn't have to leave them behind, Professor. They know we're up to something big, and could be useful in emergencies."

"I'm sorry, dear," he said. "They're too valuable to risk, and could be more of a hindrance than a help in case of trouble. All right, everybody? Then let's separate in twos and threes, mingle with the festival crowd, and meet again backstage at the Fremont Theater, according to plan."

Rhoda accompanied him from the house, followed at

short intervals by fragments of the crew of young bodybuilders, experienced yachtsmen all. She located Domino and Dominique in the vicinity of the morning room, and wished she could somehow have reassured them that they would be well cared for during her absence, even if she never came back. Then she was among the crowds milling along Legendary Lane and had to resign herself to not seeing them again for a long, long time.

Tim Waverly was the last to depart, and Verna nearly had to shove him out the front door to send him on his way. She ascended the stairs to her bedroom, uncertain whether she was touched or exasperated by his old-fashioned protectiveness. Exactly when Maximo would return from the theater with Graziella would depend upon events. But she should have ample time to don the spare maid's uniform she had worn when she first arrived here.

Domino and Dominique were taking their first language lesson. Exchanging crude noises seemed to them an inefficient means of communication, certainly compared to telepathy, but they had lately decided there was no other means of signaling their needs to Earthlings. So they sat down in the morning room to learn cat.

"Meow," said Lakme, after being encouraged with a swat across the chops.

"Mwoop," Domino tried unsuccessfully to imitate the sound.

"Mwoop," Dominique came no closer.

For several minutes they sat with their heads together, perplexed by their inability to enunciate. Many hundreds of generations had passed since their ancestors, selectively bred for starship service, had needed any form of communication but telepathy. Their vocal faculties had so atrophied that not even as kittens had they mewed. They decided at last that they needed more practice.

Simultaneously they pulled Lakme's whiskers, and again she mewed.

"Mwoop," said Domino.

"Mwoop," said Dominique.

Their ears were conditioned to detect the faintest irregular sound, which might indicate some shipboard malfunction, and each knew how far she still was from speaking good cat. Yet this momentary setback did not blunt the keenness of their other perceptions, and both sensed at the same instant that there was a stranger in the house. They left Lakme sitting, and darted like twin shadows to the door, and peeked out.

A bend in the hallway screened them from the vestibule, but they sensed that the Earthling who had escaped captivity with them was there, and that her distress was becoming more and more poignant. They could usually discriminate the growling of Earthlings familiar to them, but the growls they now heard were utterly strange.

Verna had been caught by surprise. Descending the staircase in her maid's uniform, she was startled when a strange man darted out of the library with a photograph in his hand. He glanced down at it, and then back up at her. Satisfied, he flashed her his badge.

"Verna Malmrose, I am Detective Ambrose Prine of the Royal Beach Police Department. I arrest you on the charge of murder." And he took a printed card out of his vest pocket, and read from it her civil rights to remain silent and be represented by counsel.

She was so stunned by this turn of events that she could only stare helplessly while the man handcuffed her to the banister, and went to the hall telephone to summon a paddy wagon. Her sole consolation was that at least she had not been recaptured by the thugs of Benton Ingles. But somehow she must warn the others, or they would lose precious time searching for her in vain, and possibly jeopardize their whole mission to Sulatonga.

Domino and Dominique had crept up to the bend in

the hallway, and with team-think perceptiveness analyzed the situation at a glance. Their Earthling benefactor had been recaptured by the same mean, ugly
type that had imprisoned her the first time. A metal
chain fastened both her forelimbs to the railing at the
bottom of the staircase while her captor growled into
the communications device on the wall. He would
certainly interfere with any effort they made to un-
chain her, possibly try to capture them, too, and they
retreated swiftly to the morning room.

Lakme had been in a nasty mood all day. Until the
advent of Domino and Dominique, whom she regarded
with instinctive dread, she had never known discipline.
If she seemed to have become a nice pussycat, obedi-
ent and affectionate, it was purely superficial. Her natural meanness and ferocity, irritated today by the
strangers and commotion in the house, still smoldered
within her like a feline volcano. The unexpected reap-
pearance of her two drillmasters soured her mood still
further, though not openly.

"Meow," she said, as they sat down on either side of
her.

But the language lesson was over, and they
marched her in step back up to the bend in the hallway. The mean, ugly Earthling was now growling at
their benefactor, still chained helplessly by both forelimbs, and they sat Lakme down between them and
concentrated.

She was comparatively dull witted, with only rudimentary senses of perception, but so strong were the
telepathic images focused upon her that her ears flattened, her fangs bared, and her fur stood on end. She
had a lot of frustrations to work off, and she now felt
them seething wilder and more violently within her,
and all directed toward the stranger in the vestibule.
Then at the critical moment, single claws prodded her
like spurs, and the volcano erupted.

"The wagon's on the way, Miss Malmrose," Detective

Prine was saying. "Don't do anything foolish, and we'll get along just—"

He never finished, for at that instant he was assailed by a screeching, clawing fury against which he could only try futilely to defend himself. A Siamese cat is a formidable creature to begin with, and Lakme had a lot of scores to settle. She marked them off on his face, as she drove him, arms wrapped over his head, stumbling and cursing, back into the library.

In an instant, Domino and Dominique were on the stairway behind the astonished Verna. One hopped onto the shoulders of the other, and moments later the handcuffs fell to the floor. Then they were all hurrying down the hallway, as the wild screeching of Lakme, mingled with Detective Prine's cries for help, echoed through the house.

Verna glanced back just as the big, clumsy man burst back into the vestibule, tore the hellcat out of his hair, and with an agility born of panic dived into the hall closet. Siamese cats are the watchdogs of the Orient, and Lakme at once sat down outside the door to watch. It would be a painful mistake for Detective Prine to emerge before the paddy wagon he had called for arrived.

There would be no hot pursuit from him at least; but then Verna noticed another man peering in through one of the sidelight sashes beside the door, and wondered who he could be. The police could not possible have arrived so soon. The porch light was evidently too bright for him to discern anything inside the house, but she could see clearly that his face was disfigured by a black eye, puffy lips, swollen jaw, and other witnesses of recent beatings. Was the spy Maximo had thrashed twice already back spying again?

Whoever he was, this was no place for her, and she overtook Domino and Dominique just as they reached the pantry. One door led down to the basement, the other out of the house. Her Los Angeles Dodgers baseball cap, which she wore to protect her scalp from sunburn while out in the garden, hung beside the latter door, and she clapped it onto her head.

An outdated maid's uniform, a baseball cap, and two exotic cats prancing along in step before her; even in California she would attract attention. But somehow she had to reach the *Sidonia* before nine, or at least alert Tedworth Vay to what had happened so it could sail at its scheduled time without her.

The brick lane behind the mansion separated the garden walls of two long rows of other Victorian mansions; but no sooner had she entered it than a police car, headlights ablaze, cherry-colored lights flashing, spun around the corner at its far end. She slipped into the entrance recess in the wall opposite, but its door was locked. The police car now barreled down the lane straight at her; there was nowhere else to hide, and it was too late to run.

But not to jump. Domino and Dominique sprang in tandem up the garden wall, disappeared over the top, and a moment later she heard the rasp of a bolt. The door yielded to her pressure, and she slipped through it and shot the bolt behind her, an instant before the police car skidded to a halt outside. Car doors slammed, and she heard heavy footsteps pounding in the direction of the Londi mansion. No doubt other police vehicles were in front of the house by now, so it would be only minutes until Detective Prine, freed from his tormentor, sounded the alarm to the entire Royal Beach Police force.

Then she was startled by a wild barking and whirled around, expecting to be attacked by some fierce watchdog. But once again Domino and Dominique were up to the challenge. They bounced back and forth with such supernatural agility that the onrushing dog stopped and stared at them in bewilderment. Then it lay down and wagged its tail and whined. In the dim light Verna saw that it was only a cocker spaniel.

"Oh, you poor little thing. You're just a pooch, not

a watchdog." She patted the dog reassuringly, and it stopped whining and licked her hand. "I hope your master isn't frightened, too. I'm not really a hatchet murderess."

But nobody was home. The porch light was on, and there was a night light beside the swimming pool, but the mansion itself was dark and deserted.

She absentmindedly continued to pet the cocker spaniel while she pondered her next move. The voyage to Sulatonga meant too much to her to renounce without at least an attempt to get aboard the *Sidonia*. Failing that, she had to tell the others why she couldn't sail with them, so they wouldn't lose precious time searching for her. In either case, she dared not stay here any longer. For all she knew, she might already have tripped a burglar alarm.

Her fellow argonauts would be assembled backstage at the Fremont Theater by now, assuming the guises of a television crew, like the one that had shot a gala beer commercial aboard the *Sidonia* just two days ago. The plan was to board the yacht tonight as though returning with it to Hollywood. But there would be police everywhere among the huge festival crowd around the theater, who might spot her if she went there, and a telephone call, with so many wires being tapped these days, was out of the question. It looked like her only chance was to proceed directly to the docks, and find some means of getting out to the yacht on her own.

But how was she to reach the docks without being spotted? And what about Domino and Dominique? They were her guardian angels; she could not leave them behind. Somehow she had to make herself less conspicuous, and debated breaking into the deserted house, at the risk of tripping a burglar alarm, and searching for some kind of disguise. In any case, she had to get moving.

The cocker spaniel, tail wagging, with playful yips, dodged round and round her as she passed the swimming pool. She noticed a striped beach towel flung carelessly over the diving board, but did not see how that might help her until she entered the garden. Upon an antique marble bench lay a gardener's smock, straw hat, shears, trowel, and a large wickerwork flower basket. That was all the disguise she needed, she would not have to break a kitchen window after all, and she hurried back to the diving board for the towel.

It was a beautiful garden, lush with peonies and camillias, and she regretted the devastation she now wrought upon it. She would apologize to the owner, if she ever got out of this mess alive. The cocker spaniel, though still playful, did not interfere. Domino and Dominique ignored it, having once established their authority, and with their inevitable good sense understood her scheme after a single demonstration, and cooperated. The pooch continued to romp and dodge playfully around her, as she circled the dark mansion to the front gate.

Colored searchlights swept back and forth across the heavens with spectacular effect from the direction of the Fremont Theater, as they had at the original premier of *Sidonia the Sorceress,* generations ago. Hawkers of festival gimcracks were everywhere, and a young woman in a gardener's smock and floppy straw hat, carrying a flower basket overflowing with fresh blossoms, attracted no special attention among the festival crowds. In fact, Verna soon realized that she could have turned a tidy profit tonight, had she known how to price her flowers, or tie them properly into bouquets.

But she stopped to sell them only when she could not avoid doing so without making herself conspicuous. Otherwise she descended resolutely through the old Victorian neighborhood toward the docks.

The gazebo in the public square was a relic of the Gay Nineties, while the gang of thugs congregated nearby were all gruesomely modern. They had long

hair and beards, and wore trendy sweatshirts stenciled
with environmentalist slogans; but except for the fact
that they did not carry placards this time or chant slogans against Delfred Bassett, they looked exactly as
they had the night they raided Lola Londi's garden
party. Verna also recognized the last one to join them,
despite his holding a handkerchief to his face, as the
man she had seen peeking in the window when she escaped Detective Prine.

Screened as they were by the gazebo, she had come
upon them unawares, and now found herself less than
twenty feet away. Among them, in a ridiculously
phony wig and a sweatshirt stenciled ANIMALS ARE
PEOPLE, was the sadistic brute who had first captured
her. From hints he had dropped while beating and tormenting her, she was certain that he was somehow involved in the death of her brother. But the stakes were
higher than personal vengeance, and she had to swallow her anger, and behave unsuspiciously like the
flower girl she seemed.

For some reason, the young people in the milling
crowd around her, mostly college students, were now
particularly anxious to buy flowers, and she sold out
her entire stock within minutes. Fortunately Domino
and Dominique, hidden under a towel folded at the
bottom of the basket, remained silent and motionless.

With her flower basket now apparently empty, there
was nothing suspicious in Verna's hurrying off to refill
it. Not until she reached the far side of the public
square did she glance back. The reason for the sudden
demand for her flowers was now apparent.

The young students had also spotted the gang of
thugs as phonies, evidently believing them to be cops
in disguise, and playfully rained blossoms down on
them from all sides.

Farther inland, the searchlights had ceased to sweep
the heavens, and now rose above the Fremont Theater
like colored pillars. That meant the opening ceremo-

nies of the Lola Londi Retrospective Film Festival were about to commence. Pulling her floppy hat forward the better to conceal her face, Verna strode resolutely in the opposite direction.

CHAPTER XVI

Angel was furious, not just at being taunted by a lot of smartass college punks throwing flowers at him and his men, but at the inability of those very men to carry out his orders. Another golden opportunity to redeem himself frittered away. His thick fists began ominously to clench and unclench as he listened to still another excuse for failure.

"I couldn't help it, Angel," said Whipple, taking the handkerchief away from his face, which was now a disaster area. "People were coming in and out of the house so fast, and then they all left—for the film festival, I guess—and finally an unmarked car pulls up, and a cop goes inside. So I go after him to check."

"After a cop?" Angel glowered at him. "Didn't I tell you the cops aren't supposed to know we're here?"

"Yeah, but I recognize this guy. Prine's his name. Used to work down at Fresno Beach when I was on the force there. Anyways, I peek into the house and see nothing. The front door's open, so I sneak inside. Still nothing. All I come across is this Siamese cat sitting in front of a closet door. So I start tiptoeing down the hall. Then all hell breaks loose." He dabbed with the handkerchief at his clawed face, bitten nose, and chawed ears. "Lucky I got out the door alive."

"You might not think it's so lucky when I get through with you," said Angel. "So you never did see this Prine, or find out what he was up to?"

"I caught a glimpse of him. This damned cat is clawing the hell out of me, and then the closet door opens, and it's Prine. He starts for the front door, but the cat spots him and leaves me alone to go after him. So he dives back into the closet, and it's me that gets out the door."

"And not a goddamn thing to show for it." Angel's fists balled at his sides.

"Yeah, I do. It's that snoopy broad, the one you caught but got away again, who everybody thinks butchered them three docs up at the Med Center. Verna Malmrose. A paddy wagon and two squad cars pull up just as I'm leaving the gate. Five cops run into the house, and I hear another reporting in on his radio. That's how I know they're here to pinch the Malmrose broad."

"Did they?"

"Not with Prine in the closet. Anyways, she can't do us no harm. With everybody thinking she's a mad slasher, who's gonna believe what she says?"

Angel looked him disgustedly up and down. "A chauffeur beats you up, then he beats you up again, then you get mauled by a goddamn cat."

"It's been a tough week, Angel."

"Not so tough as it's gonna get, once I get you back to Ingles City. All right, the rest of you." He brushed a peony out of his false hair. "Let's get going. There's nothing more we can do here."

They stalked from the public square and up the street to where they had parked their cars. The playful crowd had run out of flowers, and most were content to hurl only taunts after them. One freer spirit, however, also hurled an ice cream cone, which splattered against the back of Whipple's head.

Lola Londi had been one of the most enterprising scene stealers of her day, and tonight, from the mobbed streets and sidewalks, from the packed grandstands flanking the theater entrance, all eyes were upon her. Maximo held open the rear door of her Packard limousine, and she emerged into the brilliant lights a vision of regal splendor, glittering with gold, silks, diamonds, ermine, and an incredible fan of white ostrich plumes.

Tedworth Vay stepped forward as her escort. He looked less tonight like the Sorcerer of a tarot deck than Mandrake the Magician of the comic strips. His black cape was lined with crimson silk, his top hat was of black silk, and he wore the order of a deposed royal house. He remained in the background as he escorted the evening's star toward the glittering entrance of the Fremont Theater.

Colored pillars of light reached to the heavens from every corner of the block. From the grandstands, jammed with golden lads and girls from all over California, erupted a wild cheering for the goddess of yesteryear. The Sons of Paradise, resplendent in their new usher uniforms, formed an aisle for her like a royal guard of honor. There was not a dry eye among them.

Just before he reached the entrance, Tedworth Vay spotted the face of an assassin in the crowd. He also noticed that Kelly, the owner of the sinister face, had a dark voluptuous woman at his side, dressed in a Los Angeles Dodgers warmup jacket, and he nodded him inconspicuously toward the alley beside the theater, which led to its stage door.

Then he was escorting Lola Londi, still using her ostrich-plume fan with effective theatricality, into the gorgeously refurbished lobby. The Fremont was a relic of the golden age of movie palaces. The motif of its shimmering decor was Hollywood-Moorish, brilliant with gilded festoons, gaudy with enameled arabesques, spangly with plaster drapery, musical with the plash of an Arabian Nights fountain. Craftsmen had labored twenty-four hours a day to complete the restoration in time for the festival, and the results were stunning. Many in the youthful audience, accustomed only to the seats-and-screen movie houses of shopping centers, were overwhelmed.

The balcony had been closed since shortly after the advent of television; but it was open tonight, and nei-

ther Lola Londi nor the faithful Sons of Paradise betrayed the least toil in ascending the recarpeted marble
staircase between applauding lines of festival goers.

The interior of the theater was like a Moorish garden
designed for a Rudolph Valentino movie: plaster grape-
vines climbed castellated walls surmounted by mock
turrets and battlements (the opulent bunches of grapes
were for some reason painted every color of the rain-
bow), there were lattice windows and tiny false
balconies at heights no lover could have reached unless
he was a human fly, and the ceiling reproduced the
heavens of a summer night, atwinkle with a thousand
stars, across which drifted images of fleecy clouds created by hidden projectors.

Vaudeville acts had once alternated here with Hollywood epics, and gilded boxes commanded the stage on
either side. From the most sumptuous of these, hung
with buntings of imperial purple, amidst a veritable
garden of bouquets, Lola Londi graciously acknowledged the cheers of the packed house.

Tedworth Vay used the opportunity to ease himself
out of public view. The Sons of Paradise, dabbing at
their eyes with moist handkerchiefs, looked on from
the corridor behind the box, and he slipped through
them and descended backstage.

Not since the heyday of vaudeville had the old
dressing rooms witnessed such turmoil. The
bodybuilders, recruited by Tim Waverly to crew the
Sidonia, were busily changing clothes, moving crates
and equipment, and packing and unpacking their luggage.

But all activity ceased at the entrance of Tedworth
Vay, and all eyes followed him as he crossed to the
stage door. For they all knew that the question he was
about to ask the voluptuous woman standing beside it,
with a man they would never want to turn their backs
on, would determine whether all they had accom-
plished so far, including the film festival itself, had
been done in vain.

"Mrs. Ingles, I presume?" He introduced himself. "My name is Tedworth Vay. We have a mutual friend in Lola Londi."

"Yes, she say good things about you. Just like my husband say bad things, which is all I need to hear." A dangerous light glittered in her beautiful dark eyes. "There is an old saying in my country. 'The enemy of my enemy is my friend.' "

"Just so. May I ask where your husband is now?"

"Sulatonga. It's an island on the equator, in the middle of the Pacific Ocean. I know because I look it up in a book. He's got some dirty business there called Nimrod. I heard him say so himself, the son of a bitch. . . ."

The rest of her expletives, while she related how and where she had obtained the information she now gave him, were in Italian, and sounded more obscene than any English equivalents. But Tedworth Vay had already heard all he wanted to know, and soon all the crew members were dispatched in television vans down to the docks. Tim Waverly alone remained behind.

"I'm worried, professor," he said. "Max should have returned with Verna by now. Should I go back to the house and check?"

"Call, but if anyone other than Max, Graziella, or Miss Malmrose answers, hang up."

But before Tim had reached the telephone, Maximo himself came hurrying through the stage door, looking harried and angry.

"Bad news, Professor. The house is crawling with cops. I figured if Miss Malmrose got away she might try to hide out at your place, so I went there. But no sign of her. So I dropped off Graziella, because maybe she'll show up later, and hurried back. A cop outside the theater told me the same thugs who raided our garden party were spotted back in town. So I don't want to stray too far from Lola, in case they try it again."

"Good idea, Max. And thanks. You did all you could."

The burly chauffeur nodded, and disappeared up the stairs that led to the corridor behind the theater boxes. The moment he was safely out of sight, Chesterville appeared through the stage door with young Rhoda, who had exchanged her fringed buckskin for less conspicuous attire.

"I didn't sense any of those robot people anywhere we went in Royal Beach, Professor," she said. "But there's so much interference from the crowds, they might be in places we didn't go." She glanced back and lowered her voice. "Is that woman Mrs. Ingles? Is it Sulatonga?"

"She is, and it is. We leave at once. Chesterville, please forward the transfer order I left in my desk to Kelly's Swiss bank account, and escort Mrs. Ingles back to my house. Graziella is already there, and can look after her until Lola returns home after the festival banquet."

"Very good, sir. Miss Londi's chauffeur will, I assume, remain here at the theater in the capacity of a bodyguard?"

"That's right. He'll drive her home after the gala, so you probably won't run into him again tonight."

"Very good indeed, sir." Chesterville departed with an ineffable look of slyness, taking Kelly and Mrs. Ingles with him.

"There's no use in my calling the house now," said Tim, looking still more worried. "But I thought the Chief of Police himself promised not to try and arrest Verna."

"I'm curious about that, too. Wait here. I'll call the house myself." He returned from the telephone a few minutes later, frowning. "It sounded as if half the police in Royal Beach were there, but I finally got through to Chief Farquarson. It seems that during his absence from the station, the deputy he had left in charge got a warrant for the arrest of Miss Malmrose.

The officer had no choice, because someone came there with information as to her whereabouts, and the demand that she be arrested immediately."

Tim hung his head. He did not have to be told who had informed on Verna, or what would become of her if she were handed over to state authorities.

"It's not that bad, Tim. They haven't caught her yet."

"You mean she escaped? From the whole Royal Beach police force?"

"Miss Malmrose is a resourceful young woman. But right now we have to escape, or it will soon be too late."

Like a quick-change artist, he stepped into a nearby dressing room and emerged almost at once in the guise of a network television producer, with the channel number and emblem embroidered over the breast pocket of his uniform blazer. But Tim had still not budged.

"How can I leave while Verna is in danger, Professor? The roads outside Royal Beach are still being watched, and she's too conspicuous to hide from the police very long inside the city."

Melodramatic organ music, punctuated by bursts of laughter and applause, reverberated from the theater above.

"Let's wait till we get to the docks before making our final decision, Tim," said Tedworth Vay, guiding him firmly by the arm to the stage door, with young Rhoda tripping along behind.

This was one contingency he had not foreseen, and he weighed alternatives as he climbed into the television van waiting for them at the mouth of the alley. By the time they reached the docks, he knew what had to be done, and went straight to the nearest telephone booth.

The crew unloading the luggage and equipment, from a van into a motor whaleboat painted "Sidonia" amidships, attracted no special attention from passersby. Television cameramen and technicians had been shooting a beer commercial in the surf, on the beach, and aboard the yacht all this week. These young men, though more robust, were dressed exactly the same. So busy were they stowing the whaleboat that few noticed that Verna Malmrose was not among them.

Tedworth Vay returned from the telephone, and immediately drew his worried friend aside.

"I've made arrangements with Chief Farquarson to hold Miss Malmrose incognito until her innocence is established. Meanwhile he will inform state authorities that she's escaped Royal Beach, and was last seen heading back to Albuquerque. He's a competent and trustworthy man. I don't like leaving her either, Tim, but we have to consider the importance of our mission. She'll be safe till we return."

"I'm sorry, Professor." Tim shook his head. "That's not good enough. If Verna is captured, we have no guarantee it will be by the Royal Beach police. What if the state police get her, or the thugs of Benton Ingles? I can't leave till I'm absolutely certain that she's safe."

"I understand, Tim. We can delay the voyage an hour or so, but no longer. It will take at least three trips of the whaleboat to freight our gear out to the yacht anyway. We can spare a few men to help you search for Miss Malmrose, provided it's done quickly and without tipping our hand."

Then an idea struck him, and he looked around for Rhoda. He found her sitting at the end of the pier, her legs dangling over the water, gazing thoughtfully out at the *Sidonia*.

"We're going searching for Miss Malmrose," he said. "We haven't much time, and need all the help we can get. Could you locate her inside a building, say, without actually seeing her?"

"I think so. The better I know people the easier it is for me to find them, even at a distance. I could find Domino and Dominique anywhere."

"Even as far away as Lola's house, when it's filled with policement?"

"Probably, but that's not where they are now."

He looked curiously at her. "Oh? Then where are they?"

"Out on the yacht."

It was not often that Tedworth Vay was flabbergasted, but he needed several moments now to regain his composure. Then he thew back his head and laughed.

"Miss Malmrose is indeed a resourceful young woman, and she has some resourceful little friends. No need for a search party, Tim. She's already out on the yacht, probably wondering what's keeping us."

The waterfront of Royal Beach was made up of public parks and beaches, alertly defended against commercial exploitation. The pier where they were loading the whaleboat was maintained by the civic yacht club. Tedworth Vay assembled his crew out of earshot of chance passersby, behind one of the unloaded vans.

"Long ago, before sailing off to the ends of the known world, Jason harangued his fellow Argonauts. Exactly what he stirred them to believe has long since vanished into the mists of time. But we may be sure that his promises had at least something to do with plunder and rapine. For though their voyage has long been gloried in legend and song, they were in the end only pirates. We, too, are about to sail forth into the unknown, on a voyage equally fraught with perils. But our purpose is rather to save our planet from the rapacity of pirates, to check depredations beyond old Jason's wildest imagining."

He paused to examine the faces of his audience, and was encouraged by their looks of integrity and resolution. Nor was it likely the first Argonauts could have boasted such heroic physiques, demigods though some were.

"Before we sail," he continued, "it's proper that we should each and every one of us understand exactly the risks involved. We all know by now the consequences of failure, both to ourselves and to our world. Nonetheless we must act. For this is the clearest instance I know of where to do nothing is to fail. Yet from this night forth we will be entirely on our own, with none to help us, with nowhere to turn in an emergency. We don't know much about the place we're going, and can't ask anyone who does know without betraying our intentions. Benton Ingles now wields more power in Washington than the president himself, and wields it insidiously and without scruple." He noticed some troubled looks and paused. "Any questions?"

"You've already warned us that Sulatonga was used for H-bomb tests, Professor," said a muscular young man. "Is that why we're bringing all this radiation gear?"

"Just a precaution. Forty years have passed since the last H-bomb was detonated on Sulatonga, so any residual radioactivity should be negligible. But we have no way of knowing that for certain. There must be some reason why the government has never allowed the native population to return, and why the island remains closed to the public, the media, and even to reputable scientists."

"It's not closed to Benton Ingles," added another muscular crewman, and there were angry murmurs from all sides."

"No, ten years ago he somehow wrangled an exclusive lease to the island from some government agency or other, in return for massive campaign contributions to several key politicians. Discovering what he's been up to there is the purpose of our quest, just as it was the purpose of the *Greenworld Challenger* before us."

The murmurs grew angrier, the faces around him more resolute, at the mention of that heroic vessel.

"We have some advantages," he went on. "For instance, while aircraft or steel ships would certainly be picked up by radar anywhere in the vicinity of Sulatonga, our small wooden vessel should be able to approach the island undetected. Also, we'll be towed there by one of the sea factories of Delfred Bassett." He quickly raised his hand to check the angry reaction to the name. "He's recently lost two ships in the area, and I've had him serve public notice that if he loses another, he'll demand a congressional inquiry. That's the last thing in the world Benton Ingles wants at this time. Most important of all, after we drop our tow, we'll approach the island from its deserted side, where the H-bombs were detonated."

"Hence the radiation gear," added the muscular young man who had first raised the question. "But what's the rest of the island like, Professor?"

"A mountainous valley, the crater of a giant volcano, dormant for thousands of years. That's where we'll find Benton Ingles, and find out what he's up to. Climb the rim, telephoto everything we see, and Fax the data back to people I have waiting for it in Washington. Only with that kind of hard evidence will they dare challenge Ingles on the floor of Congress."

"Have you any idea yet what he's up to on Sulatonga?" asked a powerfully-built young man with rimless spectacles. "Except that it has something to do with the space program."

"The sole clue I have so far is that his master plan is called Project Nimrod. That's something we can all ponder, during the voyage. Nimrod, the mighty hunter. Exactly what Benton Ingles intends to hunt, beyond the aggrandizement of his personal wealth and power, is what we're voyaging to Sulatonga to find out."

There were no hurrahs, no pep-rally cheers; the resolution of the crew was shown in the vigor with which they finished loading the whaleboat. Tim Waverly was at its bow when it reached the *Sidonia,* and he scrambled anxiously up the ladder to assure himself that Verna was indeed safely aboard.

* * *

"You screwed up, but I'm the one who has to face the Big Guy," said Angel, his heavy browridge lowering with menace. "You'll have time to think about that while you're in traction."

Whipple knew this was no idle threat. His face was already a Balkan map of knobs, bruises, swellings, bites, and claw marks, and he gazed out the window of the speeding automobile with a rising sense of desperation. Had the black limousine not been doing ninety down the freeway, he might have been tempted to jump.

"Can't you go any faster?" growled Angel. "I got a plane to catch, and some things I gotta do first."

"I got it floored, Angel," said the driver. "We'll be there in a few minutes. Do you need anything at your place, or is the baggage you got in the trunk enough?"

"Just take my bags out to the RZ, and load 'em aboard. But first drop me off at the campus."

He peered thoughtfully out the window. The smokestacks, concrete, asphalt, painted cinderblock, neon, industrial parks, and absence of greenery in the landscape rushing past told him he was fast approaching Ingles City—and a confrontation with Benton Ingles himself.

The orders to report at once to the RZ, for a night flight to Sulatonga, had come over the scrambler not forty minutes ago. Was he being taken for commendation: nothing had happened at Royal Beach except a festival for some dotty old broad who made movies a hundred years ago. Or was he being taken there for punishment: the Malmrose bitch was still at large, and Tedworth Vay was still in a position to jeopardize Project Nimrod.

In the dog-eat-dog world of B.I.T.E., there were top dogs and there were underdogs, and those who did not eat were eaten. It was time to challenge the topmost dog of all, or he would himself be torn down and destroyed. Chief Grotten had failed, and so was vulnerable himself. Was it a sign of better things to come, that the once mighty Chief of Operations was being left behind, while he himself was flying to Sulatonga?"

"Just drop me at the corner," he said, as the limousine cloverleafed off the freeway and turned down a boulevard leading to the UCIC campus. "I'll hitch some kind of ride out to the RZ, later on."

Whipple sank mouselike into the cushions as the car pulled up at the curb, hoping he had been forgotten. Alas for his bruises, he had not. Angel dragged him brutally from the front seat, and the heavy-fisted pummelling he received left him sprawled woozily in the grass.

"Take him to the Med Center."

"No, no, please not that, Angel," he cried pitiously through his loosened teeth.

"Don't worry, it's just to get you patched up. I'm gonna give you one last chance."

"Gee, thanks, Angel." Whipple groaned as he felt a stitch in his kicked ribs. "You won't regret it."

"Let's hope you don't. Next time I won't be so nice."

He left his underlings to drag Whipple back into the limousine, and waited till its red tail lights had disappeared around the corner. Then he made a beeline to the Administration building, and to a door marked AUTHORIZED PERSONNEL ONLY, in the remotest corner of the seventh floor. He entered without knocking.

"Hello, boys," he said, wasting no time. "Gimme that pen and paper there, Harry. This is big smoke, so you're gonna want this in writing."

Hunched at a table littered with audio cassettes, he painstakingly inscribed a note of authorization in his roundish, illiterate hand. The four old men who tended the computerized switchboards and banks of automated tape recorders looked quizzically at each other, frowning and scratching their heads.

"Here you go." Angel handed his note to the nearest gaffer. "This will cover your butts if there's any trouble. There shouldn't be, because my authority comes straight from the Big Guy himself."

"Whew!" The gaffer raised his eyebrows. "You weren't kidding about big smoke, Angel. Take a glimpse at this, boys."

The other three whitey-bald heads converged over the note, and suddenly all looked very old and frail. But they had no choice under the circumstances, and reluctantly pulled several undocketed cassettes from the shelves.

"A guy could get in big trouble for this, Angel," said old Harry. "Really, really big trouble."

"Relax, boys. You got your written authority, so nobody can blame you." Angel slipped one of the cassettes into a player, and listened intently over a set of earphones. "This is it, all right."

Stuffing the cassettes into his pockets, he strode from the room without another word. This was indeed it, and he pondered the reaction of Benton Ingles to the contents of the tapes all the way to the airstrip in the Restricted Zone. He hoped he'd be given the job of taking custody of Chief Grotten and, eventually, handing him over to the surgeons at the Med Center. It was a pleasant thought, and a grim smile twisted his lips as he boarded the plane.

Then everything changed in an instant. For there sat Chief Grotten himself, brooding alone in a seat overlooking the right wing, in the forward lounge.

It was a two-engine jet, luxuriously appointed with special-purpose modules, though not the colossal flying palace reserved exclusively for Benton Ingles. There were no other passengers aboard, and Angel continued warily up the aisle.

Chief Grotten was not aware of his presence until he was nearly upon him. His startled reaction was barely perceptible, and he recovered in an instant his cop suspiciousness and belligerence. But not before he had betrayed his apprehension. The grim smile again twisted Angel's lips, and he dropped confidently into the seat opposite.

"Hello, Chief. I didn't know you were on this flight."

"Didn't know it myself, till an hour ago," said Grotten, having now completely regained his composure. "My guess is that Mr. Ingles wants us all there for the big show."

"Looks that way," said Angel.

The cassettes in his pocket gave him confidence, but his animal cunning warned him that he could not safely match wits with the man seated across from him, and so he dropped the conversation.

This suited Chief Grotten, who had much to brood about. In a way, he, too, could feel confident, because his personal spy in Royal Beach, Whipple, had furnished him with regular reports about Angel's bungling there. Yet he had bungled also. No woman so conspicuously beautiful as Carla should have eluded his dragnet. He had marshaled every police resource at his command. That she had nonetheless vanished without a trace, was a thing that would not be easy to explain to Benton Ingles.

It had all started with those damned cats. They had mysteriously disappeared, and though he at last knew where to find the Malmrose bitch, she was still beyond his reach. But their gravest peril was that Carla, her passions outraged, might rouse some kind of public outcry, whether in Congress or the media, before Project Nimrod could be safely launched. Mechanically he fastened his seatbelt as the plane taxied down the runway for takeoff.

He was still brooding as the plane winged southward over the dawning Pacific. Thousands of feet below he could now make out the fishing fleets putting out to sea, the colossal oil tankers coming down the coast from Alaska, and the freighters bringing the manufactures of Japan to flood the American markets. There was even a yacht in full regalia moving down the California coast toward the equator.

CHAPTER XVII

It was an empty world, where all through the day the sky merged with the sea in an endless vault of blue, where the sun now declined from gold to amber to the deepening reds of twilight. Tunnies, bonitos, and dolphins gamboled about the yacht as it was towed inexorably against the equatorial counter currents, ever westward from the Revillagigedo Islands, into the immensity of the Pacific Ocean.

"So much for romance," said Verna Malmrose, donning a blue work shirt over her bikini. "Our South Seas cruise looks like a race to dump us as soon as possible. The *Tuna King* couldn't tow us any faster if Delfred Bassett himself were on the bridge."

The towering fantail of the sea factory, churning the water some fifty yards ahead, looked increasingly sinister in the declining sunlight. Its operations were computerized, to shrink labor costs, and no human being had yet been seen aboard.

But Verna realized that she had little to complain about. She was housed in Lola Londi's personal suite, a fantasy of opulence and luxury, the only woman among a crew of young Apollos, engaged in the adventure of a lifetime. Her hair was now a decent length, and vigorous daily workouts had restored her figure.

She sat in the deck chair reserved for her between Rhoda and Tim Waverly, among the crewmen who had gathered to watch Domino and Dominique put on their evening show.

"The faster we get there, the better," said Tim.

"Whatever Benton Ingles is up to on Sulatonga, it must be nearly ready to go. I just hope we're not too late."

"Professor Vay is worried about the same thing," she said. "He listens to every news broadcast, and is always checking our supplies and equipment, and double-checking to see that everybody knows what to do in any kind of emergency. I think he's an incurable romantic at heart, but right now he's all business."

"So are Domino and Dominique," said Rhoda. "They never miss, just like at Nintendo."

"They're Nintendo freaks," said Verna, laughing. "Too bad the only game we have on board for them is chess."

"That is too bad," muttered Tim. "They never miss at that either. At least when they play me."

"Watch out!" Rhoda alerted them. "Here they go!"

Just as at Nintendo, the two cats divided their efforts for a common purpose. Domino stood on her hind legs, peering intently over the gunwale at the surface of the water, while Dominique sat poised like a coiled spring on the foredeck above her. Then suddenly they burst into action. The instant the flying fish broke the surface, Domino calculated its trajectory, and Dominique sprang with lightning agility ten feet into the air, with precise timing and location, and batted it down.

"Score one!" cried Rhoda.

Beginning at dusk, and continuing all through the night, a veritable rain of flying fishes leapt from the water, to escape the ravening dolphins below, and sailed over the yacht—unless intercepted by a mast, a window, a bulkhead, or an unerring paw. Domino caught Dominique's first fish as it bounced off the deck, and deposited it in the galley bucket, ready to be filleted for dinner.

"They taste a lot like trout," said Tim. "I think our little friends prefer them even to salmon."

"So do I," said Verna. "You'll have to show me how to cook them some time. I never knew you could do so much with fish. That recipe with lemon butter and pasta you prepared a couple of nights ago, for instance. Absolutely delicious."

"I learned early," he said with a touch of embarrassment. "My mother and father took me along on their fishing trips when I was a kid. They caught the fish, and I cleaned and prepared them for supper. It was good training for me, I guess."

Verna glanced sympathetically at him, but she did not comment.

"Heads up!" cried Rhoda. "Here they go again."

Another perfectly timed leap, another unerring swipe of her paw in midair, and Dominique batted down another flying fish, which Domino again caught on the bounce and deposited in the galley bucket. Encouraged by the applause of their spectators, the two cats, exchanging roles every few fish, soon had a catch large enough to feed the entire crew. Then they washed themselves thoroughly, and pranced off in step with Rhoda for a pre-dinner game of chess.

Tim hefted the bucket, and started for the galley to help prepare the evening meal. "I wish I could play chess as well as I can cook," he said, and smiled good-naturedly at Verna's merry laughter.

"You've never beaten them, have you?" she said, still laughing.

He shook his head. "Professor Vay is the only one who ever beats them. He says their moves are sometimes too aggressive for conditions, especially in their middle game, but I don't see it."

What they all saw, beginning the following day, was a dramatic increase in the number of birds. Boobies, with five-foot wingspreads, circled round and round overhead, or settled out on the sea. More and more frigate birds appeared in the sky, dropping like plummets to snap up flying fish, though without nearly the accuracy of Domino and Dominique. Deafening bird cries shrieked and squalled all through the night.

The richness and variety of ocean life was a pleasant surprise to everyone on board. The huge sea factory towing them continued to churn relentlessly onward, greedy to resume its despoliation of coastal fishing grounds. It followed the equator as though tracing a line across the globe, and those with sharp eyes could soon detect a vague greenish cast in the blue of heaven, looming above the horizon.

It was at this time that Domino and Dominique formed the resolution that was to be the salvation of them all. Their instinctive service to the Masters had long since been transferred generally to their Earthling benefactors, but now they decided to concentrate their efforts more specifically on Verna. The reason for this decision was that everybody seemed so worried about her.

The fantail of the yacht had been screened off as a kind of sun deck. They joined Verna here each day when she worked out with dumbbells, or performed aerobics to music, dressed in a string bikini. But all the while they performed their own exercises, they noticed how the other Earthlings on board continually watched over her, if only in stolen glimpses, and concluded that there was a general concern for her safety. That she was prone to getting herself into trouble they knew from their own experience, for they themselves had rescued her already from deadly peril. Wherever they were going, or whatever challenges were afoot, they resolved to be more diligent in looking after her.

Their first intimation of peril came late the following afternoon, and it was Verna herself who detected it. She had been performing an aerobics dance to some yowling, thumping music, when suddenly she snapped it off, a puzzled look on her face.

"Listen," she said to the two crewmen who happened to be wandering past at that moment (their third appearance on the fantail inside of thirty minutes).

"What?" said one of them. "I don't hear anything."

"The birds," she said.

"Birds? I don't hear any birds," said the other.

"Yes, but you should. It's been like a rookery these

last couple of days, and now all of a sudden it's dead silent. What's become of all the birds?"

"Look." The first young man pointed due west. "Here they come now, a whole big flock of them."

She picked up the binoculars. It was indeed a big flock, rushing straight at them out of the declining sun. All other life had vanished from the sky. The birds appeared to be some species of gull, though not even in the Marquesas had she seen gulls this size. They looked like eagles.

"We must be nearing land," she started to say, but was distracted by something tugging at her, and looked down.

Domino and Dominique had wrapped their forepaws around her calves, and were trying urgently to tug her toward the nearest companionway. Her first impulse was to laugh, but the very urgency of their manner checked her. Why were they so anxious to get her below deck? Again she raised the binoculars toward the onrushing flock, which now seemed immense. The boobies and frigate birds might have soared from islands hundreds of miles away, but not gulls.

"I don't like this," she said. "Let's get everybody under cover. Quick, give the alarm!"

They were not quick enough. Verna refused to take cover herself until certain that everyone else on deck had been warned. She never saw the huge bird divebomb her from the blind side, its sharp beak aimed at her skull like a javelin. But Domino and Dominique, true to their new resolution, were hovering protectively nearby, and leapt simultaneously from the deck and batted down the gull like a flying fish, both its wings broken.

It flopped violently back and forth, shrieking hideously, snapping its beak, its beady eyes glittering with malice. But the deck had by now been safely cleared, and Verna watched appalled through a porthole in the after bullhead, as gull after gull dropped with cannibal ferocity on the crippled bird, and tore it to pieces.

"What are they, Professor?" asked Rhoda, standing on tiptoes at the next porthole.

"One of the reasons, I suspect, why the Atomic Energy Commission has never repatriated the native population to Sulatonga. The residual effects from the nuclear detonations may not be what we've prepared for," he added thoughtfully. "Fortunately there was nobody on deck when the birds struck."

"Fortune had nothing to do with it, Professor," said Verna. "It was Domino and Dominique. See the way they're looking at you now. They may be trying to tell you there's more danger ahead."

He smiled. "I've seen that look before. One challenge has ended for them, and now they want another—a rematch at chess. What they really may be trying to tell me is that they've worked out the problems in their middle game, and are ready to hand me a drubbing. We'll see about that, but not for a few days yet. Right now, I suggest we get to bed early. We drop our tow line tomorrow, and it will be a big day for us all."

Before retiring, he radioed the *Tuna King* to see if its crew had sustained any casualties from the gulls, only to discover that they had known about the danger beforehand. He found it curious that they had not bothered to pass on this information, and wondered what else they might have withheld. The true position of the ships, for instance. Gulls never ventured far out to sea. Their appearance could only mean that land was much nearer than reported.

Throughout the voyage, he had relied upon the instruments of the *Tuna King* for exact reckoning; but now he became suspicious. There were experienced yachtsmen on board, capable of reading their position; though not with the sun so low upon the horizon. He would set them to work with charts and compasses the moment the stars came out.

His suspicions were reinforced by the behavior of the gulls themselves. Their ferocity was appalling, and

he watched them savage one of the small sharks that
followed the ship and fed upon its garbage. They
caught it too near the surface and pecked out its eyes,
tearing gobbets from its writhing body as it floundered
blind and helpless in the water. They abandoned their
prey only when other sharks arrived, and began a feeding frenzy of their own.

In the reddening twilight the entire sea appeared to
be stained with blood. But only now did the immense
flock of gulls turn and wing back toward the setting
sun. That they had waited so long to depart, before
rushing home for the night, seemed to confirm his suspicions that the true position of Sulatonga had been
misreported by the *Tuna King.*

He would know for certain when the stars came out.
Meanwhile he retired to his cabin, and the new edition
of Propertius he had long looked forward to reading.

Domino and Dominique awoke at the same instant,
rolled out of their hammocks, and removed the sleeping caps Rhoda had sewn for them out of surgical
gauze and the ends of plastic squeeze bottles. Rhoda
herself was also awake, and quickly huddled on her
clothes. They found Tedworth Vay on the bridge with
Tim Waverly and two crewmen.

"We're dead in the water, Professor," said one of
them.

"Any luck yet raising the *Tuna King?*"

The other young man shook his head angrily.
"They're listening, but they won't acknowledge. I
can't believe they'd just cut the tow line, and desert us
in the middle of the ocean without warning."

"I can," said Verna entering the door. "Delfred
Bassett was miffed over not being invited to sit at
Lola's table at the festival banquet. Deserting us may
be his way of revenge."

"It's more than just being deserted, Miss
Malmrose," said Tedworth Vay. "We've been deceived

about our true position from the beginning of the voyage, and not by your Delfred Bassett."

She gasped. "You mean Benton Ingles has agents aboard the *Tuna King?* Then he knows we're here."

"Exactly where is here, Professor?" asked Tim.

"About two hundred miles closer to Sulatonga than we were led to believe. If Benton Ingles does, in fact, know we're here, we still have until morning to escape him. These are dangerous waters. He won't risk searching for so small a ship as ours in the dark, and the moon doesn't rise until a couple of hours before dawn."

"Then these waters must be dangerous for us, too, Professor," said one of the young men.

"They are. Sulatonga itself is of volcanic origin, but it's surrounded by an atoll of coral reefs and islets, and we have no sonar. We'll just have to keep a sharp lookout."

"I'll get everybody going, Professor," said Tim, undaunted. "There must be a passage through the reef big enough for us to slip inside, at least in the whaleboat. We could hit the beach, scale the rim of the crater, get all the telephoto evidence we need, and Fax it to your people in Washington before the sun rises."

His enthusiasm was contagious, and within the hour the entire crew stood ready for action. The engine, like the yacht itself, was an antique; but speed was not now of the essence, and lookouts were posted at the bow and atop the mast, and relieved over half hour to insure alertness.

Black masses of water rose and fell about them; tropical stars glittered in the moonless black sky; phosphorescent plankton shimmered like a sea of embers. For hours they picked their way ever westward through the shoal waters, until at last the moon rose out of the sea behind them like a ball of silver.

Again it was Domino and Dominique who signaled the alarm. For no apparent reason they both ran to the starboard railing, stood on their hind legs, their ears

peaked forward, and peered intently off into the night.
A rumble like the sound of distant trains grew louder
and louder.

"Reef dead ahead!" cried the lookout from the bow.

But that was not the direction Domino and Dominique were peering. Then they were all startled by a
cry from the lookout atop the mast.

"Motor boats, north by northwest, approaching at
high speed!"

The next minute three search lights converged on
them, and the night exploded with machine-gun fire.

"Duck!" shouted a dozen voices at once, and everybody on board scrambled for cover, including the two
cats.

Tim found Verna crouching protectively over young
Rhoda behind the cabin bulkhead, and pulled them
both along the port rail to the motor whaleboat. The
approaching roar of launches and the rattle of machine
guns were echoed on the opposite side of the yacht by
the splintering of wood and the shattering of glass.
Slamming the winch into gear, he lowered the whaleboat into the water.

"They won't be filming beer commercials on the
Sidonia for a while," said Verna, as she and Rhoda
scrambled over the side. "Poor Lola."

"Poor us, if we're caught," muttered Tim, casting off
the lines.

"No, no, wait," pleaded Rhoda. "We can't leave
yet."

"We have to, or it will be too late."

He was just pushing off, when two furry shapes
dropped out of nowhere and landed together amidships. And there sat Domino and Dominique, looking
up at him with feline expressions uncomfortably like
reproach.

"Sorry, young ladies."

But there was no time for further apologies, or for
anything but getting away from the *Sidonia* with all
possible despatch. The outboard putter of the whale-

boat was drowned by the roar and clatter of the attacking launches, and the rumble and crash of the sea.

"Verna, Rhoda, keep a sharp lookout for reefs," Tim shouted, working the tiller. "See if you can spot some place where we can anchor till morning."

"Better pull farther out to sea, Tim," Verna called from the bow. "We're getting too close to a line of breakers."

"Look, look, that way." Rhoda pointed excitedly. "The water's dark and not white and splashy. Maybe we could anchor there."

Within minutes Tim maneuvered them into what he guessed was not a passage through the reef but only a small bay or inlet. Only morning light would tell.

"Now what?" shouted Verna over the roar of the breakers.

"Now we wait," he shouted back. "We're not beaten yet. We've got all the telephoto gear on board, as well as a good radio. It takes only one good man to get the evidence."

"One good *man?*" she shouted. "Now don't start talking like a chauvanist pig, Tim Waverly. I'm in this, too, you know."

"Of course you are. I never meant to imply ... I mean, it's just, well, a manner of speaking. Of course we're all in this together. We have been from the start."

"That's more like it," she called back. "How long till we can see well enough to get past the reef?"

"Yes, and how long till those nasty gulls can see us?" Rhoda started to add, but then fell silent. "Listen. Can you hear it?"

Through the crash and rumble of the breakers they could now all hear the sound of a cruising motor launch. It was hard to place exactly, but seemed to be several hundred yards out at sea, well clear of the reef, and moving slowly south.

"They're searching for us," said Verna, slipping closer to Tim so she could keep her voice down.

"Somebody must have spotted us pulling away from the *Sidonia*."

"Let's hope they don't spot us in the morning," he said.

"They won't if they keep going," added Rhoda. "They must think we kept going, too. Oh, look." She laughed. "With all this excitement, Domino and Dominique are asleep."

"The world's most practical cats," said Tim. "Nothing's happening now, so they recruit their energy for when it's needed."

The two cats lay with their paws wrapped over their heads, sound asleep on a sack of emergency rations, barely visible in the moonlight. There were two other sacks of rations nearby, and Verna gingerly opened one so as not to awaken them.

"We'd better recruit our own energy," she said. "I suspect a lot will be happening to us, and very soon. But really, I wish you hadn't reminded me about those gulls, Rhoda," she added, distributing small food packets. "As if we didn't have enough to worry about."

"Domino and Dominique will knock them down if they attack us again." Rhoda opened the smallest packet, and sampled its contents. "Yummy, it's like a candy bar. I thought the rations would be only crackers and biscuits and junk like that."

The motor whaleboat also had oars, and Tim broke one out and used it to fend them off the surrounding reef whenever they drifted too close. The waves rose ever higher, crashing ever more violently against the immovable wall of coral, accompanied by ever more ominous hissing, sucking undertows. But not until the first roseate light of dawn were they aware of their true plight.

"We'll never get through the reef here," said Tim, refitting the oar into its bracket and restarting the engine. "See those foaming ripples ahead? The reef is just below the surface. Let's hope this motor is strong enough to pull us out of here."

It was, but just barely. With the throttle twisted wide open, rising on the crest of onrushing waves ten feet above the surface of the sea, sinking into troughs ten feet below, they forged their way inch by inch out of the jagged bay, which looked in the morning light as if some colossal sea monster had bitten the reef.

Tim zigzagged along the endless wall of coral while they searched for an opening; to have run parallel would have put them broad side to the onrushing storm waves, and risked being swamped. The crashing roar of the breakers was now like thunder. But if there was a storm anywhere on the vast planetary ocean, it was a thousand miles away. There was not a cloud in the sky.

"Tim, I see something," cried Verna through the thunderous roar, pointing to starboard.

So do I," cried Rhoda, pointing in the opposite direction. "Look at Domino and Dominique."

The two cats were wide awake now, their forepaws propped against the port gunwale, gazing out to sea. Everybody looking immediately in the same direction. It was the motor launch they had heard searching for them earlier, its throttle now open, bearing down upon them out of the rolling green waves.

"Where are you going?" shouted Verna. "There's the opening, that way."

But they had been dangerously near the reef when she spotted the passage, and Tim had no choice now but to zigzag back out to sea, to avoid being broadsided. Even when he turned again toward the gap in the coral wall, he knew he was running at a dangerously acute angle to the sea.

"Watch out!" Rhoda shouted a warning. "They're shooting at us."

Her child's voice was barely audible over the thundering, hissing crash of the breakers. In the dawning light the face of the reef was a white and red speckled wall; its exposed surface, between the crests of green water hurling forward and the boiling white masses hurled back, was like the rusty slag of a steel factory. The suction currents, as Tim angled nearer and nearer, made it increasingly difficult to steer.

The motor launch, with its more powerful engine, cut along the reef at a sharper angle still, until it was racing nearly parallel with it, hellbent to overtake them. Its roar was now audible over the thundering crash of the breakers, and they heard a burst of gunfire.

"There's the opening, Tim!" Verna pointed from the bow.

"Here it comes!" shouted Rhoda, pointing the opposite way.

As he threw his weight against the steering arm, Tim glanced back out to sea. A towering wall of green glass, the highest storm wave to assail them yet, rose up with the entire force of the ocean and shot them forward through the gap in the coral. The same wave caught the motor launch broadside and also hurled it forward, but it had not yet reached the gap, and was smashed to matchsticks upon the reef.

"We made it!" Verna clapped her hands in relief. "Well done, Tim Waverly. A splendid piece of seamanship."

"A splendid piece of luck," he muttered, still unsure how he managed it. But he was proud of himself nonetheless.

"Oh, look, Dominique was hit." Rhoda scrambled amidships to see if she could help.

The tropical lagoon inside the barrier reef was as smooth and placid as the ocean outside it was wild and tempestuous. The inner wall of the reef was a rock garden of red, green, yellow, and white anemones and corals. Miles away loomed the dark volcanic mass of Sulatonga. The putter of the outboard motor grew louder and louder as the whaleboat moved away from the crashing breakers.

All eyes were now upon the two cats. A stray machine-gun bullet had nicked the tip of Dominique's tail, and Domino gently held it in her paw, so they could both examine it. Their mutual prognosis was evidently favorable, and they took turns licking the wound until satisfied it was safely cleansed.

"She'll be all right," said Rhoda, also examining Dominique's tail. "It's just a scratch."

Then she realized that both Verna and Tim were gazing apprehensively toward the approaching island. Green coconut palms swayed gently in the tropical breeze over a luxuriant hedge of undergrowth; the bright sand beach was scattered with dark blocks of coral; jagged blue mountains, the outer rim of the giant volcano that eons ago had raised itself from beneath the sea, cut across the middle of the island like a colossal wall. All along its face thousands of huge white birds fluttered ominously.

"We'd better get under cover, and quick," said Verna. "It looks like their getting ready for breakfast."

"The trees and underbrush on the island should screen us," said Tim, guiding the tiller toward an open stretch of beach. "The big problem will be getting the whaleboat under cover. The motor launch was sure to have radioed back to headquarters that they had spotted us."

Verna agreed. "They'll probably send a helicopter, if only to check for wreckage. There's a coil of rope on board. Maybe we could rig some kind of winch, so we could pull the boat off the beach. It's too heavy to push."

"Yes, I think we could use the oars as levers, or rig some kind of block-and-tackle system with those grooved cannisters. But we'll have to work fast."

"Oh, oh," said Rhoda. "We've got company. Watch our for your eyes."

A lone gull spiraled slowly downward out of the morning sky, but seemed more curious than aggressive. Tim picked up one of the oars, and Domino and Dominique sat poised on the center thwart; but the bird did not attack. After circling only a few feet over their heads, it emitted an angry squawk, and headed swiftly off in the direction of the crater wall.

"It must have been a scout," said Verna. "So it'll be back soon, with lots of hungry friends. I didn't know gulls could be so big and mean."

"Brace yourselves," said Tim. "Rhoda, hold onto Domino and Dominique. I'm going to run us as high up the beach as I can. We have to get the whaleboat under cover before the gulls come back."

Twisting the throttle to full speed, he squared up the bow with the stretch of beach where the trees and undergrowth crept nearest the water. He was concerned about injuring the others; but they turned out to be more firmly seated than he was, clinging to their thwarts while he himself landed on the seat of his pants, as the boat jolted to a stop halfway up the sand.

"Quick!" He snatched up the coil of rope and scrambled over the side. "The gulls will be here any minute."

He tied the rope to the bow ring, and paid it out to the nearest palm tree; but he had no pulleys he could rig, so he held the oars first one way and then the other, trying to figure out how they might be used as levers. The boat was far too heavy to push or drag up the beach by brute force.

Then he noticed Domino and Dominique sitting side by side, watching him. The moment he caught their attention, they both pointed to the oar lying on the sand nearby, and then at the rope in his hand. When he still didn't catch on, they demonstrated: Domino stood on her back legs, Dominique grasped her about the hips from behind, and they both leaned forward.

"Okay, I get it." He quickly tied the rope a third of the way up the stout oar, pulled it taut, and jammed the blade as deep as he could into the sand. "Verna, give me a hand here. Rhoda, keep a lookout."

Leaning their combined weight against the oar, with its blade cutting straight ahead, he and Verna levered

the boat a couple of feet up the beach. Then he taut-
ened the rope again, jammed the oar blade into the
sand further along, and they levered the boat another
couple of feet forward. Working as a team, they
walked the heavy whaleboat into the concealing undergrowth.

"Here comes somebody," Rhoda shouted from the
beach. "From the crash, I think."

A thickset, heavy-bearded man in the rags of a
green-and-gold uniform staggered halfway out of the
surf and collapsed. Before Tim or Verna could go to
his assistance, a swarm of huge blood-red landcrabs
emerged from beneath the coral blocks strewn the
length of the beach, and scuttled hungrily toward the
helpless man.

Tim could not let even an enemy die so hideously,
and left the shelter of the trees to rescue him. But
Domino and Dominique leapt into his path, and held
up warning forepaws toward the crater wall. Thousands of voracious gulls were now descending upon
them out of the sky.

Retreating into the rankest undergrowth they could
find, beneath the broadest palms, they awaited the on-
slaught. But the birds had easier prey, and there ensued
a spectacle of such primordial savagery that they were
appalled. Even Domino and Dominique, sitting side by
side at the edge of the trees, seemed disconcerted by a
violence that exceeded anything they had yet seen on
this violent planet.

Whether mercifully dead or just unconscious, the
man sprawled in the surf was unaware of the ravenous
landcrabs converging upon him, brandishing their terrible claws. They would have stripped him to the bone
in minutes, had they not been fallen upon first by the
no less ravenous gulls.

The battle raged murderously up and down the sand.
Screaming, pecking at the hard carapaces of the
landcrabs, piercing their eyes and brains with
piledriving beaks, the gulls wrought an appalling car-

nage. Some birds became careless in the feeding frenzy, and were seized around the leg by tenacious claws; then all their frantic attempts to get airborne again were futile. But these were exceptions. The gulls were in their element, the landcrabs out of theirs, and the carcasses of the dead and dying soon littered the beach.

"They got greedy for a meal and ended up as a meal themselves," said Rhoda.

"Let's pack up and get moving, before we end up a meal, too," said Tim. "Better take a couple of days' rations, just in case."

Helping Verna strap on her pack, he glanced back through the trees. The man sprawled in the surf was still alive, and a voracious white mass of gulls fluttered savagely around him, tearing him to pieces even while he tried futilely to rise and defend himself.

"Ugh! What a nasty place," muttered Verna, as they picked their way inland through the thickening undergrowth. "Some of these plants look like bloated funguses. I'll bet every one of them is poisonous.

Reds, greens, purples, yellows, and violets shimmered with a sickly phosphorescence from the low fungoids, some of which looked disgustingly like human flesh. The emerald foliage above was covered with blossoms like giant chrysanthemums, which exuded a cloying sweetness. The tropical breeze wafting through the palm fronds overhead sounded like the hissing of serpents. Spider webs of extraordinary breadth forced them again and again to detour; the rock formations were strangely crystallized; the very ground beneath their feet was leprous with green scales, where the sandy soil had been fused to glass. The vegetation grew ever ranker and more hideously fungoid.

"Look, there were people here at one time." Verna pointed to a stone idol, squat and ugly, looming out of the sickly undergrowth.

"The native population was evacuated for the

H-bomb tests, and never allowed to return," Tim reminded her. "But it's obvious radioactivity couldn't have been the reason, so I guess there was no need to have brought all that radiation gear."

Examination of the idol showed that the side facing the same direction they were going had been glazed by a searing blast of heat. Fleshy growths extruded around it through fissures in the scaly ground.

"I wish we'd brought binoculars," said Verna, "so we could see where we're going. Rhoda, do you remember the map of the island Professor Vay showed us?"

"I could draw it for you, if you like. But I think we're going the wrong way, because straight ahead is where part of the island was blown away by H-bombs."

"That's definitely not the way we want to go," said Tim.

"Whichever way we go, let's keep the jungle above us," said Verna, gazing up through the crown of the trees. Gulls circled directly overhead like squat, white vultures. "Though down here we have to watch our step for nasty things slithering out at us. Snakes, for instance."

"You know, I was just thinking it's funny we haven't seen any other birds or animals on the island," said Rhoda. "But anyway, Domino and Dominique would protect you, Verna. It looks like they've decided to watch out specially for you."

"So I've noticed," she said wryly. "I hope they don't think I'm such a klutz I have to be watched over every minute."

They turned westward toward the ancient volcano, looming thousands of feet above them into the tropical morning, where a myriad of gulls soared and dived and fluttered along sheer volcanic cliffs, or shuttled between the sea and their nests with neverending voracity. For some mysterious reason, however, the birds shied from the rim of the crater above, and never tried to surmount it to the other side.

Both the trees and the undergrowth thinned about them as they approached, and the gulls circling vulturelike overhead dropped ever lower and lower, until they fairly buzzed the treetops. Domino and Dominique stationed themselves on either side of Verna.

"What's that under those trees over there?" She pointed toward a grove of palms rising on the far side of a broad clearing. "It looks like a building of some kind. Oh, I wish I had binoculars."

The vague outlines of a low dark structure, of indeterminate size and shape, were visible on a hillside beneath the palm grove. Tim stripped off his backpack.

"Wait here. We have to know if Ingles has any of his thugs on this side of the island. If I'm captured or, well, don't come back, return to the whaleboat and radio for help."

"Be careful," said Rhoda, pointing up at the circling gulls. "That clearing is a long way across."

"Distract them if you can," he said, and slipped off toward the clearing, using the densest trees to screen himself from above.

Meanwhile Verna and Rhoda stripped off their own backpacks, and waved shirts and handkerchiefs where they would be clearly visible from the sky. Catching on at once, Domino and Dominique leapt up and down into the air and wagged their tails. The circling gulls at once converged directly overhead.

Then one of them squalled a warning, and they all darted back toward the clearing, but too late. Tim, running for dear life, was already at the other side and into the safety of the palm grove.

His next sprint across the clearing, some twenty minutes later, caught them all by surprise, including the gulls. He arrived out of breath.

"What kind of building is it?" asked Verna.

"It's not a building at all. It's the wreckage of a B-29 bomber. The tail section is broken off, and there are patches of rust, but otherwise the fuselage seems intact."

"A safe haven for the night?"

"Exactly what I was thinking," he said. "We can't approach the crater wall in daylight, let alone scale it, because of the gulls."

"That means a night ascent, when the nasty brutes are in their roosts." She followed his line of thought. "But the moon doesn't rise until a couple of hours before dawn."

"Right, and that's when we'll have to try it."

"I can't think of anything better," she said. "But it won't leave us much time to take our telephotos and get back down again, before the gulls come out."

He gazed speculatively up at the crater wall. "We'll take food and water. Maybe we can find a cave or rock overhang, where we can hole up during the day, and come down the following night. That would give us more time to get the evidence we need."

"There's still the problem of getting across the clearing," said Rhoda. "Also, the problem of what I'm going to do while you're gone. No, that's all right. You don't have to explain. I understand the situation, and can look after myself. With the help of Domino and Dominique, of course."

"There are more gulls now." Verna looked up through the trees. "Your dash across the clearing must have attracted them, Tim."

"We'll all have to dash for it, and right now," he said, picking up a stick he could use as a cudgel. "Give me your backpack, Rhoda. I'll dash straight across the clearing. You two go back through the trees a hundred yards or so. When the gulls come after me, make a run for it. Don't stop, whatever you do, and watch your eyes."

With continual glances overhead, they slipped off through the trees in opposite directions.

As the golden sun rose higher into the tropical

blueness, a wispy wreath of clouds began to form around the jagged volcano peaks of the crater. The equatorial heat was already oppressive, and the rank vegetation exuded sweet and musky perfumes. The floor of the clearing was a black tongue of lava on which only shallow patches of grass so far managed to take root.

Tim glanced down the line of trees to where Verna, Rhoda, and the two cats had concealed themselves. The number of gulls now circling close overhead was intimidating, and he had a good fifty yards to sprint, carrying an extra backpack. But the others had no chance of getting across the clearing unless he drew the gulls away from them and burst into the open.

This time the birds were not caught unaware, and scores of them, with harsh and angry squalls, dropped on him out of the sky. The footing across the weathered lava was rough and treacherous, and he knew that if he fell he would probably never get up again. But he was a conditioned athlete, if not a track star, and his dash for cover lasted only seconds, carrying a cudgel in one hand and Rhoda's backpack in the other.

He was within ten yards of safety when the first gull struck; he dodged its sharp beak, and was battered on the side of the head by powerful wings. Then a second gull came divebombing straight at his eyes, and by reflex he swung his cudgel, knocking it down. This distracted the rest of the attacking flock just long enough for him to dive under an outlier palm, and then into the shielding grove beyond.

Meanwhile Rhoda, with the fleetness of a young Indian and unburdened of her backpack, sprinted unscathed across the clearing. Verna was neither so fleet nor so lucky. Running as hard as she could over the rugged lava, she could see a commotion of white a hundred yards up the clearing, where a crippled bird was being savaged by several others. The rest of the flock now hungrily turned on her.

Domino and Dominique could easily have been across the clearing and back by now, but they did not desert her; one loped along at her left side, the other at her right. She flinched and threw up her arms as the first gull attacked; too late to have saved her eyes had not the two cats, like twin catapults, already launched themselves to intercept it. Their simultaneous swats in midair broke both its wings at the same instant, and it fell floundering and snapping to the ground.

"Run, Verna! Run! Don't just stand there!" Rhoda shrilled at her from the trees ahead, jarring her into movement.

Not until she had reached the shielding grove did she again look back. This time Domino and Dominique had not stayed with her, but had lagged behind as a rearguard. Nor were they in any hurry to leave the clearing. There were now two crippled birds on the ground, being savaged with cannibal ferocity by the flock; while other birds, with squalls of anger and frustration, dived futilely again and again at the two cats. But they only continued to trot leisurely through the tropical sunlight, their tails held tauntingly in the air, dodging the furious attacks with feline playfulness.

"They think it's all just a big Nintendo game." Rhoda clicked her tongue in exasperation, amused in spite of herself."

The B-29 bomber had evidently been trying to land on the island, when it slammed into the side of a hill and broke in half. An overgrowth of trees, vines, and tropical shrubs camouflaged it from the air.

"It's not a hotel," said Verna. "But until we figure out our next move, we'll at least be out of the sight of gulls, landcrabs, Benton Ingles, and whatever other nasties this nasty place has roaming about."

At that instant they were all startled by a strange

roaring and commotion from the direction of the volcano, and looked up in alarm. Such was their astonishment at the apparition which met their eyes that they were unable to speak, move, or even guess what was happening.

A monstrous face had appeared without warning over the rim of the crater, and seemed to glower menacingly down at them. Thousands and thousands of gulls exploded from the towering cliffs, fluttering in wild panic to escape. Dozens plummeted dead out of the air, as roar after roar erupted from the monstrous face. Then without warning it vanished.

Minutes passed in utter bewilderment, before Verna at last broke the silence.

"And that's the wall we have to climb to take pictures? Let's talk this one over, Tim Waverly."

"All right, but let's do it under cover. Whatever that thing was—and I can't even imagine—we definitely don't want to stay out in the open."

They entered the wreckage through the broken tail section. A rear compartment door was open, but all the other doors and windows of the forward section were intact. There was a musty smell inside and patches of mold over everything organic, but in the dim illumination filtering through the cockpit windows the interior of the old warplane seemed almost like a museum exhibit.

"Definitely not a hotel," muttered Verna.

"Stay right here," said Tim, and entered the cockpit alone.

Several minutes passed before he returned, looking anxious and distraught. "The wreckage has never been discovered. Some of the crew may have gotten out, and later perished in the jungle, but the pilot and copilot are still here."

"Ugh!" Verna made a wry face. "How much is left of them?"

"Just their skeletons," he said. "The bones have been gnawed by sharp teeth."

Verna, too, now looked anxious and distraught. Meanwhile, Domino and Dominique separated and systematically began to reconnoiter their new surroundings.

CHAPTER XVIII

"Seize him!" commanded Benton Ingles.

Chief Grotten, for the first time in many years, was caught utterly off guard. He had inspected the damaged yacht, interrogated the prisoners, and completed the arrangements for transporting them back to the Med Center at UCIC. Of the casualties, none had been seriously wounded. Once their personalities had been surgically readjusted, their exceptional strength would make them all highly profitable servitors of B.I.T.E. He had expected praise for his efficiency, not a death sentence.

Nor was there any hope of escape. He recognized the audio cassettes stacked on the desk; they were the same brand used by the wiretap unit at the Administration Center; he had signed the vouchers himself. Each month he personally erased all recordings of his own telephone conversations, and in the meantime took precautions against anyone else gaining access to them.

The sadistic gloat on Angel's face told him who had defeated these precautions. But only when he was actually seized did he realize that the other four men in the room were loyal to Angel, and not to himself. He should have noticed that but had not.

"This is not the time for recriminations," said Ingles. "You have been useful to me, Kurt, but are no longer so. The important thing now is to uncover the extent of your conspiracy against me. I want names, and I want numbers."

"Let me handle the interrogation, sir," said Angel. "I know just how to get it all out of him."

"No doubt you do, but we haven't time for the usual methods. Take him to the infirmary and have him injected. Countdown is scheduled for tomorrow morning. I must know if the conspiracies of this ingrate threaten the launch."

Ingles sat behind an oversized gray desk, a sanitary distance from the cluster of men near the door. The gauze surgical mask he wore over his nose and mouth, to filter disease germs from the air he breathed, so muffled his metallic voice that he sounded like a recording played at too slow a speed.

His private office was antiseptically scrubbed twice each day from floor to ceiling. It dominated the observation deck atop an ugly sprawl of laboratories, workshops, control rooms, foundries, hangars, fuel depots, and living quarters, constructed mainly of raw concrete, cinder block, all-weather plastic, and corrugated iron, in accordance with the cost-effective standards of B.I.T.E. The window behind him overlooked the entire crater.

Eons ago, a gigantic volcano arose from the floor of the sea, directly athwart the equator. Its fountains of molten rock at last ceased to flow, and for thousands of years now its crater, some ten square miles in area, had lain dormant beneath the tropical sun. Above a rank scrub forest loomed a circle of unbroken cliffs. From the far western rim, dipping to the valley floor, running for miles, and rising again at a steeper angle here at the eastern rim, extended the track of a colossal electromagnetic catapult. There was an airstrip below the observation window, and beyond it, on a shunt from the main track of the catapult, stood a monstrous face, larger and more hideous than the stone effigies on Easter Island.

Evening shadows now stretched from the western rim, looming black in the red-violet glow of the setting sun, across the crater below. Teams of men and equipment, work lights glowing in the gathering dusk,

moved up and down the catapult track in a final inspection before the launch.

"Get this traitor out of my sight," said Ingles. "Angel, I want a full report before morning."

"Yes, sir,"

Chief Grotten knew that any resistance would only
make his torments more excruciating. Nonetheless, he
was sadistically mocked and beaten by Angel all the
way to the infirmary. No policeman in California had
administered more brutal interrogations than he had,
even to women and children; but the prospect of under-
going the ordeal himself was more than he could endure, and he broke down and began to scream and
plead for mercy as he was being strapped to a chair.

Angel laughed and spat in his face; but he was under
orders, and stood aside while an orderly injected
Grotten with a heavy dose of scopolamine.

Ingles meanwhile changed his gloves, dropping the
old pair into a lidded canister filled with a strong antiseptic solution. Tropical diseases were the most deadly,
and with slow robotic movements he moved about the
room spraying the air with a germicidal mist.

Animals were the most deadly carriers of disease.
After Project Nimrod brought him a world monopoly
of communications, his first endeavor would be to
bankrupt and discredit all animal rights organizations,
silencing forever their every forum of dissent. Henceforth all animal species not useful for food, apparel,
medical experimentation, commercial product testing,
or some service vital to human beings would be relegated to museums. Human beings themselves, through
universal DNA testing at birth and subsequent personality readjustment, would be relegated to those func-
tions in society where they would be the most
serviceable.

Neither individualism nor disobedience would
henceforth be tolerated in society. But how great minds
could be rendered the most serviceable to his new
world order was still an open question. Geniuses were

not really necessary to its working, only competent technicians. But could the personality of a great mind be so readjusted that it would be serviceable without dissent? Surgery on the renowned Tedworth Vay, fortuitously captured along with a whole crew of other conspirators, should provide the answer. It would also be an appropriate punishment for his conspiracy with other enemies of B.I.T.E. to thwart its aggrandizement.

He would have enjoyed interviewing him after his capture, but prudently decided to forgo the pleasure at this time. Tedworth Vay was indubitably a brilliant man, but he had lately been in close confinement with too many other men, in unsanitary conditions, and therefore carried a high risk of contagion. In any case, interviewing him after the success of Project Nimrod, when he had been sterilized for surgery at the UCIC Med Center, would be infinitely more gratifying.

His observation window was of one-way glass and bullet proof, and he gazed through it across the darkening valley. In a camouflaged hanger atop the western rim his great rocketship Nimrod, a miracle of electronic capability, sat poised for the hunt. Tomorrow would begin a new day—and a new world order.

Hours later, Verna and Tim also gazed through a bullet-proof window, this one bleary with decades of grime and tropical weathering. The first blankets they had found inside the wreckage fell apart in their hands, but they found others in a sealed compartment, and with them covered the skeletons in the cockpit. What had gnawed the bones was now apparent. For peering through the window at them with beady-eyed malice was the face of a giant rat.

"We closed all the doors, didn't we?" asked Verna. "Maybe we'd better double-check."

"I already have," said Tim. "All the windows in this section of the plane are intact."

"Remember how anxious the gulls were to get back to land before dark, when they first attacked us out at sea?" said Rhoda. "Now I think I know why, and why their nests are so high up the side of the volcano. No wonder we haven't seen any other birds or animals anywhere on the island."

"Looks like we've got a war here," said Tim, "eternal and without quarter. Gulls, rats, and landcrabs, each defending their own time and space ferociously, devouring the weak and careless at any opportunity, and always hungry."

"Ugh! Look at that nasty thing," said Verna, staring back at the giant rat. "It's almost as big as Domino and Dominique."

"Mwoop! Mwoop!"

They were startled by the strange sounds coming from somewhere in the compartment behind them, and looked at each other in wonder. It was like no other animal sound they had ever heard before.

"Mwoop! Mwoop!" The sounds were more urgent now.

"Stay here, Rhoda," said Tim, and he and Verna hurried from the cockpit.

He shone his flashlight around the compartment, and their first impulse was to dive back through the door and lock it behind them. A dozen giant rats already swarmed the floor, and more were even now wriggling through a small, obscure hole, gnawed or rusted through the fuselage. But for Domino and Dominique, the whole plane would have been overrun by now.

"Hold this!"

Tim handed Verna the flashlight, snatched up a metal locker, and slammed it down on the hole, crushing a rat that had wriggled half way through it. Then the battle was on.

First, the rats tried to corner Domino, but she was far too quick for them; then they tried to corner Dominique, and paid the price of turning their backs on Domino. Though the apparent odds were ten to one, the actual fighting odds were always a reverse two to one. For each rat, snarling and hissing and baring its fangs, found itself beset in turn by two cats at once. Swiftly the apparent odds narrowed, too.

"Watch out!" cried Tim.

A rat leapt through the beam of the flashlight straight at Verna's face. But Domino and Dominique were indeed watching out, and one swatted the brute out of the air and the other landed on it, breaking its back. The mopping up was over in minutes.

"Amazing," said Verna. "They're like a pair of feline Bruce Lees. Are there any more holes in the fuselage?"

"That's what I'm going to check right now," said Tim. "Here, give me back the flashlight."

"First check to see if there are any more rats." Verna shuddered.

"No need. Your guardian angels have already checked."

"Lucky they warned us," she said. "But that's the weirdest sound I've ever heard from a cat. In fact, it's the only sound I've ever heard from either of them."

"I think they're trying to meow," said Rhoda, emerging from the cockpit. "They're just not very good at it yet."

"Good enough to save our bacon," said Tim. With a look of distaste, he gathered up the dead rats into another metal locker and closed it. "Now we have to save our strength. By some means, I don't know how yet, we have to get our evidence before dawn, and get out of here."

"We might scale the wall in the moonlight," said Verna. "But now how are we going to get to it, with the island crawling with big, slimy rats?"

"Just make a dash for it again, I suppose," said Tim. "There are thick army boots here, and we could wrap our legs with heavy padding. Once we hit the crater wall, we should be safe." He glanced at her.

"Don't worry, Tim Waverly," she reassured him. "I won't slow you down. My brother and his friends, some of whom were my friends, too, sacrificed their lives to stop Benton Ingles. So did Professor Vay and your friends from Royal Beach. If we don't succeed in warning the world in time, they will have all died in vain."

"Get some sleep," he said, proud of her spunk and tenacity. "I found some old binoculars in the cockpit, so when the moon comes up in a couple of hours we should get a better look at the crater. Meanwhile I'll keep watch—just in case."

To his surprise she kissed him full on the lips. Then she snuggled up on the floor in one of the musty blankets. Domino and Dominique also wound themselves podlike into a blanket, wrapped their forepaws atop their heads, and instantly fell asleep. That reassured her there was no imminent danger.

The tropical starlight was the brightest Tim had ever seen; but though the vintage binoculars were still serviceable, he could not pick out details in the crater wall. The details of the cockpit gave him a vague sense of déjà vu, until at last he understood his feelings more clearly. It was like reliving scenes from his favorite of all World War II movies, *Thirty Seconds Over Tokyo*. Though in that epic film Van Johnson flew a B-25 bomber, small enough to take off from an aircraft carrier, which the larger B-29 could never have done.

The scurry of tiny paws over the fuselage was unceasing, and thrice more during his watch he became aware of hideous rat faces peering in at him. He did not look forward to dashing through hundreds of yards of hungry rats, weighed down by photographic equipment, but try as he might he could think of no better plan.

In a metal locker he found several pairs of heavy combat boots, and in a chest of survival gear some canvas pup tents, which he cut into strips so he and Verna could wrap their legs to the knees, until they were bite proof. There were also cans of C-rations, but he decided to stick to the fresher rations they had brought from the whaleboat. Eating what might be his last meal for many hours, he waited for the moon to rise.

Its bright arc had just lipped the rim of sea when he was surprised to see lights brighter still. Snatching up the binoculars, he peered through them toward the base of the crater wall. A stream of electric torches appeared to emerge out of solid rock, and at last he was able to pick out a file of men in B.I.T.E. uniforms. The scurry of tiny paws over the fuselage became momentarily more frantic, then ceased altogether, as if every rat on the island were now converging upon the mysterious file of men.

This changed everything, and he slipped back into the rearward compartment of the plane and shook Verna awake. Rhoda was already yawning and knuckling her eyes, and Domino and Dominique sat nearby with their heads together.

"Are we leaving already?" Verna blinked sleepily up at him.

"We all are. Hurry, we haven't much time."

He handed her the flashlight, and quickly readied their backpacks and photographic equipment for transport.

"I can manage the climb," Verna assured him.

"We're not climbing the wall, we're going through it," he said. "And nobody's being left behind. Come, I'll show you."

The moon was higher now, and the electric torches concentrated in a tight circle. Verna peered through the binoculars a few seconds, then gasped.

"It's him," she cried. "The goon who captured me the first time and has been after me ever since. This is terrible news."

"No, it's good news. It means there's some way into the crater, without having to climb thousands of feet over the top. A cave, a tunnel, maybe some kind of door."

"That makes sense, but what about the rats?" Verna continued to peer through the binoculars.

"We'll leave just before sunrise, when the rats are slinking back to their dens."

"And with good reason," she said. "That's when the gulls come out. Oh, now I see what you mean. We'll catch them between shifts."

"Something like that. Right now we'd better eat, though. I don't know when we'll get another chance."

"Good idea. Say, where have I seen that man before, the one the goon is tying up?"

"Tying up? Here, let me see." He peered through the binoculars. "I can't believe it. That's Mr. Grotten. He's Benton Ingles' Chief of Operations, the second most powerful man in all of B.I.T.E."

"How the mighty have fallen. Too bad it isn't Benton Ingles himself they're tying up. Looks to me like that bald-headed goon is now in charge. What's he doing now?"

"They've hung Mr. Grotten with his arms twisted behind him, so he dangles about a foot off the ground, and Angel and the others are jabbing him with long knives. What a miserable way to die."

"They won't kill him, Tim," she said.

"What do you mean?"

"Angel likes to torment people. I know from first-hand experience. But if they just wanted to stab the dirty swine to death, why bring him out here?"

He was silent a moment, then nodded. "So that's why the rats are all scurrying in that direction. This must have happened before."

"It will be happening to the whole world, and worse, if Benton Ingles has his way," she said, her jaw set with determination. "My brother died fighting him and his kind, so did Professor Vay and many other wonderful, valiant people. I'm ready when you are, Tim Waverly."

He had discovered a pistol lying beside one of the skeletons in the cockpit. All but one bullet had been fired, suggesting a grisly end for the two men who had died here. After forty years of tropical heat, the bullet might now be a dud. Yet the pistol itself could still be used as a club, and he stuffed it into his belt.

The moonlight was now at its brightest, and they watched through the cockpit windows until at last the file of electric torches disappeared again into the base of the volcano. False dawn now tinged the eastern sky.

"Looks like we're on," said Verna, tightening the straps of her backpack. "No, thanks, I don't want to look through the binoculars again. I can pretty well guess what's happening to the poor wretch, dirty swine that he is."

"Look," said Rhoda. "Domino and Dominique know we're leaving. They're waiting by the door."

"Yes, they seem to figure out our moves before we do ourselves," said Tim, adding wryly: "Just like when we play chess."

"Wait a minute," said Verna. "We don't know what's on the other side of that door. There may be millions of giant rats on this island. They can't all have run in the same direction at once."

"Stand back," said Tim.

Throwing the latch, he opened the door a crack. There was no wild eruption of snarling and hissing, so he opened it a little farther, then farther still. He shone the flashlight onto the dark hillside below. A single giant rat squatted in the beam, evidently a scout.

Before Tim could react, Domino and Dominique shot past him. Then there was only a single dead rat on the hillside, and the two cats separated and reconnoitered the vicinity of the wreckage. Minutes, later, they reappeared in the beam of the flashlight from opposite directions, but at the same instant, and together looked up at him as if to report "All clear!"

False dawn had passed into the first orange-purple blush of true dawn as they left the plane, but there were stretches of black shadow all along their path. The two cats again separated.

"Hey, where are they going?" said Verna. "I can't see them any more."

"They're not far away," said Rhoda. "They're moving along with us out there in the darkness, one off to the left and the other off to the right."

"Looks like they've posted themselves as flankers." said Tim, while they hurried down a long volcanic gulley.

A burst of angry snarls and hisses, cut off by a stunned silence, erupted in the shadows off to the left; then twenty yards farther on a similar eruption broke out on the right. This altercation was repeated several more times along their route.

It was brighter as they emerged from the gulley, and they recognized Dominique as she shot across their path out of the darkness on their right. A moment later, somewhere off to their left, erupted a squealing, snarling, hissing commotion of battle, and they all stopped to listen.

It did not last long. There was an abrupt silence. Then Dominique trotted back across their path, her tail held triumphantly in the air, and resumed her post on the right flank.

The going became steeper and more rugged, the dawn ever brighter. They were within a hundred yards of the crater wall when they heard the first ominous cries from above. The gulls were beginning to leave their roosts for the morning hunt.

"Run!" cried Tim.

Scrambling and leaping and dodging over the rugged terrain, they dived into the last clump of shrubbery that could effectively screen them from above. They were now but a short dash from the sheer volcanic wall.

"There it is," said Tim, pointing to a dark opening in the rock. "It's too regular to be a natural cave. But it may be guarded."

"Oh, how horrible!" Verna turned her head away.

Hundreds of giant rats swarmed over the dangling corpse; those which dropped sated to the ground were at once replaced by others hungrier still. Then a wild panic erupted as a gull fell upon one of the sated rats, killed it with a jab of its beak, and began feeding. Other gulls circled close overhead.

"We can't wait," said Tim. "We'll have to risk that the tunnel isn't guarded. We have no chance at all out here. Ready?"

Giant rats had begun swarming all around them, no longer as a ravening pack but squealing in terror as they fled the death now dropping upon them out of the dawn. Gulls were also driving the rats from the dangling corpse.

Domino and Dominique dodged through the scurrying rats on the flanks of their benefactors, but now guarded mostly against attacks out of the sky. Several gulls swooped past and might have attacked, had the dash to the opening not been so short and swift.

Tim was the first to enter, a flashlight in one hand, the pistol in the other. His surmise that the opening was not a natural formation proved to be only parially correct. An ancient vent had been bored and reinforced into a tunnel which sloped ever deeper into the volcano. Its exact purpose, other than bringing those who had offended Benton Ingles to a gruesome death, was not apparent.

"It may be guarded farther down," he whispered. "Wait here."

"No, Tim." Rhoda caught his arm. "Domino and Dominique are already checking. Oh, there they are now."

The two cats trotted in step back up the tunnel, and sat side by side in the beam of the flashlight as if with another report of "All clear."

"The tunnel can't be very deep if they're back so quick," said Verna.

In fact the vent may have extended for miles into the earth, but artificial tunneling ceased at a steel door in the northern wall. The two cats had evidently not bothered to explore beyond this point.

Tim trained the flashlight beam all around the door. It was rounded at the corners like the watertight hatches of a warship, and seemed to be bolted shut on the inside. There was no lock or handle, and no ready means of prying it open. Domino and Dominique leapt up and down on either side of it, but then sat with their heads together. If they had a report this time, it was "No way."

Tim looked questioningly at Verna, but she could only shrug. He thought vaguely about camping out farther down the vent, in hopes the door would be left open while some other poor wretch was dragged out and thrown to the rats. But that could be days, and by then it might be too late.

It was the alarm shown by Rhoda and the two cats that made him suddenly apprehensive about alarms or electric-eye sensors here in the tunnel. But before he could react, the door burst open and an avalanche of uniformed men overwhelmed him, wrenching the pistol from his grip, and throwing him to the ground.

"Kill those goddamn cats," ordered Steve Heinsohn.

He had been supervising a maintenance crew, in the underground hangar where Benton Ingles stored his private jet, when the loudspeakers boomed that an outer tunnel had been invaded. The whole crew of Brainers reacted quickly to his order, but Domino and Dominique were through the door and gone before anyone could so much as bend over to grab them.

"Damn it!" Heinsohn cursed. "This isn't my job. I just happened to be closest."

Too close, in fact. Not long ago, at the hangar back in Ingles City, a forklift driver named Hal Larmer reported seeing rats. Then he disappeared, and the next time anybody saw him he was docilely operating his forklift out in the warehouse, his personality readjusted. Heinsohn knew better than to make any such report himself.

"You never saw any cats," he ordered his crew. "You never saw animals of any kind. Got that, all of you? Okay, then tie up these two and bring 'em along with that kid."

Tim and Verna, their arms pinioned by leather cords, were hurried up a tunnel with tracks down its center like a miniature subway tube. Domino and Dominique were nowhere in sight, though Rhoda located them not far away. She was not bound with cords, but a close-cropped young man held her firmly by the arm.

Deeper and deeper they penetrated into the crater wall. Naked electric bulbs of low wattage cast a dim light; the unventilated air had an unwholesome smell like dirty laundry. Not a word was spoken until they reached the underground hangar where Benton Ingles kept his private jet fueled and ready for emergency departures, twenty-four hours a day. He personally screened the few granted access here.

"This will do," said Heinsohn, stopping before an unoccupied office. "Take 'em inside and tie 'em to a chair. No, not the kid. She can't hurt you. Let's see, you four should be enough to guard 'em. The rest of you get back to work."

He personally locked the office door from the outside. But now came the tricky part. Angel might not like it if this matter were not confided solely to him, which ruled out using the telephone, all of whose messages were recorded. On the other hand, Benton Ingles would definitely not like hearing that a crew chief had left his post, especially so sensitive a post as this one, and might suspect that it was part of a conspiracy against him. Tricky, very tricky.

He frowned and scratched his head, as he shuffled across the hangar back to his own office, pondering the ticklish situation. A wrong decision, and he could end up one of his own crew. So preoccupied was he, in fact, that he never noticed the two cats emerge from the tunnel he had just left and glide like twin shadows to the door he had just locked.

Domino and Dominique were not sure what their benefactors had intended doing here, before their capture by enemies. More insight might come from more knowledge of their surrounding. But first they had to be certain their benefactors were in no immediate danger, and they sat down outside the office door.

They located all three just on the other side, and sensed that their small friend was aware of their presence out here. None seemed to be overly stressed or anxious, so they were probably safe for now. Springing the crude lock on the door would have been simple, but they had seen four big Earthlings enter it as guards. So springing their benefactors at this time would be anything but simple. They needed more information, and separated for a systematic reconnaissance of the hangar.

It was dominated by a colossal green-and-gold jet, standing eternally poised for flight. There were no surprises among the stores, tools, equipment, or machinery marshaled elsewhere in the hangar, and the two cats met again outside the office door, and put their heads together to share impressions. Both had sensed the presence of many more Earthlings somewhere above them, among whom seemed to be the entire crew of the watercraft that had bought them here. That meant they would have to expand their reconnaissance.

How to reach the upper levels was the problem; there were no stairways, and an elevator, even if they could figure out how to activate it, would be too dangerous to use. But there were numerous ventilation shafts and primitive tools everywhere for the taking, so they took a screwdriver and a pair of pliers, and set to work.

The shaft was screened by machinery from observation, and removing its grate and filter unit needed only minutes. Its interior offered no footholds, but by rebounding acrobatically from side to side, carrying the tools in their teeth, they ascended to the next level without difficulty.

The filter unit here formed a narrow ledge, and they again set to work with screwdriver and pliers, removing the grate from the inside. Replacing everything exactly as they had found it, just as they had the grate on the hangar level, they crept into an empty room lined with gray metal lockers. Ramps and stairways led upward from this level, so they secreted the tools in one of the lockers, and sat down to plan in detail their next reconnaissance. Then they were off.

Like mobile television cameras, they recorded and transmitted everything they came upon with an accuracy no crew of human technicians could have matched. Level by level, corridor after corridor, from one module to the next, they soon had a virtual schematic of the entire complex. And it was a mutual schematic, for they would pause every few minutes in their reconnoitering to exchange telepathically everything each had seen.

Nothing delayed them. The Earthlings were so clumsy and noisy that they might just as well have blown whistles to announce their approach. Besides, they all seemed to be very busy and preoccupied with some forthcoming event.

The first big discovery was made by Dominique: the Earthlings who had brought them here over the water were all being held prisoner in a remote cell, heavily guarded. She then came upon a vast room filled with electronic devices, mostly computer terminals, before which uniformed Earthling technicians sat waiting tensely. The entire room was sealed off by glass panels, and its single entrance also heavily guarded.

Elsewhere, Domino made the discovery that was to prove decisive. What first attracted her attention was the monstrous face she had seen come roaring over the top of the crater rim, then disappear again. Its purpose still bewildered her. But through the same observation window she saw an Earthling spacecraft, similar to the one which first brought her down to the planet, poised atop the far rim of the crater. Dipping from the heights, running for miles through scrubby vegetation, and rising steeply at this side of the crater was the track of what she recognized at once as an electromagnetic catapult. From her rescue and maintenance training, she

knew that the Masters launched their far greater and
more sophisticated spacecraft by similar means.

She sat on the protruding flange of a girder, invisible
to the Earthlings passing below, but with a clear perspective through observations windows of both the distant spacecraft and the monstrous face nearer by. It
rose grotesquely above the tropical thorn scrub of the
valley, on a shunt from the main track of the catapult.
Neither she nor Dominique, to whom she transmitted
her impressions, could form any notion of its purpose.

They could both sense the tension mounting
throughout the complex. That the spacecraft atop the
distant crater rim would soon be launched from the
electromagnetic catapult was evident. Just ahead,
Domino could see a glass-walled cubicle, whose banks
of instrument panels indicated that it was some kind of
control center; its observation window looked directly
down on the monstrous face. No keen analysis was
needed to discern that this was where it was operated.

But for what purpose? That was still the question.
The small control center was unoccupied, so the monstrous face was not about to be put into operation.
Domino pondered and pondered. Dominique, two levels below, pondered and pondered. They had been conditioned by the Masters never to abandon a problem
until it was solved, and they sifted their data, exchanging guesses, speculations, and hypotheses back and
forth with instantaneous speed, abandoning each in
turn as it proved unworkable, from the first roaring appearance of the monstrous face over the rim of the crater, which sent a myriad gulls shrieking to escape,
while dozens more fell dead to the earth.

They even considered going out into the valley and
examining the monstrous face close up. There was not
a single gull visible, and the teams of Earthlings moving up and down the catapult track seemed uncon-
cerned about attacks—and that gave them the answer.

A few moments of telepathic exchanges with Dominique, to cement their plans, and Domino strutted

down the girder, her tail held proudly in the air, and took up a position that looked directly down into the glass-walled cubicle. It would be like the Nintendo games they played with the small Earthling, the one whose mind was the most compatible with theirs. The scale was far vaster, and it was real and not electronic simulation; nonetheless this new game should be fun.

CHAPTER XIX

"I really hate to do this," said Rhoda, looking sadly at the four scrubbed, close-cropped young men in the office one after the other. "But there's no other choice."

Tim and Verna, bound with cords to office chairs nearby, looked questioningly at her. She did not meet their eyes. Because she was only a child, her captors had not bothered to tie her up, and she rose and addressed them in an authoritative tone:

"The police inspector wants me to ask you a few questions. We are going to send all of you to the police station for a special medical examination. The police doctors are going to X-ray your skulls."

With each statement she made, the four young men looked more and more disoriented; spasms twisted their features, and their limbs began to twitch with odd contortions.

Rhoda continued relentlessly: "Your examination by police doctors will give us the evidence we need to incriminate Benton Ingles. Come with me now, the police inspector wants to question you."

Tim and Verna looked on in shock as the four Brainers began to twist back and forth in wracking paroxysms, convulsions rippling their features, as if they were being jolted again and again by electric shocks. None of them emitted a sound, until with a last violent tremor each slumped in turn against the walls and furniture.

"Professor Vay said that they're all programmed to self-destruct, whenever they're discovered," said

Rhoda. "And that none of them are really alive in any meaningful sense. Still, it's an ugly thing to do to them. I wish there'd been some other way."

"Untie us, quick!" said Tim. "We haven't much time."

There turned out to be less time than he supposed. No sooner had Rhoda squatted behind his chair, and with a scissors rummaged from the desk begun to pick at the tight knots, than the door burst open. Neither Angel nor Steve Heinsohn noticed her as they stormed int the room.

"You again!" Angel glowered furiously at Verna. "You got away from me at Ingles City, you got away from me again at Royal Beach, but now it's for keeps. I didn't have time to do a proper job before, but now I got all the time I need. Weeks, months, as long as I want. I'll save just enough for the surgeons at the Med Center."

"Hey, Angel, look at these guys," said Heinsohn. "What the hell's happened to 'em?"

While the two men looked in wonder at the Brainers slumped against the walls and furniture, Rhoda finished unknotting Tim's bonds, and slipped unseen behind Verna. She now had the knack, and picked at these knots more efficiently.

"I dunno," said Angel, glowering at Verna again. "But this snooping bitch had something to do with it. Never trust a broad, even when she's tied down." A sadistic leer twisted the corner of his mouth, and his meaty right hand balled into a fist. "Here's a little taste of what you're gonna get later, bitch."

His punch was aimed sadistically not just to hurt her, but to disfigure her beautiful face—but he never got to throw it. Tim flung aside the unknotted cords, leapt up, and caught him square on the jaw with a blow that staggered him. Another blow, then another, sent him reeling backward against the wall.

But then Tim himself was staggered by a punch to the back of his head. He whirled around to defend himself, just in time to see Verna bring her chair crashing down on the head of the pot-bellied crew chief. Heinsohn dropped like a sack of meal. Nor was Verna finished, for she crowned Angel's bald head with the chair as well, also dropping him to the floor.

Tim looked at her in some confusion, and not just from the blow he had received. Whatever illusions he may have begun to fantasize about rescuing a damsel in distress were dashed in an instant. Verna was disconcertingly capable of taking care of herself, and he could not really picture her melting into his strong and manly arms for protection. Still, she really was splendid.

"This is no time for Marquess of Queensberry." She gave Angel a swift kick in the slats, for good measure. "Let's tie up these goons and get the hell out of here."

Tim complied, gagging both men with their own handkerchiefs, though he was not sure how long mere cords would hold Angel, no matter how tightly knotted. As he rose to his feet, he saw a look of horror on Verna's face. She pointed to the Brainer slumped against the desk.

His face had begun to swell hideously; then his entire head burst into flames. The other three Brainers self-destructed in the same way, and a greasy smoke began to choke the air.

"Outside, quick!" Tim snatched up a fire extinguisher from the wall.

He looked pale and shaken when he rejoined Verna and Rhoda out in the hangar a few minutes later. No fire alarm had sounded, and the crew of scrubbed, close-cropped men in B.I.T.E. uniforms continued to toil docilely at Benton Ingles' private jet as if nothing had happened.

"Are you all right, Tim?" Verna examined him with concern.

He took a deep breath and nodded. "Whew, that was awful. But so far, so good. No alarms that I can hear."

"Yes, but there will be alarms if we try to go back through the tunnel, Not to mention those nasty gulls."

"This hangar is underground, but it must open onto an airstrip out in the crater. Maybe we could escape that way." He peered across the hangar toward huge sliding doors at its far side. "But first I think we should go back into the tunnel, alarms or no alarms, and see if we can find where Domino and Dominique are hiding."

"They're not in the tunnel," said Rhoda. "They're above us, and they've split up. I can always find them, and usually people I know, if they're not too far away."

"Is there anybody else you know above us?" asked Verna. "Professor Vay and the crew of the *Sidonia,* for instance."

"There's something familiar up there, but I'm not really sure. It's hard to describe. Ghost Eagle used to call the feeling 'Spirit Voices.' That is, voices you know are speaking but you can't quite hear them."

"What if they were closer?" asked Verna.

"Then I'd know for sure. Anyway, we can't just desert Domino and Dominique. Not after all they've done for us."

"But what are they doing now?" asked Verna. "And how in the world did they get above us in the first place? I don't see any stairs."

"Those doors over there look like elevators," said Tim. "How a pair of cats might operate them, I don't know. But nothing about those two astonishes me any more."

"Elevators are death traps," said Verna. "I read somewhere that no Chicago gangster will ride in one, because you never know what's waiting when the door opens."

Tim picked up a combination wrench, nearly the length of a crowbar. "We'll have to take our chances. The elevators are the only way up."

"I hope that wrench does us more good than your one-shot pistol ever did," Verna said dryly.

"Attention! Attention!" boomed a strident voice from a nearby loudspeaker. "All personnel take your stations. Zero plus twenty minutes. Repeat. All personnel take your station."

"That means us," said Verna, rummaging through a canvas hopper filled with soiled rags and uniforms. "These are filthy and they don't smell very nice, but everybody else is wearing a uniform. I think we'd better put these on."

The elevator ride was longer than they expected. Tim had pushed the "D LEVEL" button, thinking that meant the lowest level. It turned out instead to be the highest, which proved lucky. He held the wrench poised like a club as the door slid open. But the corridor was deserted, and they stepped warily out of the elevator in their soiled and wrinkled uniforms (Rhoda's was rolled up at the wrists and ankles and hung on her like a clown costume), looking both ways for trouble.

"Attention! Attention!" They were startled by a loudspeaker directly above them. "Zero plus thirteen minutes. Repeat. Zero plus thirteen minutes."

"Thirteen minutes to what?" said Tim. "Sounds like the countdown at Cape Canaveral."

"They're launching something," said Verna. "Probably the evidence we came here to get. Too late for that, but you've got a wrench there. Maybe we could still throw it into the works. Anything to stop Benton Ingles."

"Domino and Dominique are together again," said Rhoda. "They're now below us, off to the right. Professor Vay and the others are here on this floor, around to the left. I can't sense any pain or stress among them, so they must be all right."

"Till they have holes drilled into their heads," added Verna. "They're sure to be guarded. But if we can spring them, maybe they could help us throw your wrench into the works, Tim."

Keeping to the left wall, they tiptoed to the next coridor. Tim dropped to his knees and peeked around the corner. Then he quickly drew his head back.

"No use. There are at least six guards."

But Rhoda shook her head. "There's only one. The rest must be Brainers."

"That's still six big, powerful men," said Tim.

"No, only one," she insisted. "The others will obey whoever gives them orders."

"Attention! Attention!" boomed the loudspeaker. "Zero plus ten minutes. Repeat. Zero plus ten minutes."

"Wait here," said Tim. "If they nail me, you're on your own."

Slipping the wrench into his back pocket, he strode with assumed nonchalance around the corner and down the adjacent corridor. The walls and floor were of bare concrete; flourescent light fixtures hung from the girdered ceiling. All six men posted outside the makeshift guardroom stared curiously at him as he approached.

"Where's the shorted outlet?" he asked.

"Shorted outlet?" A stout, swarthy young man, who differed markedly in manner and appearance from the other five guards, eyed him suspiciously. "What are you talking about?"

"I got a job order here," said Tim, reaching around to his back pocket. But instead of pulling out a requisition chit, he pulled out his wrench, and brought it down on the guard's head with a resounding "thonk."

The man dropped at his feet and lay motionless. The five Brainers, who were indeed big, powerful men, looked blankly at him. He had anticipated that they would have orders to stop anyone trying to break out of the guardroom, but none regarding someone trying to break in. Like computers, they had to be instructed about every task they performed.

"All right, break out the cleaning gear," he ordered them. "This place is a mess. I want this whole corridor swept and swabbed, right now. Move, I say."

Docilely, the five scrubbed, close-cropped young

men proceeded to a row of lockers just down the corridor, and began distributing brooms, mops, and buckets. Tim meanwhile fished a ring of keys from the pocket of the unconscious guard. He was just fitting the key into the guardroom door as Verna and Rhoda hurried up.

"Bravo, Tim," said the former. "But I just thought of something. These guys might have orders to stop any attempt at jailbreak, and they look mighty big."

"Yes, I thought the same thing," he said. "We can only hope the crew is in good enough shape to fight them. There's no time for anything else."

"Then let's give them something to fight with," she said. "Those mop handles look lethal enough. Rhoda, give me a hand."

"Attention! Attention!" boomed the loudspeaker. "Zero plus seven minutes. Repeat. Zero plus seven minutes."

"Three spare mop handles, two brooms, and a pair of foxtail brushes," reported Verna, returning. "Not much of an arsenal."

"We'll have to rely on numbers," said Tim, unlocking the door.

"Tim, Verna, Rhoda," exclaimed Tedworth Vay, as they entered. "Marvelous! But explain later. It's seven minutes to blast off for Project Nimrod."

It was a single bare room, without so much as a bench to sit on; a single bulb of low wattage glowed feebly from the ceiling; the air reeked of confinement. The entire crew of the *Sidonia* was present; several had been beaten or wounded, but only three were hurt too seriously to walk. Arrangements were quickly made to carry them.

"Here, take these." Verna distributed her arsenal. "These aren't much to fight with, but the enemy isn't armed any better."

Tedworth Vay looked questioningly at them, and got a quick explanation. It seemed to depress him out of all proportion to the challenge.

"It's the time I'm worried about," he said. "Not that I should be any more. All we can do now is try to escape the island. I had hoped somehow, some way. . . ." He shrugged. "Too late. All right, men. Let's rush them."

The five Brainers had indeed been ordered to prevent any attempt at escape, at the cost of their lives; but they were overwhelmed by strength and numbers, and locked with their unconscious leader in the very room they were supposed to be guarding.

"Attention! Attention!" boomed the loudspeaker. "Zero minus four minutes. Repeat. Zero minus four minutes."

"How did you get in here?" Tedworth Vay now turned to Tim and Verna.

"Forget it, Professor," said Verna. "The gulls that attacked us out at sea rule that side of the island. What became of the *Sidonia?*"

"It was raked by machine-gun fire, but not seriously damaged. That might be our best hope. The Fax equipment on board is still intact. There's nothing we can do now to halt the actual launching, but we may still be able to get the evidence for which we came. Though I see we've lost poor Domino and Dominique."

"No, we haven't, Professor," said Rhoda. "They're here with us. At least, here in the same building, just below. We can't leave them behind."

"By no means. We'll rescue them and make a dash for the *Sidonia,* while Ingles and his goons and automatons are concentrating on the launch. Lead the way."

"Attention! Attention!" boomed the loudspeaker, as Rhoda led the rush through the deserted corridors to the stairwell. "Zero plus two minutes. Repeat. Zero plus two minutes."

Domino and Dominique sat with their heads together on the girder overlooking the glass cubicle. Their surmise about the monstrous head had proven correct, for they had seen it in operation.

Two men in white coveralls had used ID plates to enter the cubicle. One logged his password into a computer terminal, while the other accessed a telephone, evidently getting clearance to proceed. Domino scarcely blinked as she fixed in her memory the exact sequence of every move they made, every switch, key, or button they pressed. Dominique rejoined her on the girder just as the monstrous face began to trundle up the shunt toward the main track of the electromagnetic catapult.

Team-think responsibilities were instantaneously divided between them. Domino continued to scrutinize the manipulations of the two operators, while Dominique observed the monstrous face ascending the steep incline of the catapult toward the rim of the crater. It behaved exactly as it had when they first saw it, from the other side of the island; though they now understood what it was.

The roar it emitted as it reached the top of the track turned out to be a rapid series of explosions, shot gunning clouds of lead pellets before it, and clearing the air of any gulls that might have harassed workmen out in the open or jeopardized the launch itself. Neither cat so much as glanced aside until the monstrous face was again positioned at the end of its shunt, and the two operators below had completed their manipulations.

A moment to pool their information, a moment more to finalize their plans, and they sat ready to act. This would be as much fun as any of the electronic games they had played, though it seemed to them a strange and extravagant means of clearing the air of bothersome flying creatures.

If the engineers who designed the fantastic scarecrow or the technicians who built it ever had such thoughts, they never breathed them aloud. For the idea had been conceived by Benton Ingles himself, and no one questioned its brilliance.

Certainly Benton Ingles himself had no doubts, as he watched his brainchild return down its siding. He sat alone before his bullet-proof observation window, in his isolated, locked, and sterilized room; its fumigated air was double filtered, and every square inch of its walls, floor, and ceiling scrubbed with germicides.

This was the moment he had strived for all his life; it would someday be recognized as a watershed in human history, and he counted off his impending triumphs on his gloved fingers. The future would henceforth be ordered out of factoids promulgated solely by his monopoly of world communications. The past would systematically be rewritten to glorify the aggrandizement of B.I.T.E. All dissenting opinions and contrary evidence would be erased from a single world data bank. Fear and intimidation were temporary expedients. Only through universal DNA testing, and the surgical readjustment of personality, could mankind be rendered permanently incapable of disobedience to superiors. The human race would be purified of its weaklings and misfits, and all those selected to live would be consequently healthier and more efficient. His new world order would last a thousand years.

One thing alone still nagged him. Where was Angel? He had been instrumental in exposing the conspiracies of Kurt Grotten and others throughout the organization. Was he now conspiring himself? He was the ideal Chief of Operations because he lacked the intelligence ever to reach for supremacy. But he should have been here by now. Where was he?

Ingles tugged fretfully at his white gloves, as though trying to draw them more protectively over his hands. He could see his great satellite hunter, Nimrod, glistening in the tropical sunlight atop the rim of the crater, miles away. He had heard the muffled announcements of the countdown echoing through the corridors beyond the bolted steel door of the room. Yet a vague uneasiness still nagged him with suspicions that someone, somewhere in the vast complex was conspiring against him. Where indeed was Angel?

Domino and Dominique knew exactly where to find

him, their archenemy on the planet. But he had not stirred from his location, levels below them, and they were having too much fun to worry about him now. Though they, too, had reason to fret.

Mastery of all the operations in the glass cubicle was of no use to them so long as the operators were still there. Would they never leave? Earthlings had ceased to shuttle back and forth along the corridor below, and the harsh growling from loudspeakers, blaring out at precise intervals, seemed increasingly urgent. Still, the operators did not budge.

At last, one of them picked up the telephone, listened, and responded with low growls. Then both rose and departed, locking the cubicle door behind them. Together they disappeared into an adjacent corridor, as the harsh growling from the loudspeakers sounded once again.

Like shadows of each other, the two cats were down from the girder and across the concrete floor below in seconds. That the cubicle was locked did not delay them a second longer, for it was constructed only of glass partitions that ended well below the girdered ceiling. In tandem they sprang to the top, balanced an instant to pick out their landing spot, and dropped as one onto the same corner of a systems desk. Instantly, Dominique took her place at the observation window, while Domino began keying the exact sequence of digits she had observed the operator key into the computer.

The growling from the loudspeakers came at shorter and shorter intervals, until it was almost continuous; then there was a final emphatic growl, and Dominique flashed a telepathic signal of her own. As with Nintendo, timing was everything, and at the precise instant Domino keyed the monstrous face into motion.

As on a colossal roller coaster, the glistening satellite hunter dropped thousands of feet from the rim of the crater, gathering momentum from the force of gravity until it reached the valley floor, where its carriage was thrust faster and faster along the miles of track by powerful electromagnetic impulses. Its rockets ignited within a thousand yards of the launch incline.

All eyes at every observation window, at each level of the complex, were on Nimrod as it hurtled at increasing speed along the catapult. Benton Ingles was among the few who noticed the monstrous face trundling up its shunt toward the main track, and he was helpless to react, paralyzed by impotent horror.

Domino and Dominique, in the glass cubicle directly below him, were now aware that their benefactors and the entire crew of Earthlings that had accompanied them over the water, were fast approaching. Normally they would have rejoiced, but their instincts had been conditioned never to let their concentration wander from an assignment, and neither so much as flicked her eyes backward.

Tedworth Vay surmised this, and halted his followers before they reached the glass cubicle. They could all see what was happening, though not one in ten could have guessed how this unexpected deliverance had come to pass.

Rhoda knew exactly, for she had seen the two cats, with this same intense concentration, roll up phenomenal scores again and again at every electronic game they played. More by reflex than with any hope of effect, she put her finger to her lips, so they would not be disturbed.

The explosion was tremendous. The launch carriage and its payload came hurtling along at thousands of miles an hour, just as the monstrous face trundled out onto the main track, an instant ahead of it. The collision sent a billowing mushroom of fire over the island, and the roar shook the entire space complex to its foundations. Then the outer walls began to thunk and bang and clatter with falling debris.

The timing had been perfect, the coordination of effort flawless; the results could not have been surpassed. Domino and Dominique simultaneously leapt into the air out of sheer glee. Then they recalled their duties, and while one logged off the computer the other picked up a wadded ball of paper and two cigarette butts from the floor, and neatly deposited them in the trashcan. Only then were they ready to leave their stations.

It was a dramatic spectacle. The world outside the observation window was a chaos of fire, wreckage, and billowing clouds of blazing smoke; the sky beyond the crater rim swarmed with thousands of white gulls, shaken from their roosts by the violent explosion.

Against this wild panorama the two cats sprang together to the top of the glass partition, dropped lightly down on the other side, and strolled calmly over to Tedworth Vay. They looked up at him as if asking, "What next?"

Rhoda wanted desperately to hug and kiss and pet them, but she knew they didn't like to be fondled in the middle of a job, and this particular job was by no means finished. This was proven when three men in B.I.T.E. uniforms came running out of an adjoining corridor toward the glass cubicle. They were momentarily stunned by the crowd of strangers, and slid and stumbled to a halt. Then they turned and disappeared again back up the same corridor.

"That answers their question," said Tim.

"But not ours," added Verna. "I'd just love to see the face of Benton Ingles right now. Then I'd like to see him standing before a judge, when he's sentenced for murdering my brother. But where is he?" She looked speculatively at Domino and Dominique. "No, this is one time they can't help us."

"They don't need to," said Tim. "I can tell you exactly where Benton Ingles is right now. Remember the big private jet we saw down in the hangar. He'll fly back to Ingles City as fast as it will carry him, and start right in covering up what's happened here. Just as he always does."

"Not this time," said Tedworth Vay. "But we'll talk

about that later. Right now we have to catch a plane. Either we can commandeer it for ourselves, or wreck it so Ingles can't use it to get away. How do we get to the hangar?"

Using two shifts of elevators, they were down at the hangar level within minutes—but even that was not fast enough. The rumble of the giant hangar doors grinding open mingled with the whine of jet engines.

"There he is," shouted Tim.

"And look who's with him," Verna shouted above the noise. "He got out of the knots you tied. You're no boy scout, Tim Waverly."

Somehow Angel had slipped his bonds, and was helping Benton Ingles up the ramp into the side door of the aircraft. He glowered evilly at the troupe charging across the hangar toward him, and bellowed orders left and right. His voice was drowned in the deafening rumble and whine of the colossal hangar, yet his orders were nonetheless perceived by the uniformed crew of Brainers. They picked up hammers, wrenches, files, pipes, and mallets, and formed a protective cordon behind the plane.

"Get back! Get back!" shouted Tedworth Vay, waving his arms and pointing at the tail jets of the plane. "Get behind something!"

His words were drowned by the noise, but all understood his meaning and scattered for cover. Domino and Dominique alone hesitated. Verna was in imminent danger.

The uniform she had donned was several sizes too big for her, and in trying to reverse herself too quickly she had slipped on the greasy floor and slid toward the cordon of Brainers like a baseball player into a base. She tried frantically to scramble to her feet, but once more became tangled in the folds of the oversize uniform, and went down again.

The three nearest Brainers started for her, brandishing weapons, and Domino and Dominique started for them. But then Tim Waverly appeared out of nowhere, snatched her to her feet, and raced with her in his arms toward a shielding forklift. They found the two cats already there, and all dived for cover an instant before the world seemed to explode in a thundering roar. The fiery backwash of four powerful engines mercilessly blew away the cordon of Brainers, and the jet roared out onto the runway outside and took off.

"Oh, he's escaped," wailed Verna, emerging from cover.

They watched helplessly as the plane circled the giant crater to gain altitude, and passed directly overhead as if taunting them. It soared over the rim of the crater at the exact spot where Nimrod was supposed to have passed, before it was destroyed in an explosion that filled the air with swarms of frightened gulls.

"Look, Professor," cried Rhoda. "It's losing altitude. It must have hit all those birds."

"More likely some of them were sucked into the air inlets of its engines. It may still pull out of it."

"No, it won't." Verna stamped her foot. "Ingles mustn't get away, or that dirty swine who beat me up. Come on, gulls! Do your stuff!"

For whatever reason, it was now obvious that the colossal jet was having trouble maintaining altitude, while its airspeed diminished rapidly; its strange angle against the tropical sky showed how desperately its pilot was trying to pull up. Then suddenly it dropped like a plummet behind the towering pinnacles of the crater, and was lost from sight.

Any sound of a crash was drowned in the raging fire and explosions of the Nimrod spacecraft out on the wrecked catapult. Nor was there any sign of smoke, which meant the plane had probably crashed into the sea.

The smoke now filling the hangar came from small fires ignited by the backwash of the jet engines, but the crew of the *Sidonia*, assisted by those Brainers who had survived the blast, were already at work with fire extinguishers.

Domino and Dominique sat with their heads together, as though exchanging opinions about the follies of this strange planet. The Masters never did anything violent or unreasonable. On the other hand, there had never been so much fun aboard ship.

"I'm so happy I showed them how to play Nintendo, Professor," said Rhoda. "I can tell they're really enjoying themselves."

Tedworth Vay nodded, wondering if their mystery would ever be explained. There were other problems before him that needed more immediate solutions, but he could see that the two cats were not the only one enjoying themselves.

Verna understood Tim's feelings. He had rescued his damsel in distress, after all, and she looked up at him with both amusement and affection.

"My hero," she said, and he took her in his arms and kissed her.

CHAPTER XX

"Look at me when I'm speaking to you, Timothy," snapped Mrs. Waverly, dragging at her menthol cigarette with brusque, angry movements. "I'm your mother."

"I'm listening," said Tim, though he did not look at her.

Instead, he glanced over the couch and chairs, slip-covered with durable plastic, over the tables, surfaced with stainproof glass; over the television room that had been the center of family existence through his boyhood and youth. He felt as foolish and harried as most grooms do on their wedding day. Yet for the first time in his life he was comfortable in his own home.

"After all we've done for you, after all the sacrifices we've made to see that you got a good education, you throw it all away to marry some female jailbird and live on the beach." She nervously tamped out her menthol cigarette in the ash tray and immediately lit another one.

"You could have done better, Tim," said his father, seated on the couch facing the television set, with a bowl of cheese popcorn on the coffee table in front of him. "Didn't I say that from the very beginning, Marge?"

"You're right, Fred." She expelled a cloud of menthol smoke. "Timothy, if you do anything so foolish, don't expect to see either your father or me at your wedding."

"I'm sorry to hear that, mother." He now looked her

calmly in the eye. "Verna and I would both like to see you there—her parents have flown in from Albuquerque—but if you can't make it, we'll send you a piece of wedding cake."

"You can't live on wedding cake, Tim," said his father, snatching up a handful of the cheese popcorn. "And the way our taxes are going through the roof, don't expect your mother and me to support you."

"You won't have to, father. Verna's parents have long wanted to open a California branch of their health-food business. Royal Beach is an ideal location, and we're going to combine it with an outlet for bodybuilding equipment, and an occult book store."

"Oh, yes," Mrs. Waverly interrupted, "I should have known Professor Weirdo would be mixed up in this somehow."

Tim looked at her, but now she was the one who did not want to meet his eyes. He knew that Verna's arrest, the moment she stepped off the *Sidonia,* had been his mother's doing. The two detectives who served the warrant at the docks had described the woman who had tipped them off, and he had no doubt who it was.

The yacht had suffered only minor damage; wood putty and varnish had repaired the bullet holes with hardly a trace, and sailors from the Navy destroyer that towed it home from Sulatonga had left it shipshape. Nor had any of the crew suffered lasting injuries from their capture by Benton Ingles. That was why Verna's arrest had come as such a shock to them all. In fact, the detectives might have been roughly handled, but for the intervention of Tedworth Vay.

He went straight to the telephone, and Verna's release from all charges relating to the massacre in Ingles City was at the police station before the detectives got her there. With telephones no longer tapped, with the blockade of Royal Beach dissolved in the night, he had been a busy man these last two weeks. In fact, he had only just returned from Washington, to attend the wedding.

The collapse of B.I.T.E. was so far reaching that it

seemed to rumble like a planetary earthquake. Events at Sulatonga were classified, but insiders in both Congress and the Media had a pretty good idea of what had happened there, and how close a call it had been for the entire human race. Benton Ingles was now being denounced in fifty languages, all over the world.

As for Ingles himself, his crashed plane had not yet been recovered. But an undersea trench dipped miles downward from the volcanic shores of Sulatonga, and many believed the wreckage never would be discovered.

This might have created legal problems for his widow, but the resourceful Carla had had her lawyers settle with the estate for permanent maintenance. It was a tiny fraction of what she might have gotten, after perhaps decades of legal wrangling, but a secure annual income in seven figures nonetheless.

Her first use of the money was to redeem her old rivals. Chastened now and thoroughly ashamed of herself, she saw to it that Miss World was released from prison and comfortably provided for; the First Runner Up now owned the Amber Light, the road house where she had toiled for so long as a mere waitress. Then Carla bought a Victorian mansion in Royal Beach, which vied in magnificence with the one owned by Lola Londi, and a fierce rivalry of sumptuous renovation and display immediately ensued. According to Maximo, their gin rummy games were like Armageddon.

Maximo himself had also married. Whatever words he may have had with Chesterville were unknown, only that the buxom Graziella was now his bride, and they had both settled down to serve their beloved mistress for the remainder of her lifetime. . . .

"Professor Vay has been generous to Verna and me, in many ways," Tim said to his mother, without reproaches or rancor. It was his wedding day, and never in his life had he been so happy. He was still amazed that so wonderful a girl as Verna Malmrose could love him. "If you change your minds," he continued,

"Verna and I would be delighted to see you at the reception. The address is on the invitation there on the sideboard. Lola Londi's garden is worth seeing in itself."

"I've seen enough of your Lola Londi," said his father. "I don't think she's all there, if you ask me. People forgot who she was, and now she has film festivals all over the country. She was on three talk shows just last week." He stuffed a handful of cheese popcorn into his mouth. "We saw her garden when she was interviewed on . . . what's the name of that show, Marge?"

" 'At Home.' "

"That's it, the 'At Home' show. I don't know why you're mixed up with people like that, Tim. You don't have that kind of money, and never will, the way you're going."

"No, Verna and I will never be rich," he said. "But we love each other, and we'll be doing work that's interesting and meaningful, so we have a good chance to be happy."

"I don't see how anybody can be happy these days," said his father, eyeing the popcorn bowl again. "If we could break the stranglehold the Royal Beach Preservation Society has on development, businesses would move in here and pick up some of our tax burden. Haven't I always said that, Marge?"

"You're right, Fred," She tamped out her menthol cigarette and immediately lit another one.

The wedding at the old church, the most venerable in Royal Beach, was memorable for all who attended. Tim felt like he was walking stiff-legged through a fog as he approached the altar, and parts of the ceremony remained forever after hazy in his memory, as if he had dreamed them. But he recalled vividly for the rest of his life the moment when he lifted his bride's veil, and for the first time kissed her as his wife.

He was grateful that Verna had abandoned her orig-

inal notion of coming down the aisle in a modernistic
tunic with love beads, and wore instead a white picture
hat, long white gloves, and a traditional wedding dress
of white satin and lace. Though he doubted that this
was because she had suddenly acquired old-fashioned
values so much as because a picture hat becomingly
hid her crew cut, about which she was still inordinately
sensitive.

What stirred Verna's memory was the woman seated
in a front pew beside Tedworth Vay; it was the same
woman whose photograph stood upon his mantelpiece.
Her beauty was of the formidable kind; she looked
more like a barbarian queen than a modern college
professor, which was what she turned out to be. An ar-
cheologist, no less. Tedworth Vay was sometimes as
mysterious as his own investigations. Young Rhoda
Dawn, another of his mysteries, sat on the other side of
him, wearing for the occasion a beaded shirt bib in
front of her dress of fringed buckskin.

Though nothing was so memorable on this day of
days as the appearance of Lola Londi as a bridesmaid.
In clouds of lavender gauze, an incredible
Gainesborough hat set rakishly over one ear, and
enameled like a Barbie doll, she stood just to the left
of the bridal pair, turned sideways to the congregation
for the better appreciation of her profile. Her pose was
dramatic, like that of a pagan sibyl gazing propheti-
cally across the years that were to be. It was a spectacle never forgotten in Royal Beach, and the Sons of
Paradise, ushers extraordinary at today's services, cried
like babies.

They were indispensable at the reception that followed. Never had Lola Londi's gardens seemed more
palatial, and the uniformed old men moved unobtrusively among the guests, with only passing lapses of
purpose, when they tried to remember what they were
doing here, serving food and drink. All glanced from
time to time at the new oaken gate, perhaps hoping it

would be broken down again, and give them another opportunity to protect their goddess from harm.

The voluptuous Carla needed no protection. Beautifully gowned and coiffeured, though less spectacularly so than her friend Lola, she circulated wantonly among the guests. She was especially flirtatious with the crew of the *Sidonia,* and with other bodybuilders in attendance. Later, she was to become the principal sponsor of the Royal Beach Strength and Health Association, and for many years to come participated actively in the doings of its members. Her gin rummy losses, which were sometimes formidable, alone nettled her existence, and not just because of the money. . . .

It was evening before Tedworth Vay at last settled comfortably in his overstuffed armchair beside the fireplace. His companion, Dr. Gelsey Nance, relaxed on the sofa opposite, while Rhoda sat on the carpet. Chesterville appeared minutes later with brandy and coffee, which he served with his usual stiff dignity from a silver salver, handing a cup of sweetened cocoa down to the child on the floor.

"Anything more, sir?"

"No, we'll just relax here for a while," said Tedworth Vay. "It's been a hectic afternoon, but all's well that ends well. By the way, it was decent of you to step aside when Maximo announced his intentions to marry Graziella."

"I take little credit for that, sir. Chivalry comes easy to a man whose rival is a heavyweight pugilist."

"You're a thoroughgoing rascal, Chesterville."

"Thank you, sir. I endeavor to do my best. Shall I lock up for the night?"

He made a point of not looking toward the woman on the sofa, but Tedworth Vay did. The question in his eyes was subtle, and so was the answer.

"Yes, you may lock up now, if you would. I don't think we'll need you any more tonight."

"Very good, sir," said Chesterville, and discreetly withdrew.

"I wish I'd known your friend Lola or Mrs. Ingles a few years earlier," said Dr. Nance. "They might have helped me with my Sicilian labor problems. The dig at Lilybaeum was the most exasperating of my career."

"But the result is a superb addition to our knowledge of Roman provincial life," he said. "I've read your book twice, and each time with profit."

"And neither time with approval of its style? No, that's all right, Ted." She checked the tactful remark she knew he was about to make. "I have no illusions about the subtlety of my prose. The critics say I write as if I were sacking a city."

He smiled at her candor. "But what about your latest dig, Gelsey? You said in your letter that you were having trouble there, too."

"Yes, dictator trouble. The ruins are in the Zagros Mountains, east of Baghdad. The summer palace of a rather mysterious court official, who flourished during the reign of Harun al-Raschid. Exactly what his function was at court is still controversial, but there's no doubt he wielded great power and was immensely wealthy. His summer palace must have been fantastically beautiful, to judge from what remains of it."

"But that's in the Abbasid period. Isn't that a bit out of your usual line, the late classical world?"

"I couldn't resist. You remember Humphrey Carpenter, chairman of the archaeology department at the University of Pennsylvania? He informed me about a wonderful new find made accidentally by surveyors sent out from Baghdad, and urged me to take charge of the expedition he had just organized. I've had to import all my laborers, because the local peasantry shuns the ruins with supernatural dread, and the central government has gouged for all it's worth. Nonetheless I've already made some fascinating discoveries. Though they may be more in your line than mine, Ted."

"Oh, why is that?"

"Magic, evil magic." She smiled at him as she sipped her brandy. "It seems the builder of the summer palace was a powerful magician named Shaymirazi, who was known as the Demon Master. Little else is known about him, except that he had an evil reputation. But some of the mosaics I've uncovered in the ruins of his palace are truly bewildering. I have photographs of them at the hotel, among a mess of logs, sketches, and notebooks."

He laughed. "A mess which I suspect is arranged, annotated, and docketed with museum exactitude."

She laughed, too. "Well, control of one's material is timesaving in the long run. With academics today, you need all the ammunition you can lay your hands on, if you intend to assault one of their precious ramparts."

"No doubt, but you still haven't explained how you got involved in the first place."

"Gall bladder surgery. Poor Humphrey Carpenter was hospitalized three days before he was scheduled to fly to Baghdad. I was the only archaeologist available with enough experience to handle the project, and there was no time to lose. The ruins may soon be bulldozed for the construction of military installations. I had to work like hell, sometimes twenty hours a day, but I got everything of major importance at the site recorded one way or the other. Dictators permitting, we can mop up there next season."

"Then comes the hard part," he added. "Are you going to write the book, or will Humphrey Carpenter?"

"We may collaborate, but that still isn't decided. As a matter of fact, I'd like your opinion of some of the material I've collected. The mosaics, for instance, portray mystic symbols nobody can decipher, and animals nobody has yet recognized. I'll bring the photographs over tomorrow."

"Bring everything," he suggested. "There are twenty bedrooms upstairs."

"One is enough, Ted." She gave him a pleasant look. "Anyway, I don't think I could be comfortable with so many tourists roaming the house. The hotel is bad enough, with so many newspaper and television people always underfoot. I stayed at the Royal Beach Astoria precisely to get away from that sort of thing."

"That's surprising," he said. "There hasn't been any commotion at the Astoria since the gangster days of Prohibition."

"They have another gangster staying there now," she said. "His name is Delfred Bassett, but it looks like the little hound is finally going to get his comeuppance. If you could have seen the destitution left by one of his fishing ships along coastal Africa." She shook her head in disgust. "It was a crime."

"Yes, and one he'll soon pay for. Both the United States Congress and the United Nations have at last taken up the issue."

"About time, too. But you still haven't shown me those mysterious cats you mentioned. Can they really play chess? And Nintendo? That's something I'll have to see to believe."

"Rhoda, dear." He turned to his ward. But she was deep in concentration, and he had to speak her name twice more before she at last looked up at him. "Where are Domino and Dominique?"

"Upstairs, sleeping. They finished all the leftover salmon I brought home from the reception, and then put on their toy helmets and curled up in their hammocks. I think I can summon them for you, if you like."

"Summon them? How?"

"I've been practicing, and it usually works. But I've never tried it while they were asleep. Let's see if it works that way, too."

She continued to sit, gazing fixedly down at an invisible spot on the carpet, just as she had gazed not long ago at a love crystal. Minutes passed in silence, and then Domino and Dominique trotted in step through the beaded curtain, and sat down before her.

"It works, Professor." She clapped her hands with glee. "Even while they're asleep. Just like Ghost Eagle taught me."

"I'm proud of you, dear," he said. "Gelsey, may I introduce you to the inimitable Domino and Dominique."

"It's them," she said in astonishment. "The breed actually exists."

She continued to stare at Domino and Dominique as if she had seen a ghost, while they, in turn, examined her in clinical detail, as was their custom with all Earthlings they encountered for the first time.

"If you know anything about these two that I don't, Gelsey, I'm all ears," said Tedworth Vay. "I've tried signs, I've tried diagrams, I've sat them down on either side of me while I leafed through picture books on everything from astronomy to zoology, and I'm pretty sure they understand what I want from them. But they seem to have some instinctive block against revealing the least clue about their origins. Zoologists I've consulted don't know what breed they are."

"This is fantastic, Ted." She could not take her astonished eyes off the two cats. "The zoologist I consulted didn't know either. You'll have to see this to believe it. Is your telephone still in the library? I'll be right back."

She returned in five minutes, and half an hour later a messenger from her hotel delivered a manila envelope. She drew from it a photograph of a wall mosaic, and handed it to him.

"Take a look at that, Ted. Can you wonder I'm astonished?"

The mosaic in the color photograph was a brilliant example of Abbasid craftsmanship; it portrayed two cats sitting with their heads together, within an ornamental cartouche of curious symbols.

"Same breed," he said.

"Same cats, Professor," said Rhoda, peering over his shoulder. "See how one has a black tip on her tail and the other a black left forepaw. Exactly like Domino and Dominique. But what are those funny signs all around them?"

"We still don't know," said Dr. Nance. "Some kind

of occult symbolism, I suppose. No expert in the field has yet been able to identify them. Ever see them before, Ted?"

"Every morning, Gelsey. Here in the upper left is a point and figure chart, of the kind used daily by Wall Street speculators. Some of these others are computer programming symbols, also used in the stock market."

"Wall Street? Computer symbols? In the age of Harun al-Raschid?" She was silent for several moments. "Is there any brandy left, Ted?"

"I'll join you."

He refilled their glasses, then put the photograph on the carpet in front of Domino and Dominique. They examined it intently, but also seemed puzzled.

"They don't recognize it, Professor," said Rhoda. "So it's nothing that's ever happened to them."

"At least, not yet," said Tedworth Vay, looking thoughtfully down at the two mysterious cats.

A feline lovers' fantasy come true . . .

CATFANTASTIC

DAW

Introducing the New DAW Superstars . . .

GAYLE GREENO

☐ **THE GHATTI'S TALE:**
Book 1—Finders, Seekers   UE2550—$5.50

A mysterious enemy is attacking the Seekers Veritas, the nation of Canderis' organization of Truth-finders composed of Bondmate pairs, one human, one a telepathic, catlike ghatti. And the key to defeating this deadly foe is locked in one human's mind behind barriers even her ghatta has never been able to break.

☐ **THE GHATTI'S TALE:**
Book 2—Mindspeaker's Call (May '94)   UE2579—$5.99

Someone seems bent on creating dissension between Canderis and the neighboring kingdom of Marchmont. And even the truth-reading skills of the Seekers Veritas may not be enough to unravel the twisted threads of a conspiracy that could see the two lands hopelessly caught in a devasting war. . . .

DEBORAH WHEELER

☐ **JAYDIUM**   UE2556—$4.99

Unexpectedly cast adrift in time and space, four humans from different times and universes unite in a search to find their way back—even if it means confronting an alien race whose doom may prove their only means of salvation.

DAW

S. Andrew Swann

C.J. CHERRYH
THE ALLIANCE-UNION UNIVERSE